BRER BABYLON

BRER BABYLON

Chris Dickerson

Copyright © 2000 by Chris Dickerson.

Author photo by Robert Souers.

Cover art by Bill Robinson

Library of Congress Number: 2001117626
ISBN #:   Softcover: 1-4010-1955-2

All rights reserved. No part of this book may be reproduced or transmitted in any form or by any means, electronic or mechanical, including photocopying, recording, or by any information storage and retrieval system, without permission in writing from the copyright owner.

This is a work of fiction. Names, characters, places and incidents either are the product of the author's imagination or are used fictitiously, and any resemblance to any actual persons, living or dead, events, or locales is entirely coincidental.

This book was printed in the United States of America.

To order additional copies of this book, contact:
Xlibris Corporation
1-888-7-XLIBRIS
www.Xlibris.com
Orders@Xlibris.com

CONTENTS

chapter one 9
chapter two 26
chapter three 46
chapter four 66
chapter five 84
chapter six 108
chapter seven 122
chapter eight 141
chapter nine 161
chapter ten 177
chapter eleven 190
chapter twelve 210
chapter thirteen 236
chapter fourteen 254
chapter fifteen 272
chapter sixteen 306
chapter seventeen 329
chapter eighteen 347
chapter nineteen 361
chapter twenty 376
epilogue 397

This book is dedicated to Stephanie, my partner, friend, buddy, lover and wife.

chapter one

Zachary first met Burly Olalla at the Southeast Bull Riding Championship in winter of 1992. He had just moved to a small suburb of Atlanta, far enough away from the city to not be a suburb properly, but near enough to make the drive to his new job something less than an ordeal. Having moved from a large northern city, and not having much else to do on weekends, he had been investigating the events and gatherings that helped shape whatever passed for culture in the local environs in late 20th century America. One thing he had not had the good fortune of doing back up north was attending a rodeo. A gathering of bulls, in this case.

The rodeo was a two night affair. Friday, was really the winnowing out night. The number of riders competing that first night would be roughly halved for the final Saturday night ride. Zachary didn't (and still doesn't), know a great deal about the ins and outs of 'rodeoing', but basically, he understood that he who has the greatest number of points is the winner, provided he stayed on the bull. And the bulls must have been a pretty cantankerous lot that weekend, because no one ever did complete a ride, though there were some small consolation prizes handed out to those few who did manage to garner any points at all. He thought the amount of time one needed to stay on the bulls was 7 or 8 seconds for it to be considered a complete ride, but he could never get it straight because he could never understand the announcer.

He wondered where they got these people. There must be a school or something out in Texas or Wyoming where you go to learn how to talk like a rodeo announcer. Preparation must consist of a lot of whiskey, chewing tobacco, and nightly viewing of old westerns. "Class, your homework tonight is 'Rustlers in the Dark', pick up your pack of Red Man chew on your way out." He imagined a lot of ugly microphones.

He went on the final night. It was being held inside the North Georgia Cultural Affairs Coliseum. Upon entering the arena, his expectations were not disappointed as he was greeted by a sea of straw cowboy hats. He was definitely out of his realm, which had until recently been clothed in khaki trousers and pressed plaid shirts, with knit ties, if at all. And no hats, they mess up your hair. Hair wasn't important here, at least not on guys. As for women, well, big hairdo's were still fairly popular.

But the duds looked good. Or maybe it was just because they were different. Nearly everyone had cowboy boots on, and some kind of jeans. The guys wore your basic blues, but the women had fancier ones, studded with glittering faux jewels and denim shirts with more glittering glass and some with swinging fringe. It made him wonder why it is that people well east of the Mississippi took on the airs of a Pecos Pete. Maybe it's the same as driving a 4-wheel drive to the shopping mall. Serengeti suburbia. Everyone wants to pretend they're really someone else. Or somewhere else.

It was pretty crowded by the time he arrived, the only available seats were right up close to the fence. For the first time in his life he was ringside! He could lean forward and rest his arms on the fence. After settling in, he looked around and noticed he was just about the only one sitting that close, and couldn't help but think people were giving him a look that had a tinge of pity in their eyes. Like, "Poor, dumb city slicker", or "Must be a Yankee." At any rate, the festivities were about to begin because the lights started to dim.

Not ever having been to a rodeo before, he didn't know how the animals were treated. In the past he knew animals were often agitated by electronic shock devices, or sharp spurs, or some other torturing device, but he figured things had changed, that we as a people had passed laws against such things, that somehow we'd graduated to the next level of human growth. He was mulling this over, absent-mindedly pushing a wad of tobacco spittle around in the imported dirt floor with his tasseled cordovan loafers when the announcer came on.

"Laaadies and geeentlemen, cowboys and cowgirls and little wranglers. Tonight, but for the grace of God, some of the most toughest, and hardest, and ding danged roughest horney toads are going to try and tame the most rip snortin' thunderous fire breathin' steamin' locomotives outta hell that God a'mighty ever did place on this good earth. They're gonna come flyin' outta that chute with arms a'flappin and knees a'knockin, perched on top of one mean and angry hombre. One wrong spill and they could be playin' harp with sweet Jesus, or worse yet, end up singin' in a boy's choir, if you get mah drift."

"Folks, tonight y'all are going to witness the last of a dying breed, the last of those chosen few with true grit. No tofu chompin' vegetarians here, these men here are your steak and potato platters of piss and vinegar . . ."

He was admiring the way he spat out 'vegetarians', as if it might catch in his throat if he didn't expel it fast enough, when movement in the back of the ring caught his attention. The ring wasn't a true ring, a circle, but rather an arc. The North Georgia Cultural Affairs Coliseum wasn't big enough to allow it to be a complete circle. Instead, the hall was bisected from one corner to another, diagonally, with the riding ring completing an arc roughly from one end to the other, and the seats set up like a large L. Well within the outer wall of fence was the small corral where they kept the bulls. Next to them was the chute where they led the bulls to be ridden and where the riders would mount them.

The public could see the bulls that were going to be ridden that night, they looked as docile as any cow standing in a pasture chewing its cud. In fact, most of them were doing just that. They appeared to suffer no stage fright, and surely they knew what their job was tonight. They didn't look like any locomotives from hell, some of them even looked rather small, and there were all kinds, from black Angus to the mostly brown and familiar Hereford with their white faces, to a few Brahmin bulls. Now those looked tough no matter what. It must be that hump that makes them look so mean and powerful.

His musings were cut short by the announcer.

"I want you folks to know that these bulls lead a pampered life. They ain't allowed to be ridden more'n a dozen times, and once they're retired, they're put out to pasture to pursue the good life of making more bulls. Don't sound like a bad way to go t'me." He followed that with a few chortles of laughter, no doubt he would be slapping the thigh of whomever might be sitting next to him.

About that time a group of a dozen or so young men made their way into the center of the ring. None could have been over 30, and they all appeared to be in good physical shape. No beer bellies here, at least not yet. And they all wore the regalia of a cowboy. From top to bottom; cowboy hats, western style shirts, blue jeans and boots. Some had little lumps under their gums or small bulges in their cheeks, tell tale signs they had a wad of chewing tobacco in their mouth. And they all had numbers on their backs. They formed a single line facing the crowd.

The announcer then began, "If I could have your attention good and kindly folks, in the center of the ring you'll see our chosen few. From within these ranks of warriors a man will emerge who stands a little bit taller than the rest. Who's a little bit tougher than the rest and maybe a littler bit meaner. A true man of courage who will have wrassled with the devil hisself, and won. Who rode one ton of dynamite and hellfire until it said 'no more!' Ladies and gentlemen, I give you tonight's Roll Call of Rodeo Champions!"

The crowd began to applaud enthusiastically, complete with catcalls, whistles and hootnin' and hollerin'. Most were stomping their boots in the stands, too. It was a thunderous reception.

The announcer asked, "Who's it going to be tonight? Will it be Bill Simpson, who drove in all the way from Oklahoma City?"

With that, the first man on the left end of the line stepped forward doffing his hat and bowing ever so slightly. Just enough to show his appreciation, not enough to in any way imply deference, merely a reluctant bend of the waist. The announcer intoned again, "Bill's been riding since he was but a babe. They say he was raised on a horse on his families' ranch. Last year Bill took first prize at the Laredo semi-finals. Let's give this cowpoke a big how-do-you-do!" With that the crowd raised a bigger ruckus, while Bill slipped back into line.

Next came Rolly Winkerton from Great Falls, Montana. "This man was all busted up just 4 months ago from a run in with one big ole ugly brute known as 'The Widow Maker', a bull that was never, ever ridden. He was just too mean, and since has been retired. Just 4 months ago, ladies and gentlemen, this boy was on crutches with an arm in a sling, and here he is tonight! Now that's what I call a man's man. Let's give him a big welcome!"

The announcer went down the line in like fashion, pointing out some item that separated this man from the boys, like Bobby Johnson, from Cincinnati, Ohio, "I didn't know they had such tough customers in Cincinnati, but Bobby here won two bronco championships, then quit, saying horses just ain't hard enough, and switched over to riding bulls, cause they're meaner. I tell you folks, this man sleeps with his spurs on!"

When the announcer was finished introducing the riders, and they had filed off to the back of the arena to be near the bulls, the lights dimmed, save one spotlight shining center ring. The announcer's voice took on a solemn tone, "Ladies and gentlemen, I want to introduce you to a very special guest tonight."

With that, a single black bull trotted out into the spot light, knowing exactly where to go—the center of the ring. It was a magnificent creature, with beautiful rippling muscles and an incredible set of horns. If you wanted to sculpt a bull, this was your model. Not only was he an imposing physical specimen, but he knew he was the center of attention. He actually turned left and right, modeling himself, giving the audience a 360-degree look. This bull was fully self-aware. He carried himself with a proudness and dignity no human could best. This bull was bullness.

Zach threw out any questions or doubts he had on how or what the bulls may have felt about being forced to take part in this ancient play. They, or at least one, enjoyed it. Even rose to the occasion.

The announcer continued, "This bull goes by the name of Sinbad, and he's one ocean of badness. Raised by a well known breeder down in Texas, outta championship stock. And don't he know it! You can tell by the way he struts around out there." The voice of the announcer deepened and slowed, becoming grave, "No one has ever ridden Sinbad, I don't know if anyone will. He's hurt a few at that. Tonight? Well, we won't know till it's over. Some poor soul is gonna draw Sinbad's number here, pray sweet Jesus is with 'em."

The spotlight blinked out, and he could see the darkness of Sinbad moving toward an open gate, to be led back to the other bulls. Then the lights came up again. The crowd started to liven back up while the riders drew bulls. He didn't know how they did that since he couldn't make out much of what the announcer was saying, who was still talking above the din of the crowd. He busied himself looking about, taking it all in. He felt excitement welling, some old and buried stones were shifting. Long gone and dissipated smoke was seeping out of closets kept closed for eons, a dance as old as memory between man and animal was about to begin and it tugged on some old strand of DNA.

The rodeo clowns had begun to work their way into the arena. He had noticed them standing off to one side, just waiting for things to get going. They didn't wear much in the way of costume, not like pictures he'd seen. One or two had hairpieces on, big red clown wigs, and one of them wore a big red nose, but that was about it. And they all had sneakers on, gotta be fast out there, he guessed. He would later realize they all had microphones on, too. In the days before this technological innovation, the audience wouldn't have been able to hear them, so they had to rely on visual props in their comedic acts. Now they tell jokes and engage in banterings with the announcer. He would rue that development given the gags they did, and the woeful jokes. They were all about bodily functions and mother in laws. But for now the riding was set to begin.

In the back center of the arena he could see one of the riders sitting on a bull, a big brown and white one. It wasn't a Hereford, more like a cross between that and a Texas longhorn. And it was big. In the chute, the bull was placid as could be, though the rider didn't seem to share that serenity, he was busily occupied making sure that the one rope he was going to hang on to, that ran underneath the chest of the bull, was secure. He seemed very particular how his hand was placed, everything had to be just so and he fussed until it was right. And then at some moment unforetold, the gate swung open. At that one moment, the bull came alive. Very alive. In one quick move of amazing agility and speed, the bull swung its massive head around to its left, sideways and up, at the same time pushing its front legs up, and leapt out into the arena. When its front legs came down, it kicked up hard with its back legs while turning its head to the right. The effect turned its spine in one quick spasm. That didn't dislodge the rider, but it had to hurt the way he came down hard on the bull's back, his buttocks were the only thing that touched down, his legs were splayed out more than perpendicular to the bull. When the animal's back legs came down a split second before the rider's did, the bull wasted no time, he pushed his hind legs up and toward his right while he pushed his front legs left again so that briefly he was in the air, writhing like a serpent. The rider was dislodged mid-air, and had the bull landed and stood still, he would have had a chance to stay on, but the bull knew the game, and as soon as he landed, he bucked one more time with this hind legs, and the rider was gone. Just to make sure, the bull ran on a little more, bucking and writhing. The rider very nearly landed on his feet, and as soon as he could, he grabbed his hat and ran to the fence, accompanied by a clown. When the bull was certain no one was on top, he quickly trotted over to the open gate that would lead him back to the pen with the other bulls. It was business as usual for the beast.

The ride lasted no more than 3 seconds, it took the bull just two bucks to get rid of the man. No points here, it would be back to St. Louis, Helena, or where ever the guy came from. Money? None. It's almost an all or none kind of sport, like auto racing, but these guys don't have sponsors. You'd think one of the tobacco companies would throw a little money in to it, Zach thought, but they seem pretty occupied these days.

While everyone waited for the next rider to get mounted and set, the announcer worked the crowd a little, getting them to applaud the courage of the last rider, though they hardly needed goading. The size discrepancy between man and bull wasn't apparent until they came charging out of the chute, and went flying around the ring. Then one could see how small the man really was. Then you could see the power and strength of the bull. Then you could see just who was in control, and that it would take more than skill to stay on top of this animal, it would take a whole lot of luck, and in some way, an acquiescence from the bull. Maybe they like some riders more than others, he wondered.

Once the announcer was finished praising the courage, guts and glory of the rider, and the awesomeness of the brute, the next rider was ready to throw his lot into the hands of fate and the beast she rode in on. It was a Will Anderson from Ocalla, Florida, riding a Hereford named Brandy. Yup, Brandy the Bull. Brandy was kind of low slung and long, so the man on top didn't look quite so small. But what Brandy may not have had in height, he more than made up in moves, spinning and turning like a dervish, like a Dachsund shaking a bee.

When the gate opened for Brandy, he jumped out of the chute sideways, which surprised everyone and no doubt the rider, too. And then, when you would have expected some kind of buck by throwing the hind legs up, instead, Brandy whipped his head around to the right, almost hitting the still opening gate. He was up on his hind legs, and everyone knew he was going to come pounding down on his front legs, slamming them into the ground and maybe the rider. The rider knew it was coming, and bent as far back as he dare go, trying to absorb the shock with his buttocks as best he could, while digging deep into the flanks of the bull with his boots. The bull came slamming down all right, nearly driving its hooves into the dirt up to the knee. The force snapped the man's head forward like the end of a whip, hitting the back of the neck of the bull. But he hung on, which seemed to infuriate the bull. This drove him into a frenzied series of pirouettes, spins and jumps that sent Mr. Will Anderson flying head over heels, landing on the upper part of his back, nearly ten feet from the bull. When he landed, his boots hit the ground, points first. The audience roared and rose, fearing he'd broken his back or snapped his neck. Two clowns went running quickly to help him while another two distracted the bull, who was still spinning and leaping, and not the least concerned with the crumpled pile of ex-rider. But Will was alright. The clowns helped him to his feet, though he was none too sure how to walk. He put one bowed leg in front of the other, slipping every other step. His head must have been spinning like a gyroscope gone mad.

He lasted a bit longer than the first rider, but it still couldn't have been more than a 4 or 4 1/2 second ride. No prize here, just a sore back, maybe only a mild headache, and God knows what strained and sprained muscles. And for what? What kind of money would he have won? Zach thought the 1st place prize was 6 or 7 thousand dollars, which works out to about a thousand a second. Which, if you figure it that way, ain't so bad. As long as you can get up and walk and talk when the ride's over.

The announcer was beside himself praising this 'tough hombre', and you couldn't blame him. It does take a pretty hardened soul to go through that kind of punishment, to have the nerves to willingly get on top of something so powerful that so clearly does not want you there, and will eagerly try to dissuade you from your notions. Ah, but the show must go on, and ne'er the twain of brains and brawn.

Or so goes the stereotype. And as there is in many a stereotype the dappled commingled current of fact and fallacy, in the rodeo can be found the disgruntled intellectual; the house hunter for a purer homestead. The seeker of a life that breathes and pulses with pain and pleasure, risk and daring.

The announcer introduced the next contestant, "Ladies and gentleman, early on I talked a bit about this next fella. Y'all remember Jimbo Hardaway, that's Dr. Jim after all. He's the fella that quit practicin' medicine cause he got rodeo fever, and a bad case a' that cause he got what you call bull-menia. Get it?"

They all got it, or nearly so, but few thought it as funny as Rodeo Rex, or whatever the man's name was.

Dr. Jim came hurtling out of the chute on a smallish looking tan bull. But what the bull lacked in size he more than made up for in his zest for dislodging the medicine man. Nothing fancy here, just flat out bucking. It didn't take long for his zeal to send Dr. Jim sliding off the back end, landing on his right side, unharmed. He started to get up, but the bull wasn't done with him yet. He turned around and lowered his head, charging the still rising doctor. This is when rodeo clowns really earn their keep. When the bull first comes out of the chute, they're not far behind, in front, and to the side of the animal. When the rider comes off it's their job to see to it that the bull doesn't get to do what this one wanted to do to Dr. Jim. When the bull got within two paces of the man, one clown grabbed hold of his tail, while another charged into his left flank, right near his rump. This turned the bull enough for another one to quickly dash between the bull and Hardaway, allowing him to sprint for the fence with the help of another clown. In a matter of seconds it was over, with the bull left standing, looking about for someone or something to lunge at.

"Maybe Jimbo's gonna go back to practicing medicine after that one," said the announcer. "He nearly paid a visit to some of his mortuary friends. Folks, now you know what I'm talking about when it comes to guts. I ain't just breathin smoke at y'all. These here fella's are facin' some serious trouble. And what about those rodeo clowns. Don't they got it tough? Let's give 'em a big hand. I want to take some time here and introduce you to a couple. That fella there with the big red nose, that's Curly Brown, one of the best in the business. Ole Curly's been runnin' round arenas longer than I can remember. How long's it been Curly?"

It was then Zach realized the clowns had microphones. Curly responded, "Don't rightly know." He was standing near the center of the arena with his hands in his pockets, looking down, with an exaggerated, ah shucks look. He was wearing huge, ridiculously bright plaid trousers.

The announcer asked again, "Come on now, Curly, surely you know how long you been rodeoing."

"Weelll", he said, "Don't wrongly know neither."

In fake puzzlement the announcer responded, "Do what now, Curly?"

"I guess as long as I been married," Curly said.

"Curly, what has rodeoing and your marriage got to do with one another?" the announcer asked.

"You ain't seen my wife. She's been riding me since we was married." Curly said.

Some in the crowd laughed, some in the crowd groaned. Zachary lowered his head, hoping the microphones would break. Gratefully, the next rider was ready.

The bull he was riding came charging out of the chute. Nothing fancy, he just came out bucking and kicking his hind legs up really high. Zachary didn't think it would take much more for this bull to flip right over. He didn't, but he got at such an angle that the rider really couldn't help himself, there wasn't any way he could hang on unless maybe he was tied. He came sliding down the bull's back and off the side of his neck. He landed on his feet and quickly ran behind the bull, who didn't show any interest in following him. The bull, who had run out of the chute straight to where Zach was sitting, had urgent needs. He stood on the other side of the fence from where Zach sat and began to urinate. This wasn't a wee or a pee, but a gusher. It splattered all over him, from feet to knees he was getting hit with a mixture of urine and mud. He leaped out of the way, but not until he was well besmirched. Only the people closest to him saw what had happened, most of the crowd was watching some of the clowns playfully teasing the rider who was climbing the fence, getting out of the arena. That didn't ease Zach's embarrassment but did enlighten him as to the reason why it was so easy to find such a choice seat.

He settled back into a seat a row up, the other attendees giving him as much room as he wanted.

The next few rides were pretty uneventful for him, though the same could not necessarily be said for the riders, one of whom got stomped on by a bull after he was thrown off. He had landed right near the bull's hind legs and the bull just continued to buck and kick. He stumbled on the poor rider, which probably saved the guy from really getting hurt. Had the bull landed on him, something would certainly have broken. As it was, he got up and skedaddled right smart, as the announcer put it.

At intermission he stayed in his seat to watch some of the entertainment the clowns provided, or rather, he meant to stay until he saw what passed for entertainment.

They brought out a flimsy looking outhouse, with a half moon cut into the door, setting it down in the center of the arena and milling about it for a while. Meanwhile, they were talking to the announcer about eating at Mexican restaurants. One of them then had to use the outhouse, and when he did, there was an explosion and all the doors of the outhouse fell off, exposing the clown sitting there, acting surprised. Zachary quickly left, knowing his fate should he stay for more.

He went out into the concessions area. The vendors were selling cow skulls, leather belts and fancy belt buckles, wallets, as well as western shirts, and of course, hats. They were also selling Native American items too, which struck him as a bit perverse to barter and trade in the goods of the conquerors as well as the conquered. History gets all mixed in to this gigantic blender of free enterprise. Add a dash of Europe, Asia and South America and pour over the marketplace. He didn't buy anything, they were all out of sacred cows, so he settled for a hotdog instead.

When the coast was clear, and the miasma of corny jokes had been sucked out by the ventilators, he went back in and sat down, the second half was set to begin.

The announcer must have taken a short break, he came on and said, "Well, I hope you folks enjoyed that as much as I did. We got some pretty funny comedians out there. But now it's back to business. We ain't had a one that's rode one of these bulls yet." Of course, they've rode, they just haven't stayed on.

And neither did the next four riders. Each one was launched by their respective bull, and each one returned to earth rather unceremoniously. A nose landing here, a belly skid there, a tailspin pirouette followed by a back flip. No one appeared to get hurt, though a few did seem a little peeved at themselves, or the bulls, he couldn't tell which. He would have been happy just to elude death by the beasties.

The big moment came when Sinbad was about to make his reappearance, with the good fortune of rider falling to a Jake Slator from Muskogee, Alabama. Big Jake, as he was called, could be seen in the chute sitting on top of Sinbad. He seemed to be spending an inordinate amount of time making sure his grip was just so, and damn sure the rope around Sinbad was tight, which probably annoyed the black bull because he kept slamming against the side of the chute, trying to crush Slator's legs. Big Jake kept having to lift his legs so they wouldn't get pinned against the fence, and that kept slowing things down.

The announcer was speaking in reverential tones about the mighty Sinbad and the relatively puny human on top of him. Zach thought this announcer must have been ringside David and Goliath. Man/boy against the giant demon. "Now folks, y'all've seen how hard it is to try and ride one of these bulls. Ain't a one been rode yet, and now I ain't taking nothin' away from any of the other riders, nor the bulls, but you purt near hafta consider them as average rodeo bulls compared to this ornery fella. I tell you folks he's a mountain of mean. I heard it that last year in the Greater Texas semi-finals, he threw a cowboy over the fence, then climbed over after him! I tell you, they almost retired that bull right there, and done it with a 30 ought 6.

"But now ole Jake here ain't nobody's fool. He can handle hisself as good as anyone else ridin' rodeo. Took first place up in Calgary last summer, and you gotta pass some pretty good mustard up there. Tells me he's got more broken bones than good'uns. Let's hope he don't change that ratio tonight."

By now all hell was breaking loose in the chute with Sinbad and his erstwhile rider. Sinbad was causing a ruckus, rearing high up on his back legs in order to get his front hooves up on the fence. He seemed to be trying to get as vertical as possible so that he could slam backward in to the fence, crushing Big Jake, but his hooves kept slipping on the metal slats. Poor Jake was doing his best to hang on without getting pancaked. The only humane thing to do for both of them was to open the chute.

When he came through the opening gate, Sinbad was up on his hind legs. The way he turned mid-air, you would have thought he was going to twist and land on his back, just getting the whole damned thing over with. He looked like some mythical beast, part lion, part bull, with his forelegs splayed out and his massive head turned sideways, mouth open in a silent roar. When his forelegs hit the dirt, he was bent nearly in half. The force of his landing caused Big Jake to lurch forward, his head slamming down low against Sinbad's left shoulder. Knowing the rider would not yet be able to recoil from the forward momentum, Sinbad leapt into the air, all four hooves off the ground, and in one blinding move, snapped his horns around, trying to gore Big Jake.

Jake must have sensed what was coming. With inhuman effort, he fought against the incredible G-forces pushing him forward, managing to push his torso back up off the bull. But he couldn't move his forearm quick enough. Sinbad's left horn bore into it just above the wrist. He screamed in pain as horn crushed bone. But he instinctively gripped tighter with his right hand, and held on.

Sinbad knew the man was wounded and it was only a matter of time before he shed the hated rider. He ran straight ahead a few paces, all the while kicking and bucking hard. He was only a few paces from the fence, about five yards from where Zach was sitting. By now the crowd was on their feet yelling and screaming. So was Zach. His adrenaline already running high, seeing this something inside of him exploded. Against his will he shot to his feet, compelled and pulled, there was nothing he could do, he no longer dwelled in his intellect, his ego, but deep down in his belly.

Sinbad approached the fence, writhing and rearing and kicking, with Big Jake hanging on, his face grimacing in pain, and his hand, broken at the wrist, flapping like a loose sail in a hard wind. The bull was only a step or two from the fence. Zach thought for sure he was going to crash right into it, or just throw his body into it, crushing Big Jake, but he stopped one step away, locked his forelegs, and threw his hind legs into the air in one awful spasm that sent Big Jake slamming into the fence, where he slid down it like something soft and sticky. Big Jake must have been back in Alabama, because he sure wasn't in Georgia. His ride was over in less than 6 seconds, not even a complete ride.

Sinbad had run back toward the center of the arena before he stopped and turned around to see the slumped over and unconscious Big Jake heaped in a pile against the fence. Then he lowered his horns. The crowd gasped, some yelled, "you sonofabitch" and other obscenities, but Sinbad paid them no mind. They had brought him here for sport and the game was still on.

Most of the clowns were scattered about the arena following Sinbad's unusual run to the fence. Only one had managed to get to the injured man, and now Sinbad was charging them both.

The clown couldn't get Big Jake up, who was just starting to come around to consciousness. So he stood up straight, alone, with his hands to his side, and looked straight into Sinbad's eyes. 'Oh God,' Zach thought, 'are you fucking crazy, he's going to kill you!' The clown didn't even look tense, no clenched fist, no hard set jaw. He looked passionless. Not fearful, not angry, not sad. Nothing. Just a look of mild concentration, like he was meditating. Like he wasn't even there. Zach could see his eyes were half closed. And Sinbad just kept coming. It was like some scene in a western, high noon and all that, only it wasn't man against man, it was man against bull. Surely, two men would die tonight.

The bull was only two feet away from goring the clown when suddenly he veered off, one of his horns grazing the clown, causing him to spin jerkily around, as if he had been rudely woken from a pleasant dream.

Gods, was he lucky! The crowd cheered and screamed while Sinbad ran on a few paces as if he intended all this for the drama. But in catching sight of another clown, Sinbad seemed to remember why he was here and chased after him. In short order the clown was well up the nearby fence. He then turned his attention to another clown, who quickly ran for safety too. Meanwhile, another clown had joined in the effort to resuscitate Big Jake, who was by now groggily starting to stir. They were frantically trying to get him on his feet when Sinbad, who had circled around, once again began to charge.

The same clown who had faced Sinbad just seconds before, turned toward him again, standing in front of the other two. He took on that same impassive look of concentration, with his arms hanging limply at his sides. And once again, in all his fury and might, Sinbad charged, but yet again turned at the last second, this time not so much as nicking the man, and ran off chasing another clown, who easily ran out of the way.

Sinbad soon circled back, lowered his head and charged a third time. Probably because of residual adrenaline and fear, Big Jake was fast waking up, and was starting to climb up the fence when Sinbad closed in on them. He and the second clown who had come to his aid were both on the fence, while the one who had been facing Sinbad was on the ground. He squared off to Sinbad and somehow managed to turn him again. But the bull ran past only a couple of paces before he wheeled around and lunged at the brave clown. In an instant the bull was in front of him, sweeping his horns upward, trying to catch flesh. But the clown had sensed something was wrong, for as soon as Sinbad had passed him, he had jumped toward the fence. He had one foot on a rail when Sinbad's horns caught him in the thigh. He was already moving up and the force of the bull's sweeping, searching horns helped propel him over the fence. Sinbad had literally tossed him out of the arena on his butt. The man landed face first in the urine and tobacco spit mud at Zach's feet, who jumped down to see if he was alright. As Zach bent down, the man lifted his head, face all splattered brown over white face powder, and through a big wide grin of pearly whites, said, "Howdy. Name's Burly Olalla."

chapter two

Several months later in his office, feet propped up on his desk, Zachary thought back on that night and that clown. Spring had come to the south, and as always, it stirred things up inside of him. There were two times of the year that made him feel anxious, or better said, brought out a yearning. One was the fall, when he thought people would feel more like hibernating, that it would be more natural to want to go into a quiet time, but for him it was the opposite. Maybe it was some hangover animal thing, the fall rut for males. Did women feel the same? Maybe things do feel anxious then, knowing a hard winter lies ahead. Perhaps the rustling leaves are shaking a raspy brittle finger at you, admonishing, "Better get a move on, better get going, hurry up now if you don't want old man snow and cold to catch you!" But now it was the time for feeling the promise held by the loving caress of a warming sun. To be embraced by the swirling golden stream of fragrances and perfumes and even pollens. It is the pulse of promise, two lovers tentatively kissing: each kiss, each touch, each tender sigh quickens, slowly, now faster, now slower, anticipation building. Spring is a child of angelic innocence, of unfettered and unquestioning love, of radiant smiles and giggly bubbly laughter and of tempestuous tempers and stormy moods. Spring is the sun pulling plants out of the ground, and robins pulling worms for baby blue eggshell chicks.

And in the south, spring unfolds in one glorious zip-a-dee-doo-dah-my-oh-my-what-an-incredible-way.

But his thoughts were on Burly Olalla. He got the sense that Burly was a very unusual bird in the brief moment they had met that night last winter. As he helped Burly off the ground, he was muttering things about the bull that Zach didn't quite understand, such as, "I should have known sooner that it wouldn't take him long to break my thoughts. That was close." Or something like that.

Zach asked him, "What are you talking about?" but he didn't respond. He was brushing the dirt and grime off himself, but then he paused, and looked Zach straight in the eye.

His eyes were coal black, which set them off rather ridiculously from the white powder and brown filth field that surrounded them. But a light danced in those eyes, a merry and mischievous light.

He laughed, then quickly turned away and said aloud, "How the hell is Big Jake?" There were plenty of people around Big Jake, who, although he was in a great deal of pain, managed to flash Burly a smile of gratitude when he caught him looking at him. "Looks like he'll be all right," said Burly, "though I don't know about that arm. Looks to be pretty busted up."

Zach then mumbled something about the wonders doctors can do today, and Burly responded with a grunt and a chuckle, "Yea, they can do sooome things!" He rolled the 'some' out like a red carpet for a delegation of doubters.

"Well, look," he said, "Thanks for helpin' me up. You ever in Arkansas City, you look me up."

Zach asked him where Ar-kan-sas City was and he said Arkansas City is in Kansas, correcting his mispronunciation. Zach was pronouncing it like the state of Arkansas, but he said it like R Kansas.

"Yea, sure will," Zach had responded automatically and with no sincerity.

Burly just laughed again and walked away, the next rider was about to come out of the chute, the rodeo still had to go on.

Zach was thinking about that time, absentmindedly turning over the triangular, wooden name plate that sat on his desk and read 'Zachary Peterson, assistant to the assistant vice-president', when his office door burst open with a knock and a rush of air.

"Hey Zach," a voice asked, "you wanna go out for lunch?" Only one person would barge into his office like that, opening the door and knocking at the same time. "Yea, sure Marty. Where you wanna go?"

"Ah thought we'd go over to Bevlyns and git some grits and such."

"Marty, I can't eat any more greasy food. I'm gonna die from the stuff."

"Oh, come on. You can git a turkey sandwich or somethin'."

Zach groaned, but relented and agreed to go to Bevlyns. He could have changed the plans, but he couldn't think of any alternative places, still thinking of Burly Olalla and that night. He thought it odd that no one, not even the announcer, who for all his bluster and store front toughness was still perceptive, but didn't sense anything unusual about how the clown had turned the bull away. They thought he somehow called the bull's bluff by staring him down and standing up to him. Oh, the announcer was full of platitudes, and rightly so, for the brave clown standing in front of that rip snortin' locomotive from hell. "Lookin' death in the eyes he was folks, but he stood there with the horn of Gabriel and blew that bull away," was one phrase, he recalled.

Marty and he walked the few blocks to Bevlyns and sat at the lunch counter. Bevlyns is kind of an Atlanta institution. It's been in the same family for generations and is named after the founder's mother, whose name was Beverly Lynn. For at least 40 years it has served up the same fare, which is southern style cooking. To Zach, that translated as everything fried, from green tomatoes to apple pie and even ice cream. Give an old-time southern cook some oil and he'll fry anything. But he liked it, in moderation.

They hunkered over the counter with the menus. The waitress who patrolled the counter, a dark haired, plain looking woman of 30 or so pushing her uniform's stitches to the limit, came up and greeted them. "Hey y'all, how you boys doin' t'daiy?"

"Hey Jess", Mary responded, "doin' all raght. Whatcha got special t'day?"

"Same as ever' Friday, fried catfish, hush puppies and a bowl a'greens," she wearily intoned.

By bowl a'greens Zach knew she was talking about over boiled turnip greens or kale with a little bit of bacon thrown in for flavoring. That's considered vegetarian.

She leaned over the counter to Zach and said in a sugary voice, "What can I get you, sweetie?"

Marty quickly said, "Now you caiyn't go flirtin' with him, Jess, he's almost a married man!"

Zach shot Marty a scowl, "What are you talking about, Marty, I am not! What in the hell gives you that idea?"

"You Yankees don't know nothin'. When a man dates a southern girl for as long as you en Emma been goin' out, y'all as good as maiyde."

Jess leaned back while bringing her hand to her mouth and said in mock surprise, "Now did I go losing out, did I let one get away? Tell me it's not true Zach'ry?"

He said flatly, "It ain't," and gave Marty another dirty look. Then he looked up at Jess and smiled, saying, "Now Jess, of course I'd let you know when the competition was getting close." He enjoyed this little game with her, they both knew they'd probably never date, but they played it anyway, just harmless flirtation. "Now how about getting me started here with some sweet tea?" he asked.

"Is that all would get you started?" she said as she leaned over.

"For now," he said.

"I'll get you anything, honey," she replied, then turned to walk away.

"Hey, what about me?" Marty asked. "Don't I get nothin?"

"For throwin' a cloud over my heart, I don't think you deserve nothin'!" declared Jess, who paused for a dramatic moment, then turned around to look at Marty with a smile, saying, "Because I'm such a forgiving person, what can I getcha, Marty?"

Zach had to admit she had one of the cutest smiles he'd seen, but there was a lot of trouble in it too. Marty just ordered a Coke, then looked down at his menu silently. Zach turned to him and said, "Marty, Emma and I have been going out for only 3 months. How can that add up to marriage?"

He shrugged his shoulders and said, "Yea, but you two don't date no one else. It's a done deal in my book."

That 'book' of his was a sea of aphorisms, colloquialisms and Southern sayings deeper than Zach could fathom; he had yet to hit bottom. Zach thought of Marty as a good ole boy, a native born Southerner. He didn't think of 'good ole boy' as having negative connotations, not in the pejorative sense, not like it used to mean. He was born in Alabama, in the tiny little town of Weogufka, some fifty or sixty miles southeast of Birmingham. His father had worked in a nearby quarry, but when it was played out, he moved his family to Birmingham and got a job in a factory. Marty was thirteen years old at the time. It took him a while to adjust to life in the city, but he adapted, eventually graduating from the University of Alabama there. He was the first in his family to even go to college, let alone graduate. His family, generations of farmers and quarry workers, had always lived close to the city in the Weogufka area. Before his father, none had left the country and in the South, country living is a world apart from city living. Maybe that's true everywhere.

"I think I'll get a salad," Zach announced, and laid the menu down. Turning to Marty, he said, "I have strong feelings for Emma, she and I have gotten really close in the past few months we have been dating. But marriage is not going to happen anytime soon."

"Ya see? You just said anytahme soon, not that it ain't gonna happen. That's muh point! Y'all as good as wed." Marty wore the smug look of someone who just scored big in a poker game. In a rhyming, lilting voice, he added, "Two mares in a stall and not a word. Add a stud and you'll git a herd."

"Aaacckk!" Zach choked on a drink of sweet tea. "Don't go there, Marty, don't go there," he said as tea dribbled down his chin.

Mercifully, Jess returned. "So what'll it be boys? Zach, does that glass have holes in it?"

"Nah, Jess, the only holes are in my friendships," he said behind a napkin.

After finishing lunch, Marty and Zach stepped out into a beautiful bright spring day. Having been disabused of his reverie over Burly Olalla, Zach was subsumed by the miasma of fragrances and buds and flowers in the little splashes of greenery that lined the street in pots and garden ways and entrances. He could almost swim back to work in the thickness of it all.

"Care to breaststroke back, Marty?" he asked.

"What on earth are you jabberin' about? Swim back?"

"You have to take advantage of this weather, before it turns thick with humidity and heat in June. It's nothing but thin air up north. Well, maybe in August it isn't. You're used to having to claw your way through air dripping with discomfort, I'm not. I want to enjoy this before summer sets in. Maybe Emma will go camping with me this weekend. It would be great to hike in the mountains."

"Yea, you take a hotel en she'll go," Marty said, "Leastways Ah would."

"She's not like that, she's adventurous. Remember, the first weekend we spent together was down off St. Simeon's island, sea kayaking."

"Yea, but you spent nights in a fancy hotel. And didn't her mama give her hell for doing that after y'all hadn't been goin' out more'n a month?"

"Times change, Marty, and her mother let it go after a while."

"Ain't the point. Maybe she don't wanna upset her mama again. Had a fit, I heard. More'n likely she'll wait until you're engaged or so."

"There you go again. Will you stop with the marriage stuff?" Zach threw his arms apart to emphasize an emotion that wasn't really there. "Anyway, Emma told me she'd try camping with me. We have a 3-day weekend coming up. What is it, Memorial? Next weekend? She's never been camping, at least not as an adult."

Marty did not share the same enthusiasm for outdoor activity as Zach did. For the most part, raised in the country, he seemed to have the natural dislike for sleeping out of doors that many a country raised folk do, unlike some of their city cousins, who relish the opportunity to leave the comfort of their urban dwellings to be set upon and perhaps be made miserable by all manners of insects, reptiles, bad weather and the occasional mammalian intruder. Oh, he'd go out fishing, and maybe spend a night in his little pop-up camper, but never in a tent. "Why on earth would I deliberately make myself uncomfortable?" was his usual response.

"That's alright, Marty," Zach continued, "you can hold your camping critique, just tell me, isn't next weekend Memorial holiday?"

"Yup, it is," he replied.

They were, by now, standing in front of their office building, which was a large, refurbished, two story brick factory that had originally been home to a tanner, dating back to 1898. The name of the original owner was still engraved in Tennessee marble on the lintel: L.C. Hazelton, 1898.

"Well," Zach said, "I guess it's time to go up and see if we can waste the afternoon away until it's quitting time."

Marty laughed, knowing the last thing they'd be able to do was fritter away time in the office. "Yea, Ah think I'll go nod out on ole J.J.'s leather couch."

Zach laughed, too. It was a funny thought, the incongruity of sleeping in J.J.'s office while he kept on working around you, his indefatigable energy humming along like some cyborg on

Prozac. "Well, let's go, I want to call Emma and see about next weekend."

J.J. was John Jenson, their boss. Nearly ten years ago he had been a very popular news anchor in Chicago at one of the network affiliates. He seemed to have all the necessary requirements for landing the top anchor job at the network for the evening news: He was handsome, well spoken, prematurely white/grey haired. He had that avuncular air about him so sought after by the newscasts. You could always trust whatever John Jenson told you, no matter what it was. And if the news was a bit scary, you felt reassured by him. He was sure to be the next Walter Kronkite, but the networks decided to take a different tack on things, to reach out to the up and coming younger generation, the baby boomers, and they all followed one another in picking younger men and they reached out to women, too, the new generation's own. And so J.J. was left out of the top plum, what would have been the pinnacle of a career, so he quit and traveled around a bit. Not long and not far, though, something less than a year, and he never left the States. Rumor had it that he spent most of his time watching television, not exactly the kind of sabbatical one would romanticize or dream about. He seemed to get a dose of the new religion of the networks, because he decided to start up his own consulting business for news shows. Now he would reshape local news to be the top draw in their market. John Jenson had the know how and savvy to turn your little hogs and corn belt farm report, gossip-mongering, weather forecasting station into a slick, professional production. Number three in a big city market? No problem there either, John Jenson would get you top ratings in six months.

And to his credit, he usually did. His success centered on his openness to new ideas. He would do whatever it took, no matter how untried or unusual, to turn a station around. He'd turn comedians into weather forecasters, or weather forecasters into comedians. He'd turn out your old white haired anchor, or pair him with a young blond. The aging beauty queen, still popular with the audience, he'd make her a roving, special reporter. Got a spunky, smart-lipped reporter not quite a national beauty treasure? No problem, make-up can do wonders, and sassy comebacks will make up for the loss of looks. Attitude counts big. And to keep himself fresh and up-to-date, to surround himself with new ideas, to insure he waded in a creative and polyglot pool, he hired people of all different stripes and backgrounds to the extent he could afford or justify. The office was a veritable zoo of humanity.

That's how Zachary fit in. J.J. hired him because he thought Zach represented, or had the pulse of, the new up and coming, suburban/urban middle class. The yuppies turning puppies (parented, urban, etc.), though he was not yet married, but close now, according to Marty. J.J. wanted him for what he thought he brought to the mix from the North, in the same way he hoped Marty brought from the equivalent generation from the South. Zach was his khaki-clad, thirtysomething, North Shore, shopping mall, Range Rover sports fan, fond of micro brews and mutual funds and certified cigar aficionado.

The two men went through the revolving glass entranceway, under the ever-watchful moniker of L.C. Hazelton, and entered into the atrium, a two-story expanse the remodelers had added during the rebuilding a few years back. They greeted the receptionist, who they knew and had gone out on the town with more than once, and got on the escalator to their second floor offices.

The upper story was originally a vast storage area, and was therefore very open. It had been partitioned into office space by glass, for the most part, so it didn't feel as enclosed as solid walls would make it feel. No matter where a person was on the floor, it felt spacious, and it was designed so that one could always see outside through windows. J.J. thought it would enhance thinking if the mind and body didn't feel confined. He had a point there. He was also clever and careful in choosing the colors of the carpeting, furniture, drapes and those walls that could be painted.

Nothing was boring, nothing insipid and droll. There were bright, but somehow muted, shades of greens, blues, purples and even ochre's and light sienna's. Everything tasteful, everything to encourage creative thought.

Zach's office was around the corner from Marty's. As they walked down the hall to their offices, they ran into J.J., who came bursting out of Marilyn Kinder's office. "Boys, boys, how was lunch? What'd ya have? Same old Friday fish fry? Was it any good? You better watch that stuff, coronary clotting crud, you know."

J.J. didn't ever really leave time for responses when he was being polite and acknowledging you, and in a hurry. Which was always, unless he was specifically probing you for ideas. That was about the only time he could sit still. It was kind of comical, really, to be in on a meeting with J.J. It was almost painful to watch him squirm around in a chair, like a child being forced to stay put for punishment, knowing all their friends were out playing in the yard.

"No, no, J.J.," Zach said, patting his stomach, "Nothing but good in the temple." J.J just laughed and sped on his way. Over his shoulder he said, "I want to talk to you two before you go home, I want to bounce some ideas off you. How's the Bradford account going?" Before they could respond, he was gone. He didn't really want an answer, he was just reminding them to keep working on it. It must be the manner of bosses to prod in that fashion, it must be taught in Boss 101. Marty and Zach looked at each other and smiled, shaking their heads, it was a classic run-in with J.J., like stepping outside into a gust of wind that braces you, then quickly spins off. "Weyull, Zach, time for a nap, hey?" Marty said. "Yea," Zach laughed, "I can use the Bradford papers as a pillow."

Zach went into his office and sat at his desk, spinning the chair around to face the window looking out, and grabbed the phone. He hit the speed dialer for Emma's number and leaned back in the chair, only to be greeted with voice mail. His enthusiasm drained hearing the auto-attendant's voice. "Yeah, yeah, thank you for calling blah, blah," he said, wading through the system till he got to the part to record. "Hey, it's me, give me a call. OK?" He set the phone down in disappointment. "Well, shit, I guess I have to get to work."

He opened the Bradford file papers and started going over them. William Bradford owned a small network affiliate in Chattanooga, Tennessee. His news hour ratings were second in the local pool of three, but slipping. He wanted to regain his ratings, and even to take over number one. Marty and Zach had come up with the idea to can his current top anchor, a platinum blond woman who looked like she just came from a country and western stage show in Nashville, (which she in fact had) and replace her with a brunette with no accent, no regional inflections in her speaking mannerisms. There are ratings in the banality of unaccented speech. They knew of an ambitious young reporter working at a small TV station in Syracuse, New York, who might take the job. They also knew of a wise ass ex-jock who would be a great sports anchor, which always gives ratings a boost. It might take a little money to get him to relocate to Chattanooga, but they thought they could convince him it is only a short drive to Atlanta and the big leagues.

Zach spent the next couple of hours looking over the station ratings, the demographics and market profile of Chattanooga with no interruptions and no phone calls; and unfortunately that included Emma. He started to get drowsy and leaned back in the comfortable chair J.J. thought was mandatory for conducing creative thought, and slipped into sleep. And in to a dream.

He dreamt he was swimming in a pool in a room with vaulted ceilings and stone walls. The light reflecting off the water danced along the walls and ceilings, each ray shimmering and moving as if by individual will, but the movement of all seemed choreographed by a larger puppeteer. There was no discernible color to the stone, but the entire room was infused in turquoise and pale rose. It looked like some ancient Roman bath. A telephone rang, so he got out of the water to answer it. Moving toward the sound, he found himself entering another room, this one a bit more spacious. It opened up into a rotunda, and he walked up to a marbled rail to look down on to a crypt. The phone was begging to be answered, but he had to go down into the crypt to get it. There was a stairway to his left, which he followed down where it opened into the crypt room. As he walked up to the sarcophagus, he was overcome with feelings of incredible awe, a consuming, trembling, emotional force. He became aware that he was in the presence of divinity, of holiness so pure and powerful he was but transparent, stripped to gossamer essence. Shaking, he sank to his knees and approached the sarcophagus in humility and reverence. Somehow he knew that it was Jesus Christ lying in there. He crawled up to the edge and peered over the rim with head bowed and saw a man lying within. A linen sheet lay draped over half his body, partially exposing his right leg to cover half his groin. His skin was oily and dark, and he was quite hairy, and all of that dark as well. He was peering over his mid-section and could have reached out and touched him had he cared to. Seeing that it was but a man, the solemnity shading to dread abated giving him some measure of reassurance. His eyes followed the bump of the man's knee up the line of his thigh, with its stubby black hair and the thighs were thick, not at all thin like he supposed Jesus' had been. He couldn't help himself, though embarrassed and shamed, his eyes were soon peering at his groin. He could see the scrotum, covered in black pubic hair, and could see the trunk of his penis, though the end was covered by the sheet. Jesus started to stir, and Zach's eyes began to move up toward his face. He didn't speak, but his words entered Zach's head like thoughts. "You see, I am a man as you are." It was taking a tremendous amount of courage and effort to look at him, Zach's head and eyes were turning to meet his gaze, to look him in the eyes but he was pushing against an unknown force, a molten stream of fear and dread, trepidation thick with foreboding. Slowly, slowly he turned, straining against the fetters and binds of loathing and doubt and uncertainty, eyes blurring and motion denied until Zach could see the outlines of a bearded face, no more, the rest seemed indistinct until through more effort he peered into the sweet rapture held by dark brown eyes. They were kind eyes, full of love, they did not hold question nor judgment, they held only love. And knowing. He could sing and play and dance and rejoice in those eyes. But he began to gain self-consciousness, ego reclaiming awareness, and as he did, his perspective began to telescope back, to become aware of a surrounding field of white, of dark islands in a sea of light flecked with brown. Memory jogged, consciousness waxing, he knew this face. Where? When? Associations: winter, riding, bulls, clowns, Burly Olalla!

He awoke with a start, nearly falling backward off his chair, feet kicking out, knocking things off his desk as arms flailed out, sending the telephone clamoring into the corner by the potted ficus. "Jesus Christ!" he yelled aloud, "What the hell!" The telephone was ringing even as it tumbled, and kept on as it stopped at the base of the pot. He groaned and bent forward, lunging at it. A knee caught the edge of the desk and he howled in pain as he went down. But he did answer the phone, yelling, "YES!?"

"Zach?"

It was Emma.

"Oh God, Emma, I'm sorry, I didn't know it was you. I didn't mean to yell, I mean, I'm not yelling, I mean not at you, I guess I am yelling, but I just smashed my knee into my desk and I fell and I was sleeping, and I had this dream, and . . . Ah, jeez, let me collect myself, I . . ."

"You allraght? Did you hurt yuh'self? Oh Zach, Ah'm so sorry. You okaiy?"

"Yea, yea, just fuzzy. I need to . . ."

"Ah woke you up?"

"Well, yea, I just dozed off. I was going over the Bradford account, and . . ."

A knock at the door interrupted them. "Just a sec, Emma."

"Everything all right in there?"

The deep voice told him it was one of his office neighbors. "Yea, Kelly, just knocked some things off my desk. It's alright, nothing broke. Sorry."

"Okay, just checking. Sounded like a bomb went off or something."

"Nah, no such luck, I'm still here."

Kelly laughed and walked away. His intrusion allowed Zach to gather himself.

"Hey," he said softly into the receiver. She responded even softer, "Hey." She drew the word out like a long kiss, a breadth of wind cupping and delicately brushing his cheek, a hey that went right to the heart. Hearing her voice calmed and soothed him, all the jangly nerves stopped sputtering. "Yea, yea, I'm okay, just nearly broke my knee trying to get to the phone. 'Course it would help if I kept it on my desk," he said, a little playfulness in his voice.

"Zacharee," she breathed with a touch of coyness, "hWhat did you do?"

"Those damn Bradford papers. They put me to sleep. When I heard the phone it startled me, so when I woke up, I kicked my desk, knocking the phone on the floor. When I reached to get it, I smashed my knee on the corner of my desk. But hearing your voice now, it's like a balm, like nourishment and sustenance."

"You're so sweet. You allraght now?" she asked.

"Yea," he said, drawing it out dreamily. "But wait, no, there was a phone ringing in my dream. Wow, I had this interesting dream, and it wasn't the phone that startled me, it was seeing Burly Olalla, I mean his face." He was starting to recall the dream.

"You mean that rodeo clown you told mc about?" she asked.

"Yes, that guy. His face loomed up at me, sort of. Oh, I have to tell you about this dream, it was really wild. Well, not wild. Any rate, I don't want to tell you over the phone, I'll tell you later. Are we going to have a later? I mean tonight?"

She laughed at the double-entendre, implied or not, that he held uncertainty like a schoolboy about their relationship. She knew he only asked about getting together that night, nonetheless, she was silent for a moment to roast him on his own petard, then she laughed again and said, "hWe 'u'll have dinnuh t'gethuh at mah place, and you can tell me all about your dream."

"You know," he said, "There is sometimes a fine line between playfulness and cruelty."

"Oh, Zacharee, Ah just cayun't help mahself when you get this cute," she giggled.

"And I get to see your mean streak. What can I bring?"

"Nothin', less'n you want t' pick up a bottle of wine."

"Mmmm, sounds good. See you when, 6:30?"

"You can come at 6:00, Ah should be home by theyn."

"All right, J.J. wants to see me, but I should be able to slip out without him catching me. If I'm late, though, J.J. caught me."

"Zacharee, you should see him if he wants to see you."

"That's your Southern sense of duty and honor. I don't have it, remember, I'm a Yankee."

"You sure ahre," she laughed.

It was time to go back to the mundane things that made up each other's work day, and so they said good bye with all the tenderness two lovers offer when parting for what will seem like an eternity, though precious few grains of sand slip through the slender neck of the hourglass.

About 5:15 that afternoon, he put the Bradford file away and gathered his sports jacket and brief case. "Quittin' time," he announced aloud. He opened his door cautiously and peered down both hallways, the advantageous view a corner office provides. He most certainly did not want to run into J.J. A meeting with him at this time could well mean a delay of up to an hour. If he wanted to go over something, it could wait until Monday. He'd had long meetings with J.J. over the color of office paper clips. No item or idea was too small to mull over and harangue to death.

The coast was clear, so with the deftness of a cat burglar, he stole down the corridor to the escalator. And just in time, he could hear J.J.'s voice, "Has anyone seen Zachary? Did he go home? Zach? Marty! Marty? Anyone seen Marty?" That man has a sixth sense, he thought to himself. He hurried down the escalator; freedom lay beyond the revolving doors. When it comes to skulking and slinking, he considered himself at the top of the class and so he was soon whistlin' Dixie under L.C. Hazelton. See ya, L.C.

Emma lived outside of the city as he did, but in a different direction. It was only about a half hour car ride from the office to her house in so-so traffic, and he'd be there right about 6:00, allowing for time to stop and get some wine. Zach decided to get three bottles while he could in case they need more over the weekend; Jesus don't like drinkin' on Sundays in the South.

Although Atlanta is a good-sized American city and cosmopolitan enough for all but the most urbanized, it doesn't take long to get from marble facade to red clay mud, from a treeless downtown to a canopied country road. Emma had chosen to live on the border of both. The town she lived in was once too far from downtown to be considered a suburb, though not any more. It still had a quaint town square, red bricked with a refurbished depot-an artifact belying the town's origin as a railroad stop. The cotton they grew down in the southern part of the state used to be shipped to the north end to be spun and woven in mills, and the old town used to have several of them, all long gone. Like carpet remnants, the industry leftovers could be seen off the interstate coming down from Tennessee. Few actually weave on the premises, fewer still use cotton.

He pulled in to the driveway of the house she rented. She wasn't home yet, her white Camry wasn't in the carport, and since a beautiful evening was unfolding, he decided to wait for her on the front porch, though he knew where she kept an extra key to the house. She loved sitting outside and she loved rocking chairs, so naturally the porch had one. She in fact had one in just about every room, as he thought about it. She must have five of them, at least. He smiled to myself about this little revealing thing about Emma. Rocking chairs are like genes, they hold the past and help adjust to the present, and lay out the future, too. You dip into the past leaning back, then roll into the present mid-rock, then peer into the future, only to slide back again. Sisyphus pushing a history book. She did that, she carried the past in her voice, the present in her appearance, and the future in her eyes. Living in a town that bordered bumpkin, burb and urburb. That she grew up in both city and country had a lot to do with it.

Her father, Broderick, was a doctor, a general practitioner in his hometown of Savannah. He was a near-stereotype with his shock of white hair, three-piece suit and old-fashioned mannerisms, and even being a general practitioner seemed somehow dated. But he was no relic, far from it. He'd been a very young medic in Germany in WWII, and returned home to further his medical studies at the University of Georgia in Athens. But he'd also studied English literature. He loved modern fiction, modern to the extent of James Joyce and William Faulkner. More than once with Zach, after a glass or two of port he often rued the loss of great talent in English and American writing. From the roar and thunder of those two and Lewis and a few others, a tidal wave of talent sounding loudly on the surf, then ebbing to a back tide, draining away, foam sucking into sand, the last few fainting cries raised by the likes of Brautigan, Vonnegut and D'Angulo. But it comforted his spirit to know that the tsunami had hit more southerly shores and reinvested itself in Garcia Marquez and Allende and others. Zachary rued away with him, though for the most part he hadn't read anyone but Vonnegut and Hemingway. The first time Zach mentioned Hemingway, Broderick took the bottle of port away, so Zach never brought his name up again. It was in one of those literature classes at UGA that he met Virginia, Emma's mother.

Virginia was the daughter of a wealthy Georgia farmer, a family that could trace their ancestry directly back to the Scottish highlands. They'd come to America in the 17th century, moving from Virginia to North Carolina, then down into Georgia. Way down in Georgia, near the panhandle of Florida. A lot of flat land there, the heat and the soil perfect for cotton. They'd built many a great plantation on the back of some other, not so eager nor fortunate, immigrants. Virginia was born on what remained of one of those plantations, outside of Thomasville. The house was huge, with great big Greek columns and spectacular entrance with stairways spiraling off to both sides, the high ceilings, twenty some rooms, the driveway bordered by oaks dripping Spanish moss. And it sat in the middle of 3500 acres of pecan, peach and turpentine pine trees. And yes, there was still some cotton. The mansion is partly run as a museum now, but when Emma was growing up, that was where she spent her summers, at Trieste. The school year was spent in Savannah, at what the family really considered home, located in the historic district, just off one of the city's many little parks on a street more inhabited by horse drawn carriages carrying tourists than by locals.

The sound of a car pulling into the driveway took Zach away from rocking chairs, genes and summers at Trieste.

"Hey," Emma yelled from the open car window, "Ah see you ran off without talkin' t' J.J."

"Apparently he couldn't find me. Don't know why," he lied with a smile that he hoped would find forgiveness, seeing how it was so obvious. "He must have forgotten."

"You ahre rotten," she smiled back.

"I know, and it's contagious," he said walking to the car. He grabbed her as she stepped out and faked a gentle hug, and instead began tickling her. "And now you've got it."

"AAAHHH," she screamed. "Let me go! It's unfaiyr, Ah can't defend mahself."

"There is no defense from the rotting working fever, but not being sadistically inclined, I shall cease and desist," he intoned like an automaton then stopped, but he still held her.

Gathering herself, she flashed that smile of hers that stuns him, opening the door of possibilities, of heaven down here in the muck of earth. "Hey," she said gently. "Hey," he responded. Their eyes locked, and eyelids slowly closed as heads drew close. Lips touched, gingerly at first, then eagerly and passionately. "Let's go inside," Emma said. She led him by the hand, quietly, only whispers of clothes sounding. Once inside she tossed her keys on the kitchen table on their way to the bedroom. In the bedroom, she went over to a window and closed the blinds, then went to the other and did the same. Zach stood next to the bed and watched. She came to him, put her arms around him, gently pulling him close to her, her breasts spreading out against his chest. For a few minutes they kissed while standing, lips pulling on lips, tongues exploring each other in silent dance, soft kisses on soft necks. His hands soon slid down her back to her buttocks, caressing, then gently pulling her hips into his, softly, almost imperceptibly at first, then with rising urgency. Hushed and barely audible moans came from her. He lifted her top off and kissed her exposed skin, circling round her breasts. Then he undid her bra, letting it fall to her feet. He massaged the lines under her breasts left by the wire in the cups, first with hands, then nuzzling them with nose and brows, then with mouth, kisses healing tender flesh, her nipples stiffening. He knelt down and undid her skirt where a clasp held it at her side and let it join the bra at her feet then pressed his cheek against the soft mound rising against her panties. Gently, he rubbed his face on her panties, first one cheek, then the other, then using the hardness of his cheekbones, each passing eliciting a soft moan. He nuzzled there, too, and smelled the loam of the earth. His hands held her buttocks, sliding under her panties, fingers massaging soft skin, kneading muscles underneath. She was swaying, pulsing like a clear note struck from string. She grabbed his hands in hers, pulling them up, wanting him to stand. As he stood, she unbuttoned his shirt and threw it on a chair and slid her hands down his sides slowly, tenderly 'till they reached his belt, which she then unbuckled and undid, along with pants and boxers, letting them pile at his feet. She began kissing him, starting from the shoulders, working her way down slowly, soft kisses and warm, languorous flicks from her tongue. She rubbed her face against his stomach, cuddling, nuzzling, kissing. Then she moved lower still, a gentle moist compress of lips and tongue. Now his body harmonized with hers, pulsing with pure tone. She stood up, placed her hands at his hips, pulled him to her, and leaned into the bed, where they fell in as one.

chapter three

"I bought a couple of bottles in case we want some on Sunday," Zach said over the rustle of bags. "A red and a blush. Which one you want?"

"Ah don't cayherr, you choose," Emma said from behind the refrigerator door. "hWhayre is the darned pickle jar? One a these days I'm goanna clean this mais up. Too many jars! hWhat's this?" Picking up a Mason jar, she examined it thoroughly, and not without a little disgust. "Ah'm afraid t' open it." She unscrewed the lid and looked in, not letting her nose get too close for fear it would be severely offended. "Oh, mama's apple buttuh! Ah thought it was awl gowne."

"Opener, opener, opener, whither thou be. I'm feeling like it's Friday, and I want some wine you see," Zach sang as he looked through the kitchen drawers most likely to hold such an item, which in Emma's kitchen, meant any one was as likely as another. "Hah, unearthed you are!" he cried triumphantly. "The great archeologist Von Zachary has discovered the key to the secrets of the pharaohs. With his willing and able assistant he will unlock the vial containing the ambrosia of the Gods, and upon drinking the magic potion, they shall join them in eternal bliss." Pop! went the cork. "Ah, the God's speak their approval," he went on, "Assistant, the medical beakers." Emma grabbed two wineglasses and slid over to his side, pressing against him. He poured the wine and handed her a glass, and they raised them in mock seriousness that gave way to giggly laughter. "Ah, the effects are instantaneous," he said, looking at her, "You know, they say . . ." he stuttered, momentarily forgetting what he was about to say, "You know, they say," he began again, then lost it again. He turned to look at her fully. "You know, Emma, you are incredibly beautiful, you're glowing like an incandescent light bulb. There is a white light bathing you. I swear I can make out little white tendrils snaking out, like from some kind of vine."

She blushed and squeezed his hand. "Ah think it's from our love makin', you have it too."

"Yea, all right, but the vine must look more like Kudzu," he said.

She laughed, but admonished him, "Theyuh you go again, don't maike fun of yourself. Ah maght get maiyhd that someone, even though it's you, is pickin' on you." At that bit of spin he laughed too. "You know, as soon as you get home you talk more Southern. Your accent comes out like, I don't know, coons at night."

She grabbed the bottle of wine and her glass and moved over to the couch. "Ah don't caiyr. Ah cun let mah haiyr down. Come tell me bout yaw dream this afternoon, bout yaw snoozing awhaiy on J.J.'s paiy."

"Jeez, I forgot all about it. What about dinner?"

"hWe'll maiyke it afta yew tell me bout yaw dream."

"Okay."

He sat down next to her and told her all about it, about the walking down the stairway with growing excitement, how he felt something portentous was unfolding. Of how he trembled as he walked up to the sarcophagus, knowing, just knowing, that Jesus was inside. Of how he looked at him, saw his humanness, saw his maleness. How he felt embarrassed and intrigued at the same time, that he shouldn't be looking at sacredness, but couldn't help but look, like he was supposed to. That that was the intent of the dream. And all the time a phone was ringing. And when he was beginning to feel almost comfortable, or maybe not as embarrassed, and was becoming aware he was dreaming, or something like that, what do they call it, lucid dreaming? he was looking into Christ's loving, dreamy eyes, so compassionate, so knowing, then the vision started to telescope, pulling back and all of a sudden, there he was, that clown, Burly Olalla. Seeing him, he woke with a start, and the telephone was screaming ringing which jarred him even more and it was her calling.

Emma just sat there looking at him with eyes wide open and unblinking. Big brown saucers in stationary orbit. She wore a smile that betrayed some mischievous event occurred that he didn't know about and was he ever missing out. Lips pulled back and thin against her teeth, nearly grinning.

"Well, what do you think? Are you going to lose those cute little dimples and say something?" he asked.

"Weyull, it's very rich in symbolism, but Ah don't know hwhat all of it means, beyond the obvious, lahk findin the Chrahst within. hWhat d'yew think about it?"

"Surprised I had it." he said somewhat matter-of-factly.

"Don't saiy nothin' of the kahnd."

Hearing her say 'kahnd' in her drawl brought a smile to his face, which bothered her sometimes depending on her mood. She knew he was about to tease her about her accent, but he let it go.

She spoke again, "You said that you felt the dream maght have been about yaw lookin' at Jesus, knowin' that he was, afta all, human."

"Yes, a man. Like me. You know, we forget that he was, or those who worship him forget, and only concentrate on his being a god. There I was looking at him, looking at his sexuality. Even I felt uncomfortable, and I'm not really a Christian. Not anymore, anyway. What was it that Paul said, 'When I was a child I held childish things, but now that I'm grown, I put them away' or something like that. That pretty well sums up my feelings on all that religion and stuff. I'm not sure I even believe Jesus existed."

She laughed, tilting her head back a little, "I can imaigine mah Granny, bless her heart, havin' that dream. Ah don't think she'd evuh tayll enyone if she did, she'd be so mortifahd."

She shifted on the couch and continued, "But it's awlmost too personal t' talk about. You know, it has so much maigic in it you don't wanna say nothin' for fear of takin' some of the maigic awaiy."

"What do you mean?"

"It's lahk a seecrit. T'ain't a seecrit if you talk about it."

"So, what are you saying, that the dream was magical or something?"

"Ah'm sayin' theyuh was a lot of meanin' and symbolism in it, and yes, you can say theyuh was a lot of maigic in it. It was so full of atmosphere and drama. And what do you maike of this Burly fellow showing up? Is that some random coincidence? Ah still cain't believe you had this while napping at the office. Diggy Selma used t'talk about big dreams, the kahnd that changes peoples lahves. You know Zachy, I think you had a big dream."

"You just put the kabosh on it," he stated, "by mentioning Diggy Selma. That crazy woman talks to rocks for God sakes! You had me going there for a second."

"They'uh not rocks, they'uh crystals," she said defiantly.

"Whatever."

An awkward moment of silence passed between them; he had said something less than flattering about one of her favorite people.

"You may be on to something," Zach said to break the silence and to regain her graces. "I'm not totally dead, you know. I know it was powerful, I can still see that white, mud-stained face looming out at me. Also, I can clearly see the pores on Jesus' legs, not to mention part of his you know what." She was looking at him sympathetically, the kind of look one gives to a child who just can't seem to grasp the task at hand, but who will eventually. Just be patient ya little yipper, you'll grow up. "But I don't know what to do with it," he continued, "I'm not on any spiritual quest, I'm not looking for the grail. Hell, I'm not even looking for a church, so it doesn't make sense that I would have a dream like that. But I sure am curious about that clown.

"That guy was interesting, something about him . . ." he let it trail off like smoke from a campfire wisping into a blue unknown.

He looked at Emma and smiled, touching her forearm. "Hey, I didn't mean to say anything bad about Diggy. I've never even met her. I know you like her a lot, she just seems to be some old character out of a bad B-movie. You know, the old hag with hexes and potions and stuff."

"That's your own stereotype, Zach. She's nothin' lahk that at all. She taught me a lot of things when Ah was growing up, when Ah spent summers at Trieste. She knows a lot of things most people have forgotten about, or don't cayerr about. She's from a different time and it don't have anythin' t' do with chicken blood or tea leaves, or whatever else your mind is fantasizin' about."

"Probably not, I just haven't run into anyone like that."

"Wayull, you will."

"Yea? When?" In his best impression of a landed Southern gentry/plantation owner voice, he said, "Are we agoin' back home, back to the plantation, Scarlett?"

She giggled, hit him with a pillow, and said, "Yeah Suh, en we'ze agoan tah n' feathuh this heayuh Yankee."

He reached over and grabbed her in her most ticklish spot, right on her side at the lowest rib, causing her to jump, nearly knocking over her glass of wine. "Unfaiyuh," she declared, then moved the glass out of the way and jumped on him, digging her hands into his most ticklish spots. "All right!" he howled, "All right!" They tussled a bit more 'til he leaned back on the couch, bringing her with him, arms wrapped around each other. Breathing hard with burbly laughter, faces close, they began to kiss. Through a mouthful of kisses, he asked, "When you tar and feather me, I'll be naked, right?" Moving on top of him after she slipped off her panties, she murmured, "hAin't no bettuh waiy."

Dressing themselves later on, in a breathy, dreamy voice Zach gently teased, "It's getting late and we haven't eaten yet. You have a taste for anything besides wine and love?"

"Ah guess Ah have to, Ah suppose we could run over to that

Chinese place on the squaiyerr, Ah don't think thaiyerr's anything left in the house t' eat. Ah have to go shopping tomorrow."

"That reminds me," he said, "Next weekend is Memorial Day, so we have a long weekend coming up. You have it off, don't you?"

"Uh hunh," she assented.

"Great. I was thinking maybe we could go camping up in the mountains. What do you think?'

"Sounds wonderful, Ah so need t' get out of town. But Mama might be opening up Trieste for the summer. If she does, she'll need some help."

"When will you know?"

"Ah'll call her this weekend, Sunday would be the best time to get hold of her."

"Okay, so we still might go camping. If we do I'll need to go over to Exurban Outfitters and get some things."

Saturday morning bloomed bright and sunny. Carolina chickadees fluttered around the bird feeder in Emma's backyard. A pair of cardinals patrolled the ground along with a pair of mourning doves, sweeping up seeds the messy chickadees knocked down in their furious attacks on the feeder. The chickadees are too small to see in the trees. Often, only little innocent cheeps in the foliage betrayed their presence, then suddenly they materialize on the feeder in a blurry flurry of wings. Instantly they set about attacking the seeds. Being very discriminating in their tastes, only one of a dozen seems palatable, the rest imperiously tossed aside. A feeder assault by a chickadee chain saw.

"Look at those little mongrels. I can't tell if they eat any of the seeds, or they just like to throw them on the ground. Maybe the mourning doves and cardinals pay them with juicy grubs later on. It's a feathery cabal," Zachary opined looking out Emma's kitchen window.

"Hmmmm," she replied, "coffee's ready." She didn't seem to have any interest in his avian observations.

They sat down at her little oak table and sipped their mugs, waiting for the caffeine to separate morning from night, a job long ago taken away from the sun and given to the little bean from South America. Emma wore her white terry cloth robe, hair not yet brushed, her eyes still not sharp as she hadn't fully returned from a night of riding dreams and exploring hidden and secret realms. Her skin seemed extraordinarily soft, the lines and contours indeterminate, like focusing a camera, then mussing it slightly. And she looked beautiful. She was aware he was staring at her, and smiled at him, a smile that escaped from a curled dimple, an embarrassed cheek uncoiled. Maybe it was the morning sun coaxing gold out of the air and limning her with threads of sunlight, or the song of contentment from the cooing doves coming through the open window, or the snowy white tendrils of love that still laced them together from their night of making love, but he knew then that he loved her. He loved her strong and loved her powerfully. He loved her softly, and he loved her gently. And he loved her forever.

Then again, it could have just been her smile.

But he could only smile back. For some reason he was struck dumb. He wanted to tell her what he was feeling, what was going on inside, how he was madly in love with her, but he could only look at her and smile dumbly, mute as a doorknob. He looked down into his coffee for inspiration, but only got a push to sip it. If he didn't do something he feared he would begin to drool. That would be just lovely. On a gorgeous spring morning in Georgia, with the birds outside cooing, his heart singing love songs to the golden glow beauty across the table, who smiles at him like a goddess, who looks like a goddess, and he looks back, head tilting down, drooling. No, no, marshal your resolve boy, show her your mettle, let her know you are what she has been waiting for all her life. "Emma. I, I," damn this stammering, he said to himself.

"Yes, Zach?"

"Emma, I, I, I think that when we're done with breakfast we should run over to Exurbans."

"Alllraaaght."

Oh, you courageous mollusk.

"hWhat do you need here?" Emma asked as they got out of the car in the camping store parking lot.

"Just a couple of things. For one, I'm looking for a good pair of hiking shorts, you know, the kind with a million pockets."

"Oh Zach, you don't need to pay these ridiculous prices for a paiyr of shorts. Why do you need to buy them here? You can get 'em cheaper at Sears or Kmart and they're just as good"

"No they're not. They're cheaper there all right, and cheaply made. When we go hiking I want something really durable. I don't want to have to worry about bending over and ripping them. Unfortunately, I'm speaking from experience. I once had to walk five miles on a popular trail with my boxers showing. Course, these days that would be fashionable. I also need a good camp stove, something small and light weight, but a good one."

"Didn't you get all that stuff before we went kayaking down at St Simeons island?" she asked.

"Mostly, lot of good it did us, especially that expensive tent we didn't use."

She laughed, "How could we have known they'd be such a wonderful little resort thaiyer. Besahdz, it was sooo romantic." Like Cupid drawing his bow, she nocked a beam to her dimpled cheek and let loose a coy and coiling smile.

Zach nudged up against her and said, "The stuff that dreams are made of."

Though it was early yet, the parking lot was overly stuffed with Range Rovers, Explorers, Jeeps and all kinds of 4-wheel drive vehicles. Everyone was stocking up on the latest techno camping gear for their weekend crusades. As they walked to the front door, they passed a well-used older Suburu station wagon. Zach nudged Emma, "That has to belong to one of the sales people here." She asked how he could know that. "Just wait," he said. "When we're inside we'll look for the geekiest, nerdiest looking guy, and ask him what he drives. He'll either be in the climbing section or the slalom kayak section."

"How do you know all this?" Emma wondered.

"Cause these guys are like Clark Kent. In the city they pass themselves off as wimps, but when they get outdoors, they're transmogrified into animals, wildmen. This is what J.J. pays me to know: audiences."

"I'll bet you're wrong," Emma challenged.

"What's the wager?"

"Loser fixes dinner of the winner's choice."

"Done. I can taste it now."

Once inside they headed to the rock climbing section. "No good," Zach said, "No suitable geek. Let's go over to the white water boats."

He saw his candidate and said to Emma, "That's him, that's Mr. Suburu."

She said haughtily, "You're too sure of yourself, a sure sign you're cookin'."

"Hah! We'll see. Excuse me," Zach said as they approached a rather mild-mannered looking young black-haired man. He wore dark rimmed glasses, which tended to give him a mousy appearance, set off all the more by his slight build and wan complexion. "I'm thinking," Zach continued, "about getting into kayaking, white water kayaking. Do you have anything like a beginner's boat?"

Green, dispassionate eyes peered out through thick lenses at him. "We have one or two. Have you ever gone out on a river before?" his soft voice asked.

"Not really, I mean, I've done some canoeing before that had some good bubbles, but nothing big. You?" Zach asked.

"Yea, a fair amount. I do some guiding down the Chattooga," he said.

Zach looked at Emma and gave her a slight nod to show her how on track he was. She looked a bit puzzled; she probably didn't know what the Chattooga river was.

"Hairy stuff there. I haven't done anything like that. I was wondering, can I get a kayak this size," Zach pointed to a nearby solo kayak, "on a small car? I drive a Suburu wagon."

"Oh yea. That's what I drive and I can get four of those on mine. You just need the right roof rack," Mr. Suburu responded.

"Cool," Zach said. "Well, look, thanks for the info, but right now we have some other things we need to get, I'll be back in a while."

"My name's Alan. If I'm not here, have me or Jeff paged. He'll be able to help you if I'm not available."

Zach said thanks and sure thing, grabbed Emma's hand and walked away. He pinched her and said, "Lobster on the grill, wood fire, no charcoal, and corn on the cob. Just vehicles for butter, baby, that's how I want it."

"You're just lucky, and Ah'm not paying for lobster," Emma said.

"Oh yes you are. You can't renig five minutes later. Too late. Dinner of choice, sore loser."

"How did you know it was going to be him?"

"Clues, Emma. You have to look for clues. First off, the car outside had a roof rack, inside there were all kinds of nylon straps and Gortex looking things. There was a bumper sticker that said something about saving some river. And the car, which is a 4-wheel drive wagon, was kind of beat up. All the other cars in the lot were expensive, no one working at Exurbans could afford an Explorer or a 4-Runner, and Suburu wagons are prized for their reliability and they can go just about anywhere. And they're as economical as any small car."

"Ok, Ah can buy that, but how'd you know it would be him?" she asked.

"Someone who really loves to be outdoors and to do really risky things like running the big rapids on rivers like the

Chattooga, or climb El Capitan in Yosemite, isn't going to look like some Wall Street tycoon walking out of Abercrombie and Fitch all duded up like the safari starts today. 'Excuse em, miss, where are the porters? Miss, the natives?'"

"Ah get your point."

"He's going to look like some average Joe, someone normal. Outward appearances don't mean much to them. Everyday is a bad hair day," Zach concluded.

"Diggy Selma once told me that inside a stone is the history of the earth."

"Uh, yea. Something like that. Here's men's clothing."

"If you only knew how to look. She also said you can talk to the stone, and it will talk back, if you know how to listen."

"Unh hunh. Right. Here's some cool looking shorts."

"Oh God! Zach, look at that price! Forty dollars for a pair of shorts!"

"Sure, there's twenty dollars worth of pockets," he said, defending them. She shook her head in a mixture of disgust and disbelief and kept quiet. If he wanted to waste his money, that was his business, was her mute message.

She kept quiet until they got to the map section of the store. On a large, square table, under which were drawers containing topographical maps of Georgia and all of the Appalachian Trail as it extended from its beginning (or end, depending on your perspective) in Georgia, to terminus in Maine, was a larger map of the north Georgia mountains. She asked, "Where's the Chattooga?" Zach pointed it out and said, "That's where they filmed the movie 'Deliverance', you know, with Burt Reynolds. It has some really tough rapids. Mr. Suburu has to be pretty good to guide down that river."

"I don't know if I ever want to try anything like that. But maybe we can go look at it some time," she said. Then yawning, "Are we about done here. I'd like to go get a cup of good coffee, I think there's a Starbucks or a Caribou around here. You ready?"

She had lost her accent, he noticed. She does that whenever they go into specific stores or certain public places, just lets it lie down like some ole coonhound lying on the floor. It'll get up later of its own accord. Looking at the shorts and some other small camping items he held, he allowed that he was.

After placating their caffeine desideratum, they headed back to Emma's. At the front door, a bluebird lit on the back of one of the rocking chairs. As soon as it saw them, it took off as quickly as it landed. "Hello, Mr. Bluebird," Emma called out as it flew away. "Anything to say? Well, thanks for the visit."

Inside the house, the answering machine was flashing its urgent message that someone had called. Emma went over to it and hit the play button. "Emma, this is your mothuh. Ah'm goin' to Trieste next weekend to open it up and Ah'd love yaw help. Give me a cawl dahlin'. Yaw fathuh and Ah will be in and out awl weekend."

"Looks lahk we'ze aheadin' deepuh in ta Dixie," Zach drawled.

"Will you go? Ah really want you to see Trieste. And you caiyn meet Diggy."

For the rest of the weekend, Emma was in high spirits, talking about Trieste and Diggy and summers and sweet tea and peaches and almonds. Even alligators. And she grilled the lobster perfectly.

"Monday, Monday. Can't trust that day." The words to The Mamas and The Papas song still rattled off Zach's tongue as he entered the office that Monday after he'd heard it on the car radio coming in. Normally he would agree with the song's sentiments, but not this Monday. He was in no bad mood, no melancholia accompanied him as he passed under L.C. Hazelton's lintel. He was excited to be going to Trieste over the Memorial holiday, but happier still to have realized his true feelings for Emma. Some fissure had cracked open inside and out poured a tidal wave of feelings and emotions. And thoughts, oh, and sentiments too. Of spending all his time with Emma. Of spending the rest of his time with Emma. Emma, Emma, Emma. Her name floated constantly in front of him, always it danced at the end of his tongue. Everyone he met on the street reminded him of her somehow. She had planted herself firmly in his heart. He heard her laughter in his soul and felt her skin inside his brain. 'Roots, roots, roots wound roundly down the sound of Emma, Emma, Emma you're deep inside my heart. Oh, God, girl, I love you!' he screamed inside his skull.

"Good morning, Zach," a voice called as he came off the escalator to the second floor.

What? "Oh, hey Gerdy." Gerdy was short for Gertrude, a first generation German-American. J.J. thought she represented the European immigrant point of view or at least could tell what might pique their interest or capture their attention.

"Daydreaming Zach? It's only Monday morning and you look like you're already AWOL."

He liked Gerdy, and gave her a dreamy smile. "I had a great weekend, Gerd."

"Something tells me it has to do with Emma," she said with a wry smile.

He could no more have hid the truth than turned into a reptile. "Yea, it does," he replied with a nod and a loony grin.

"Oh my, you're head over heels in love, aren't you!" she laughed.

"I'm a'rollin and a'tumblin and there ain't no end in sight!" he said.

They stood a bit and enjoyed the moment. She was happy for Zach, though there was a tinge of envy because she was still looking for a partner. Her loves hadn't worked out, and while that led to inevitable disappointments and all too often heartache, Gerdy did not lack in zeal nor persistence. Something of the German in her, Zach guessed. He asked her to not spread the news around the office that he was so smitten so that he didn't have to spend all his time fending off queries, gaffs and guffaws. And especially don't tell Marty! Being for the most part a private person she readily agreed, though she held doubts that he could hide his condition. "Better go right in to your office and close the curtains," she advised.

He heeded her advice and slipped quickly, but quietly, down the hall. As he turned the corner to his office, he ran smack into J.J. "Zachary! How are you my young man? How was your weekend? Boy, I had a great one, went fishing off the coast of South Carolina. Caught a ton of fish! That captain knew his stuff! I'll have to give his name to you. Say, I need to talk to you about something but I can't remember what it is. I'll remember soon enough. Well, anyway, we'll meet up later, gotta run. Ta ta."

He breathed a sigh of relief. With J.J., you don't really have to talk, just show interest, smile and nod a lot. He would really only take notice of you if you had an advanced case of leprosy or some other such malady, or if you actually engaged in the conversation. Zach opened his office door and slid in. 'Safety! Solitude!' he thought. His mind was racing, tormented by his emotions. 'I should call Emma! No, she probably isn't at work yet. Anyway, we talked late into the night. But on the phone!' He hadn't stayed at her house Sunday night, she said she had some things she needed to do, one was to talk to her mother. He agreed, he didn't want to seem possessive or appear insecure like the lovesick teenager that he was. 'Don't want to spook her yet. But I think she loves me, doesn't she? Wouldn't she have asked me to stay last night if she really wanted me? Maybe I'm just a boyfriend to her. Maybe she really hasn't fallen for me like I have for her. God, could it be I'm crazy about someone who isn't crazy about me? Isn't that a lopsided love? Don't people end up going off the deep end in situations like this? The object of revered adored worshipped love jilts the love soaked fawning worm who ends up stalking her. No! Emma has strong feelings for me. I could feel that, I know that. She thinks I'm funny, but maybe that's all, I'm just funny to her. Yes, I go out with a clown, He's soooo funny, but I could never take him seriously. He's not like a doctor or a real professional. I'm not going to marry him or anything like that. Wait a minute. Where am I here. I'm going to drive myself nuts. Get a grip!'

Love is an invading force that seizes command central, terrorizes the ego, without mercy teases and tortures the body like some debilitating and debasing drug, ransoms rationale and only gradually loses power like a dying empire. Holy Roman amour writ wee.

Zachary decided he needed to stick his nose into work. 'Where the hell was that Bradford account!?' First, he needed some coffee, but that required a trip to the break room, and it was guaranteed that on a Monday morning it will not be devoid of life. Someone, and most likely that would include Marty, hell, he's there every morning, will be there. Could he handle Marty now? Sure.

Putting on his best mask, the one that reads everything's a joke and maybe even you, he fearlessly left his cocoon and walked out to the break room, wearing his grin as a shield.

Only two people were getting coffee, Marty, of course, and Larsen Grebe. Larsen always kept a veil around himself, never letting anyone in, always hanging back, so he was safe from him. But Marty would get uncomfortably close. "Hey guys," Zach greeted them. "How was your weekend?" Take the offensive, he encouraged himself. "Marty, did you put on a few pounds this weekend? What'd you do, eat a couple pounds of ribs? Wash it down with a gallon of beer?" Zach slapped Marty's ample stomach, "Better let some air out of that tire, Pudge, it's gonna blow." He didn't like to be called Pudge, and Zach knew it would annoy, and thus distract, him.

"Ah, hell, Zack. This is full a' good times. Took a lot of work to get it to this perfection. You just caiyn't appreciate a livin' museum is all."

Larsen was chuckling at the exchange. For one, he knew the two to be close, and secondly, it didn't involve him, someone else was being made fun of. Larsen had a bit of a mean streak wrapped up in his need for distance from others. Hard to tell which came first, the whole or the sass.

"Yea, living museum," Zach charged on. "More like operational cafeteria. I'm gonna slap some credit card logos on there and hang a sign, 'Open for Business.'"

"Do what, now?" Marty said.

He was smiling, but better not press, thought Zach. "Hey Lars. Anything good come down the pike this weekend?"

"Same old, same old," Larsen replied with a shuffle to his feet, revealing absolutely nothing. 'The guy could have rode in to work with aliens and you'd never know,' Zach thought.

"Let me into this coffee, boys, give my foot a push, as maestro Zappa said."

"hWhat's got you all riled up this mawnin'?" Marty asked. "Lahk a hound got caught a scent."

"Just glad to be back to work, you know. Like J.J. Two days away and I start pinin' to be back," Zach said with an exaggerated sigh. "And now I can get back to the Bradford account."

Larsen muttered, "Yea, right," while Marty tried to look him in the eyes and which Zach tried to avoid.

"No," Marty said, measuring his words out, "Ah thaiynk somethin' else is up here. Yew come in haiyerr all fussy budgy lahk a kid needin' t'pee, with eyes all lit up. Usually they'ze a bit on the dull side come Monday mawnin'. hWhat's goan' on Zack. This got t' do with Emma?"

"Who?" Zach innocently said, but he sensed trouble, Marty's accent was getting thicker.

"That's it. It do. Y'all gettin' married ain'tcha ya now?"

He said it as fact. "Marty, don't start." Damn him, how could he tell!?

"You caiyn say hwhat yew want, but Ah kin tayull. Yew gone crazy in love. Set a date yit?"

"Marty, you have my word that I have not discussed marriage with Emma." That was a truth he could hide behind. "And should that time arrive, I stress 'should', I will most assuredly let you know, the very first in the office."

"Allllright, aaallllright," he said while pouring himself more coffee. "Yew don't have to tayull me, Ah understand this Yankee reticence. Y'all have yo' little privacy needs, even from friends. Just thought Ah'd have somethin' t' tayull Karen. Yew know how she likes yew, and wants to keep up with yew."

It was a rather cheap and obvious ploy to appeal to Zach's warm feelings for his wife, who he liked a lot. When he first came down to Georgia, Marty and Karen where his only friends, and they opened their home to him. "Well I tell you what, Emma wouldn't be nearly as unfortunate as Karen," Zach said. They all laughed at that, Zach was throwing the ball back into Marty's court, another deflective move. "Boys," he said, "I think it's time to get to work. We'll have this little chat again." Zach poured himself more coffee and walked out of the break room.

'So much for my mask', he thought as he walked down the hall. He knew Marty would be in his office within an hour to really get the low down. He could imagine Marty sliding quietly through his door, as if he were a burglar, and in a hushed voice asking him what was up. It made him smile to imagine the portly grown man sneaking around like a juvenile delinquent. He looked at his watch when he got to his office; time to call Emma.

Emma worked in the programming department for the Atlanta Public Broadcasting Corporation, and usually didn't get to work until after 9:00 a.m. and often didn't leave until well after 6:00 p.m. But it was now near 9:30, and she should be in by now. He speed dialed her number, and got voice mail. Damn! Well, don't leave a message, it might seem overly much, like he needs to speak to her and damn the truth of that. He leaned back in his chair, spun it around to look outside, and slipped back into the weekend.

There are moments in one's time on this spinning orb that one can sense an interconnectedness running through life. Where one can sense the presence of what we call fate. Through dim perceptions we catch fleeting glimpses of threads intertwining individual life courses, sown by unseen hands of some master sower. Maybe there is more than one, like the mythologies of old Germania. Three women; one young, one middling age, and one old. They weave a tapestry of stories and events that comprise the lives of a person. Maybe they in turn are guided by another encompassing force. Zachary was able to catch the faint scent of two thin plumes of fumes, two fates, his and Emma's, slowly coiling, like grape vines around a post. Vines loop out into air, then turn back in to retouch, bracing against one another, using each other for support in order to grow out into the nothingness of air, the unknown of future. Slender green tendrils reaching out for experience. Maybe the vines are our souls and the grapes become our memories, our experiences shared, his and Emma's. Part hope, no doubt, and part truth. And lurking in the ink black mise-en-scene of thought unrealized and wholly formed was a certain white faced clown, rising nearly to the surface of clarity like some undiscovered cetacean, which was both troubling and bothersome, so he returned to his feelings for Emma. Just thinking of her smile he filled with her essence, filled with the joy she brought him. It started in his heart; a warmth that spread quickly outward, to shoulders and stomach and groin aye yie yie, and into arms and up into head, filling it thick and cottony. How lucky, he thought, to be able to feel this; this is ambrosia, this is the fountain of youth, the golden apple, this is the ALL.

He turned slightly to reach for the mug of coffee just in time to catch Marty sneaking in the door, like a kid stealing out of detention. "Hey," he whispered. "Hi Marty, come on in," Zach answered.

Marty gave Zach a quick appraisal and said, "Look at yew all glowy eyed lahk some fawn. Now it hain't none of mah business, but yew know Ah'm doin' mah job fur someone eiylse. If Ah don't git the lowdown on yew en Emma, Karen'd be madder'n hell with mu-ie. Ya see where Ah'm comin' from."

Zach knew Karen, and she probably would be. She had taken on the job of seeing him wed and had set Zach up with more than one bad date. He don't know if it was a Southern thing or not, but she couldn't stand to see an unwed man over twenty-five. Somehow it upset the balance of the universe. And someone at thirty needs help fast, the firmament is cracking.

Zach was cornered and Marty didn't deserve a lie. "Marty, jokes aside, I'm not getting married. Really. I'd tell you. I had a great weekend, but that's as far as it goes. Next weekend we're going down to Thomasville to see the old plantation. I guess I'm all excited about it."

"Y'all ain't talkin' 'bout it or nuthin?"

"You have my word as a Southern gentleman. We haven't even discussed it."

"You ain't neither Southern or a gentleman."

"Come on, Pudge, you're getting too serious on me. It ain't happening." Zach swung his arms out for emphasis. Nothing to hide.

"Okay. Okay. Karen'll be happy y'all are gittin' along just fine."

"That we are."

Changing the subject with a shrug, he asked, "Yew making any progress on that Bradford account? Yew want me to get a'hold a'that gal in New York?"

"Nah, but thanks, I'm the one with the connection there. Hey, you could call that ex-jock we ran into at that CNN party. What was his name? God, was he drunk."

"Yea, but everyone else was too. No one noticed, 'cept for Ted."

"Ted saw him? You sure? How do you know?"

"The way he looked at him. Turner's the kahnd of man what don't speak with his body, he's got a poker face. But Ah was near enough him when Barnes, that's the man's name, dipped his beer mug into the punch bowl, and Ted's eyes said it all. 'That man is a fool.' But that ain't the worse of it."

"Shit! There's more?" Zach cried. "Maybe he doesn't remember. Don't remind him when you talk to him, I was going to try and use Atlanta as leverage to get him to take the sports anchor in Chattanooga. You know, the old 'Well, lots of people go from there to Atlanta, and CNN is here.' Damn! What'd he do next?"

"He asked Ted how Barberella Jane was doin' only it come out, 'Bob Rella' so at first Ted just kahnda smahled at 'im, didn't know what he said through his slurred talk. You know, most people don't like her call her Hanoi Jane. When Ted finally caught on what he said, he just glared at the poor drunken fool and moved away. Ah guess they was mo' pity in 'em than anguh."

"Barberella? What's that?"

"Some cheap movie she did in the 60's, playing some sex kitten or somethin'. Not what you call high art. Must'a needed the money."

"Well," Zach said, "This certainly mucks things up a bit. You don't suppose Barnes forgot all that do you?"

"He was pretty soused, he just maght'a. Ah can cawl him en feel 'im out. If he sounds excited about the possibility of wuhkin' near Atlanta, he'll show it. And he'll also let mu-ie know if he thinks he screwed up any possibilities to'des that end."

"Karen is a lucky man. My thanks, oh wonderful one."

"Ah ain't toast, leave the buttuh alone," he said and turned to leave Zach's office.

"Lunch is on me," Zach said to his back.

Marty turned around in the doorway and grabbed his belly, "Good. Ah'm gittin' real hungry, the restaurant is open for business."

"You're going to make me pay for that comment, aren'tcha Pudge?" Zach observed.

"Yup," he said as the door closed.

Soon after Marty left, Zach's phone rang. It was Emma. She said she had just got in and couldn't wait to call him, she just wanted to hear his voice. His heart went super nova.

chapter four

"It's getting pretty hot. Let's roll the windows up and turn the air conditioning on," Zach yelled over the roar of air rushing into the car. "Oh, but it feels sooo good. Let's leave them open for a little while longuh," Emma replied. "hWa'm aiyuh can feel like a comfortable ole coat, lahk a nice big hug."

It was late Friday morning, the holiday weekend just about to unfold. They had both managed to get the day off in order to stretch the three-day weekend by another day and had left the city early that morning. A road trip holds the excitement of discovery and possibilities. No matter how mundane the object of the adventure, it becomes a journey into the unknown by drawing upon some long slumbering and forgotten human migratory pattern, a genetic coelacanth of human history. But the two riders did not seem to share the same atavistic ardor. Their conversation in the early morning hours did have an air of whimsy, though try as he might, Zach could not steer them around to what he really wanted to talk about: Emma and him, though that alone was not all that was on his mind. An hour earlier they had gotten off Interstate 75, which plows straight down through Georgia coming out of Atlanta, running south until it dead ends at Alligator Alley in Florida. Not far south of Atlanta, the land starts to change. The rolling hills open up and flatten out. The forests of north Georgia give way to long-cleared fields, the remnants left to make do in copses and hedges and the occasional overgrown, busted flat farm. Down in the flat lands of the coastal plains, white and red oak become swamp and live oak, the latter so named because it never sheds its leaves, nor Spanish moss. Hickory, sweetgum, white pine and hemlock become turpentine pine and pecan trees and the red earth soil bleaches out, turning to a true blond, flecked with sand, eventually turning into sand in the pine-barrens of deep Georgia. Here and there the evidence of the old economy of The South could be seen in small forgotten towns. Huge wire cages, some still carrying stragglers of the previous year's harvest; little white tufts that got snagged in the wire like stars caught in the sunlight, sat out in front of some forlorn old farm building. Cages piled neatly and cages tossed haphazardly, all waiting silently to fulfill their once a year duty of hauling precious cargo to the Turnerville Gin, or the Moultrie Gin, or the Milledgeville Gin, all for the master of old Dixieland; King Cotton.

True it is that as one drives south from Atlanta, the land loses elevation, but it's too gradual to really notice, like driving down a mountain. But one feels something very akin to it, like moving down into a sunken desperate valley from a cool alpine meadow, or stepping into a hot tub. The air becomes thicker, more viscous, atmosphere resistant, energy expended merely leaning into air. It's a bubble, tactile sensations push against skin. Touch the air, there's tension, it flexes on your touch. Everything seems to slow down, birds, animals, people.

Stories of a lingering and evil past crept in on the outer edge of Zach's thought. 'Maybe it's just my prejudice', he thought, 'having been raised in the North, educated about a war fought down *there* in a time and place far away against people enslaving other people. Plantation life and stereotypes, massive wrongs and little rights. Then Selma and Oxford. George Wallace and Martin Luther King. It took a long time down here. As if we had nothing like it in the North. Yea, right', he nearly said aloud. Still, an uneasiness was present. Somehow, he did not belong. He looked over at Emma. She had her bare feet stuck out the window, wiggling her toes, each little pinky dancing in some ecstatic trance, unmindful of its neighbor. She was going home, and she was happy.

She was humming some unfamiliar tune, with the seat tilted back, arms behind her head to tilt it forward so she could see all the familiar surroundings, and dressed for heat in a tank top and shorts. His eyes followed her bare skin from her toes down to her thighs, where it disappeared underneath green linen shorts. Every now and then the wind would buffet them, exposing white panties with little blue flowers on them. Cool little puffs of air to skim the heat off. He thought of doing the same.

"What's that tune you're humming?" he asked.

"It's an old spiritual Diggy taught me."

"What, like a church song or something?"

"Ah guess. It's one of the songs they sing at this ole church Diggy goes to now and theyun. She doesn't go all the time, just on occasion."

"I thought she was a pagan or something."

She laughed at him, "You do live in a world of your own makin', don't you? And stubborn 'bout it, too. Why Zachree, Ah think yaw half mule." She thought her little joke pretty funny. "Ah think Momma's got some ole mules left at Trieste, Ah'll be glad t' introduce you t'ole Henry, Ah think he's still around." She was giggling and her own merriment set her toes into a frenzy of movement.

"Henry the mule. That's quaint. Zachary and Henry," he said somberly. "Why do they still have mules? Didn't the tractor replace them in like the early part of this century?" he asked with a little bit of sarcasm.

"Yes, but they kept 'em on anywaiy. They'd use 'em for haulin' logs outta the woods, the turpentine woods. Sometimes the trees'd die if they wasn't scored proper, and then you cut 'em down and use 'em for fahrwood. They'ze so full of pitch, they burn lahk they was soaked in gas. Anyway, Momma likes to keep some things around that remind her of when Trieste was a working plantation, a real farm. And the mules do that. She keeps some horses and cows too."

"I don't get one thing," he asked. "Why does she open it up during the summer, when it's hottest? I'd think you'd spend winters down there and summers in Savannah, where at least there's a sea breeze."

"Wayull, pah'tly cause of me and my brother and sister. The schools were a little better in Savannah, at least that's what Daddy thought. And besides, since part of Trieste is a museum, most tourists come up from Florida in the winter, so summers the off-season theyuh. Even though it was Momma's idea to let the county take over part of Trieste to help defray the cost of keeping it, she can't stand to see it overrun with tourists. It's still her home, that's where she grew up. When she talks about openin' it up, it's the livin' part she's talkin' bout, she goes theyuh when things'r slower and she can spend time visitin' with Diggy and her other friends."

"Diggy?" he asked, "What has she got to do with it?"

"She lives theyuh, in the house that used to be the caretaker's house. I guess that's what you could call her now. She runs the museum."

"That's interesting, I had this image of her living in some shack out in the country."

"Oh, God, Zach, you are terrible! She went to college you know."

"Another myth shattered. Is nothing sacred anymore? So the crystal gazing herb woman is a college educated church goer too?"

"I don't know if you'd call it a regular church. She only goes there on special nights, usually on Saturdays, when they have shouts."

"A shout? Is that a noun?"

"More like a verb. A shout is an old time spiritual revival-like event that goes back to the time of slavery. Diggy says the black slaves combined some of their old beliefs and spiritual practices from Africa with the church practices of the Christians. It was a bit too weird for them, she says, to just sit there in a pew and quietly pray to some God that was somewhere up and away.

She says they had to get more involved, feel the Holy Spirit raise up in 'em."

"Kinda like a Baptist meeting?" he asked.

"Something like that," she said distractedly. Her gaze was caught by something out the window. "Oh no, they've ruined it!" she shouted. "Look, they put a Wal-Mart up where Sam Carter's farm was!"

They had just reached the northern outskirts of Thomasville, the land mostly comprised of small farms but off to their left loomed one of the nearly ubiquitous, late 20th century versions of the general store. The huge gray building sat out in a large field like some dry-docked aircraft carrier. A true USS Enterprise.

Emma leaned back in her seat, disappointed that America had finally come to Thomasville. "I hope they don't drive Blainey's out of business," she said, flatly.

"And Blainey's would be . . . ?" he asked.

"A hardware store downtown. This is probably going to hurt the downtown too. That's one of the things that maiykes this town so special. The downtown is still alive, it ain't rolled over and died yet, or turned into some T-shirt tourist trap. Keep 'em in Florida."

"It'll be a hard go to compete with Wal-Mart. People shop for deals," he stated.

"Yea, Ah know," she said with resignation.

"Do I keep going straight here? Remember, I don't know where I'm going."

"Yep, we take this downtown, then turn right on the main drag, Broad St., and take it out of town for a few miles."

The highway narrowed to two lanes as it passed under a canopy of oaks covering the street. It was unusual that the city had left the road narrow to accommodate the trees, and not to accommodate the automobile. The city planners hadn't fallen prey to mobile America's desire to be able to drive anywhere they want and with plenty of room. Standing back from the tree-lined street stood quite a few nice old Victorian homes in decent shape, as well as a few 1940's style bungalows. As the commercial buildings that marked the main downtown section came in to view, Emma suddenly said, "Turn right here! You hafta see this! It's a huge oak tree, the biggest in the U.S., Ah think."

They drove a couple of blocks till they came to what appeared to be yet another tunnel of green limbs. Flashing yellow lights warned of low clearance, but Emma's Camry slid right underneath the tree limbs, though not by much. To their left was a preposterously huge oak tree, its great limbs bigger round than the trunks of most trees Zach had seen. The trunk itself looked as if several other oak trees had been bound together to make the one. Some of the limbs branching off swooped so low to the ground they had been propped up by metal frames so they wouldn't block the street. The tree itself spread out over two city lots, though, as with most live oaks, it wasn't that tall, being much wider in proportion. Spanish moss hung from nearly every limb and cables had been rigged throughout the tree to ensure it wouldn't break apart in a wind storm, or just collapse under its own weight. Zach pulled the car over to check the monster out.

They stood in the shadows cast by this magnificent giant, reading the plaque the city had erected. With the usual American habit of comparison, the metal tablet related that the tree was as wide as Niagara Falls was deep and was the biggest oak tree east of the Mississippi. It had begun life mid-17th century, and was now over 300 years old. Zach was left to wonder what this tree had witnessed from its vantage point. It silently watched as man as Indian walked under its branches, then man as white settler and man as white slave holder and man as black slave, then man of either color, free of past constraints. Or nearly so. What ugliness had it seen? Had it seen master whip slave, had it seen lynchings? Had it also known sweet talk and hid caresses of young lovers? Had it been admired by older couples, out for an evening stroll? He kicked at an empty quart beer bottle. Maybe it had sheltered a drunk, giving him security and comfort for a time, maybe beautiful dreams. Or maybe it was some kids exploring the magic of alcohol for the first time. The tree as gatekeeper, a sentinel if you will, to altered consciousness, though in this case, a common tool for an altogether very common consciousness. But the thing had presence, and if that means a force, then the tree had, what would that be? His thoughts were distracted by a car noisily bumping by. The tree was now surrounded by houses, some big, some small, in a hot, quiet, sleepy Southern town. It was Friday and only one car had driven by, no one walked the sidewalks, no one worked in their yards, everyone inside, everything, if anything, was occurring inside. He remembered something Emma's father had told him, a quote from William Faulkner maybe, that he now got a sense of. In the South, history is not the past, it is not even past.

When they got back to the car, Emma was quiet, she just wanted to get out to Trieste. Zach thought she might be reconciling Faulkner with Wal-Mart.

They drove west of town through pine barrens for seven miles, until they crossed the Ochlockonee River. Soon after they came to a green wooden sign on the north side of the road that read, in elegant white script, *Trieste*. "Don't turn in there, go round back," Emma said. But Zach protested, "I'd like to go in the main entrance, see what the grand entry is like."

She relented so they turned by the sign. Immediately they were on a long narrow lane comprised of compacted sand, vaulted over entirely by live oaks dripping with Spanish moss. "Gods, Emma, this is like a movie set."

"Momma won't let 'em pave over it, says it would suffocate the tree roots. The county historical society are glad for it, but worry 'bout traffic tearin' up the ole road."

"Do you get a lot of tourists out here?" he asked, driving very slowly down the shaded lane.

"Not so much now, but it gets more every ye-uh. Raght now, most tourists go to Melhana or Patsy's ole place down theyuh at Pebblewood. You haf t' remembuh that very few of the old plantations are open to the public. Most are still lived in by the rich Yankees or their descendants who came down here in the early 1900's and bought them for a song and dance. So's they could 'Own their own goddamn plantation'. Truth of it is, that's why most are still around. They would have just rotted away 'cause folks couldn't afford to keep 'em up and cared for. Mah family managed somehow to keep Trieste going. Anyway, momma only let the county come in in 1990, and so not a lot of people know about it yet. But as they find out, they're comin'."

Emma kept on talking, pointing out things they drove by. Just beyond the trees on both sides were open fields, all grass now, what used to be cotton fields, she said. Beyond them were groves of pecan trees, also on both sides. Then the land was a quilt work of various groves of peach trees and other fruits of lesser quantities, and those gave way to vast woods of turpentine pines, the product of which really kept Trieste afloat in hard times, according to Emma.

"They don't make turpentine here any more, but momma leases out land to local farmers to grow cotton and also pays 'em to take care of the fruit trees. She loves her peach trees, and sells most of the crop. She also likes her big ole pecan trees and gets a mess of nuts outta theyum. All and all she makes enough money off the land to pay expenses and taxes, but just for the land. She had to get the county involved to keep the house kep' up."

Zach was listening to her, but filing it away for conversation and questions later on. He was too mesmerized by the drive, it was easy to imagine himself in another time, riding in horse drawn carriages to the grand old estate for a fox hunt, or to discuss the war effort about the Northern aggressors. The lane wound around a garden brimming with roses in full bloom, along with irises and petunias and many, many more flowers that he didn't recognize. Emma said the flowers were really the result of the museum caretakers, her mother didn't have enough time to fool with those, at least not to keep it up like it is now. The garden itself was started by her great grandmother when she was just a little girl, on the eve of the Civil War.

Zach first caught sight of the house, or more properly, mansion, as they passed by the garden. It had been partially hidden by the huge willow trees that flanked it, as well as the line of magnolias that grew tall and wide twenty yards in front of it. It was startling to come upon so large a structure so quickly, that something so big could be so well concealed then suddenly appear as if it had been stalking you, the rock rising to sink the fog bound ship. Or the tree the car.

"Zach!" Emma yelled, "Watch the road!"

Awestruck by the house, Zachary had drifted a little too close to one of the blossoming crepe myrtles that had by now replaced the oaks.

"You hit one of momma's crepe myrtles and Ah don't think she'd ask you back. 'Specially the purple ones, they're her favorite."

Dear reader, you would get a better description of the house and grounds by contacting either the museum at Trieste, or the Thomas County Historical Society, and have them send you a brochure, or guide you to books wherein Trieste is discussed, but here follows a necessarily limited sketch.

Standing right smack in the middle of the front of the house, you look at granite steps gently ascending to the double-door front entrance. The spacious entryway is guarded by very immense columns, as is the style of many large Southern homes even to this day (even many a ram-shackle trailer can be found colonnaded). On either side of the entrance are large rooms, with very high windows. These adjacent rooms are themselves adjoined by somewhat smaller rooms with a second floor that sits above this section of the mansion. At the end of the second room to the right, there is a passageway that leads to a room that is otherwise apart from the house, the library, which had only one floor. Above the main entrance is a very large window with an immense chandelier hanging behind it, and the balcony that overlooks the main foyer. As you step inside you have your choice of stairways, to the left or right, both go up to the second floor balcony. Were you to instead walk directly from the front doors to the end of the main hallway, you would end up in the kitchen. The front of the house is occupied by various sitting rooms, a tearoom, a breakfast room, and of course, the dining hall. There is even a gentlemen's smoking room with a billiards table. To the left side of the house is another entrance for guests or owners to use in inclement weather. Presumably, that would be used in full summer, too. It is a beautifully constructed vestibule supported by columns, and large enough to drive a carriage under. Most bedrooms are upstairs, along with a nursery and children's play room, and various guest rooms too, but the master suite of rooms and bedroom is on the first floor, near the secondary entranceway. The back of the house is comprised of the kitchen and service and storage rooms. They are of recent construction, as the original kitchen was detached from the main building, as was the laundry building, which is now two rooms, one for clothes, and one for cleaning and storing table linens and bedding.

The house itself looks somewhat like a cross between The White House and Thomas Jefferson's beloved Monticello, sharing the Federalist styling. The exterior walls are brick (made from the red clay of North Georgia) that have been white washed, but never too thick as to actually cover the brick, only to brush it, as it where, like a thin, wispy cloud. It is not a common exterior finishing these days, and does give it a preciously old looking appearance.

Since the house is still used by the owners, truly a living museum, the only sections of the house off limits to tourists (and guided tours are the only way they can see it) are the master suites. And they are quite substantial, the floor spacing for them alone exceeding 3000 square feet.

Emma had Zach drive around to the back to a parking lot reserved for the family. Grabbing their luggage, he said, "This place could be listed as an American castle." To which Emma replied, "Ah think it is."

Zach had met Emma's mother before at the Savannah home, but meeting her here was making him a little unsettled. She carried herself with dignity and pride, but it did not lend itself to haughtiness or vanity. He wasn't sure why he was edgy, as if he were meeting some American icon, or legend, or memory. Emma just said, "Oh, Zach. It's only momma."

"Yea, momma in her 30 million square foot double wide."

They walked toward an indistinct white door that for all the world could have lead to a potato cellar, when they were hailed by a woman coming out of the main rear entrance. "Emmy! Emmy!" she yelled.

"Diggy! Hey!" Emma yelled back, waving her arms and bouncing on her feet. They both walked quickly toward each other while Zach stood with the suitcases, mute and grinning.

They hugged each other like old friends, occasionally pulling back to get a better look at each other as people often do when they haven't seen each other for a long time. Zach couldn't hear what they where saying, but when they started to look at him and laugh and smile, he figured it was time to leave the bags and go over to them, if nothing else, to check possible slander in progress.

Diggy was a slender woman not so much older than Emma and Zach. She was a bit on the small size, maybe an inch over five feet. Her skin was a deep, soft copper brown and as he got closer, Zach could see that her eyes were azure blue. And she was strikingly beautiful.

"So this is the Yankee you brought down to tar and feather," she said to him through a mischievous smile while glancing a look to Emma. Her voice was somewhat flat, though it had a distinguished air of command to it. 'So that's why they were laughing', he thought. 'Emma was having a little fun'. Diggy extended her hand, "I'm very glad to meet you. I'm Diggy Selma. Emma has told me a lot about you."

Her handshake was unusually firm for a woman. Zach's immediate impression was of a no nonsense type of person. Straight up and neat, almost military. "Well, I hope to get the time to clarify some of her comments. And I have heard a great deal about you, I'm truly pleased to meet you finally," Zach returned her cordial greeting. He enjoyed looking at her marvelous eyes, and it did not make her nervous one iota, she did not look away as so many people do when someone looks them in the eye. She returned the gaze, unflinchingly. 'Gods, this woman knows who she is', he thought. He was the one who eventually looked away, to Emma, who spoke next. "Zach showed a lot of interest in your church when I told him about it."

"Really," she said as a big smile spread across her lips. "Well, you can come with me tomorrow night, if you wish."

"Are you having a shout?" Emma asked.

"Yes, we are," Diggy replied.

"Oh, good. What do you say Zachree, wanna go?" she said to him with that little tease of daring-do in her voice that made it impossible to say no.

"Sure, why not," he said in a non-committal voice that hid true uneasiness. "I mean, this is Thomasville, and if that is the entertainment for a Saturday night, then, when in Rome . . ."

Emma knew him well enough to know what he really meant. "Oh, it'll be fun. Yew'll love it. hIt ain't lahk goin' t'a Cath'lic mass er nuthin'."

To Diggy, his dry response caused a bemused grin to break out on one side of her face, raising a dimple in the process. She leaned back ever so perceptibly as if to take better measure of him. To change the subject, he said to Emma, "Ever since we got south of Macon, you've been talking mo' Southern!"

"Ah don't have t' hide it so much now that we're out of Atlanta, with all them Yankees runnin' round. En that a Southern city!"

Her comment reminded Zach of one her worst experiences when, after high school, she went to a women's ivy league college in upstate New York. She lasted just a year there. Her father wanted her to go to a good school, not some Southern finishing school, as he put it, and his alma mater, in his eyes, had become an institution of higher ignorance, graduating drunks and business school dope heads. He was not without his opinions. But he ended up sending Emma to what was in her eyes essentially a Northern finishing school, Vassar, in Poughkeepsie. It was a low point in Emma's life, she had difficulty making friends, they all thought her accent and mannerisms, so different than theirs, as funny and backward. They stereotyped her as a Southern Belle, and so she withdrew into her books and studies while learning to hide her accent and eventually herself. She made it through a year but then went back home and sat out for the fall, enrolling in Emory University in Atlanta in the spring.

"Diggy, you know where momma is? We better go let her know we're here." Emma said.

"I haven't seen her since this morning, she was on the second floor, getting the turquoise room ready for Mr. Zachary," Diggy replied.

"She's gonna put him up theyuh? It's so far away from wheyuh Ah'll be and it's in the museum part of the house. What's he gonna do if some tourist wakes him in the mornin', or he wants t' take a nap? Ah'll have to get her to change her mind."

"She said the museum doesn't open until 10:00 and he's bound to be out of the room by then. And I don't know that she thought anything about naps."

"Wayull, let's go hunt her down, Zach. Oh, Diggy, it's so good to see you." Emma wrapped her arms around Diggy and gave her a warm embrace. She asked Diggy if she had any dinner plans, which she did, so they left it that in case they didn't run into her, they'd see her at the church service Saturday night, and then went in search of her mother.

Entering the house felt peculiar to Zach. On the one hand, it was a home, and though used sparingly now, it had the feeling of familiarity that provides, at least to Emma as indicated by the way she moved about. On the other hand, it was a museum, so it felt antiseptic. It was of course, beautifully and tastefully decorated with antiques, many of them brought in by the historical society to make up for the relative dearth of the family's heirlooms. When times were tough, many had been sold to raise cash, Emma had said. The historical society had also supervised the repainting of much of the interior, matching colors to popular hues in antebellum Thomasville.

They found Virginia in the master suites, sitting down and enjoying a sweet tea, Southern summer water.

"Momma, what's this putting Zach up in the turquoise room?" Emma asked without pause to say hello.

"Lovely to see you too, mah child. Hello Zachary," Emma's mother said with a friendly smile.

He walked over and gave her a gentle hug. She looked somewhat noble lounging on a light green armchair with her feet propped up on an Ottoman that had golden tassels hanging limply from its base. He told her how resplendent she looked. "Yaw're a flatterer, Zach. But don't think Ah don't cayhr to hear it," she said dryly, swirling her glass of sweet tea. "Now, mah precious Emmy, hwhat is it you are not lahkin' about Zachary's arrangements? If you have a better solution, Ah'm willin' to listen."

Virginia talked slowly, like a long train coming, choosing each word carefully, measuring out the words for emphasis and clarity. Her drawl was very aspirated, so care is almost three syllables; kayh-yuhr-uh. It is a very pure South Georgia accent, becoming rare through the commonizing influence of TV, movies and popular music. Emma's accent was stronger, not by any influence or geographical quirk of living in northern Georgia, but in her lack of concern for grammatical correctness when speaking, or letting 'muh haiyr down', as she puts it. She also talked faster than her very deliberate mother. Virginia also moved as slowly and measured as she speaks, casting her chalk white arms out languidly, liquidly, for emphasis, like an empress motioning to her retinue.

In a peculiar twist of tongue and geography, many people coming up from Tallahassee, not an hours drive south of Thomasville, have to learn to speak Southern.

"hWhy can't he stay in the room next to mine? Theyuh's three bedrooms here," Emma averred.

"Ah know, darlin', but that is a bit too close. Ah know propriety these days, such as it is, would hold that proper, but Ah am not of these days. Besahdes, Huntuh and Jenna just maght drop by. Then hwhere would Ah put theyum?" she asked.

Hunter was Emma's brother, a lawyer in Savannah and the oldest of the three children. Jenna was his wife.

"And just what did Hunter say? Was it, 'We maght be comin down,' or "We'll try.' Come on momma, he's just being polite, he ain't comin'. He's got too many backyard barbeques to attend. Evuh since he got this noble public servant idea in his head he spends his time rubbing shoulders with the powers that be so they might smile upon him and get him elected to the state house or make him some kinda judge."

Emma's comments about Hunter quieted Virginia, she found herself yet again wondering about her son and his newfound desire for public office, espousing hackneyed ideas of a political nature that seemed so trite and cliché-ish to her and more than a bit at odds with his former libertine life style. She worked that over a while before brushing it off as immaterial to the discussion of sleeping arrangements. "Just the same, Emma, they maght drive down and bring yaw fathuh, tew."

Options closed on that, so Emma retreated, she and Zach threw her bags in her room, then she gave him a quick tour on the way to his room.

The turquoise room, where he would be staying, was always intended to be for guests and was still upholstered to display that purpose by the museum people. It did not take much work on Emma's mother's part to get it ready for Zach, just a change of sheets and some fresh towels in the adjoining bathroom.

"I've never slept on a canopied bed before," he said to Emma, setting his bags down. "I don't think I've even kissed on one before."

"And that's all your gonna get on this one," she said with a smile as she draped her arms around his shoulders and kissed him. "Momma's probably going to leave all the doors open between the suites to keep an eye on me so Ah don't go sneakin' off in the middle of the night. Propriety, you know."

"You may be right," Zach said, "But this place is pretty big. I'd think having someone around would make you feel more comfortable. Maybe she's just not used to sleeping alone, at least not here. I can imagine some could find this place a little intimidating, even spooky at night."

"Listen, momma grew up he-yuh, this is home. Any spooks runnin' 'round is relatives," she said with a laugh.

"Probably. Probably," he replied. "Hey, you've got to show me around some more. I want to see the gentlemen's room, and the kitchen and that library. And we haven't seen anything outside yet."

"Okay. Let's put your bags in the closet so tour groups won't see 'em. Then we have to go back and visit with momma, Ah don't know what plans she has."

In the hallway outside their room they could hear the voice of a guide lecturing a group of tourists coming toward them, so they ducked out through a door leading to another hall that ran perpendicular to the one they had come in from, and took a back stairway that led down into the breakfast room, a set-up that would allow guests to go down to eat their breakfast in solitude, or have a late night snack as (formerly) staff would have left small trays of food for a visitor's comfort and need.

Virginia was in the hall outside the suites that now comprised the family living quarters, near the side entrance to Trieste. She was giving instructions to one of the museum staff about something when the two approached. "That shed is a wreck but Ah suppose we could get it cleaned up for the walkin' tour. Ah believe it is locked as well. Ah'll look for the key presently." Dismissing the staff person with an peremptory nod of her head, she turned to Emma and Zach. "Emma, darlin'. What is it? Zachary, dear. Are yaw'r accommodations satisfactory?"

"Five star, Virginia. And much cheaper."

"Good. Ah am happy that is settled. And Emma, do see that you don't parade around durin' museum hours in denim cut-offs and a T-shirt. Try and look nice like Zachary."

With a small sigh of exasperation revealing a history of mother-daughter tussles, Emma replied, "These are not denim, mother, and *they are not* cut-offs. They are called shorts. And Zachary is ovuh dressed out of politeness."

"He appeah's to be a propuh gentleman, at least for current tahmes."

Zach enjoyed the comments bolstering his ego, but ego is mere Icarus wax, and Emma as sun said that he wasn't altogether a gentleman. He gave her a hurt look at which she just rolled her eyes.

"Mama, Ah've come down he-uh t' he'p you, not get a dressin' lesson. What can Zach en Ah do for you? hWhat needs t' be done?"

"hWell, Ah suppose nothing raght now. Let me look for the key t' that shed next to the ole ovuhseer's house. Ah want to open it up for the museum walk, but it hasn't been opened in ye-uhs, not since Daddy died. Lord knows what's in theyuh. You can help me go through it, but in the mean tahme Ah suppose you could show Zachary around a bit mo'."

They left her there to look for the key and went outside to tour the grounds. Walking away Emma wondered aloud that she wasn't altogether sure that it was an admirable trait of her mother to always be concerned with propriety and appearances. "Ah know times was tough at Trieste when she grew up. Granddaddy didn't make much money farming, en Ah know she wasn't much better off than some of the dirt poor farmers round he-uh. She just had a bigger shack. Zach, this place was run down thirty years ago. It was fallin' apart. If momma hadn't married daddy, Ah don't think Trieste would still be in the family. She wasn't fed with no silver spoon growin' up round these parts."

"You mean she's not a Southern belle? I'm crushed."

She laughed a little. "Yaw tryin' t' cheer me up, Ah appreciate that. Yew always do that, that's what Ah like so much about yew, Mr. Zacharee Peterson." She took his hand and turned to hug him. Her face was moist from the humid mid-day heat, little beads of sweat clung to the fine white, downy hairs that ran down her cheeks and across her upper lip. A fine, barely visible mustache laced with little crystals. She looked gorgeous, so vibrant and sexy. He nearly seized up pressing those little crystals to his lips.

While Emma gave Zach a tour of the grounds, she told him how Trieste had been saved from the auction block and from being parceled up like so many plantations had been after the Civil War by the hard efforts of her great-granddaddy and his wife, the struggles of her granddaddy and grandmama during the Great Depression, then finally of how her father had put more than a little capital into Trieste. As his medical practice grew, and thus his income, he pretty much saved the place from the auction block once again. "Mama may be a Southern belle, but she ain't no ivory queen. They's plenty of dirt unduh her finguhnails. She just lahkes to put on aiyuhs"

chapter five

"So tell me, Zachary. hWhat do you think of ow-uh little home?" Virginia asked as they all sat drinking wine, waiting for dinner to be cooked.

Zach set his wineglass down and said, "I'm not sure I would describe it that way. Parts may be little, but certainly not the whole. It's charming, in a grandiose sort of way. When we walked around outside, I felt like I was walking through a history book."

Emma's mother had insisted they take dinner in the dining room, despite it being part of the museum now. She often did that when visitors came to the mansion and her fidelity to an unnecessary decorum flattered Zach.

It was a beautiful room; rare hand painted Chinese wall paper of colorful exotic birds in stands of green bamboo decorated the walls. The plates were decorated with birds, too, hand painted from Audubon prints. They drank out of antique Viennese crystal goblets and set them down on a very large, and very rare, ornately carved Queen Anne table made from English oak. Were it not for their modern appearance, the diners could be part of a scene from one hundred and fifty years ago, an antebellum vision, but with another and perhaps more telling difference: there were no servants, they made dinner themselves. Or rather Virginia had. And later on, Emma disabused Zach of further romantic notions when she told him that her mother had acquired both crystal and china twenty years ago when the family was financially secure enough to spend money on furnishings, and not just the house itself. But at that dinner, he was slipping into the past.

"One thing that I've been wondering, Virginia, is about slaves. I assume, this being a plantation, that it had slaves, right?" Zach asked.

"Yes. At one time great granddaddy had 300 slaves, or so. He was wealthy in that regahd."

"Wealthy. Okay. Where did they sleep? I haven't seen any slave quarters, or housing."

"They would have lived in wooden cabins, and they just rotted away ovuh tahme. Wood rots fai'ly quickly down he-uh if unattended. But you can see the remains of some of the stone fahrplaces some of them had. They would have belonged to some of the mawre impo'tant slaves."

"Not all of them would have had stone fireplaces?" he asked.

"Oh, heavens no! That would have been too costly and tahme consumin' to build. That would have taken them out of the fields. Most had wattle and daub fahrplaces."

"Wattle and daub?"

"Sticks and mud."

"Oh. Where'd they live?"

"About a qua'tuh of a mahle no'thwest of the stables. You can make out the outlines of some of the fahrplaces in the grass yet."

"That'd be interesting to check out. Do you know where they are, Emma?"

"Sure. We use to play around there when we were kids. Theyuh's a little creek theyuh that flows into the Ochlockonee. Ah guess they put them theyuh, the slaves, so they'd have a watuh source. Ah don't think Ah ever saw it run dry," she said.

Virginia cut in, "No. Never has. It's spring fed from up to'des \ttapulgas."

"What a name, Attapulgas. Do you know what that means?" Zach asked Virginia.

"No, Ah don't. Some Indian word Ah've always thought. Creek, Ah would suppose."

"Speaking of names, what does Trieste mean?"

"Well, Ah don't raghtly know. It's Spanish, though. The story goes that great-great granddaddy found a breastplate from a Spanish soldier's suit of arms down by the rivuh. Stories tell that DeSoto had come down the Ochlockonee aftuh wanderin' through No'th Georgia. I'd always thought it meant breastplate, or coat of arms, something like that."

Zach didn't know Spanish, but he remembered having come across a similar word in a French phrase. "Chasson triste means sad song in French. Chasson is song, so I suppose triste means sad."

Emma pursed her lips as she thought for a moment then said, "That jogs mah memory of mah high school French, you're right, triste means sad and gloomy."

Zach laughed and said, "Do you think Trieste was named by the slaves?"

Virginia didn't laugh with him. Somewhat abruptly, she announced, "Ah think Ah'd better check on dinnuh," and excused herself from the table.

As soon as Virginia was out of hearing range, Zach said in hushed tones to Emma, "Uh oh. Then it's just irony." Leaning over and whispering, he asked, "Does your mother have any, um, latent or lingering, umm . . ."

She smirked at him. "She's not a racist, Zach, if that's what yaw gettin' at. But she's no apologists for the family and what they did neithuh. She'd just tell you it was a different tahme. People lived a fah cry different from the way they do nowadays. Besahdes, she probably did need to check on dinnuh, and left at just what seemed an awkwuhd tahme. Ah should go see if Ah can he'p her. Don't worry, you didn't say nuthin' wrong." She slid her chair out from under the table and left the room, leaving him to look at the walls.

She returned not two minutes later, saying, "Don't drink too much of that wahne, Diggy just called. They gonna have their church meetin' tonight. Ah said we'd be ovuh theyuh round 8, if that's alraght. You still wanna go?"

"Yea, sure. Maybe I need more of this, though," he said, setting the nearly empty glass down. Checking his watch, he said, "Jeez, that gives us an hour to eat, get ready, and go. How far is the church?"

"10 to 15 minutes, if Ah remembuh right. Momma's got dinnuh ready now, thank goodness."

Her mother came in to the room, carrying a large platter that smelled exquisitely delicious. "Ah hope you like roast pork, Zachary."

"I grew up on it." he replied with obvious eagerness.

They ate a quiet dinner leaving Zach to wonder if his attempt at levity concerning the etymology of Trieste wrapped a dark, gauzy mood around the meal. But at least it was over soon, as he and Emma had to hurry and did so despite Virginia trying still to regulate her daughter's victuals velocity intake.

"Momma, it ain't gonna hurt ma stomach, en promise you'll leave the dishes till Ah git back?"

"Don't worry about it, darlin', Ah don't have much to do this evening anyway. Run along and forget about it."

They left her at the table with many thanks for a wonderful dinner, especially on behalf of Zach, and quickly they went to their separate quarters and got ready. In a short time they met back at the dining hall, then went outside to the car.

Emma's memory of the way to the church was nearly perfect; they only missed one turn driving there. The roads they drove on were dirt and gravel and mostly in pretty good shape, not torn up with ruts and washboards, so they could keep up a decent speed. It was pretty much smooth sailing through a patchwork of farm fields and pine-barrens. A lot of turpentine had been taken out of those woods not too long ago, and the trees stood testimony to it, many still bearing scars. A lot of the small farmhouses they passed, along with the ubiquitous trailer, could have used some of the cash these trees had generated at one time. With sunlight shading to the golden hues of a sunset, they soon came to a little clapboard church in a clearing surrounded by huge old live oaks, limbs overly burdened with Spanish moss. The white paint of the old building was chipped and faded a dusky white, rimmed for three feet above the ground a dirty light ochre from splashing rainwater. There was a small dirt parking lot at the front where they parked, the lot filled with cars old and new, mostly old. The two were running a little late, and it appeared that the service had started. They opened the old grey door carefully and peered inside. To their surprise, a voice called out, "Emma, you came! Come on in! And Zachary, we're glad you're joining us!"

It was Diggy speaking, and everyone turned to see the newcomers. The room had been arranged so that all the seats, and what pews there were, formed a circle. Nearly forty people were in the small church, the insides painted the same flat white as the outside. They were of all ages, from the very young, to some obviously very old folks, pushing ninety perhaps. And everyone was black. They looked at the two white people with genuine friendliness, but there was also a bit of amusement in their expressions. It was a rare event to have white folks in their church, but a few recognized Emma. Some of the old women reached out and pressed her hand as she and Zach walked by to reach two available chairs, and Emma knew many by name.

They weren't too late, the service, or 'this thing' as Zach called it, hadn't started. Diggy quickly introduced them, explaining that Zach had shown an interest in witnessing a shout. Since he really didn't have any idea what was going to happen, he just smiled a lot and nodded in agreement with her. Emma could sense the uneasiness behind his forced smile. She had decided not to explain to him what a shout was, she thought it better for him to experience it. She told him, "Sometahmes it just don't do no good to explain things. Sometahmes it's bettuh to just go on en jump raght in the thick a'things."

Diggy sat down and motioned with a slight nod to a large, heavy woman wearing a tight, sleeveless black dress made of thin glistening rayon. Her enormity pressed and overflowed everywhere it could gain advantage on the fabric, which was as successful in its task of containment as saran-wrap would hold a lake. As she rose, the congregation shifted in their chairs, as if to ready themselves. Her sheer size alone was enough to warrant everyone's attention, but she also had that air of command that is so hard to define in a person, yet is so apparent in some. Zach realized she must be the pastor or minister, whatever they called the leader of this 'flock'. He didn't even know what denomination this church was and in point of fact, did not feel like he knew a whole lot about anything at the moment. And Emma was of no help, she was as rapt as everyone else.

There was no pulpit, the woman just kind of rolled out into the middle of the floor like a safe on wheels. She looked out over her audience with eyes that would brook no tomfoolery, tolerate nothing but the most serious of efforts from these folks. She turned slowly in the center of the room, appraising everyone individually. Zach hunkered down in his chair hoping she would not notice the white boy in the room. The woman's eyes came to Emma, who just smiled back at the mask of imperturbability. Then her gaze fell on Zach. He squirmed, but looked right back into her coal black onyx eyes. 'Man', he thought, 'did she look mean with her jaw stuck out, and three chins underneath to back it up'. He broke out into a nervous grin, which broadened into a bigger smile. All nerves. She held her gaze, then moved on to the next person without a flicker of emotion, recognition, or anything passing for warmth or friendliness. As she moved way, his body relaxed but was re-tuned to her, like iron filings after a magnet passes.

After circling the crowd, she paused for a moment, then flung one huge arm out, the flesh quaking and quivering in protest, and yelled out in a full, rich, baritone voice, "Lord sez you bettuh git ready! De Lord sez you bettuh git ready!"

While Zach recoiled from the sonic boom that was her voice, the crowd repeated what she said in a rhythm which she picked up and hurled back at them, but with a different line, "Cause there gonna come a judgment day! Cause there gonna come a judgment day!" which the audience sang back to her twice.

Then, "And he gonna come back, too! And he gonna come back, too!" she shouted with more belief than Zach held in his own name referring to himself. The congregation sang it back to her, then she shot out, "Gonna look inside your soul! Gonna look inside your soul!" like the voice of doom. After the audience sang that back to her twice, there followed a few "Amens!" then she broke into an old spiritual, with everyone joining right in, including Emma, hand clapping and singing loudly. They all stood up and swayed to the tune. Zach tried to look like he knew what he was doing, and more that he was enjoying himself. Letting go in church was new to him, hell, letting go anywhere was new to him. He tried not to be too stiff, didn't want old whitey to look bad.

She led the congregation in at least five more songs, each one being sung with more fervor than the last. People began shuffling their feet, some began turning around in tight circles where they stood. Gradually the singing and clapping grew louder and louder and people started stomping their feet on the wooden floor. Sweat started to trickle down many faces, Emma's included, while the noise was getting thunderous. Hallelujah's started crackin' like lightening. Zach looked around, most had their eyes closed, those that opened them did so only to look upwards and gesture to the sky, often letting out an Amen! or Hallelujah! He was surprised that Emma could get so involved, let herself go; she was prancing as ecstatically as everyone else.

Big Mama in black was working the circle, walking around and urging everyone on. She'd walk up to someone who was fervently singing and praising and yell things at them Zach couldn't hear over the din of singing, shouting and amen-ing. Sometimes the person would suddenly stop and stand still, eyes closed, and smile, beatifically stoned, others would sing and praise all the more jubilantly.

This went on for at least half an hour before she got everyone to start shuffling and dancing around in a circle, even some of the old people, instead of sitting down to rest, jumped right in and joined in the fray, as foot loose as some of the twentysomethings there. The circle went counter clockwise, at first at an agreeable pace but that soon quickened to a near trot, with some people turning and spinning in circles within the circle. And all the time the clapping continued, and the foot stomping and the singing and praising. Around and around they went, once, twice, thrice, eight, the ninth, Zach lost count. It was getting hot, stifling hot, he wished he could take his shirt off. He tried to catch glimpses of Emma behind him, and when he could, she was focused somewhere else, her eyes tiny slits looking at her feet or looking through him when she looked up. But she was smiling from here to Attapulgas.

After who knows how many turns of the human wheel, people started to spin out of the circle, and either drop to the floor, or sag into a chair, there to be left to recover, or go to whatever lands their addled ships took them, distant shores for sure. Meanwhile, and all the while, Big Mama in black was in the middle orchestrating and administrating. Once in a while she'd close in on someone and shout right into their face, sending them off, mind separated from body. It was getting hotter and hotter, Zach was getting dizzy and tired. He still tried to keep up the singing and praising, all the time his mind jumping between the absurdity of this, the downright silliness of dancing in a circle shouting and whooping, and the necessity of focusing so that he didn't trip over his own feet. 'Hadn't I done this as a child?' he wondered, 'Spun around to get dizzy, a natural form of getting high? And it was adult proof, they couldn't take it away. Oops, a near trip, gotta keep my focus.' As he caught his balance after yet another near stumble, Big Mama in black was upon him, looking at him with those coal pits for eyes. He started to mumble an apology for tripping, when she shoved her face within an inch of his nose and shouted, "*Who* got a dream!?"

Something sharp was poking Zach, but it seemed far away, an irritating nudge dig thump. Yet each jab brought him closer to consciousness. He became aware that he was lying face down on the ground, grass sticking in his mouth. He could feel the sharpness of the blades, the spiny texture, feel them catch on his tongue as he ran it down the stem, and tasted the chlorophyll. How can grass taste green? Can you taste a color? He stirred to spit it out and the poking stopped. He felt groggy and heavy, drugged, a dentist's shot to the brain. He started to push himself up but gave up for the effort and sank back down. Turning his face sideways, he opened blurry eyes to perceive some kind of woods, trees all around. Daylight. 'Where am I?' Dim recollections of heat and tiredness, and movement, strangers dancing in a circle, drifted like flotsam across his mind. Groaning, again he tried to lift himself. Too much. He lay on a forearm and tried to think. A high pitched squeaky noise caught his ear, but it was no more than background noise, jibberish, nothing he could understand. It was faint, a long way off and receded like shadows just as quickly as it had come. What could he remember? Nothing. 'Boy, must of tied one on last night', he thought. But he didn't feel that old familiar headache from too much alcohol. "I don't remember drinking last night." he mumbled aloud. That brought back the faint whisperings. "Hey!" he yelled out when he was jabbed again, "That hurt!" He rolled over on his back to look up and see a large furry something looking down at him. 'I must be dreaming', he thought. 'This thing, a rabbit? was wearing some kind of old farmer's clothes. A rabbit wearing clothes?' Its nosed twitched. 'God, it was a rabbit, no, someone doing a damn good imitation of one.' Zach sat up and dropped his head between his knees and rubbed his eyes, hoping to erase whatever they were hallucinating, hoping the rabbit would be gone, or the game over. Either way, just not-what was. But then he heard the voice again, this time he could understand some of the words, and they weren't far away, they were coming from Mr. Bunny. 'Did I take drugs last night? Did some one give me drugs and I didn't know?' He opened his eyes and looked at him/it/she/whatever.

The rabbit said, "Hey, yo, Mr. Man. I tukkin you was dade. But I seedz dat you ain't, leastwaze not yit, which I'ze bleedze you ain't. How yo comin t' be er?"

He was stunned and couldn't respond. A rabbit, say about 4 foot high to the tip of its ears, standing on its hind legs, dressed poorly in rumpled, patched, coarse woven clothes, but with a fairly decent vest on, had just spoken to him, out of the side of its mouth to boot. Zach turned away, he couldn't handle the realism of this trick, he was disoriented enough as it was. This was too real. Too real. This wasn't funny. 'I don't know who's up to this, but I'll find out, and they'll pay. Pudge? J.J.? Emma? Where's Emma?'

The rabbit spoke again, "Es yo def? Ef'n yer is, I kin git hep kaze I node der's some dat kin signs. Mr. Man, is yo def?"

Then he poked Zach, and Zach realized that the rabbit had been jabbing him with the long nails, or claws, of one of his paws.

"Ouch! Damn you, you do that again and you'll regret it!" Zach warned the rabbit, who quickly jumped away, landing easily three or four feet away. "Well, tooby sho, you kin talk jist lik reg'lur folks." He then spit out a long stream of putrid looking brown juice. "Co'se, if'n yo def, how you larnt t' talk?"

Zach didn't saying anything, just sat and watched as the rabbit reached into one of his trouser pockets and pulled out a dark brown wad and bit into it with long, curved and very stained, incisors. 'Tobacco. He's chewing tobacco,' he realized. They quietly appraised one another, Zach marveled at the creature's eyes as it studied him and his clothing; they were eyes filled with curiosity and intelligence, and a good deal of wariness and maybe mistrust. 'God, they looked like big brown rabbit eyes.' Only different. And his ears, that was a great makeup job, they must have been wired to some little computer or something because they moved around very naturally. Easily the best special effects he'd ever seen.

It was time to stand up, try and get his blood flowing, maybe that would clear things up somehow. The rabbit jumped back another couple of paces as he did so.

"Heyo, yer!" he squeaked. "W'at I gwine do wid you? I dunner dey got mannerz you come fum, skeerin folks dat way."

He put one paw up to his chin while resting his elbow on his crossed front arm, a pose Zach would usually associate with deep thinking, al a Rodin, but this was a rabbit, or something. His eyes looked very mistrustful now, gone was the curiosity.

Indignantly, he said, "I ain't ne'r year'n no Mr. Man talk like you duz. Mebbe you ain't fum er, and yo is too biggity to confab wit ole Brer Rabbit."

"Brer Rabbit?" Zach said incredulously.

"Co'se. Whysomever you look 'stonish? All de creeturs no dat." He ran his paws down his clothes to smooth them out.

"Brer Rabbit?" he said again.

"Der you iz."

"I suppose Brer Fox is here, too?"

His eyes narrowed and his ears laid down towards the back of his head, "W'en you seed im? You he fren? I got 'spishun you might be. He up to sumpin, dat why you play Brer Possum?"

"No. Uncle Remus sent me," Zach said sarcastically.

"Onless I dism'mber, I ain't familious wid Unk Remus. He fren un Brer Fox too?"

Zach didn't respond, he was getting tired of this game and wanted it to end. 'Brer Rabbit! Right!' Maybe if he just walked out of this wood, he'd recognize something, or come to a highway and hitch a ride into whatever town was nearby. He couldn't see anything through the trees, so he asked Mr. Rabbit, make that Brer Rabbit, where a road would be.

"Da big road right er der," he said pointing the way, so Zach started heading that way, leaving the rabbit standing by himself. Walking away he was full of thoughts of how real that rabbit had been. Someone did an incredible job making him, down to his tobacco chewing. 'Ugh! I'll have to complement them after I yell at whoever was behind all this.'

He soon came to a wide, dirt road. He looked for tire prints, but saw none, only a host of animal tracks running both ways.

Being as adept at reading spore as the average urban dweller, he could name none of the animals that made the prints, it was a maze of hoof prints big and little, and many a paw print too. Some had to be from a bear they were so big, but no shoe prints. 'So this is the big road,' Zach thought. ' Wonder what he calls the expressway. Now, which way to turn?' Any way seemed as good as the other, so he veered left.

The land looked vaguely familiar to him. It was mostly flat, sandy soil with a great number of pine trees, probably turpentine, he thought. Here and there a giant oak tree would be spread out, taking up a 1/4 acre or so, and fairly festooned with Spanish moss. He walked for nearly an hour, without any change in the scenery, just trees, trees and more trees. He was getting hot and thirsty, the sun beat down unrelentingly. He'd passed and jumped over many a small stream, some had clear water running in them, but he wasn't about to drink from a stream, what with all the pollution nowadays. He'd never even heard of anyone drinking out of a stream or river. Not even a pond. He was getting very agitated because he couldn't come to any understanding of how he had come to be there. Not one fleeting ghost of a memory, not a sliver of an idea, not one echo of a spark of a synapse in his brain could be called forth to bear news of his arrival, only vague apparitions moving in a dark room. 'Emma? Emma? Where are you? I was with you, right? Didn't we, didn't we, didn't we diggity, Diggy? Diggy. I know her. Didn't we see Diggy? "Oh, damn it! This isn't fun anymore!" he yelled out to whomever was doing this. "Damn you! Can you hear me?" he yelled much louder. "It's gone on long enough! You've had your fun, I give up! You win! Okay? OOOOKAAAAYYYY?"

Nothing. Not even an echo, the trees swallowed it up. Dejected, he walked on.

And walked for another hour until he came to a field, or rather a clearing, he couldn't make out what, if anything, had been planted in it. He didn't care, it was a sign of people. His pace quickened as hope bloomed and twined around revenge.

Presently, a path intersected the road and he followed it to the left, out into the field and over a small rise where there was evidence of a garden, but any fruits of someone's labor had been gone for some time. Down the path another hundred feet he could make out a small cabin and what appeared to be a well. "All right, water!"

He made his way directly to the well without concerning himself at all with the cabin. A bucket with a rope tied to it sat on the edge of the well, which he lowered down until the saving sound of it hitting water was heard. It was as good as tasting it. He hauled it back up as quickly as he could and drank the sweetest water he'd ever had. Setting it down after slaking his thirst, he drew his attention to the cabin. It was really small, not more than one room with a small shed attached, and it couldn't have been more than five feet tall. Maybe they were midgets, or dwarfs, or something, he wondered. Well, it doesn't matter, they were still people, and they could help him out, though sometimes these back country people can be skittish when strangers come to their doors. 'Just no guns. Don't need guns pointed at me,' he muttered as he knocked.

The door swung open with the first rap of his knuckles. He peered into the one room, dimly lit by two small windows, one directly across, the other to his left, which opposed the fireplace. He could make out several small chairs and a table and in one of the corners, a bed. There were various items hanging from the rafters: some dried herbs and animal skins, and various kitchen utensils. Pretty primitive, he thought. His mind drew forth some pictures of poor people with raggedy clothes and dirty hair and unwashed clothes. And awful teeth. He yelled out, "Anyone home? Hello? Is anyone here?" Silence. He stepped inside, ducking his head but thankfully, it was taller than he first estimated. Calling again, "Anyone here? I'm lost, I need some help. Hello?" Nothing. 'Well, you've as good as broken in now,' he thought. 'Don't shoot, folks, don't shoot.' He fought memories of farmer's daughter jokes and scenes from 'Deliverance' as he looked about. There was another door at the back of the cabin that he could not have seen from the front door. It was slightly ajar, as if it hadn't been closed properly. Or some one had left in a hurry. He walked up to it and swung it open, looking out into the backyard which was cleared off of brush and timber for about twenty paces. He couldn't make anything out in the bushes and trees that were naturally thick at the edge of the clearing, the leaves fighting for the sunshine. He called again, "Is anyone there? I'm not going to hurt you! I need some help! I'm lost!"

He paused for a moment then turned to look back inside the cabin. He had the sensation of being watched, and he swung around in time to catch something quickly disappear behind a bush. "Hey!" he called out. "Please, I'm not here to hurt anyone, I just need some help. Can you hear me? I know you're there. Please, please, come on out."

He waited silently and patiently as the bushes rattled a little bit, then watched as the rattler emerged. "Holy shit!" he exclaimed.

Out stepped a large red fox dressed in clothes similar to that rabbit, only this fox didn't wear a vest, just a coarse spun white shirt that had no collar, and he had suspenders that held his pants up. He was shoeless and had his trousers rolled up just like Mr. Bunny, and walked upright, too. His long pointed ears were pitched forward, alert. He stuck his paws into his pant pockets and shuffled out from behind the bush. "Good God, is this never going to end?" Zach moaned. "Who the hell is doing this?"

"Scooze me," the fox said in an alarmingly normal sounding voice. "I wuz des checkin' somfin out behime er. I din't node I'd compnee."

"And you'd be Brer Fox, I suppose?" Zach asked with a bit of annoyance.

"I might node im. Who axin?"

Zach didn't respond, he carefully scrutinized the fox who stood some 15 paces away. He was unbelievably lifelike. He held his long pointed face down, but his eyes were looking up at Zach in a sort of shy, ah-shucks manner. He was a very handsome looking animal, as foxes go, with a beautiful red color from the top of his long snout to the back of his hind legs, and a very lustrous white underneath. He had nearly black markings on his face, but just small ones, like accents. He was tall, standing close to five feet to the tip of his tufted ears, that he stood on his tiptoes (tippaws?) probably exaggerated his height. He was lithe and lean looking, even through his baggy clothing. A magnificent bushy tail twitched nervously back and forth.

"Nummine. Mo' samer t'me, I des kuse."

Zach still did not say anything, though joke this may be, it seemed rude not to respond. "My name is Zachary Peterson and I'm lost. If you could get me to a telephone or a highway I would be indebted, and I would reward you. Do you know where I could borrow a car? I can pay you."

At this the fox pulled a paw out of his pants pocket and scratched his head. "I got no reckembembunce un a ca. En I ain't ne'er year'd no telfone ne'er. But less'n I'ze a-gone gump, din't yo des come fum da big road?"

His black eyes held more honesty than Zach had ever seen, like Emma's without the mischievous-ness. And he appeared to really want to settle his mind by knowing for fact whether or not Zach had just come down 'da big road'.

Cold fingers of an icy awareness slid around Zach's throat. Maybe this wasn't a dream, maybe this wasn't someone's complex, Byzantine idea of a joke. The humanness of this animal's query, the curiosity and even emotion behind his desire to know a simple matter, a simple fact, was compelling. 'Had I not just come from the road?' He studied the fox with a little more compassion, reflecting that he had some different personality traits than the rabbit, he seemed a little shyer, and at the same time perhaps a little more honest, or rather, less dubious. What is the quality he was thinking of? Yes, he was an ingenue. He thought of all the Uncle Remus tales where the rabbit was always outwitting the fox. Zach could see now how it could happen, he was too trusting.

And that rabbit had a lot more cunning in his eyes. The rabbit was disingenuous, at least in the stories, and maybe here. Here? It was getting difficult trying to explain away these creatures as parts in an elaborate hoax. Wherever the hell here was, he was. He resolved to just keep looking and accept. Just accept. Surrender to whatever was moving these creatures about and whatever had built this place. 'Whomever or whatever, I'll go along with you. For now at least.'

"Well," Zach finally responded, "it doesn't matter. Something will turn up. And yes, I did just come from the big road, and I'll be heading down it again. Thanks for your help."

He turned to leave and started walking away around the side of the cabin. The fox asked, "Iz yo hongry?" Zach had to stop and think about that. He couldn't remember his last meal, so he couldn't go by time to tell, since he often ate by the clock, but the grumbling in his stomach said it didn't need a watch. "I am. I'd be indebted to you if you would give me something to eat."

"Tooby sho," the fox said with obvious glee as he sprang toward the cabin. "I hongry myse'f an bleedzd t' cook sum bittle fer yu'n too."

He broke into a big smile, which due to his muzzle, looked more like a sneer with his long, sharp teeth exposed, and the corners of his mouth snugged up. But his eyes were all aglitter as he pranced and jigged his way to the cabin. Standing at the door he turned to Zach and said, "I'ze monstus bleedzd des fer compnee since my 'oman and chilluns went fer t' visit wif her sist'r."

Zach followed him in and sat down in one of the small chairs at the table, which obviously served as desk, work table and kitchen table. He couldn't imagine a family in the one room no matter they be foxes or not. Zach didn't want to force an uncomfortable silence exaggerated by his watching the fox's every move, so he asked him how big his family was while he moved about getting the coals in the fireplace stoked up and then swinging a big black cast iron pot over it. The dexterity he had in the use of his paws as hands was astonishing.

"Dey's my wife and fo' chilluns, n' dey all tree yer ode. Dem young un's got a good medjun of the whully-win's, dats fo shoo. And how yo fambly? I spec' yo got un wife and chilluns back whe'e yo fum? Where iz yo fum? I ain't ne'er year'd talk'n like dat yo do. Co'se, t'ain't nu'my bidniss, des kuse. Now my 'omans fambly, dey talk diffint too, and dey got diffint mannerz too . . ."

Brer Fox was a talker, and he kept right on rolling, Zach didn't have to say much of anything, just respond now and then in the affirmative or negative, just indicate that he was listening. As the fox kept on chatty rattling, the aroma issuing from the black cauldron was causing Zach's mouth to water in anticipation. It smelled delicious. Brer Fox told him it was his "fambly's speshul stew, fum he great-granpappy." As he talked and talked, the aroma snaked out the door like a homeless wraith and into the surrounding woods, haunting someone else's nose. Pretty soon there came a knock at the front door.

Brer Fox said, "Ef dat don't bang my times, I got mo compnee," as he moved to the door.

He opened it to find Brer Rabbit standing there, who said loudly and senatorially, "Brer Fox, I year'd yo was feelin' po'ly, so I sez, sez I, dat I'd rack o'er er and ax if'n yo be needin' anytin. How duz yo sym'tums segashuate?"

Brer Fox took a step back, and eyed him dubiously. "Slanchendickler, I 'speck," he said slowly. "Who sedz I come 'long po'ly? Dis ain't got nuf'in do wid dis er stew duz it?"

Feigning hurt, Brer Rabbit said, "Ah-yi, I ain't projickin' wid you, I'ze serrous kunsun. Fust I year'n yo got de agur fum de gals up t' Miss Meadows, I come gallin o'er er, un you is disbeleefin' me. I'ze a Friday-born fool fum who lay de rail fo t' keer fo you. An er I stanz all bellust and yo jubous." He lowered his ears and dropped his head for dramatic effect.

Brer Rabbit looked up just a little to see if his words and actions had any effect on Brer Fox, which, if they did, Zach couldn't tell. The fox's attitude toward the rabbit was already one of mistrust, a far cry from his genuine friendliness toward Zach, who wanted to applaud Brer Rabbit's obvious performance, but he let it go.

The rabbit continued, "Well, I 'speck I'ze bett'r git on home fo it git dahk n' de dinna bell, doe I ain't kotch my breff." He started to act as if he were leaving, but seeing that it was having no effect on Brer Fox, turned back around and said, "I seedz yo got compnee, en got no truck wid ole Brer Rabbit. Bimeby, dat de same fell'r I seedz up t' Miss Meadows."

"Dat so," said Brer Fox, casting a glance toward Zach, who shrugged his shoulders and said "I don't know a Miss Meadows."

Brer Rabbit quickly responded, "Weren't at de house, but en de woods wha's roun'. Ax im ef dats de troof."

Zach spoke before Brer Fox, "I woke up this morning with him poking me. So, yes, we did meet before." Brer Rabbit folded his arms across his chest at this small triumph.

With a heavy sigh, Brer Fox said, "Well, mo' samer t'me yo met b'fo. Un 'spect on coun un my frenliness n' hosspetall'erees yo kin come in fo some stew, but I des wan yo shorance I not regrettin' afterwards."

"You kin shoot yo' shekels on dat," said the rabbit with gusto as he brushed by Brer Fox and jumped into the cabin. Sauntering up to the kettle he said, "Hooey, it smell d'lishus. Less 'ave a-bait er un dat."

He reached for the ladle that hung over the stew, but Brer Fox quickly moved between Brer Rabbit and the pot. "Ez ter dat," said Brer Fox, "des drap in un dem dar chars en I git de pot to de table."

Brer Rabbit spun around and launched himself into a chair. Grinning, and full of renewed hope and energy, he began thumping the floor with his foot while drumming on the table with his paws. Zach asked him if he was nervous or something.

"Nooo. I des splimmy-splammy dat my ole fren Brer Fox ain't got de agur. Dey's folks what git da croops n' dies."

"Get the what?" Zach asked.

"De croops n' coffs. Nat'ally, I bleedz he ain't got 'zeaze. Brer Fox, iz dat stew ready? I'ze monstus hungry fum rackin down er two-fo'ty on de shell road."

The stew was hot enough to eat, and so Brer Fox ladled each out a bowl full. Conversation came to a stand still, but the noise level didn't change. That rabbit made more sounds than a barnyard of swine while he gobbled up his food, and by the time Zach had finished his first bowl, Brer Rabbit was well into mauling his second.

"Brer Fox, dis de mos' bodayshush stew I e'er et," he said while looking up for a brief moment, "my compelerments t' de chef." His face was speckled with stew, which he removed now and then with his arm sleeves. Brer Fox and Zach ate more leisurely, though they all ate their fill.

It was getting dark when at last they pushed their bowls away and leaned back in the chairs. Brer Fox struck a match, lighting an old oil lamp on the table, which cast a golden hue around the cabin. He then got a pipe down from the mantel above the fireplace, stuffed it full of tobacco, and lit it. Zach was glad to see that Brer Rabbit didn't seem to want any of his chew right then. He could tell they both wanted him to talk, to tell them about himself. Brer Rabbit even asked if he was from the "de big wa'der."

"No, I'm from a big city. Have you ever heard of Atlanta?" They shook their heads. "It's not so far from here, but I don't know which direction it's in, I'm kind of turned around. I'm hoping you'll be able to help me out on that score."

They both looked at each other, eyes as big and blank as newborns. "Well, you must know someone who might be able to help me."

Brer Rabbit spoke up, "Dey's Brer Wolf, he run 'round e'erw'ere. En Brer B'ar too. He talk mighty biggity, 'zef he bin all roun de worl."

Brer Fox added, "Ole Jack Sparrer, dey ain't nuffin he don't node bout. He allers chirripen sumpen bout dis o' dat gossip."

"En Brer Tukkey Buzzud allers flyin up dar in de elements, he ain't ne'er see t' miss nuffin ne'er," added Brer Rabbit.

"I don't think they're the ones who'll be able to help me," Zach interjected. "Do you know of another Mr. Man?"

"Lessee," said Brer Fox, "dey's ole John oe'r dar by de big 'simmon trees. En Toby w'at live on de big crick by de gals, en . . ."

Who lives the closest?" Zach interrupted.

"Brer Possum do," said Brer Rabbit.

"No. I mean, between ole John and Toby."

They both shrugged their shoulders and shifted around in their chairs.

"I speckeleck ole John," Brer Fox finally said. Brer Rabbit quickly refuted, "I not want t'quoll wif my good fren Brer Fox, speshul he des cook de bestes' supper, but it mo'n lakly Toby."

Brer Fox looked at Zach, "Brer Rabbit good et many a teng, en he monstus good et trouble, but he don't no nuffin bout dis er teng."

Slapping the table and standing up in his chair Brer Rabbit yelled at Brer Fox, "Dat de mos splendiferus slandus lie I e'er year'd. You de one's dat 'sponsbul fo de trouble. Who dat who make de Tar Baby? En who dat who jist bout e't my chilluns?"

"Dat wuz Brer Wolf," Brer Fox shouted back. "En dat Tar Baby tuk t'me, not you. En I cain't see ter me nose ef I ain't lookin at de feller who stole dat er side er beef fum me w'at we stole t'gedder fum Mr. Man."

"I to'd you he tuk en cum back fer it, en wukked me o'er good wid a battlin' stick. Dats de hon'st troof."

"De hon'st troof? Dat w'at you sez t'Brer Tarrypin w'en you stole he quills?"

"I ne'er stole he quills, dey was barried."

Brer Fox let out a howl and snickered, "Dey was barried. Der you go 'gin, Mr. Wull-er-de-wust."

"Hey! Hey! Hey!" Zach said, jumping in to the fray. "That's

enough! Pardon me for being a little self-serving, but I need the help of both of you. If you start fighting, I won't get anywhere."

That quieted them for a moment. They sat back in their chairs and pouted, looking down at the table. 'Kids!' Zach thought, 'They're just like kids!' Brer Rabbit got up and walked over to the fireplace, rubbing his chin. He was working something over in his mind, scheming, no doubt, to fix Brer Fox up. The glowing coals gave him a little bit of a sinister look. Eventually he spoke up, "In de mo'nin, we kin set out fer ole John's and Toby's sepprut'. De fust dat gits back iz de un dats right."

Zach could see that Brer Fox liked the idea, the poor dim sap. "No, that's not going to work," Zach said. "No one's going to go wasting time running around in the woods, or not going anywhere, for that matter," he said, looking at the rabbit, who looked away angrily, or rather, pretended to be angry.

Zach watched Brer Rabbit standing by the fire, the last of the flickering flames and dying embers dancing and shadow boxing around his form. He was deep in his scheming again, one arm wrapped across his chest, the other propped on it, rubbing his chin, his furrowed eyes looking deeply into the red coals. It dawned on Zach that since he wasn't getting anywhere with these two, he had to dig a little more, go out on a limb, in order to find a way back. "Maybe I need something a little stronger than just directions," he said aloud. "Do either of you know a doctor or a . . ." he stopped. Asking for a psychologist would definitely cause too many difficult questions with indecipherable answers. "A doctor, do you know of a doctor?" he asked.

Nope. No such luck.

"How about a priest, or a minister, a medicine man. Any medicinemen around? A holy man? How about an astrologer?" Their puzzled looks gave him the answer. "What I think I may need is some one who can do a little magic. Someone outside the fold, you know, like a, like a, medicine man. Or a witch, yes, a witch, a potion mixer, a conjurer." They both drew back and gasped, Brer Rabbit saying shakily, "De conjun woman?"

"Yes!" Zach cried, "Bingo, a hit! You know a conjurer!"

They looked at each other with eyes as big as moons, cowering in the shadows cast by the light of the oil lamp.

"Does she live far? Do you know the way to her place?" Zach asked both of them.

Neither spoke for a long time, until Brer Rabbit weakly said, "Brer Fox de un dat duz, I ne'er bin dar. En I 'speck I bes' be rackin' on home, de Missus be wondrin' bout me fo sho. Tankee, Brer Fox fo de mos' bestes' stew I e'er e't." While Brer Fox shook his head in obvious disagreement concerning his knowledge of the conjuror's whereabouts, Brer Rabbit was backing up towards the door, while speaking, "Mos' bleedzd t' meet wif you, but I bes skaddle. It all-night-Isom fo dis er rabbit." He turned to grab the latch on the door, but Zach launched himself from his chair and slammed the door shut just as Brer Rabbit opened it. "Yiiieee," he screamed as he jumped clear across the cabin.

"Oh no you don't," Zach said. "You're not leaving just as I'm about to get somewhere in this crazy story. Now, let's sit down at the table and discuss this." Brer Rabbit made a move to leave out the back door, but just a step in his direction by Zach stopped him. Quick as the rabbit was, Zach was much bigger, and he realized it didn't take long for Zach to move from one side of the cabin to the other. Dejected, he sat down at the table and started complaining, "I be mos' happy fo t' hep, but I don' no nuffin, en my po' chilluns iz prolly sta'vin, en my 'oman be worrin' t'def, en . . ."

"Brer Rabbit, shush. If I remember right, you've spent many a night away from your family, and this won't take long. You and Brer Fox will take me to the conjurer's tomorrow, and after that, you can do as you wish. I need you just for as long as it takes to get there. Okay?"

Brer Rabbit eyed Zach suspiciously, "How you no bout me en my fambly? You mighty kuse, Mr. Man."

"Never mind, it wouldn't make much sense to you," he replied. "Now, who knows the way to the witch?"

They both pointed to the other.

"That is why we're all going," Zach said in mock gleefulness. "Brer Fox, what do you know?"

"Des pa't de way der, en on'y fum w'at folks sez. I ain't ne'er bin der, dats de troof un it."

"I believe you. And what do you know Brer Rabbit?"

"Lak I sez, nuffin. Don' no nuffin, ne'er year'd nuffin, ne'er seed nuffin. Mr. Man, Brer Fox jist sed he de un dat no's sump'en. He de un you wa'n't. Hon'st."

"It's hard for me to believe you don't know anything. You've had your nose in everybody's business for ever."

Brer Fox guffawed loudly. "Dat fo sho, tooby sho."

"How you no so much bout my bidniss?" Brer Rabbit asked. "Speshul we jist confabb'd dis mo'nin?"

"I know you much better than you think. But that's for another time to discuss. Brer Fox, what do you think of what Brer Rabbit is saying, that he doesn't know anything?"

"He on'y let on w'en it 've'nyunt fo he t'do so. Dey's a story dat one time ole Brer Rabbit dun got hese'f ne'er cook'd by de wi'ch. Dat he wuz kotch up spyun on her en she groppted he up en tho'd 'im inter un pot wif ballin' wa'der, dats w'at dey say."

"Der you iz 'gin wif dem lies!" yelled Brer Rabbit.

"So you were spying on her?" Zach asked.

"I no spy!"

"Okay, you aren't a spy. Okay, I believe you," Zach said, reassuringly patting his paw. "What was in the pot?"

"Inguns en carr'ts," Brer Rabbit said absentmindedly.

On account of his furry face, Zach couldn't tell if he blushed, but he was sure that's what he was doing after he as much as admitted to having been to the witch's place. Brer Fox sniggered and snuffled through his muzzle. "You sump'en, Brer Rabbit, you sump'en e'ss," he said.

It took nearly an hour before they settled on who knew what. Brer Fox would be able to take them most of the way based on what he'd heard, and Brer Rabbit would be able to take them the final steps. He'd stumbled upon the conjurer's house once after having been chased by dogs. He'd gotten lost in the woods fleeing from them, and had finally escaped by breaking into her house, which he thought looked empty. He then found himself jumping from the pan to the pot, as it were. The 'witch' was fond of rabbit stew and it had taken all of Brer Rabbit's wits to talk the conjurer to distraction so that he could make his break. And he did, a tribute to his wily ways.

"All right," Zach announced, "I'm dead tired and need to sleep, and I don't care where I do."

Brer Fox said that he could sleep in the bed, while he'd "cu'l up n'er de fa'r," and Brer Rabbit could do the same. Trusting Brer Rabbit to bolt, Zach said he'd have to sleep nearer him, that he was going to tie a string to his finger, and the other end to Brer Rabbit's arm.

Arrangements made and Brer Rabbit secured as best they could over his undying protests that he could be trusted, which Brer Fox and Zach never thought for a minute was true, they all soon fell asleep, the cabin filled with nighttime snores and grunts and snarls and growls from the dreaming occupants, at least for the two critters. Zach, too tired to care that he slept with a hare, fell into a dreamless, deep sleep, a night spent in a black hole of heaviness. Waking late to the sound of birds through the open window, he saw Brer Fox still curled up by the fireplace, and the other end of the string tied to a bedpost. Brer Rabbit was gone.

chapter six

Burly Olalla looked up at the fading sun. Pink, purple and orange pastel hues colored the western sky. A few ragged cirrus clouds sent long probing tendrils out, roots searching for water, seeking the path for a thunderstorm to follow. "Cracks in the vault of heaven," he chuckled to himself. "But I don't think you'll be leaking any water tonight."

He was standing on a small hillock in the Flint Hills of southeastern Kansas, on the ranch he owned some twenty miles outside of Arkansas City, Kansas. The ranch wasn't huge, by Western standards, still, at 1700 acres, it was plenty big for his uses. The hillock he stood on was near a small creek about half a mile from his house. He needed the water, muddy as it was, to douse the fire that had been burning for an hour and a half. But it needed to burn another half hour or so first and when he finally did pour the water on it, it would be but glowing coals if all went as he hoped.

He wasn't alone on his little mound. His best friend, Donovan Littlefeather, sat crossed legged on the prairie grass, playing a mournful tune on a flute carved out of fragrant Western cedar. The notes drifted away on the prairie wind, lingering only when a gust curled up around him, caressing him for a song played in its honor. The flute was adorned with a single tail feather from a Cooper's hawk, which twisted wildly in the wind, a weathervane for spirits.

And in the plains, the wind spirits come roaring out of the Rocky Mountains, challenging anyone or anything that dares to stand up to them. 'Give me time, and you'll bow to me, whether stone, bone or wood', it boasts. A turbulent, but unbiased, spirit.

But Burly and his friend weren't there to placate the wind gods, at least not directly. They would soon appeal to them, and all other spirits, to intercede on their behalf for the healing of Burly's maternal uncle, who lay in a hospital bed in Wichita, cancer eating away at his lungs.

They had built a sweat lodge on the little hill in the fashion favored by the plains tribes. Slender cottonwood saplings had been tied together to make a small domed structure, much like an igloo, but without the long entranceway. Over the saplings, blankets had been carefully placed so that from inside the lodge, no light could be seen, it would be pitch black save for the light cast by glowing rocks that were now red hot in the fire that burned not a dozen feet away. If the fire was hot enough, the rocks would be nearly white by the time they were brought into the lodge.

Between the lodge and the fire was a small mound made from the earth that had been removed from the center of the lodge, where a pit had been dug, and where the rocks would be placed. On this mound lay several sacred objects belonging to both Burly and Donovan. There was a small coyote carved out of turquoise, several hawk feathers tied together with colorful thread, two small leather medicine bags that probably contained a little sage and cedar, maybe a small twist of tobacco and perhaps another small fetish. One was Burly's and the other was Donovan's; the contents personalized by the owners. Also on the mound lay a bundle of sage and cedar wrapped together, and a plait of sweet grass about a foot long, braided like a ponytail. Laying on the sweet grass was a long pipe, some sixteen inches long, belonging to Burly. The bowl was carved from a single block of red stone, taken from a sacred mine in Minnesota, the stem from a cottonwood branch, beautifully adorned with beads of various colors, though yellow predominated. And, perhaps most importantly, there lay a huge buffalo skull facing west, directly into the east-facing doorway of the sweat lodge.

As a symbol, there may be none more powerful nor meaningful to the plains people as the buffalo, though it now lives in only a couple of national parks and on a few private ranches, yet it still retains an exalted place in the cosmology and history and hearts of the people who at one time lived as nomads on the vast plains of America. The buffalo was both sacred and secular: they ate the god they revered.

Burly had a small herd of his own, about 130 animals. He raised them in honor of his ancestors, the Kiowa and Kansa. His mother is a full-blooded Kiowa, while his father had been half Kansa, the other half of mixed European stock. He'd been dead now for twelve years, having run his pickup truck off the road into a cottonwood tree on his way home after drinking in town at his favorite bar. His white half killed his Indian half, Burly always said.

His mother lived in a small trailer on the ranch, not far from his own house. She had given Burly his unusual name because at the time of his birth, she and her husband happened to be traveling in the state of Washington. She started having contractions while they were driving on an Interstate and the exit they got off was for two towns; Burly and Olalla. They weren't sure which town to go to, and Burly entered this world in the car half way between both. His surname was Smith, but he had long ago given that up, well before he started traveling the rodeo circuit.

Donovan was Kiowa and a little Apache. His mother had been a flower child in the 60's, who lived briefly in San Francisco, just long enough to develop a drug dependency that took years to shake out. Her favorite musician had been Donovan in those days, and she named her son after him and her two twin daughters Jennifer and Juniper Littlefeather after one of his songs.

Burly bent down and picked up a pitchfork lying next to the fire. One of the burning logs had fallen over, exposing a couple of red-hot rocks, and he deftly covered them back up. The task of the firekeeper was to keep the rocks covered as best as possible, until the wood was burned, and even then, to keep the rocks covered in coals.

"This should be ready in 20 minutes or so. It'll be perfect, it'll just be getting dark," he said to Donovan, who set his flute down. Donovan's stomach growled in response, he hadn't eaten since yesterday, fasting all day in preparation for this evening. "Good thing, too. I don't think my stomach wants to go much longer without something in it."

Burly laughed, "We'll soon give it smoke, steam and heat. That should quiet it!"

"Unh," was the only response that came from Donovan. Although he had participated in many sweats, they were hard on him. He just couldn't get used to the temperatures, which often reached upwards of 140 degrees, sometimes even higher. He rarely ever had to leave them, to ask to be let out of the lodge before the ceremony was over, still, the next day was often spent recuperating on a sofa in front of a television set. But he still did them, and he never turned Burly down when he needed help with a lodge. And tonight he'd be pulling stones for Burly, who was holding this lodge for his sick and dying uncle.

Burly knew it was hard on Donovan, but he didn't have anyone else to ask. There wasn't anyone that he trusted for a lodge as special as this one for his favorite uncle. Ever since he was a little kid and as far back as he could remember, his favorite had always been Uncle Remo. He usually spent his summers on Uncle Remo's small ranch outside Anadarko, Oklahoma, helping him with his farming chores, putting up hay, fixing fences, feeding cattle when it got so dry the grass wasn't worth a damn, and running after those damn hogs of his. The thought of it brought a smile to his face. Uncle Remo and his hogs. Slopping hogs, castrating hogs, separating hogs, butchering hogs, he'd done just about everything with those hogs. 'That's why I don't have any now,' he laughed to himself. And now Uncle Remo lay dying in that sterile room in Wichita. 'He'd probably get up and walk out if I could bring a hog up there,' thought Burly.

The sun and the fire were now the same: The last of the sun was just a swath of reddish orange glow on the horizon, the last of the fire a pile of glowing embers.

"It's time," said Burly. He took all his clothes off and grabbed the smudge of cedar and sage and stuck it into some coals at the edge of the fire. It ignited instantaneously. He blew the flames out and a rich aromatic smoke arose. He then took a fan of turkey feathers and blew the smoke over Donovan, now standing naked in front of him, then fanned the smoke over himself. In this way, he cleansed them of impurities, made the profane sacred. Holding the turkey fan, he grabbed a rattle he had made from a turtle shell and a small pouch of tobacco and another of cedar and sage, along with a towel and his sacred pipe, he entered the lodge from the left side. Sinking to his knees, he uttered a brief offering of a prayer in Kiowa, "Ada domgaga," 'I am one with the earth.' He crawled around the pit clockwise until he came to the other side of the entrance, where he sat down.

"Hand me the water, would ya?" he called out. Donovan swung the five-gallon plastic bucket into the doorway, water sloshing out over the sides. "Careful," said Burly, "That's less heat and steam, as if you didn't know." He said it with mirth, so Donovan was in no way offended, he knew his friend. Burly would never intentionally hurt him, or even be sarcastic for that matter, he was just ribbing him about his sensitivity to the heat. "Oh. Hey, the ladle isn't in here. It's over by my shoes, which are somewhere behind me," Burly called out again. The ladle retrieved, it was time to bring the stones in.

Donovan picked out a stone from underneath the coals with the pitchfork. He then set that down and brushed the stone with a pine bough, knocking embers and ashes from it, then carried it to the lodge. As the stone entered the lodge, Burly welcomed it, "Welcome, Grandfather. We are blessed to have you join us." He then guided it to the pit, making sure it found its way into it without mishap, using a forked antler from a deer he had killed several years ago, an antler reserved just for this one special use.

Then he sprinkled some sage and cedar on it, fragrance erupting along with sparks as the dry mixture touched the hot rocks. In all, seven stones were brought in one at a time, the rest Donovan covered back up with coals. Upon entering the lodge, Donovan said in English, "All my relations," then pulled the door blanket down, adjusting it so that no light, even from the outside fire pit, could be seen. Inside the lodge, only the faint glow from the seven stones cast a light, not enough to even outline Burly's form.

Burly began singing a song in Kiowa, and though Donovan didn't know the words, not knowing much of his native tongue, he knew that it was a song welcoming the spirits, inviting them to come join them, to spend this time with them in this ancient and sacred ceremony. Part of the song would plead with them to listen to these poor and humble humans whose hearts were open to all that the spirits might offer, or would accept if they choose not to listen, if they chose not to come. That would be all right too. As a human, there are things we do not, and can not, understand. And we sit here tonight to merely ask.

> "Dagya gehde, dagya gehade,
> Dagya inatagyi, dagya inatagyi,
> Dakinago abatea, dakinago abatea,
> Dakinago dakantahedal, dakinago dakantahedal."

While he sang, Burly shook his turtle shell rattle, keeping beat to the song he learned long ago from the medicine man who taught him about sweat lodges, who taught him about his heritage, who taught him how to be a human, a real person, in his own tongue. Of how to be a red man in a white man's world. They aren't exclusive, he was taught, they are inclusive. They had to be. His uncle is a very wise medicine man.

Burly's voice sang out into the prairie, rolling up and down the Flint Hills, it dug down into the ground and it reached up into the heavens. When Burly sang, his whole heart and his whole being sang too. And tonight, there was more urgency than normal.

Tonight he sang for two; himself and Runs With Many Horses, his uncle's real name. Tonight he wanted to make sure his voice reached all the spirits. As he sang he would take a ladle full of water and spill it over the stones, each time releasing a wave of heat and steam flung from the stones to wash over him and Donovan. To Donovan, they were blasts of endurance, and even now, at the beginning of the ceremony, he found himself hugging the ground, sacred Mother Earth, for cool comfort.

When Burly was done singing, he set his rattle down. There followed a long silence. It was the silence of asking with your heart for the spirits to come. The heart spoke much louder than the tongue, and the spirits heard that above all else.

Burly broke the silence by asking how Donovan was. "I'm all right, I'm all right," he responded. "It's not so hot yet. I can still find some cool air down here close to the earth."

"Good. Let me know if it gets too hot. This is not an endurance test. This ain't the Sun Dance," Burly said.

"I know. I will, I promise."

"Good, good."

They sat in the silence a little longer, listening to the hiss of steam on the rocks at the bottom of the stone pit. Burly spoke, "I feel the presence of a lot of spirits, many familiars, like Hawk and Coyote and Buffalo, and I think the Thunder Beings are here too. But I also sense some new ones too. I'm not sure who they are yet. Maybe they'll let us know. HOH!" he cried loudly, signaling the doorkeeper, Donovan, to open up the door flap.

The cool night air rushed in from outside, while smoke and steam billowed out. They sat for a moment, allowing the fresh air to cool them off, but not too long. Soon enough, it was time to continue.

"How's the fire look," Burly called out to Donovan as he poked around to pick out another stone. "Great. There's a lot of hot coals, the stones are staying real hot. Hey Bur," as he called his buddy, "Shouldn't the buffalo be facing the same way as the door; east?"

"Yea, but it just didn't seem right tonight. Every time I placed it that way, it didn't seem to want to stay there. It felt wrong, so I turned it in to face the lodge."

"Does that mean anything?" Donovan asked as he brought in a stone.

"I dunno. We'll see. Welcome Grandfather!"

In all, he brought in seven more stones, seven more grandfathers. Each one was individually honored by Burly. With the flap closed and the lodge secure, they were once again alone with the glowing stones, once more they were back in the womb of Mother Earth, for the sweat lodge is not only a purification and a means to ask for divine intervention in the mundane affairs of man, it is also the return of the body to the womb that gives birth to all: the warm moist womb of the Great Mother.

The second round was one of thanks, of gratitude for all that one had, whether property or person, loved one or despised one. A person opens their heart and gives thanks for their very life, for the breath the air gives them, for the food the earth gives them, thanks to the animals for their flesh, to the plants for their flesh, and to the trees for their body and bones. To the stone people for the firm place to set a foot, and to those sacrificing themselves in the heat of the fire pit, and releasing it for the two men inside this womb. Burly's voice sang with all his soul, for with all his soul he was grateful for all that he had, and in his gratitude, and in his joy, he poured ladle full after ladle full of water upon the hissing stones.

When he was done singing, it was time for Donovan to offer his prayers in silence or aloud, the choice was his. The waves of heat had sent him to the ground to hug as closely as he could cool Mother Earth. It was hard to find gratitude in his heart when he wanted so much to escape the unbelievable heat, the intense smell of cedar and sage that now nearly nauseated him, the steam burning his naked flesh, his lungs gasping to fill with air. But he did. He had plenty to be thankful for, and he listed them loudly, finishing with a resounding HOH! Burly rattled wildly and poured more water on the stones to insure the words of his friend were sent skyward, toward the spirits, so they would echo in the heavens.

Then it was Burly's turn to give thanks, his singing had been merely a prelude, a sounding to let the spirits know what was forthcoming. His list was long and it was delivered with tears from his soul. He, too, sent his words skyward with more water, while Donovan only wished his friend's thanks were complete. This sweat was one of the hottest he'd been in.

When Burly was finished, he called out for the door to be opened. He knew it was a very hot sweat, he knew that his buddy would be very uncomfortable, maybe even close to passing out. It was his job as pourer to be alert and aware about everyone's condition, and besides, they were only half way through and though it truly was not an endurance test, it would be better if Donovan was able to stay inside the entire ceremony.

With the flap open, the two men lay on their backs, letting the cool night air wash over their steaming, sweating bodies. In the distance they could hear the low growl rumble of thunder. Inside, their breathing and the hissing rocks made the only sounds. Eventually Burly sat up and offered Donovan a ladle of water to drink. The water was God-fully refreshing, and sweet tasting, too. The taste and character of water often changed in sweat lodges, it became sweeter and somehow lighter, certainly more refreshing. Burly said it was because it had become holy water. Right now, as Donovan eagerly drank it, it was indeed holy, saving his life as far as he was concerned. Burly offered him another ladle, which he poured over his head, the chill of it caused him to shiver, but he was too hot to raise chill bumps.

"You okay, Do?" Burly asked him, using the nickname he'd called him since they were boys growing up together in Oklahoma.

"Yea, I think I'll live, but damn, Bur, this is a cooker."

"There must be a reason, I'm not doing anything that doesn't feel right. The spirits are prodding me, is all. I'm just going along with 'em."

They stayed in the darkness for a while longer, before it became apparent it was time to continue on. Donovan got up wearily and went out to the fire pit. "Hey Bur," he called, "ain't a cloud in sight. I can see stars all the way around."

"Hmm," replied Burly softly, "the spirits, the spirits." He grabbed his rattle and started to sing, and sang even as Donovan brought seven more stones in to the lodge.

The stones properly greeted, and the door flap closed, the third round began. This was the round where one asked for healing, usually for another, but it was okay to ask for healing for oneself. Certainly it was proper to ask for guidance from the spirits to help keep one on their path, not to be deterred, not to veer off, and though we often do, it is because we are mere humans and need the guiding hand of the spirits to keep us from being wayward. And to open our hearts to others, to hear their heart, hear their needs, and to learn to listen to that little voice within, often it is the spirits whispering to us. This was the round where one declared the reason for their coming to, and holding, the sacred sweat ceremony. This was the round for pleading to Grandfather and Grandmother, the learned wise ones, and The Great Spirit.

When Burly had completed the songs that let the spirits know that heart-felt cries would be coming, his 'crying for healing songs', and he'd poured more water on the stones, it was Donovan's time to ask for intercession on behalf of this two-legged.

If he'd been hot in the first rounds, he was boiling now. His head swam in a whirlpool of dizziness, nausea and pain. He could hear himself speak, but it didn't seem like him, as if he stood outside of his body. The words he heard coming from his mouth were slurred and drunken. But his heart broke through and cried to the spirits, to the Great Spirit, for healing for his loved ones, and for Burly's uncle, and for himself. He cried and he choked and he gasped, but his words reached up and lifted from his heart like the flight of the hawk. His pleas finished, and him nearly spent, he let out a barely audible HOH! then collapsed to embrace the cool breasts of Mother Earth. Outside, the clear and cloudless night rumbled and clashed.

Burly knew Do was having a tough time, and only poured one ladle of water on the stones to send his missives aloft. He'd saved more for his own turn, because the main reason for this sweat was his Uncle Remo and he wanted plenty of help sending his prayers aloft.

He began by asking the spirits to look out for his mother, she needed their help sometimes when she got sad and confused, and called out for her husband, dead now for all these years. Then he asked that they look out for all the people and all the animals, and all the living things. All things need the love and guidance of the spirits. He asked for healing for Mother Earth, she suffered from the ways of the humans, they need to know, show them how to love and care for She Who Gives So Much. Awaken the human to the wisdom of the ancient's, show them again the things they have forgotten, the proper way to love and honor her. Bring them forth so we two-leggeds can walk a good path into the future, one of understanding and tolerance. Then he asked and pleaded through tears for the healing of beloved Uncle Remo. He listed all the good things of Runs With Many Horses, his always helping his own people, the Kiowas, that he would help anyone who asked for and needed it. He would give it if he could. He was never known to have turned anyone down who needed help. This is a good man, please keep him here on this plane longer, so that his goodness touches more in need. Or if you are to take him to be with you and his relatives, then take him soon, relieve him of this great pain that tears apart his chest. Let him die then in peace. Lastly, with a sad and heavy voice, he asked they keep him, Burly, on his rightful path, and that Grandfather and Great Spirit hear his prayers. He ended with a great splash of water upon the stones, sending yet another blast that sent poor Donovan closer to the earth. If he could dig in, he would have, save he lacked the energy, he could get no flatter. Burly cried out "HOH!" and flung the door flap open himself.

The stars danced in to the lodge. Little tiny white lights floated and spun and whirled around, some zipping over to the far side of the lodge, some circling the stones in the center, some floated over and drifted above Donovan's head. And some drifted over to Burly and hovered at eye level, as if they looked into his head and heart. Burly looked back with love and awe, this wasn't the first time they had blessed him, but that was at a different ceremony, never had he seen them with the door open at a lodge. He thought he'd seen them before in sweat lodges, but he couldn't be sure. This was a gift from the spirits, a blessing and a gift from the Creator. Donovan hadn't seen them yet because he lay on his belly with his head buried in the crook of his arm. Some primal instinct or sixth sense caused him to roll over, and as he did, he looked right into the many lights that hovered above his head. He didn't say anything, nor did he gasp. He just smiled stoned.

The two men were enraptured for an hour, it seemed to them, children of the universe enthralled in the moment of miracle. In truth, the lights were there only a few minutes. Such is time when spent with spirits and wonders. In unison, like a flock of birds, the little spirit lights darted out of the lodge, leaving Burly and Donovan shaking in gratitude, overcome with feelings of love.

"Aye," cried Burly, sobbing, deep breaths racking his frame. "Ayyyyeeee," was all he could say. Donovan sat up, rubbing his face with his towel, clearing the sweat and grime from it. He said nothing, just crawled out of the lodge to get more stones.

Weary, exhausted and spent, he crawled on all fours to the fire pit, using the pitchfork to help him stand. He managed to get a stone on it, then nearly stumbled as he brought it to the lodge. Burly was still overcome by the appearance of the spirit lights, so Do had to say "All my relations" to get his attention. The task of performing ritual brought Burly back in to focus. He greeted the stone and guided it onto the mound of hot rocks. When all of the stones, seven more, had been placed on the mound, instead of closing the door flap, Burly said, "It is time to smoke the pipe, in thanks and in gratitude. The spirits have heard us, but this is the way it should be, to send our prayers to the sky with the smoke, that they should rise like this sacred tobacco smoke."

Before he lit it, he sang and rattled a song of thanks, the first song his uncle had taught him so many years ago. The words were of thanks to the spirits for listening to them, should they have, and thanks if they didn't. It did not, and does not, matter. It is one and the same, the choice is always theirs, and he and Donovan as humans could not begin to fathom the mysteries and reasons that guide the Creator and the spirits to do things the way they are done. Tonight they had been blessed with the spirit's presence, that was enough. That is always enough. Hopefully though, they had heard their prayers asking for healing.

He lit the pipe and offered it to the four directions and to the earth and sky, then took four deep pulls, then offered it again to the four directions and the earth and the sky as he let the smoke escape from his lungs and mouth. Then he passed it to Donovan, who repeated the rite.

In this, the fourth and final round, the last of the water is poured on the stones, the last of the heat from the fire is released into the lodge so that those inside would suffer mightily at the end of the ceremony to show their sincerity, to show they are committed to this healing. For the love of others they suffer this little death, this is their sacrifice. And they also honor the water and stones and wood that had offered to sacrifice to help make this ancient ritual possible. It was always the hardest round. As he sang and sang and rattled, and poured ladle after ladle of water, and threw sage and tobacco and cedar onto the stones, Burly rocked back and forth while Donovan clung to the earth. Burly sang songs that not only thanked the spirits but also let them know the ceremony was over. They could leave now, they could return to wherever they dwelled. He thanked them all, those that he knew by name: the Creator, Grandmother and Grandfather, Hawk, Eagle, Buffalo and Coyote, relatives who came, the ancient ones, the Thunder Beings, the dancing spirit lights. And those he did not know the names of, those who watched quietly and participated but who he did not know. He thanked them all. Then he collapsed on to the ground, his face kissing Mother Earth.

They lay a long time in the suffocating smoke and the burning steam, in the stultifying paralyzing heat, too exhausted to move, even to open the door. Donovan had nearly passed out, perhaps he had, the distinction was hard to make. Burly was trying to gather himself so that he could open the door and let the cool night air in. The ceremony was over, he just needed to open the door flap, but merely getting up on his hands and knees was difficult. As he struggled, he heard an unrecognizable cough. It was too high pitched for Donovan, or at least it seemed to be. He lay still for a moment. Nothing. Perhaps it was a hallucination, perhaps he hadn't heard anything, senses are certainly put to the test in a sweat lodge and sometimes it is a fine line between spirit and illusion. When he tried to raise himself again, a very peculiar and slightly shrill voice called out, "Hit monstus hot n' er."

chapter seven

"Zach. Zachary! ZACH! Wake up! Come on, it's time to wake up." Emma was shaking him, trying to rouse him. He could hear her but she was far away, her voice tumbling down a long tunnel. "Hey, come on you!" She shook him some more. Gradually, he became aware of her, began to feel her. He realized that his head was nestled in her lap, he could smell the familiarity of her, of Emma-ness. "Mmmm," he murmured as he buried his head deeper in her lap. He was still far away, but her fragrance and body odors and her touch and voice were bringing him back, like a siren calling to a lost sailor. His mind was swimming in images and thoughts and emotions. One big soup, a seething stew of color, noise and smells. A stew of . . . what was that? A stew of potatoes, carrots and greens in a big black pot. "Ooohh," he groaned. "Emma, Emma," he groggily repeated. He rolled over and opened his eyes to look up in to her face, her beautiful face, framed by her dark hair like a halo. "Ah, my guardian angel."

She laughed lightly, "That's very sweet. Ah'm glad to see you decided to come back. Ah was beginnin' t' wonder 'bout yew."

He raised his head slowly, gingerly, as if it ached, just to get his bearings, to see where he was. The room was familiar: The church, the people now standing or sitting, some lying down. He remembered being dizzy and needing to lay down. "Must'a konked out, how long was I out?" he asked.

"Not too long, maybe fifteen, twenty minutes tops. Ah kinda lost track muhself."

"Did you pass out?"

"Not really, just got a little disoriented for a spell."

"God, did I have a time, I can't begin to tell you. I was lost and I couldn't find you. Man, that was something, you wouldn't believe it. So real . . ." his voice trailed off.

She squeezed him, pulling him closer to her, cradling him in her arms like a baby. He reached his hand up and stroked her face softly, lovingly. They held each other's gaze, exchanging silent love letters that had gone unsent and unopened verbally, things they hadn't said to each other were transmitted through their eyes, brought forth from the fear of separation. He could see that his feelings for her were mutual, just unsaid. In this moment of tired dreaminess, on this noisy night of sweat and song and dance, their hearts were speaking. Words, his stumbling words, weren't getting in the way. They were alone in a roomful of people, two lovers clutching each other, a veil of woven breath, emotions, love, lips, eyes, aromas, hormones and hearts surrounding them, cloaking them. Suddenly, a large dark shadow loomed over, blocking the light and breaking the moment, but not their bond there on the church house floor. It took him a moment to realize it was Big Mama. "What did you see? Did you meet Spirit, Mr. Peterson?" she asked him. Her voice was flat, dissonant and nearly disinterested. Part of this woman was removed from life, he thought, though the larger part was still here.

"I guess," he said softly, embarrassed to speak too loudly. "If you count Brer Rabbit and Brer Fox as Spirit."

Her eyes widened and a big smile blossomed across her round fleshy face. She let out a deep laugh that erupted out of her belly like some dark creature let loose from primeval bonds in a volcanic explosion, her fat quaking in seismic rhythm. "The white boy done met Mr. Brer Rabbit," she said aloud, laughing deeply. A few nervous little laughs broke out and scattered across the room. No one seemed to think it as funny as Big Mama. "That's all right, honey," she said to him. "I'm not laughing at you. It just seems funny is all." She reached down and patted him like a child, "You all right? You did good, you did good." Clucking to herself, she walked away to look after other people, some were still out.

Emma pursed her lips and spoke to him like one would to an infant, "Did the little white boy really meet Brer Rabbit?" For added effect she rocked his head, still cradled in her arms and lap. "And what did ole Brer Rabbit say to the little boy?"

"Eat mo' possum," he replied, grabbing her below the ribs. She squeaked and slapped him playfully on the head. "You're a bad little boy," she smirked.

People were now beginning to get up and walk about, the hum of conversation grew louder, the energy livening up. The lights were brought up full and the brightness forced Zach to sit up to keep it out of his eyes. Before they stood, he said to Emma, "Em, the bizarre truth of it is that I did meet Brer Rabbit and Brer Fox, and it was as real as you and I sitting here. I'll tell you the whole story on our way home. I was out only fifteen minutes or so? It seemed like a long day to me where I was. Or wasn't, I guess." She didn't say anything, just looked at him with eyes full of love and trust, a visage he'd never seen before, at least not directed at him. Holding hands, they helped each other stand. Something had shifted; Zach felt a palpable change in 'them'. They'd crossed over some barrier, some Rubicon of experience that bound them together all the more, like the first time they made love, but deeper. More personal? he wondered. 'I don't know, making love is pretty personal.'

Diggy walked up to them and squeezed Emma's hand, smiling at both. "Hey," she said softly, less militarily, he thought. "What do you think of our little church shout, Zachary?"

"Well, I can't see it at St. Peter's basilica with the pope as head honcho screaming in people's faces, but a good dose of it might raise Sunday attendance. Could be a hard sell in the suburbs though."

She gave him another of her appraising type looks, with a smile, of course, and turned to Emma, "How'd it go, Em?"

"Wonderful, Ah'm so glad you called us Diggy."

"I'm so glad you came." They gave each other warm hugs but Big Mama intervened, asking people to get in a circle and hold hands to praise the Lord and to sing to end the evening. Everyone joined together and after praising Jesus for all and everything, she led them in a beautiful rendition of Amazing Grace. Somehow the song got under Zach's skin and rattled him, bringing tears to his eyes. Holding his hand, Emma could feel the convulsions in his body as he fought back the emotions. She smiled with a great deal of satisfaction.

Outside it was dark and cool. With no town lights for miles, the stars shone brightly, crackling and winking with not a cloud in sight. Somewhere in the distance Zach could hear what he thought was thunder. "Heat lightning," Emma offered. It seemed to be moving away and to the west.

They rode in the car with the windows down, the insects and tree frogs and all manner of other night creatures loudly proclaiming their lives and whereabouts, creating a din that one almost needs to shout above in order to converse. Zach drove slowly so that they could talk without having to fight the wind noise and the critters of the night at the same time. Emma said she hadn't really experienced anything that evening, so she listened quietly to his story. When he finished, she asked him where he thought Brer Rabbit had gone. He replied, "Does it matter? It wasn't real." She said she wasn't so sure about the things that happened in a shout, she'd heard some pretty amazing stories. It may sound silly, she said, with Brer Rabbit and all, but there was likely some meaning in it.

Driving slowly it took them twice the time to get back to Trieste, but they didn't care, it was a beautiful evening. They decided to go down to the river, the Ochlockonee, that flowed through the plantation east of the great house. They went to an isolated spot, Emma's favorite, a clearing on the river north of the house and around a bend, hidden from view.

"Who'd you bring here?" he teased as they parked.

"Lots of boys, and got lots of kisses." she laughed.

"Is that all? Just kisses?"

"Not even that, really, Ah only spent summers here, silly. Ah didn't get much of a chance t' meet the town hunks."

They walked down to the river. Zach was tremendously impressed by the night sounds. They were awesome, almost eerie in the volume, like some old black and white jungle movie sound track gone wild. Huge live oaks hung their limbs far out over the river's edge, Spanish moss brushing the surface. Out over the black ribbon of water, unseen splashes goaded imaginations, begging to be known to avoid possibilities. "There's gators out here, aren't there?" he asked.

"Yes, but they don't get very big. They won't bothuh us," she assured him. They sat down on a fallen log at the edge and listened to all the sounds.

"It's like some kind of symphony I can't understand," he said. "There's a definite rhythm to the noise, I can hear a pulse, an ebb and flow, but I don't know the language. Insects and frogs over here calling to those over there, across the river, and they answer back."

"It's the same in the swamp, the Okefenokee ovuh near Waycross. Lots of times driving here, or going back to Savannah, Ah'd stop in theyuh just t' listen t' the night. It's so beautiful, so ancient and prehistoric." Emma spoke quietly, almost secretively. "It always takes mah troubles from me, grabs 'em and takes 'em down into the black water, under the lily pads and down into the murk and alligator dens. I don't know," she continued wistfully, "this place and the swamp, they make the world bigger, they make the world not all known and discovered, prodded and poked and photographed. These places make me think that some things might still be unknown and wild. Especially at night. That's the best tahme t' feel it."

"Yea, it's kind of spooky too," he said. "Fertile ground to get your imagination rolling. Reminds me of earlier tonight, you know, setting atmosphere, getting things right so that you're suggestive. That shout, it's like participating in some old ritual. I couldn't help but think of us as Africans dancing round a fire and all that, or Indians. You know, shouting and whooping and all. The only thing missing was drums. And Big Mama, man, she was something."

"Big Mama. You ahre so bad, Zachree. Her name is Esther Rollins," Emma rebuked him. "She's a wonduhful person, Ah've known her for years. She's good friends with Diggy, too. She's a sweetheart."

A large splash on the far bank startled them, causing them to jump. "Jeez, that had to be something really big," he said, "You sure these gators are small?"

"I hope so," she said with a trace of concern.

They stopped talking for a moment, straining to see out over the water into the darkness. They couldn't make anything out, just bats flying in close then veering off in their disjointed and erratic flight, skimming the water for insects.

"So you think the shout is set up to make people suggestible?" Emma asked.

"Well, yea. There's all that praising to Jesus and singing and all that. I think it sets people up to see or meet or feel Jesus or spirit, whatever they're calling it. That's okay, don't get me wrong. I just think they get what they're looking for."

"And were you looking for Brer Rabbit?"

"I don't have any idea how that happened. I mean, I wasn't even a special fan of Brer Rabbit and all those stories growing up. I couldn't read it, I couldn't understand what they were talking about."

"You mean the language? You had trouble understanding the language?" she inquired.

"Yea, it was too differmint."

"I know who that is, that's Albert Alligator, from Pogo! That is differmint! Did you like Pogo too? God, Ah just loved him, he was my favorite."

"Yea, me too. I was a little young, and when I got old enough to understand Walt Kelly, I began to really appreciate his genius. His political satire was brilliant. But that was at the end of the strip, as soon as I was old enough to understand him, he died."

"They should teach him in school, if they don't already," she declared.

"Yea," he agreed, "But back to this Brer Rabbit stuff, I don't know where that came from, but it was so real, I thought someone was fooling me. I thought it was a trick, and I even wondered if you were involved, it was so good."

"Me? You thought Ah might be pullin' a trick on you? Zach!"

"Emma, it was so real I can still taste the stew that Brer Fox cooked!"

"You just said it wasn't real."

"I know, but it lingers like an intense dream."

Another large splash not a dozen yards from them, and on the same side of the river, brought them to their feet. "Maybe we oughta sit in the car," he suggested, not even pretending to hide his nervousness.

"Yea, it sounds like a feeding frenzy out there," she agreed.

In the security of the car she asked him if he had felt any fear while on his little venture, his little dream.

"Not fear, I wouldn't say that. But I did feel anxiety and frustration not being able to get back to you and back to what I know as normal. It was like one of those dreams where, say, you're being chased, and you can't open a simple door, or you're in quicksand and you just can't grab anything solid, only in this case I couldn't find a road or a phone. And simply put, I missed you. There was this small, but growing, fear that I might not see you again." He squeezed her hand when he finished speaking.

She smiled sweetly, and he prepared for a kiss, but instead, she spoke, "Ah was feeling a little anxiety too, while you were out. It looked like you were sleepin', just lahk ever'body else that was on the floor. And it seemed to go on a long time, but Ah knew you'd be all raght. Ah've nevuh seen anyone who wasn't.

You know, it doesn't sound at all like it is giving people what they're looking for, it didn't work that way for you. Something entirely different happened to you, something you didn't expect at all."

"But I had no expectations. I didn't know what I was getting into."

"Well, maybe those people who've been goin' to that church for years, and shouts for just as long, don't have any expectations. Maybe they just go and let whatevuh happen, happen. Maybe that's why they keep going to it, keep coming back. Maybe that's why they still do 'em. What good would it be if you knew what was going to happen? Why do it?"

"I know what's gonna happen when I drink a bottle of wine! That's why I keep going back to it!" he reasoned.

"These folks ain't gittin' high. It's different."

"I don't know, maybe not, but there sure are some similarities."

"Well, you're right in that they are doing something to get out of the ordinary, to escape. But they do it to connect with God, with Spirit."

"Where you going with this, Emma? What are you trying to say?"

"I dunno . . ." she sighed and looked out over the river.

"Why do you go to them, the shouts? It didn't seem like anything happened to you, least not tonight," he asked.

"It's always different, tonight nothin' really did happen. Maybe I was thinking of you too much. But Ah go cause it's different. Like you said, it feels ancient and primitive. It ain't somethin' you think about, it's somethin' you do. It ain't some priest standin' in front of his flock going through tahred ole rituals. And it ain't some damn intellectual exercise talking about God in the subconscious, or some stupid philosophical discussion about God and existence. Yuk!"

"Yea, boring stuff there."

"Ah nevuh had anything really weird or unusual happen at a shout. Ah never saw spirits or speak in tongues, nothin' lahk that. Ah just get good feelin's goin' theyuh. When Ah get tahred or dizzy, or hwhatevuh, and lay down, Ah get ovuhcome with love sometahmes, very intense feelin's of being loved by something or someone. And it feels very close. That's why Ah go, to get those feelin's. It ain't something Ah've felt anywhere else but doin' those shouts with Diggy and Esther."

"I'd say that's worth the price of admission."

"Yes, it is worth the price of admission," echoing his comment. With a beguiling smile, she grabbed his hand and said, "Ah'm so happy you wanted to come, Zach. It means a lot to me, Ah've never had anyone want to come to a shout, they've never shown an interest. They'll all make excuses, good ones, too, but in the end, Ah think they're afraid. It might have to do with goin' to a black church, Ah don't know. That's one of the things Ah like about you Zach, you're not afraid t' try new things."

He thought of some wise cracks, but checked them. She was getting to know him too well, and would know that for a defensive gesture or as an inability to receive a compliment. "I do have my fear thresholds," he finally said.

"And what would those be?"

"Crossing your mother would be one. Crossing Big Mama would be another."

They shared a laugh with Emma protesting the appellation 'Big Mama', though she did not argue the point about crossing either one. Their laughter soon gave way to long and passionate kisses. He slid over and sat in the passenger seat, with the back all the way down, the side door open for room, and the moon smiling down at them through the open roof. They took their clothes off, then she got on top of him, straddling him, her head framed in the glow of the moon and the twinkling stars. The sounds of the night were their music, from the wild spooky splashes in the river, the humming of the insects and the croaking frogs, to the lonesome call of the owls in the distance.

In the sweaty laboring spent moments after lovemaking, Emma lying curled on him, her knees pressed into his ribs, he ran his fingers through her matted wet hair. "We went somewhere tonight, didn't we?" he whispered in her ear. Without opening her eyes, she nodded, and held him closer.

The next morning, sitting at the breakfast table within her suite of rooms, Emma's mother asked Zach how he liked "that old fashioned church." He didn't know how much she knew about what went on there, and he sure wasn't going to talk about Brer Rabbit and what had happened to him. Instead, he said it reminded him of what he thought a Baptist gospel revival would be like, with singing and clapping and dancing and what not. She said she knew all about shouts, she'd gone there a long time ago with Diggy. She had thought it amusing to see the Negroes practicing their Christian faith in such a unique and different manner. Being Methodist, it was quite a shock, but she had reminded herself that these people needed an outlet to let loose their frustrations of being second-class citizens. He thought her ideas pretty enlightened for a woman of her generation, but that is where her thinking stopped, that it was just a way to shake off frustrations through energetic worship. She didn't think of it as a way of actually connecting with and feeling God. "Emmy's been goin' theyuh fo' so long Ah'm surprahsed she hasn't braided her haiyuh in dreadedlocks, or hwhatevuh it is they waiyuh these days," she said.

Emma looked at her with the frustrated look that only a daughter can give a mother. "Those people are conservative, not unlahk yourself, mama. They'd just as soon waiyuh dreadlocks as you would. Even the younguh ones."

"Now Emma, de-uh," Virginia replied, "Ah am not critisizin' them, Ah am only illustratin' the fact that you have spent many a night over theyuh. Ah am not in-sin-u-a-tin' eh-ni-thin'." She rose to grab some butter out of the refrigerator.

Zach leaned over and whispered to Emma, "Mighty quaint customs those Negroes have." She smirked and shook her head. "Sometimes Ah wonder if she's learned anything all these years," she whispered back.

"He-uh we ah," Virginia said, setting the butter down on the table. "Darlin', you know Ah am not prejudicial in any way, and Ah won't stand t' hear anythin' of the sort. Why, Ah consider Diggy a very good friend, Ah helped secure her post here at Trieste."

"Mama, Diggy got the job here because she was more qualified than anyone else. She got the job on her own merit."

"Whatever, Ah'll not quibble with you. Zachary, Ah just want you to know that my daughtuh's opinion to the contrary, Ah hold no biases in these old southe'n bones. Black people have earned the raght to be equal under the law. They've made great strides, just look at all those wealthy sports stars."

"Yea, we pay our gladiators handsomely these days," he said. "Times do change."

"They most certainly do," she said idly as she fixed her attention on her breakfast of fruit and English muffins with jam.

Conversation had by now ebbed, drained by subject matter and crowded out by breakfast. After they had finished, Virginia announced that as soon they had attended to their morning needs, they were to take the key she had and clean out the shed discussed yesterday, but not to throw anything out unless she had seen it. "That shed has not been opened in so many years there's no tellin' what yaw'll find."

Emma followed Zach to his room, where he was going to change into clothes more suitable for the work they were about to do. It was the first time of the morning they'd been alone together, and they quickly embraced. "Hey," he said softly, leaning back a little to look her in the eyes. "Mmmm," was all she would say as she buried her head in his chest. "You okay?" he asked.

"Oh, mama can be so obtuse sometimes. It just frustrates me a little. Ah gave up long ago tryin' to change her. It was the old story of the child trying to change the parent, trying to mold the parent in the child's image. Sometimes Ah slip back into those teenage years, though Ah don't want to. It's a waste of time and energy, Ah should just enjoy her as she is."

"Yea," he said, "I think I tried to change my dad once, but being the lawyer that he is, I didn't get very far. I quit arguing with him at a very tender young age. Let snipping dogs lie, became my motto."

She chuckled, and it made him feel good that he had lightened her darkening mood, the latter to be avoided at all costs, in his mind. "Now, let's go rummage round in the past, shall we?" he said.

She looked up at him and smiled warmly and lovingly. "You like to make me feel good whenevuh Ah start getting sad. Ah love that about you, but there are tahmes when Ah need to stay in the moment, stay mired in whatevuh Ah'm feeling blue about. It's the only way to get to some understandin' on things sometimes. Ah'm not sayin' this is one of those tahmes, Ah'm actually happy you made me smile."

"Anytime you want to feel bad, let me know. I'll help. Really! I'm good at making people feel bad," he said in as much earnestness as he could muster.

"I'm not so sure about that," she said. "Ah think yaw more naturally inclined to want people to feel happy."

"We is met the enemy, and they is us!" he exclaimed.

"More Pogo! Theyuh you go again, tryin' t' make me feel good!"

"Incorrigible, aren't I?"

"Yes, you ahre," she said, smiling flirtatiously. She kissed him tenderly, the taste of sweet butter still lingering on her lips. Pulling away, she asked him how he'd slept last night, if he had any dreams. He hadn't. Last night's sleep was a black hole, he couldn't remember anything, he'd fallen right off to sleep. "A pity too," he said, "I was hoping to hear some of your relatives rattling around the halls and haunting the place. Not even a creaking door, I'm afraid." He pulled her back close to him, "Yesterday was one of the best days in my life, last night by the river, with the stars and the moon, our lovemaking . . . was . . . was . . . magical."

She didn't say anything, she didn't have to. Her eyes and her lips told him everything he wanted to know.

"Hand me that can again, I think it needs another squirt. It still won't move, the lock's still jammed."

Emma handed him the can of WD-40 and he gave the rusted old lock another spray of oil. "These tumblers are pretty well stuck. How old do you think this lock is? When we get it off, assuming we get it off, your mother should donate it to the museum. There, that got in there, that should do it. Let's give it a minute to work."

They were attempting to open the lock on the old shed Emma's mother wanted them to clean out. It hadn't been opened since God knows when and Virginia wanted it open as part of the tour. The shed, not much bigger than a large chicken coop, which is what it may have been at one time, was situated at the back of the barn out of sight of the house and like the barn, was constructed of bricks, which is likely why it was still standing; many of the other original structures had been made of wood and had long ago rotted or had otherwise been torn down. As they waited for the oil to work on the rusted lock, Zach tried to peer into an old window that was next to the door, but something was blocking his view. The unbroken windowpane was old; the glass had begun to sag, as if it were melting. "You ever been in here?" he asked Emma.

"No, its been this way as long as I can remember. It was just forgot about, Ah guess."

"Surprising, it seems to be a solid building."

"Well, momma and them didn't need it, what with the big barn."

"Hmmm. Let's give it another try." He put the key in the lock and worked it around. Eventually he could feel the tumblers give a little, but they still held firm until he torqued on the key as hard as he dared without breaking the darn thing. Finally, after a lot of work, the rusty old lock relented and quit the job it had been holding for umpteen years. But the door was not about to open so easily either. Zach could see that paint had been sloshed right over the crack between door and doorway, so he used a knife to clear the paint away and free the door. "All right!" he exclaimed. "After you, madam," motioning for Emma to enter first.

"Yuk! Look at all these cobwebs," she said after taking one step inside.

"Here, let's swing the door wide open for more light, this place certainly hasn't been wired for electricity," he said while nudging her in a little more.

"Hey, don't push, they's no room in here."

She was certainly right about that, he realized. There was junk everywhere, all manners of crates and boxes and barrels. All kinds of riding equipment and horse halters and work yokes hung on the walls. Covering the front window was an old wooden cabinet. The two large doors comprising the upper half were wide open, revealing more riding equipment like bridles and horse shoes as well as some old hammers and pliers and other assorted tools. A box of old-fashioned nails sat rusting and fusing together in a small wooden pail.

"Jeez, it's like some old hardware store in here. Look at this stuff! I can't believe no one's been in here," he said.

"You'd think granddaddy or my uncles would have used this stuff."

"They might have, look at this." He picked up an old tin that had a date of 1932 on it. It was a tobacco tin and he could read some of the lettering that hadn't yet flaked off: 'Chieftain Tobacco-The Redman's Pride'. "Indians revenge is more like it," he said, "We take their land and they give us tobacco, which in turn gives us cancer and kills us."

"Look at this," she said excitedly, "It's an old saddle, a woman's side-saddle!" The leather was green from mold, but the mold had died, or at least had stopped growing before totally devouring the leather. Silver metal still lined the horn and edges of the saddle, and some filigree of copper or bronze, burnished green, was emblazoned in it. "Look, there's some initials on it, can you see 'em? They're my grandma's, Ah bet this is mah grandmama's old saddle!"

"Cool. Hey, look it this. This is an old beaut." Zach held up an oil lamp of elaborately formed glass, the lower part of which had a pastoral scene hand painted on it. "This must be worth something." Looking about the room he said, "This must have been a tack house, or whatever they would have called it, where they kept all the things for the horses."

"Ah s'pose, but they's a room in the barn that we've always called the tack room. Ah think stuff just got thrown in here, and most of it just happens t' be related to horses and oxen, if Ah'm raght about that yoke hangin' ovuh theyuh." She pointed to a large wooden yoke hanging by one end in a corner.

"I suppose we ought to make piles, one for stuff that your mother would clearly want, like this oil lamp, and what . . . there must be half a dozen other lamps. And the saddle and stuff. Then there's this stuff," he said, kicking a pile of what may have been rags, or old burlap sacks, "This stuff would clearly get thrown out. But I don't know about some of these old wooden chairs, they don't look like anything special to me, but you never know."

"We're probably gonna have more things mama'll want to look through than not, so let's start by makin' some room in here. Chairs and some of the larger crates we can set outside for now, that'll give us more room. Where'd Ah put those plastic garbage bags? We can throw these old sacks in 'em."

They went about the work of sorting through the junken treasure of the past. They found all kinds of interesting items; from a pail of antique marbles made of glass and clay to a box of buttons and even an old clay pipe which could be quite ancient, and many an old tool-some whose task was long forgotten, other's raison d'être folded into the slurried path of progress. Everything was covered with a coat of dust that protested the violation of its dormancy by roiling up and clogging the atmosphere in the old shed, and the lack of a cross breeze made it difficult to breathe. Given the humid climate of the deep south, most things were in pretty good condition, owing in part to the concrete floor. That had helped keep the room fairly protected from the elements, that and the dozens of coats of paint sealing any crack or crevice. Though the little building had been shut for years, that hadn't stopped it from getting a fresh coat of paint every other year or so. At some time or another, the brick had been painted, too, so everything was sealed inside, like a mausoleum.

On toward lunch time, Emma's mother paid them a visit. She hadn't come to work, just to call them to lunch. Poking her head through the doorway, she exclaimed, "Mah goodness, look at all this dust. How can y'all breathe? Oh, look! Mama's saddle from when she was a young lady! Ah wondered what come of it."

"So it was grandmama's! When did she get it?" Emma asked.

"Daddy gave it to her for her 24th birthday. They were already married, yaw Uncle Travis must have been nearly five years old by then. Ah wasn't bo'n yet, and Lewis was nearly one, Ah guess. She was always proud of that saddle, rode on it even when Ah was a teenaguh."

"Didn't you have cars then? I mean, it wasn't that long ago," Zach inquired.

"Oh yes, we had cah's, and mechanical tractors too. But the roads were sand or crushed shells, if they weren't dirt. Roads weren't paved until the 1940's in most of the county, and when it rained, you had to get around on horses, the roads were impossible to drive on. Besahdes, mama always lahked her horses, she always had some through thick en thin. That was one thing daddy lahked t' spoil her with, beautiful horses."

"Do you think it'll clean up?" Emma wondered.

"Lord knows, darlin', but you can try if you want to. You can have it if you lahk. All this other stuff Ah'll go through once y'all get everythin' out t' where Ah can see it. Now, Ah came down he-uh t' get you two fo' lunch, but y'all er too filthy t' come in the house. hWhy don't Ah bring down some sandwiches. Would that be all raght? T' eat down he-uh? Ah'll make a nice picnic basket for you."

"That'd be fine with me," Zach said. Emma agreed that it would probably be better that way, as dirty as they had gotten.

Virginia gave the cabinet a long hard look before she turned to leave. "Ah believe Ah can recall seeing that in the kitchen in the house that Diggy now occupies, the old ovuhseer's house. Or at least one that looked just lahke it."

"It's full of horse shoes, nails and tools. Stuff like that," Emma told her.

"Wayull, it looks like it's an old kitchen cabinet. Daddy must have hauled it down he-uh t' store things in. Can you two move it so we can try and get that window open, it's dreadfully dusty in he-uh."

Zach told her that since they'd cleared some things out and had room to shuffle it around, it shouldn't be a problem, they'd move it before she came back with lunch.

After she left they took everything out of the cabinet; boxes of nails, horse shoes, old pliers, a couple of hammers and tins filled with screws and other odds and ends. There were two drawers on the bottom that they took out, too. They were filled with just about everything one could imagine from an old workshop, from old rusty screwdrivers, and tins of nuts and bolts, to carpenter tools like angles and wood chisels and planes and what not. Totally empty, it was light enough for the two of them to move. With Emma on one side, and Zach on the other, they half-carried and half-dragged it out from in front of the window. As it was moved, something inside of it rattled, which puzzled them because they thought they had cleared everything out-the drawers weren't even in it anymore. Setting it down, Zach bent over and looked into the empty spaces where the drawers had been. He couldn't see anything. They picked it up again yet the rattle was still there, something heavy and metallic was moving inside, some where. They looked in the empty cupboard but nothing was there. Emma wondered if there might not be some hidden drawer somewhere. She bent down and grabbed at the fascia board that ran parallel to the floor at the bottom of the cabinet. Grudgingly it opened up, with much squeaking and groaning, to reveal a shallow hidden drawer. She slid it out, and there sitting on top of some old papers was a pile of chains.

"What the hell is that?" he asked.

Emma picked them up carefully and said, "They're chains."

"I can see that," he remarked.

"Chains to hold humans, Zach. Slave chains."

"Christ!" he said in disgust.

She held them out, showing them, pointing out this part probably went around the wrist, that part around the ankle, and this could be connected to both ends, so the slave couldn't stand up straight. She spoke perfunctorily, flatly. She laid them down gently, then spoke, "Ah guess they was put in theyuh long ago en just forgot about."

They were both silent, shocked at having discovered things grisly and disgusting, the evil of it rolling down through the years to defile the present. The present, so far removed from something so vile, yet now arrested in the rank mist of a past. The past was present.

Wanting to shift the mood, Zach wondered aloud what the papers were and reached into the little drawer and gathered them up. They were lists, lists of names like Billy and Sally and Old John and Little Tom and Hannah. Slave names, and next to them were numbers, the prices paid for them bought and sold along with the date of purchase and date of sale from and to who and where. The bill of goods for a plantation.

He handed them to Emma without saying a word. She quietly thanked him and said, "Ah'll give these to Diggy, they'll be of interest to the museum. Ah can't imagine mama wantin' 'em."

He looked around in the drawer before closing it and noticed something tucked back in the corner that for all the world looked like a small cigar. He picked it up and held it out between them. "What the hell, a rabbits foot!" It was remarkably preserved-though dried and shrunken-it showed no signs of rot. The end of it, where it had been separated from the unfortunate rabbit, was wrapped tightly in cloth, still colorful after who knew how many years.

"I don't know who this belonged to, but I'd venture to say it wasn't any one of them," he said, nodding to the list of names. "Few probably had any luck."

chapter eight

"Do!" Burly hissed, "Was that you?"

A very alert Donovan quickly and sharply replied, "No! Was it you?"

"No! It wasn't me, man," Burly answered. As controlled and as evenly as he could, Burly called out, "Who is with us? Are you spirit?"

The voice spoke again, "Dat w'ut I bleedzed t' no. Iz you h'ants? Ef you iz, I mos' sholy lak t' git gone, az I mo's perlite en leaf yo to do yo h'ant bizniz. I got nuttin 'gin h'ants, daze some un de frenliest folks I node, yasser. Ef you ud des sho me de do, mo speshually hit monstus hot n'er, I mos' 'blige. Des sho me de do."

There followed a long spell of silence. Burly didn't know who or what was in the lodge. It didn't sound like any spirit he'd had in a sweat before. Come to think about, he hadn't ever heard of any spirit that sounded like this, that talked in such an odd way. He could hear two breaths being drawn other than his. One he knew to be Donovan's, who was drawing air fast and furious. The other was even quicker, though shallower. He'd felt the breath of spirits before, but he'd never heard them talk, at least not so clearly.

The strange, high pitched voice spoke again, "Heyo, h'ants, iz yo der? I 'clare I 'bout ready fo de graveya'd ef hit ain't gwine cool off nun n'er."

Burly realized he had to open up the door at the risk of the spirit leaving. He had to think of Donovan, too, who was surely suffering, and the spirit was going to leave whether the door was open or not, such is the whim of spirits. He cried out HOH!

and Donovan quickly flipped the door open. There was a scream, "Aaaaiiieee!!!" and the spirit tore past him and crashed through the flap as the first light of the dying coals appeared outside. "Yow!" Burly hollered as whatever ran past him dug something sharp into his thigh in its mad plunge to get out. Donovan yelled too, the thing hit his arm while he pulled away from the door, but his was the cry of surprise, not injury.

Brer Rabbit leapt over the bed of coals, clearing a dozen feet with his jump. He kept on running down the small rise and launched over the creek, landing halfway up the next hill. Gaining the top of that he kept on running pell-mell down the other side of it, not sure where he was going, too scared to stop and get his bearings. Those ghosts weren't going to use any of his body parts for no conjurin'! There he was, fast asleep, lying next to that nice fellow Mister Zachary (though he did begrudge him for tying him to the bedpost, and for not trusting him, though that didn't bother him too much, since no one really trusted him anyway) and the next thing you know 'he uz lyin' some'rs redik'lus hot wid two h'ants conjurin' som'n up wid 'im. W'at I do 'serve dis?' he wondered.

He ran steadily for three hundred yards before he dared look back, afraid he'd see those two ghosts flying after him. No sooner had he turned around than he ran right smack into something big and furry. "EEEE!" he screamed. The huge thing gave out a tremendous bellow and jumped three feet to its side. Brer Rabbit was knocked flat on his back. Too scared to be dazed, he got up quickly and ran off in another direction, pleading for the h'ants to leave him alone.

He ran another three hundred yards up and down hills, as fast as he could, his legs pumping furiously. Coming down a small draw, he saw a small grove of trees ahead and ran to them. Upon reaching them, he collapsed from exhaustion and lack of breath, and from very badly jangled nerves. Ranting out loud for the h'ants to leave him be, he crawled toward what appeared to be a hole at the base of one of the trees, and finding it big enough, crawled in, pleading to be left alone by the conjurin' h'ants. He was able to squeeze a couple feet up in the hollow, and thus wedged in tightly, felt some measure of comfort and safety. Alternately pleading for his life and begging forgiveness, and swearing that he'd change his wicked ways and never ever take advantage of anyone anymore, or make trouble for anyone ever again, and make special friends with Brer Fox, in this delirious moaning ranting raving mumbling maddened frantic state, he eventually fell asleep, his night of terror coming to a close.

The next morning, after he woke and got his bearings, shuddering at the previous nights memories, he slowly and gingerly let himself down out of the hollow. He listened carefully with his sensitive ears for signs of anyone or anything outside. Satisfied there was no imminent danger, he stuck his head out from the base of the tree and looked around.

Each way he turned his head, it was the same: treeless hill followed by treeless hill. He'd never seen anything like it before, having lived his entire life in the wooded southeast. 'Dis er iz sump'en', he thought to himself, 'some fa'mer got hisse'f un monstus big paschur.' Cautiously he made his way to the top of a rise, only to have his breath taken away by the immensity and vastness of the prairie. He whistled, then said aloud, "Tooby sho, I not reckembembunce dis t'all."

He felt vulnerable standing out in the open grassland, with no cover to duck in save a few scattered trees here and there. But he was thirsty, and getting hungry too. Smacking his dried lips together, he remembered the creek that he'd jumped the night before, and set out to find it, walking the small ravines and dry creek beds for what small cover they provided.

It all looked the same to him, one hill after another; nothing looked familiar. Granted, last night he was beside himself with fear, but odds were he'd stumble upon something soon. He walked for a long time, certain he was heading in one direction, but the little draws he walked brought him into a great big circle and he soon found himself back at the grove of cottonwood trees where he'd spent the night. 'Dis mos' 'culiar,' he thought. He realized that despite the danger, he'd have to head out on the tops of the hills if he was going to have any chance of finding anything. And so he did.

He walked in one direction as best he could for half an hour before he got the distinct feeling he was being watched. Every now and then he'd turn his head ever so slightly to try and catch a glimpse behind him. He pricked his ears up too, but not so that they would alarm whoever was trailing him, to let his possible follower know Brer Rabbit was on to him, but just enough for him to hear. The grass, green and moist from spring rains, didn't give any hint of footsteps, and what wind there was muffled any other noise. Instinctively, his great trait of self-preservation, indeed, Brer Rabbit's natural state of grace, readied his body for flight or flight faster. He allowed to himself that no one was going to 'kotch Brer Rabbit.'

And so he began to swing his arms, hum a tune and skip a little, acting as if he hadn't a care in the world, until he came to an abrupt drop off into a ravine that he couldn't see until he was right on top of it. There were some bushes in the little draw that he quickly jumped into. He was going to surprise whoever was following him, 'skeer 'em des de way I skeer't de creeturs back home de time w'en I wuz de wull-er-de-wust.'

Landing in the bushes he came face to face with a snarling coyote. "Heyo," he gasped, "W'at fur you a'skeer'n me? I node you wuz er, I des shakin off dem dat uz atter you. I heppin, z' all," he lied, while backing up, the coyote leaning in on him, fangs dripping saliva. "Dey's a truck un um bak dere."

"Hon'st, I heppin. Why you no talk t'me? You des gonna gobble up ole Brer Rabbit wid out sayin nuttin? Man's got a right to node who gonna e't im. Who iz you?" Brer Rabbit was talking fast, but the coyote kept pressing in on him, snapping and baring his fangs. "I heppin, dats de trufe. Iz yo Brer Fox brudder? Yo bigger'n im. Mebbe yo Brer Wolf kin, but no 'fense, he bigger'n you iz."

The coyote yipped at the mention of Brer Wolf, then narrowed his eyes and crowded in on Brer Rabbit. Still backing up and talking fast, Brer Rabbit said, "I t'ain't much t'et, I so little. I node a monstus big cow we kin kotch up terge'er, n'you kin 'ave mos' un em." The coyote lunged at Brer Rabbit's outstretched paw. "Okay, you kin 'ave all un em. W'at you say? Why you no talk?"

Brer Rabbit kept on asking the coyote why he wouldn't talk, why wouldn't he give Brer Rabbit what may be his last request, "to confab wif un dyin' man," until finally, after trying hard to grab hold of the rabbit, the coyote relented and halted, then began to hack and cough. His eyes lost their anger and fierceness as he tried to clear his throat, but he did not for a second let them stray from Brer Rabbit. It took a long time and a lot of effort before he finally spoke, "I," he began, but his throat burned, he worked his jaws like he had something caught in his mouth, like he was choking, "I," he began again in a guttural, phlegmy voice, "don't talk . . . haven't talked . . . . in . . ." He spit and coughed and cleared his throat again, "in a long . . . (ack, cough) time, because . . . no one . . . has . . . talked to me."

Brer Rabbit grinned and said, "I des de man fer t'hep you."

"Not . . . if I . . . eat you," hacked the coyote in a hoarse, broken voice.

"Dat de way t'talk t'de man w'at des saved yo life?" Brer Rabbit lied.

"You didn't . . . save my . . . life," the coyote responded, his voice straining, the pitch rising and falling with the effort. "That was me . . . following you . . . you liar."

"I 'clare t'grayshus, you de mos' disperlite en owdashus creetur I e'er seed."

"And hungry, too," added the coyote.

"Whysomever we no wuk terge'er? Hit's de hon'st trufe, las night I seed de biggity'st cow I e'er seed wif deze er eyes. We go in cahoots, we bound t'git mo truck den you kin 'majun."

"And why should . . . I..trust you? You've already . . . been lying . . . (nnnggghhh, cough, cough) up a storm. Besides, it was probably a . . . . buffalo, and no way are we going to bring a buff (ack) alo down."

"Des leaf dat up t'ole Brer Rabbit, deze er buffo ain't seen de laks a'me b'fo."

"I'm sure they haven't. Listen, rabbit, I need to rest . . . my tender voice . . . while I decide how to eat you. In . . . the meantime, you go with me to the creek, I need water for my throat." With that the coyote pointed the way with his muzzle, and jabbed Brer Rabbit to get him moving.

"I bleedzed t' year dat, I iz, I'z bout dried out m'seff. Dey jis one mo thing. What I call you, what yo name?"

"Coyote," he rasped, then shoved Brer Rabbit hard.

They made their way to the creek via gullies and ravines, the coyote knowing every twist and turn of every little rivulet. It was getting hot as the sun climbed high into the sky, and Brer Rabbit was looking forward to a drink of water. That didn't stop him from scheming and planning his escape, but every time he turned around to say something to the coyote, to try and catch the coyote off guard for some ruse or trick, the coyote would bare his teeth and growl, like he knew Brer Rabbit's own mind. "You sho do lak t' flash yo toofies, coyote," he said.

"I know you'll understand the message," was his reply.

Arriving at the creek, they both drank eagerly, Brer Rabbit slurping and gurgling and getting himself all wet, while the coyote was more delicate, perhaps owing to his sore throat. He let the soothing water slowly trickle down over his burning vocal chords, unused for years, now hard pressed by this damn gibbering jabbering talkative rabbit.

After slaking their thirst, they moved into the shade provided by a small willow tree. To the annoyance of the coyote, the rabbit kept smacking his lips in satisfaction and shaking the water off himself. "Dat wuk my 'membunce loose," he said, "I uz hongry ez ole Brer Bar atter he sleep thoo de win'ner."

"Me too," the coyote leered.

Brer Rabbit drew back a step. "Dem biggity cows mos' lakly right roun' 'er some'ers." Smacking his lips loudly, he said, "I kin des 'bout tas' dem dar staks on de bobbycue right 'er bout now, en I node de bes' way to cooks um. Folks alluz sayin' ole Brer Rabbit, he de bes dat w'at kin cook dem dar staks, tooby sho." He eyed the coyote to see if he was in any way effecting him.

"You're full of more bullshit than a slaughter house," Coyote said.

"Den ef you e't me, w'at dat mek you?" Brer Rabbit reasoned.

The coyote laughed, his voice a choking, gargly gasp.

Brer Rabbit took advantage of the point. "I de wuss tastin creetur dey iz. Ef you not beleefin me, ax Brer Wolf. He kotch me un time, en he tuk en tuk a bite un me, en he spit me out, he did, as sho es you er sittin dar. En der uz time ole Cousin Wildcat, he tuk en tuk a lik un me, en he got de agur, he did, en ef . . ."

"Shut up!" yelled the coyote. "Shut up! You talk too much. And where did you learn to talk like that? Tell me, but in five words or less." He bared his teeth emphatically.

"All de folks talk lak dis w'er I fum."

"And where is that?"

"I dun'ner, but hit got lots mo trees den er. I aint ne'er seed sech un big paschur."

The coyote muttered to himself, "Must be towards the sunrise, beyond the big river." Then addressing Brer Rabbit, "How'd you get here? How were you traveling?"

"No, suh. I des sleepin nex t'Mist'r Zach'ry, en de fus' news I git, I uz wif some h'ants in some monstus hot den. Dey uz fixin t'do some conju'n wid me, but I racked out'n der de fus chance I gits. Dat uz w'en I run lippity slippity in t'de biggity cows. Now 'er I iz bout t'get e't by de only fren I haz en de whole wi'e worl'." Brer Rabbit started sobbing, which he worked up to crying, which he then elevated to bawling loudly, holding his arms up and crying into his shirt sleeves. But all the time he kept an eye on the coyote from under his sleeve.

The coyote didn't seem to be paying him any attention. He was thinking, putting together the information the rabbit just gave him. 'Very hot den of h'ants, conjuring, running into buffalo. Hhhmm.' Not much happened on this land without his knowing about it, and he soon realized that Brer Rabbit must be talking about Burly and Donovan, he knew they held a sweat lodge the previous night and the rabbit probably thought they were ghosts or something, h'ants, as he called them. And the big cows would have been Burly's buffalo. But how did this rabbit get in there? Did he crawl under the coverings? Did he just appear out of thin air? If he did, he must be powerful medicine. Maybe he better not eat him, at least not yet. Not until he's sure who and what he is. Maybe he better take him to Burly, and if Burly lets him go, he'll be right there to end this story with a fine dinner of loquacious rabbit over sage.

He looked up at Brer Rabbit, who was blowing his nose in a handkerchief. 'But I better keep an eye on this hare, he's a slick one,' he thought.

"Okay, brother rabbit. You've got a deal. If you can bring down a buffalo, I'll let you go," he announced to Brer Rabbit. 'This way I can get you close to the house without raising your suspicions,' he thought to himself.

Brer Rabbit jumped up and hit his heels together and twirled around in the air, his long ears twining together. "You en me terge'er, dem cows doan stand un chance. You gwine be de mo's happy fell'r dat e'er wuz." He rushed up to the coyote and gave him a big hug, and, since to Brer Rabbit, going too far is just a geographic mistake, he added, "You en me iz des lak fambly. We lakly kin."

This time it was the coyote who backed up. He grimaced at the rabbit and told him, "My good nature has limits. Leave be, rabbit, leave be."

The coyote knew that some of the herd would be close to the barn right now because during the winter this was the time of day Burly would have fed them, and though the grass was very green and there was plenty of forage in the fields, some still came by the barn, just in case something could be had. If he got the rabbit near the barn, Burly might see them, and somehow Coyote would detain the rabbit until Burly could get him, then he'd slip away. He didn't have it all worked out yet, but he would figure something out once they got there. "Let's go!" he ordered.

They traveled right on the hilltops, in plain view, the coyote not giving a wit if they were seen. This made Brer Rabbit a little nervous, but he didn't have any choice in the matter. After walking for what seemed many nervous miles to Brer Rabbit, they came upon the buildings that comprised Burly's ranch; the one big barn, several smaller structures and then a small ranch house with a trailer not far from it. It was a far bigger layout of buildings than he'd ever seen, and the sight of it excited him. "We gwine t'town! Dat we er! Mr. Coyote, we gwine 'ave some fun!"

The coyote hushed him, "Shut up! This isn't a town, it's someone's house. And if they see us, they'll shoot us."

"Shoot us? Den why we en de open lak dis?" Brer Rabbit asked.

"Never mind. What we came for is over there," he said, pointing to a lone buffalo.

It was as he hoped. At least one buffalo was hanging out near the fence gate where Burly would bring hay in during the winter. It was the younger of two bulls Burly had, the older would no doubt be with the herd. A good thing, this was a very spirited young bull, eager to show his virility and prove himself. He'd chase after this silly, dressed up rabbit in a heartbeat.

They moved over to the fence and followed it towards the bull as quietly and as stealthily as they could. The coyote didn't want to spook the buffalo too soon, he wanted it to chase the rabbit a little bit, that would be more apt to get someone's attention.

As they neared the huge animal, Brer Rabbit could finally get a good look at the size of the bull. He hadn't seen anything this big before, and it was much bigger in the daylight. "Dat er mighty suvvigus creetur, en dem's awful big hawns. W'at I 'pose t'kill de beast wif? I ain't got nuffin, not e'en un knife!"

"That," said the coyote, spotting a pitchfork leaning on the other side of the fence not ten paces from them.

They slipped through the fence rails and cautiously made their way towards the pitchfork. The bull had his back to them and couldn't see them approach, nor had he smelled them yet. Once they reached the pitchfork, Brer Rabbit grabbed it and said to the coyote, "Des wait er til I shows you how er man git he brekkus."

With that he crept along the fence until he got close to the bull. Whispering, he called out to the bison, "Heyo, Mr. Buffo, do'n be skeer't, I des un lil' rabbit dat kin do no ha'm t'big fell'r lak you." The buffalo turned to look at the curious little creature that was talking to it and rumbled a warning from deep within its chest. Brer Rabbit shook in the aftermath of the sounding, but it didn't deter him, he went on, "I'ze in need er some hep. Now, doan be 'larm'd, but der dis coyote dat kotch me up en won' lemme go 'til I kilt a buffo, but I sez, sez I, dat I don't keer if I duz kilt a buffo, dey ain't done nuttin t' ole Brer Rabbit. I got nuttin gin 'im." The buffalo swung his massive head and bellowed out loudly at the mention of coyote's name. "Doan be mad, Mr. Buffo, I got plans dat we kin fix 'im up good. W'at say you? Talk low, do, he ne'rby."

The buffalo ambled over to the rabbit, if more in curiosity than in active agreement to participate. He wasn't exactly a friend of coyote though, they'd been going after each other forever, and small though the coyote was, comparatively, sometimes he did make off with a young buffalo calf.

Back down the fence line, the coyote watched intently. Brer Rabbit had his back to him, so he couldn't tell he was talking, and when the buffalo came over to the fence, he wondered just what was going on. He started to creep closer to the two.

Brer Rabbit said to the huge animal, "Ef I uz t'come in dar wif you, promise not t'hurt ole Brer Rabbit?"

The buffalo nodded its gigantic head in agreement.

Brer Rabbit slipped through the fence rails, dragging the pitchfork. The buffalo stood not five feet from him, dwarfing him in size, the tip of Brer Rabbit's ears just reaching the top of the buffalo's head. "Ef you lemme chase you round dat dar shed, en den do es I sez, sho nuf, dat er coyote come gallin' round de cornder, en den he all yo's. Dat 'greebul?"

The large young bull nodded in agreement again. This seemed like a good chance to even some old scores with Coyote, and if this was a trick, this goofy looking rabbit would pay dearly. With a loud snort, he spun around and ran toward the shed, his tail held high. Following close behind was Brer Rabbit, shaking the pitchfork menacingly, and yelling, "Des stanz still so'z I kin run you thoo, stanz still you big cow'rt! Des stanz en fight lak er man!" And with that they disappeared behind Burly's tractor shed.

The coyote couldn't believe it, couldn't believe that scrawny, gangly, garrulous hare had a buffalo on the run. What followed then shocked him even more. From behind the shed came the sounds of battle, the buffalo bellowing and the rabbit screaming, god awful bloodcurdling yelling and hollering and squalling. Finally, there was only one voice, Brer Rabbit's. He was proclaiming loudly, "Dat w'at comes t' folks dat mess wif ole Brer Rabbit, bofe big uns en lil' uns. I ain't e'er met er man er creetur dat come out'n er quoll er rippit on top er ole Brer Rabbit. Dat I ain't. En dis w'at un man haz fer brekkus, ah-yi!"

The coyote couldn't believe his ears, he trotted out into the barnyard, the bragging of Brer Rabbit reeling him in. He broke into a run and came tearing around the corner of the shed, only to come face to face with one angry, and opportunistic, young buffalo bull, who bore down on him. Coyote's forward momentum gave him no choice but to jump up on to the buffalo's huge hump to avoid being crushed. From there he tried to jump up on the sloping roof of the shed, just a mere foot above him now. But the roof was made of corrugated metal, and he couldn't get a foothold. He clambered and dug and tried vainly to get his claws to dig in. Meanwhile, the buffalo was trying to get his fore legs up on the side of the shed to try and snag the coyote with his horns, but his hooves kept slipping. There they were, the coyote frantically digging and clawing, the buffalo snorting and bellowing, jabbing at the tail end of the coyote with his horns, and Brer Rabbit standing to the side, hooting and hollering, urging the buffalo on. "Git 'im, Mr. Buffo. Dat de vilyun dat say dem tearbul tengs bout you en yo's. Git 'im good now, doan let dat rascal git 'way." Eventually the coyote's battle against gravity failed, and he fell backward off the roof, back on to the buffalo's hump. Twisting sideways once he landed, he leapt to the ground and tore away as fast as he could. As he ran away from the barn, he caught a glimpse of the rabbit rolling on the ground, holding his stomach and laughing hysterically. But he didn't have time to think of revenge, he could feel the buffalo's breath on his tail.

Sitting inside his kitchen eating an early lunch, Burly heard the commotion down in the barnyard, and came out onto his back porch to see what the devil was going on. When he did, he caught sight of a coyote being chased by a buffalo. "What the hell is that all about," he said aloud to himself, and to Donovan, who was lying on the couch, recovering from the previous night's events. He watched the two disappear down into a gully, then saw a rabbit come walking out from behind the shed on two feet, wearing odd clothes. He was brushing dirt off his shirt sleeves and laughing. "Hey Do!? Do!! Come here!" he yelled in to the house.

They hadn't been able to come to any agreement on what manner of spirit had come to them last night in the sweat lodge. Burly thought it was maybe Fox spirit, or Coyote. Especially Coyote because of the magical way he materialized in the lodge, spoke to them with that strange accent, then ran out screaming. An odd thing for a spirit to do, but then, with Coyote, you never know. There had to be some teaching in that, but he couldn't determine what. He lay awake last night trying to think of what the spirit had meant asking if he and Do were h'ants. H'ants. It wasn't a word he'd heard before. Some old word used by people in the long ago? A spirit word? Maybe the spirit was telling them they should be more like a h'ant. If only he knew what a h'ant was. By running out of the lodge, maybe the spirit was telling them if they weren't, then they should be avoided? Are spirits avoiding them now? Hell, maybe its as simple as he shouldn't of gotten drunk last weekend. Sometimes it was just too hard to understand spirit. That old trickster, Coyote, was up to something, trying to teach him something, but he couldn't fathom it. Donovan, on the other hand, swore it was some little gnome-like man. He'd seen clothes, and the creature ran upright, like a man. He thought it was some elf spirit wearing a hat that had two big feathers in it, like some spirit from Iceland he'd read about in National Geographic, or that he'd heard lived in Ireland. They went to bed puzzled and woke up just as mystified, as neither had any dreams that might have clarified the matter. One thing Burly did know, though, it had been a very powerful sweat, and a very healing one. He'd gotten a message from the hospital that morning that his uncle was feeling a lot better. He'd gotten up this morning and walked right on out of the hospital before he could be caught and confined to bed again. They were going to do a biopsy the next day to check on the progress of the cancer and they warned Burly not to get too optimistic because patients often suddenly feel better right before they slip down the final path to death. Burly didn't believe them. That his uncle had recovered consciousness meant that he was alive and on the road to recovery and damn the diagnosis of the doctors. He promised the spirits he would make a special sacrifice in thanks for this miracle, for their obvious intervention. He just hadn't made up his mind yet what that sacrifice was going to be.

Donovan stumbled out of the kitchen onto the back porch, squinted his eyes to see what Burly was pointing to, and said,

"What the fuck is that? Am I seeing this? Is that what was in the sweat last night? But that's no little man, that looks like a goddamn rabbit! And look at the way he's dressed!"

"And look at the way he's walking, like a man," Burly said. "I don't know if he's real or not, but we have to check this out."

"I don't know Bur, I gotta quit coming up here, this shit's gettin' too weird," Donovan shook his head despondently.

"Come on, before he gets away again." Burly was already halfway to the barn.

They didn't have to worry about it running away, as soon as he saw the two men coming towards him, the gregarious rabbit waved to them, calling out, "Heyo dar! How you come along?" then he froze, remembering the coyote's warning that if they were seen, they would be shot. But they didn't have any guns, least not that he could see, and besides, that coyote couldn't be trusted, that much he knew for sure. Maybe he should be polite to these two men, he might be able to get something to eat, and maybe they could tell him how to get home. One of them had a big friendly smile on his face, but the other looked a little worried, he'd keep an eye on that one.

Brer Rabbit didn't recognize them at all from the previous night, but they knew he could only be the same spirit that ran out of the sweat lodge. There was no mistaking that, and the clincher came as soon as he opened his mouth and spoke.

"We come along fine," Burly said warmly, with a smile, "And how do you come along?"

"Mighty po'ly, mighty po'ly," answered Brer Rabbit.

"Why is that?" Burly asked in a genuinely concerned voice.

"I not familious wif de lay er de lan roun' er, en I monstus hongry on top er dat," he answered truthfully. He didn't like the way the two men looked at him so closely, with so much scrutiny. They were looking at him like he was a h'ant himself, or they were hungry too, only they saw him for dinner. Their staring made him very uncomfortable, and he was about to make excuses and tear out of there when the smiley one said, "I would be honored if you were to come to my kitchen and let me fix you whatever you like to eat. And I'll try and help you get home as best I can."

Brer Rabbit didn't know what was going to come of this, but he liked this smiley fellow. "Dat mighty nice er you, mighty frenly, en I mos' 'bliged."

Burly swept his hands towards the house, and they headed that way, Brer Rabbit leading. Behind him Burly was beside himself with delight for having met this magical, marvelous, exquisite creature and spirit. Donovan wasn't so sure, he was dubious that any good could come of it.

Halfway to the house, Burly asked the rabbit what name he might call him. "E'erbody call me Brer Rabbit." The two men froze.

It was an electric shock to Burly's brain, a hard rap from a hammer, a stunner. Brer Rabbit? Brer Rabbit? Brer Rabbit? Brer Rabbit? How the hell can that be? He's a cartoon figure. No a children's story, no a fable, uh, uh, uh, he's a fake, made up. He's a story, a myth a tale a lie. Can't be, can't be. This is another test by the spirits, he's had them before. This is Coyote medicine, that's what this is, and wasn't that a coyote he'd just seen running off down into the gully? Yes, this must be Coyote, The Trickster, teaching him something. Something. Something. He looked over at Donovan, who shook his head, and said, "This is it Burly, no more. I can't deal with this shit any more." Burly took another close look at the rabbit. Yes, there was no doubt he was a rabbit, and yes, he was dressed like some old farmer or something, and yes, he talked like Brer Rabbit, though he couldn't really be sure because he'd never heard Brer Rabbit speak. Hell, no one had. Had they?

"Brer Rabbit?" he stammered.

"Iz you un nudder dats ha'd er yearin?" Brer Rabbit asked.

"No, I can hear fine, I can hear fine," Burly replied airily.

"Dat good. En w'at bofe yo names?" he asked the two men.

Burly answered for both of them, "I'm Burly and this is Donovan. How, how did you get here?"

"Bleedz ter meet wif you two fin' gennermens, I mo's sho'ly iz. Kin we git t'de bittles now? I need sump'n n'er t'eat, I'z monstus hongry, den I'll tell you my 'speunce."

They made their way to the kitchen, where the rabbit proceeded to amaze the two men with his dexterity using eating implements, and with the amount of food he could consume at one sitting. That he ate anything and everything surprised them too.

"I thought rabbits only ate carrots and lettuce and things like that. You're supposed to be vegetarians," observed Donovan once he got over his initial uneasiness.

Between mouthfuls, Brer Rabbit replied, "I lak um des es much ez de nex' man, but I ne'er et no vegtar'n. Leasways not dat I reckembembunce. Less 'ave some mo er dat dar ham."

While he ate, Brer Rabbit told them of his meeting with Coyote, and how the coyote was going to eat him until he agreed to let Brer Rabbit try and kill a buffalo for food. If he succeeded, he'd let him live. But Brer Rabbit cunningly foiled the coyote's dastardly plans by persuading the young buffalo bull to work with him and Brer Rabbit turned the tables against the wicked one, that was why they saw the buffalo chasing the coyote. Brer Rabbit relished telling the story, embellishing it whenever he could, such as telling them that he helped Mr. Buffo get on top of the shed, only to watch as that cowardly coyote jumped off the other end, and then he had to help Mr. Buffo down, "so dat he cud chase on atter 'im."

After he had eaten his fill and then some, they sat down in the living room, Brer Rabbit plopping down on the sofa, his belly swollen grotesquely. Donovan thought he could prick it with a pin and he'd deflate, spinning around the room like a balloon letting loose the air within. Brer Rabbit was enthralled by the house; it was furnished and decorated beyond his wildest dreams. This was the lap of luxury. He thought Burly the wealthiest man he had ever heard about, certainly that he'd ever met. As he told him, "Buhly, you de richis' man I node, sholy yo some kind er king!"

Burly told him that far from being a king, he was a common man, living a very normal life. To that Brer Rabbit just whistled, he said he was a common man too, but there was nothing like this back home.

Brer Rabbit was feeling mighty comfortable, he felt very safe in Burly's presence and in his house, and even though Donovan was nervous, Brer Rabbit knew he wouldn't harm him. There were so many new and incredible things to know and explore here that it was all a bit of an overload to him in light of the morning's events, and that on top of last night's scary doings, now he was feeling drowsy from all that he had eaten. Soon his drooping eyelids refused to stay open, and he fell fast asleep on the couch.

Burly and Donovan were still pretty much awestruck. They sat and stared at the sleeping rabbit, now snoring away on Burly's couch. They were quiet, vigilant monitors, witnesses to an observational flexible reality, Burly with a far away look and grin on his face while Donovan fidgeted. They sat for a long time until Donovan finally spoke, "Burly, I don't know how to say this, but do you know that Brer Rabbit's asleep on your living room couch? Listen to me! Do you know that Brer Rabbit is really, really asleep on your sofa. Here! Right now!?"

"Unh hunh. Yep. Unfucking real," Burly said.

Donovan continued talking, more to himself than to Burly, "This is getting out of hand. I dunno, maybe I'm just not cut out for this path. Maybe it's not my road. I'm no medicine man. I'm gonna quit the church, no more peyote for me. No more sweats, no more vision quests. I'm turnin' white, man, I'm gonna turn white."

"What?" Burly asked.

"I said I'm going white. This is it, this is what all the teachings, all the lessons, all the fasting, all the work with spirit, this is what it has all come down to: Brer Rabbit sleeping on your fucking couch!"

"We have to find out how he got here," Burly said, not responding to Donovan. "When he wakes up we have to find out how he got here and why. Maybe there's no way of telling, the way spirit works sometimes, you never know, but we have to try and help him. He's come as a gift from spirit, that much I know."

"What kind of gift? He's no ancestor spirit, or White Bear. He's not medicine, what is he?" Donovan wondered.

"I don't know. You're right, he's not Satethieday, but he is a gift and he is medicine. How else can you explain Uncle waking up from a coma and walking out of the hospital? You've been around, you know those things don't just happen."

"Yea, yea. But . . . aaaarrggg, fuckin' Brer Rabbit! Man, I need a beer," Donovan said in frustration. He got up from his chair and went into the kitchen and got a cold beer out of the refrigerator.

Their voices woke the rabbit up. Rubbing his eyes and yawning, and smacking his lips together, he greeted Burly, who sat staring at him, then got up and walked into the kitchen. Donovan was leaning against the kitchen counter, drinking his beer. Brer Rabbit asked him what he was drinking, and being told it was beer, said he wouldn't mind if he had some too. Donovan asked him if he'd ever had beer before. "Tooby sho. Up ter Miss Meadows en de gals, we allurz drinkin' un gamlin' un carrin' on. I got some t'backer some'ers," he answered. He searched through his pockets until he came up with a twist of chewing tobacco and offered some to Donovan, who politely declined. Burly came into the kitchen, and upon seeing the rabbit drinking beer and chewing tobacco, felt his conviction that Brer Rabbit was a gift momentarily waver.

The beer loosened a tongue not entirely bound by timidity or truthfulness. The rabbit related his story to the two men as best he could, which is to say, with many digressions and ornamentations and a few outright lies. Sitting on Burly's back porch, he told them he had gone to bed the previous night tied to Mr. Zachary's toe by a length of string, and had woken up in that "monstus hot place". And no, he hadn't run out of there because he was afraid of h'ants, he just needed to get some fresh air, he was having trouble breathing, and he screamed just to fill his lungs up. "Why were you tied to Mr. Zachary's toe?" Burly asked. "De nex' mawnin' we uz gwine ter de conju'n woman's so dat Mr. Zack'ry cud git home a'gin. I uz tied so I din't wanduh off 'n my sleep lak I sometimes duz. Dey need'd my he'p fo' d'reckshuns."

"And who is Mr. Zachary? Where does he live?" Burly asked.

"He nice fell'r w'at visit'd me'n Brer Fox. Hit Zach'ree Peterson dat live up dar en place call Lanty."

"Lanty? Lanty? Could that be Atlanta? He must mean Atlanta," Donovan said.

"Dat w'at I desh shed," replied Brer Rabbit in a voice getting thick from the beer, making it more difficult for the two men to understand him.

Suddenly the rabbit's ears pricked up, he heard a noise coming from a shed that stood some fifteen yards from where they sat. It was a small wooden doorway built as the entrance to a storm shelter, an underground safe haven from the many violent thunderstorms and tornadoes that often ripped through the plains. As the door slowly creaked open, the rabbit's body tensed, any trace of drunkenness gone. He was ready to fly at the merest whiff of danger.

Burly and Donovan looked at each other with concern, they weren't sure what was going to happen next, what the rabbit was going to do. Burly reached to grab him, to hold him steady, but Brer Rabbit quickly and easily moved away. "What dish yer teng? Dish dat coyote 'gin? Yo in c'hoots wif dat vilyun?"

"No, no, it's nothing like that," Burly said, trying to ease the tension and calm him down.

Brer Rabbit's eyes danced back and forth between the two men and the doorway, with one ear tuned to the shed and the other tuned to them. He placed one foot in front of the other, ready to roll. The door opened agonizingly slow, creaking and groaning as it did. He could see a dark, triangular object pushing it open, then a large black webbed foot appeared on the top step, followed by a black beak limned in yellow, then the body of a creature emerged out of the darkened doorway, the likes of which he'd never seen before. It was about four feet high, black with a white belly; the triangular object was a flipper. As it came out into the light and saw them staring at it, it gronked and trumpeted. Brer Rabbit flinched at the sound, the spasm knocking the small drip of tobacco juice that hung from his open mouth to the ground.

"Brer Rabbit, meet Bart the penguin," Burly said.

chapter nine

Dinner was quiet that evening at Trieste. Gone were the simple, curious questions of history posed by Zachary, gone were his little chatty and slightly cynical observations. Even mother and daughter had left their needles elsewhere. It wasn't entirely a somber and morose repast, conversation was just tilted toward the trivial and familial, such as what the two young people were going to do tomorrow now that they had the shed cleaned out. Virginia would go through what was left in the morning with Diggy. Emma's father, expected sometime around noon, could also help sift through the bounty, such as it were. No, they were free to do as they pleased Sunday, but they had to be back for dinner. Virginia was going to cook a ham, one of her husband's favorite dinners.

The conversation that preceded the evening meal had smudged the dining hall with an unpleasant bouquet. A beautiful amber jewel of Trieste had broken, and the ancient air released was odious. The talk had concerned the chains. Of course, slavery had been acknowledged and discussed the previous night, and Zachary still wanted to see where the slave quarters had been, to kick around the stones still piled there, but the black metal devices held the past in his face like a fist, an unavoidable reminder of the human capacity for injustice, which is merely another euphemism for evil. Zach thought sardonically that if slaves were considered wealth, were chains the bank? For Emma, they took the shine off that past and gave it to the moon, who lurked outside, searching for the sun.

Emma's mother thought they belonged to the overseer, and had probably been lying there unseen for over one hundred years.

One hundred years of soliloquy. That was when the last official overseer had died, thirty years after the Civil War ended slavery and the plantation system. He had been an Irishman, Francis Donaughy, and that in itself was unusual for the time, that he would be given a job so critical to the health of the plantation. People didn't think much of the Irish then, and the lousy, back breaking work of building rail beds and laying rails through the hot, malarial swamps of the south often fell to Irish and black crews, but never as one crew, never working together. It was either the only work the Irish could get, or no one else could be paid to do it. The Africans had no choice. The Irish had someone to look down on, the Africans didn't.

For Virginia, the discussion of the chains had no effect. They were a good museum piece, and she was sure Diggy would be happy to put them on display. She looked forward to giving them to her tomorrow along with the list of names, the bill of sale. Emma and Zach scheduled a conflict; they'd be elsewhere tomorrow, in town, in point of fact. Emma was going to show Zach around Thomasville.

The rabbit foot was another mystery. Virginia had no idea what that was about, if she had put it in there as a child, she certainly had no recollection. Zach could have it if he wanted; she couldn't imagine it having any historical interest. It was an early evening for Zach and Emma. Moods soured by the return of history, and dead tired from finding it, they bid a good evening to Virginia and gave each other perfunctory kisses at Emma's door. Zach went to his room and tossed the rabbit's foot into his small overnight bag and forgot about it, falling quickly into a deep and satisfying sleep, too deep for dreams.

Thomasville closes up on Sunday. You can walk down the center of North Broad St. and not have to dodge but half a dozen cars. If you're lucky you can get a cup of coffee, but it won't be on that street, you'll have to jump over to Madison, and that they would be open depends on just how the owners are feeling that day. They might come in, then again, they might not. But if they are open, the coffee is good, and you can even get a cappuccino if you like. On weekdays, the cafe in the same old building serves good, even modern, cuisine. Like most buildings in downtown Thomasville, this one has a history. It was originally an old steam laundry, with very high ceilings to keep the heat off floor level, and huge wooden vents two stories up to release the steam to the outside. Zachary was looking up at one of the vents when Emma brought hot drinks to their little table. Waiters, they do not have.

"Well, we've walked all of 10 minutes, and we've covered downtown," Zach observed. "And everything's closed, even the famous hardware store. What shall we do next?" He leaned back, put his hands behind his head and stretched his legs out.

"We can git back in the cah en drahve around and look at some of the ole Victorian homes, some of 'em ahre quite remarkable. Few ahre really homes anymo', they been turned into doctor's or lawyer's offices, especially 'cross the tracks. Too bad it's Sunday, some ahre museums now and ahre worth a little tour," Emma said without enthusiasm.

"Just as well," Zach responded, "I don't feel like poking around another old house. God knows what we'd find somewhere else. Look at this." He reached down and from a rack picked up a tourist pamphlet entitled 'Black Heritage Trail Tour Guide'. "Says here that Thomasville is the birth place of the first black American graduate of West Point, a Lt. Henry Ossian Flipper."

"Ole Bessy Flippuh was one of the women at the shout the othuh night, she's a great-great somethin' or othuh of his," Emma said.

"Hmm," was the only response she got from him while he thumbed through the pages. She was thinking of Diggy, and that right about now her mother would be triumphantly handing the chains and the papers over to her. 'A significant historical find', she would probably be saying. 'A great gift to the museum.' She hoped Diggy thought so. Why was she feeling so guilty? she wondered. It was as if she felt the guilt of her ancestors, the guilt of their having treated people so poorly, so horribly, so inhumanely. And it would be to people just like Diggy. She couldn't imagine being anything less than an equal to Diggy, couldn't imagine ordering Diggy to do something, to have her look back at her with eyes full of fear, or hatred. That thought hurt. She'd felt this guilt before in a slightly different capacity when she had gone to school up north. Then she felt guilty for just being who she was, a southern girl. How and why should she feel guilt for the sins of the past, even though they were her ancestors? It just didn't seem fair. Even those spoiled little Yankee girls seemed to blame her for slavery. Part of her knew it wasn't fair, part of her knew she carried no culpability; she had no part in the affairs of people long dead. Her mother's words floated to the fore of her mind, 'Times were different.' Those were her mother's defense barriers, her little comfort pills, her mantra that allowed her mind to wander away free, to seek safer ground, away from that murky bog of guilt and the past. She tried to pass them on to her daughter, but now they didn't seem to hold any power, not when confronted with the cold metal reality of those chains.

"Hey," Zach said softly. "What are you thinking about, you look terrible. You okay?" He reached out and touched her hand.

"Oh, Ah dunno. Ah was just thinkin' bout those darned chains, en how terrible they made me feel en now momma's gonna give them to Diggy lahke they was some kind a prize. Ah just can't help but feel bad for Diggy."

"Maybe she'll think they're great, a real find," he said.

"Maybe, and on some level she will think they're great to have. But Ah guess it all makes me feel guilty or somethin', Ah feel awful, like we dug up something that was best left alone, best left in the past."

"I know what you mean," he said, "I feel it too. The minute we realized what they were, our joy and happiness were torpedoed by some submarine. Some ugly, dark, wretched, little submarine."

"Yes, they's been a cloud ovuh us since yeste'day en Ah don't lahke it, don't lahke it at all." She was gaining on something, if not determination; he could hear it in her voice.

"Soooo, what do we do? Just forget about it? Let it go, like we never saw it or heard it. Like see no evil, speak no evil, hear no evil?"

"No, that nevuh works, pushing somethin' down that should be aired. It just bubbles up somewheyuhz else, like a darned weed. It's lahk squeezin' a balloon in yaw hand. It squirts out somewheyuhz else. No, best t' turn the spotlight on it," she declared.

He drained his coffee and pushed the empty mug away, then groaned. "Self inspection begets self loathing; the wisdom of the talk show."

"It is not! That's ridiculous! Are you turning male on me?" she asked with no hint of a smile.

"Oh, God no!" he replied in mock horror.

"Zachary, I'm serious."

"I know, I know," he said. "I'm sorry. Can I get you a refill?"

As he got them more coffee it dawned on her that somehow the matter had infiltrated their relationship. He was annoying her, he wasn't taking her seriously. It wasn't condescension, but by not really listening to her, he was indirectly telling her that it wasn't important enough to him. When he sat down again, he was greeted with a cold smile.

Not dwelling entirely on another planet, though prone to occasional off-world forays, he realized he had some work cut out for him. The first thing to do was to find out what he had said or done that bothered her, and try to pull it back. "Emma, I'm really sorry. I know this is something we have to unearth. I don't like the way it has interfered with us either, how it has cast a shadow over us. I didn't mean to be flippant, and I sure didn't mean to diminish your needs in any way."

She was surprised. That was good, she thought, that was very good. He's willing to admit mistakes and apologize, and he also knew what he had done wrong. That was an unusual thing in her experience, for a man to know where he had transgressed. Especially in the field of needs, her needs, more precisely. Feelings soothed, she could return to the matter of guilt. They tried to climb down the ladder of logic and reason to arrive at justifications for the onerous burden of guilt. Neither could come up with any substantive basis nor cause for them to feel guilt over a situation wherein it was so obviously out of their personal sphere of influence and control. It wasn't until Zachary related a story from his high school days, of his feeling sorry for a kid that his own friends had beat up and he'd been embarrassed by his friend's actions that she realized it wasn't guilt they were feeling, it was shame. Not personal shame, but a universal shame, a human shame. Shared shame. It was a revelation. They were elated to find they were racked not with remorse or guilt, but shame. "God, it feels so good to feel shame! I love this shame! I embrace this shame! I have shame!" Zach proclaimed.

His ministrations returned giggles to Emma and their brief journey into the heart of this little darkness returned them to their previous state of grace with one another. And it was now, on the other side of this turbulent river, that Emma realized that she truly loved Zach, and come what may, she always would. For his part, Zach was just glad to get the hell out of the river.

They took the long way home, via side streets and by grand old homes Emma wanted to show Zach. For a small town near practically nothing, Thomasville had a lot of big Victorian houses. Emma told Zach the story of the town's former grandeur. Near the end of the nineteenth century, northerners came in droves to breathe in the pine scented air thought to have restorative effects. They came by the thousands, and two huge hotels were built to accommodate them. Thomasville became a hot item for hot money, the 'in' place to winter for the rich and near rich. Ironically, they built huge homes in and around town, which made the pines a bit scarce. But no matter, they soon discovered that for a pittance they could buy their own southern plantation thanks to the plunge in the price of cotton and the rise in (or mere existence of) labor wages in the aftermath of the Civil War which forced nearly all of the original builders into bankruptcy or to sell off parts of the land. Many seasonal visitors then moved outside of town. Even though the end came for Thomasville when Miami was discovered and developed, many of the descendants of the Yankee plantation usurpers still lived in and around Thomasville, or just south of the state line in Florida.

When they got back to Trieste, they drove in the back way so they could get close to the area where the former slave cabins had been. They parked next to a large magnolia tree, and walked out over a field to the site by the creek where the cabins had stood. They quietly walked around the stone piles marking where the fireplaces and chimneys had been as if listening to the wind for voices, reflecting on chains, sales receipts and shame. The ruins were shielded from the big house by the barn and other similar structures, but also by a line of ancient live oaks. They were all immense, easily a couple of hundred years old. No doubt, many had sheltered the little cabins those many years ago. Zach wondered what they would say if they could talk. Would they tell of cruelty and suffering? Or would they talk of laughter and joy and singing and ordinary everyday things people do? Would they tell of overhearing stories of rabbits and foxes told on cold winter nights around warm fires? Would it be Brer B'ar and Brer Alligator tales told in the stifling summer heat under its cool branches? Of barbecues and picnics and children playing and climbing on the many limbs? He wondered about these things as he walked around and kicked at the stones, half hoping to unearth some old relic of life on a Georgia plantation for a black person, something that spoke of a life, not of a system. A breeze brought a song to him, and he began to hum an unknown, unfamiliar tune. At first it was just a fragmented melody he hummed as he walked around the stones, but soon it blossomed like a morning glory greeting the day and words started to come, little grains of pollen gifted by honeybees, flakes of gold rising to the top of a gold miner's pan.

> There, 'fore the night is gone
> My love, I do, I see her run
> O'er fields now wet with dawn
> She comes to me
> She comes to me
> Like a dream so sweet
> I only wake for thee

He stretched his arms and gently spun and swayed with the rhythm of the song, let it take him out on an air, singing out loud as he sang it over and over. He turned and twirled with the coaxing of the warming sun and soothing breeze, with the oaks keeping time with their branches, sunlight glittering through the leaves turning into tinkling crystals flooding him with thoughts and images that seemed like memories. A dark skinned woman with hair pulled back tight and covered with a colorful scarf bade him to come forth and dance with her. She smiled sweetly, he knew the name she called, Jubal, and he knew her name, Sadie, but her real name was different, it was African. She came up to him and whispered in his ear, "What's the matter, Jubal, forget about our date? Did you think Folasade would let you get away that easy? Not when she has her eyes on something." He was filled with desire and longing and love for this woman, this specter. His heart beat wildly, but it throbbed too, from anguish and grief. He felt the pain of separation, of loss, of being torn from her, taken from her, icy fingers squeezing him, the sting of lash upon his back, the feel of metal around his hands and feet. He did not want to see her go again, he clutched at her but she began to fade. He shouted, "Noooo!" but he thrust and pawed at air, she was melding back in to the trees and stones and grass from which she came, smiling warmly, lovingly, seductively, at him.

Crystal sunlight once again dappled the leaves as the last of her blew away like tiny spiders on gossamer threads. He was alone again, a heart walled in darkness.

His arms fell to his side, he had already stopped dancing, and as consciousness tried to regain control, he slowly turned to see Emma staring at him intently as she sat under one of the oaks. He looked at her not as a person, a personality, but as the thing she meant to him, what she was to him. He looked at her as the embodiment of love. His love, now. She smiled and said, "That was lovely."

He sat down heavily and sighed. He told her what had happened, how real it seemed, how clear she was, this Folasade, of the pain he felt, the searing anguish that cut him, crushed him, as she faded away. In the moment, he could have sworn she was standing right here. Now, mere minutes removed, it was a dying memory as he, Zach, came to the fore of his mind. It made him see ego as an appendage that didn't really dwell there, it only rented the space. He shook his head and said to Emma, "I don't know what's happening to me, all these strange things this weekend. On the one hand I can explain them as merely creations of my mind, of an overactive imagination. On the other . . ." he let his words shove off from shore, bobbing in the surf. Emma was silent. He spoke again, "I feel like a personality in a bag, a body suit. This, me, Zach, feels like an adornment, like all the things that make up Zach are like clothes, or jewellery. Here on my wrist is the wristwatch memory of my second grade class, and here on my earlobe is an earring that is my junior year in high school. My pants are all that I know of what society has taught me on being a man, and how that has been personalized by Zach. A Zach. This thought or memory or whatever of Folasade has jangled me, shook me like a coin in a piggy bank, only the coin is me, but that part of me I'm not aware of, and the piggy bank is personality. But my heart still aches from seeing that woman, it burns with pain."

"Diggy thinks we all have past lives, we've all lived before," Emma said. "Do you believe that? Do you think you're having memories of some past life? A life lived here on this plantation?"

He exhaled loudly, "Sheeeewww. I don't know, I don't know," he said. "I just don't know anymore."

Emma noticed that the little glint of light in Zach's eye that signals he's alert and on call, the mischevious playful Zach, was out. But there was another light pulsing ever so faintly.

"Let's say that was a past life memory, that I, Mr. White Kleenex Middleclass Babyboomer Suburban Safari White Picket Fence man was a slave named Jubal 150 years ago. And I had a lover named Folasade, a beautiful black woman fresh off the ship from Africa. And apparently I was sold and had to leave her or she was sold. Does that mean I had other lives too? Why can't I remember those?"

"First off, it wasn't uncommon for families to be broken apart, husband and wife to be sold to different plantations, different owners, even theyuh children," Emma said. "As for othuh life times, why not? And what good would it do to know them, to remembuh them? What would you do?"

"I don't know, you'd think it might help you in this lifetime," he replied.

"What if we had the memories of all past lifetimes in us? Do you think one human would be able to stand it?" Emma wondered.

"An interesting thought. God, how could a human take it, all the memories of all the awful things we've done. We'd probably all kill ourselves, one big mass suicide," Zach said.

"Or we'd all love each othuh 'cause we know we're the same, like all the great teachin's say. How about one big mass love-in instayud?" Emma responded.

"I like that outcome much better," he said smiling and reaching for her. They embraced for a moment, then Emma lay her head in his lap, where she lay a long time, Zachary gently running his fingers through her hair. They spent the rest of the afternoon trying to coax stories from the oaks.

"Hi Daddy!" Emma gave her father a big hug, kissing him on the cheek. Always somewhat embarrassed by displays of affection, he stood it tolerably well, being less wooden than usual owing to the fact he was tired. Having arrived from Savannah some five hours ago, he'd been going through the items in the shed with Virginia since. He turned to greet Zach, "Hello Zachary. How are you finding your stay at Trieste?"

Zach smiled and extended his hand to shake the doctor's, "Great, Broderick. It's been great, like a vacation. How was your drive down this morning?"

"Usual, I'd say. Usual. Damned state government has too much money and needs to keep spending it on superfluous highway construction."

Sympathetically, Zach said, "I take it there were a lot of construction delays."

"As I said, usual. Usual."

Zach made further small talk with the doctor while Emma went over to Diggy, who was still helping out and gave her a very warm embrace. The intensity of her feelings gave way to a little tear, and her emotions took Diggy by surprise. "Why, girl, what's come over you? There, there now, it's okay. What is it, Emmy?" she asked.

"Nothing," Emma said, "Nothing, I just want you to know that I love you."

"I know that, honey, I know that. I love you too." She patted Emma on the back reassuringly. "Everything all right between you and Zach?" she inquired.

"Oh no, it's nothing like that. We couldn't be better. He really is wonderful," she replied, to which Diggy said, "That's great to hear. I'm really happy for you two." She didn't want to press Emma, so she didn't ask her any further questions. Emma's mother came up to the two women and said, "Well, you timed it just right, Emmy, we were about to quit and go inside for some drinks."

"Good, I've done enough cleaning out here for the weekend," Emma replied.

Virginia said to Diggy, "You're going to come too, aren't you?" Diggy said it sounded very refreshing, she'd join them for drinks, but declined the extended dinner invitation as it was Sunday; she needed to spend time with her family.

They made their way up to the house and sat on the screened-in porch at the back of the family quarters. An overhead fan kept them cool while Broderick mixed gin and tonics for all.

"What is that extraordinary smell?" Zach asked aloud. Emma told him, "That's momma's ham she been cookin' all afternoon."

"It doesn't quite smell like ham," he said.

"Well, it isn't normal ham. She takes a country ham, you know what that is, don't you?"

"That's the real salty one, right?"

"Yes. She buys one of those, a whole one, and soaks it in a bathtub for about a week. That takes a lot of the salt out of it. Then she rubs it with her special honey and molasses mix, and cooks it slowly for hours. It's really something."

"Sounds like it," Zach said, then turning to Diggy, "You're going to miss that?"

She smiled at him and said, "I've had it before, it really is delicious. I'm sure you'll love it."

Having just come back from checking on her ham, Virginia said to Diggy, "Oh, Diggy, did you tell them about the chains? She just loved them, she thinks they're a great thing for the museum, and she thinks the papers have historical significance."

The two young people were silent, taking refuge in their drinks.

"Here you are, dear," said Broderick as he handed Virginia a drink. He sat down, and after getting himself comfortable, said to Emma and Zach, "Diggy thinks the bill of sales will help a lot of people trying to fill out their family tree. Since no records were kept of slaves except for these receipts, it will be a great help. Birth records were virtually unheard of until after the turn of the century. For black citizens, that is."

"How far back do the records go?" asked Zach.

Diggy spoke, "A cursory look over them indicates they cover roughly the 1800's to 1830's, a thirty year period. But I haven't had time to really study them closely. Hopefully, they will have a broader sweep,"

"And the chains?" he asked.

"What about the chains?" she said.

"Well, um, what do you think of those?" he asked. He was uncomfortable; it was difficult for him to look her in the eye and talk frankly and candidly about an object that so clearly represented the subjugation of blacks by whites.

She put him at ease with her response. "Oh, they'll be a great addition to our collection in the library, what we call our "Life on a Georgia Plantation" exhibit. Our prize specimen has been a first edition printing of the famous book by Fanny Farmer. That's where we took the name from, her book. The chains will sit right next to it, I would think."

Conversation turned to the booty of the shed, and for the next twenty minutes, they discussed things that would go to the museum and things that the family would keep, and the children could look through for anything they might want. At length, Virginia got up to go into the kitchen again, and Broderick followed. Emma took the opportunity to ask Diggy for the papers, which she still had with her in a manila folder. While she leafed through them, she told Diggy what had happened to Zach while they were examining the stone piles at the old slave cabins. Diggy was very impressed, and told Zachary that he had a gift and should look to work with it, bring it out, define and improve it. Zach's response was subdued. He told her this was all new to him, that he felt it all a bit too strange. She got him to smile when she slapped his knee and said, "But you a brother now!"

Emma wasn't finding what she was looking for, so she handed the papers over to a laughing Diggy, and said, "You have to look at them, you're used to reading this old handwritten stuff. If it's not off a computer anymore, Ah can't read it."

"What are the names again?" she asked her.

"Jubal and and Folasade."

While she was looking through the papers, Broderick and Virginia returned to the room bearing appetizers. Everyone crowded about the patio coffee table save Diggy, who was busy looking at the records. Emma's mother asked Zach what he had seen in Thomasville, and his answer and their subsequent conversation gave Diggy ample time. Eventually she announced, "I've got something." Emma's parents looked up quizzically.

"Look here," she said to Emma. She showed her the name of Folasade, scribbled as 'Full Sadie', and the entry of 'strong healthy young woman, 20 y.o.a., English bad'. At the end of the line was the amount paid for her, '$235'.

Emma said excitedly, "That has to be her. Is there a date?"

Diggy leafed backward through the delicate, crumbly yellowed papers until she found a date for all the entries at that time. The date was March 22, 1823. "She was probably bought in the spring for work in the upcoming planting season."

"Who was bought?" asked Virginia.

"Oh, no one momma. We just heard about this name and wanted to know if evuh theyuh was a black woman with a similar name at Trieste." With a furtive look to Diggy, she asked her to keep looking. Zach took shelter again in his nearly empty glass of gin and tonic, electing to get up and make another.

"Well, let's see," Diggy said, "We'd have to give them time to meet and fall in love, so we'd have to go forward in time to see if there is an entry on the selling of either of them."

"The selling of whom?" Virginia inquired.

"Nothin', momma. Just someone we read about somewheres."

Virginia contented herself with asking Zach if he'd make her another drink too.

As Zach sat back down after handing Virginia her drink, Diggy said, "There he is, October 27, 1823. 'Sold; large strong field hand, Jewball, to Henry Connery, $260.' Sold him after the harvest, it appears."

Emma and Diggy looked at Zach with knowing eyes, to which he responded by rolling his in his head and engaging Broderick in a discussion that ranged from hunting practices on the old plantation to breath mints.

After dinner that evening, Emma and Zach took a walk down toward the river to pay one last visit to that dark continent of mystery on the edge of the plantation. It was a quieter night over the water; perhaps it was too early, the creatures of the evening hadn't all woken or stirred for their night of feeding on each other. The two lovers were quiet. The dinner small talk had tired and bored them and the events of the weekend were weighing in too. They walked to the river's edge and took in one last breath of its wildness and sacred ineffability, one last sup of its proffered feral ambrosia to fortify Emma, and Zach, too, against the civilized version of a Darwinian mud puddle they would find tomorrow back at their jobs.

They soon returned to the house, having taken comfort and solace in the quiet walk and each other's presence, like old lovers. They bade each other a good night's sleep with warm embraces and a passionate kiss, then went to their separate quarters to retire early, intending to get up early and return to Atlanta.

When they got back to the city, they decided to spend the night together at Zach's so they swung by Emma's house to pick up some clothes for her to wear to work, finally arriving at his apartment in the late afternoon. Tired and sluggish from driving in what turned out to be a hot day, they prepared for nap. But before they did, Zach decided to play the one message that was blinking urgently on his answering machine. A voice he didn't recognize at first, and whom he was about to dismiss as a salesman, said, "Uh, yea. Hello. Is this Zachary Peterson? My name is Burly Olalla. I'm calling from Kansas. This isn't a joke, though it may sound crazy to you, but I got someone here who needs to talk to you. His name is Brer Rabbit. Give me a call." He then left a telephone number.

Neither Emma nor Zach felt much like napping.

chapter ten

"You don't look like y'all had a good weekend," Marty said to Zach as they sat in his office. "You sleep in a briar patch or somethin'? You all raght?"

"Yea. Yea. Born and bred in a briar patch," Zach replied.

"Do what, now?" Marty asked.

"Nothing, nothing. Never mind. I'm all right. Just didn't get a wink last night. Couldn't sleep, you know. Musta been the moon or something," Zach responded vacantly.

"Muh granny alwaiys said a person caiyn't git a good night's sleep on the full moon. Said they's too many spirits about," Marty said. "But come to think of it, weren't a full moon last night. It was just a little bitty slice a' pie."

"Well, must of been spirits anyway," Zach said as he slumped over his desk. It was true, he and Emma didn't get much sleep the night before. It wasn't that they were up talking, it was more shock and disbelief that had kept them awake. In lieu of counting sheep, he counted "Unfucking believables". They had finally drifted off around 3:30 a.m. The two bottles of wine they drank wasn't helping Zach much either this morning and he hadn't exactly split them with Emma. What was on his mind specifically this morning, aside from the obvious (possible) life of one particular rabbit, was the agreement he and Emma had made last night; they had to get to Kansas. They had called the number left by Burly Monday evening but there was no answer, so they were going to try again tonight. In the meantime, they were going to set up a trip out west as soon as possible.

"Hey, man. Can I get you 'nothuh cup a' coffee? Maybe that'll heyulp," Marty offered.

"Yea, that'd be great, Pudge. I appreciate it."

As soon as Marty left, Zach dropped his head back down on his desk. When he was awake and able, he'd go down to J.J.'s office and find out when he could take his vacation. All they needed was a week, but two would be better. Three better still.

Marty returned with two mugs of coffee for Zach. "Thought Ah'd save you a trip," he said as he set them on Zach's desk. "You're the best, Pudge. Karen's a lucky man, I mean woman," Zach corrected himself.

Marty gave him a dirty look for the unintentional slight. "Ah'll leave you for now, but Ah want to know what y'all did down theyuh in Thomasville," Marty said backing out the door. "Somethin' happened down theyuh, Ah kin see it in ya."

"Oh God! Oh God! How can this be?" Zach mumbled to himself as he set his head back down, not that he'd lifted it that far off the desk, just enough to swallow some coffee. His mind was a very murky, thick porridge of memories, dreams, real life events, imaginings and present thoughts. Somewhere in there was the twain of it all, the crossroads of two streams of consciousness, one real, the other not so real. He wasn't entirely sure which was which. Had he dreamed a phone call from Burly Olalla? Was that a memory of him and a rodeo, or some imagined event, a daydream? Brer Rabbit was a book he'd read. No, he'd seem him on a talk show, Oprah or Rosie O'Donnell, couldn't remember which. He'd seen a play about two slaves, Jubal and Folasade, a tragedy it was, starring Denzel Washington and Cicely . . . no, not her, someone else . . . he'd had a dream about finding some cat's cradle chains that belonged to Kurt Vonnegut, no they were awful chains that lashed out and tried to grab you, they were evil, they were possessed, they killed people, they were alien chains . . . where was his lucky rabbit foot? He'd had it forever, got it at a circus . . . saw Burl Ives in a black and white movie about a swamp, Emma was in it . . . where was he this weekend? Where did he go? He jerked his head up and momentarily wondered where he was. Of course, in his office, and he'd been down in Thomasville over the weekend with Emma. Wonderful Emma. Thoughts of her steadied him, he smiled and drank more coffee and remembered he had to steel himself for a meeting with J.J.

For the first hour and a half of his work day, Zach busied himself with drinking a lot of coffee and looking through his papers, trying to find an alternate reason for going to Kansas should J.J. not let him take his vacation so soon. He found a long dead proposal from a small TV station in Wichita that had asked J.J. to come up with a marketing plan to improve their ratings. At the time, two years ago, nothing came of it, they weren't able to pay the kind of money J.J. wanted. That was before Zach had arrived, and he suspected that J.J. was stretched a little thin back then and threw them a bid that he knew was too high. But now they could do it, and do it profitably. Armed with this as a backup, he readied himself and went to J.J.'s office.

J.J. was in true form, up and running on this first day of the business week. He was holding court with Gerdy, Matt Samovar, the firm's business manager, and his secretary Louise Coughlin, all the while talking long distance on his telephone to someone. For the first time he could remember, he was aware of the energy that J.J. exuded. It was visceral and palpable, almost too much for his drained and racked system. He could put a finger on it, tag it and name it. Seeing Zach, J.J. managed to smile broadly while engaged in two, maybe three, different conversations. He thought of coming back later, but with J.J. there might not be a later, and besides, he wasn't sure how long he'd be able to keep himself together as tired and wired as he was, so he took his position in line.

He sidled up to Gerdy. She turned to him and whispered, "God, Zach. You look positively awful. You and Emma fighting?"

"No, no, nothing like that," he said as quietly as he could. "Just a long weekend." She gave him a smirking smile of disbelief. To Gerdy, everything boiled down to personal relationships. Happiness, joy, sadness, satisfaction or anger were all a result of how well one was getting along with another human being, especially a lover. That may in some way explain why she never had a solid relationship; she looked for her needs to be met in another, he thought.

J.J. hung up the phone and asked Zach what he wanted, after asking how his weekend was. Zach didn't really have to respond as J.J. essentially had one long conversation running with himself all the time. But he did tell him that he needed to talk to him in private, to which J.J. said to hang around, he wouldn't be long with Gerdy or Matt and Louise.

Watching the manner in which J.J. quickly grasped situations and adroitly and adeptly dealt with them had always been one of Zach's favorite pastimes since coming to the firm, but it seemed like empty machinations right now. He just wanted to go back to his office and put his head down on his desk. He didn't have to wait long, thank god, as J.J. quickly dispatched everyone back to their respective offices. Zach wondered how this man had sex.

"Well, my boy," J.J. began, "You are supposed to come back from a long weekend looking refreshed, not like you've been out carousing with the commoners at a tavern."

"It's nothing like that, I just couldn't sleep last night. And it kind of brings me to why I'm here. J.J., I need a vacation. Do you think I could take two weeks soon?"

"How soon is soon? And where are you planning to go? Europe? Africa? Sailing?" he asked.

"Next week and out west."

"Next week, next week, out west, next week . . ." J.J. was rubbing his chin, a good sign to Zach that he just might agree.

"How close is the Bradford account to being completed?" he asked.

"There are some stumbling blocks. I'm trying to get someone to move to a town they don't want to live in, then I can offer a job to another person, who would have to be convinced a lateral job switch would be an improvement, and they'd have to move as well. These people just need some time to make up their minds." He wasn't exactly lying, but he wasn't giving full disclosure either. J.J. didn't have a fast response, which was a bad sign. Worse yet, he told him he'd have to think about it and let him know later, perhaps today but possibly tomorrow. Zach thought of pulling his trump card, but thought it better used as a last resort. He'd wait until J.J. came to a decision. He was certain that he would bite on the idea of a working vacation, though Zach didn't really want to have to think of work and Brer Rabbit. And Brer Rabbit. That sounded so strange here in the office under fluorescent lighting with all the monitors and TV's that were always on and the computers. He and Emma thought the phone message had been a joke, then they wondered, how in the devil did Burly Olalla know anything about Brer Rabbit and Zach? Who would have called him and told him that Zachary Peterson had dreamt or visited or daydreamed about Brer Rabbit? Big Mama? Diggy? Anyone in the church? That was as implausible as the very idea of Brer Rabbit running around in Kansas. And Burly Olalla didn't sound like he knew who Zach was, like he didn't remember they'd met at the bull riding event the past winter or that he had invited Zach to visit. Well, now he was going to Arkansas City, but not for any reason he could have imagined. No, a hoax by Mr. Olalla just didn't make sense, not that any of it did. In the end, he and Emma just had to follow through with it, and if Zach had to make it a working vacation, so be it.

Returning to his office, he found a message on his voice mail. It was Emma. She had been able to get the time off with no difficulty, in fact, it worked out better for her to take her vacation now rather than later.

He returned her call, and by good fortune, she was still in her office. "Hey," he said to her, "It's me. That's great, you got the time off, so we're half way there. J.J. hasn't agreed yet. He has to think about it. I might have to make it a working vacation, though."

She was disappointed at the prospect, but was now so intrigued by the whole thing, true or not, about the possibility of meeting what may be Brer Rabbit, something right out of a fable, that it didn't matter how they got there, just that they got there. And soon. She hadn't of course told anyone per their agreement, who would believe them? but the more she thought about it that morning, the more excited she had gotten.

Zachary seemed a little less enthused. His world was coming apart, the world as he knew it and had been taught about, and which he had carefully nurtured and supported brick by brick with ideas, consciousness, perceptual focus and awareness, all guided by the force of his desire to have it conform to all that he could see and feel and know by rational thought and all he'd been told by other people. A great big edifice of reality supported by nearly every single person he had met in his life, their biases and prejudices, all the media; scholastic textbooks, radio, TV, especially TV and the nightly news. He could see now how it reinforced a view of life on this planet far from what's possible, from what may be a truer reality. And politicians and talk shows and ugh . . . it was depressing to him now, all of it. He seemed to be gripped by a fatalistic view now that all is not as it seems, so ALL really doesn't matter. In one long weekend a wrecking ball had smashed his kingdom of Zacharydom with its well-established bounderies that moved in and out of the realms of Americadom, TVdom, Wall Streetdom and dom and dom and dom. He had a void now that had been left by the exiting of that king and his subjects, the tyrant had fallen and chaos now ruled the land. Enter a newly appointed head of state, a jester in brown fur: Brer Rabbit.

Emma was so jazzed she talked right through Zach's dark cloud and said to give her a call after he and J.J. talked next, otherwise she'd meet him when he swung by to pick her up. She had to go, lots to do, gotta move, see you later and I love you . . .

She hung up. He was stunned. Had she ever said "I love you" to him? No. He'd remember if she had. A little bit of white perked up in his black existential angst. That felt good, that felt like something to hear again, worthy of a return trip, made it better to be here now. That could give him reason to live. Smiling, he set about to work, if only to get through the day so he could ask her to repeat that.

The afternoon found Zachary sleepy and drowsy. It was hard to keep his head up and no amount of coffee would help. Only a nap would do. He'd had a lunch of meat and potatoes that was adding to his drowsiness. He and Marty had gone to the old standard, though he hadn't returned the flirtations of the waitress, which irked her. Over lunch he told Marty only about working in the shed, the cleaning, dusting and moving, and finding the chains and the register of names. He told him about the church shout but only so far as the dancing and singing, making it sound like a lively Baptist meeting, which was familiar to Marty, a Southern Baptist himself. Of rabbits and Folasade he said nothing.

As is often the case for those who seek naps, when he was about to join the company of Lord Nod, J.J. burst through the door, a pot of coffee not offering as much buzz as he.

"I have the most splendid news, my young executive," J.J. said, calling Zach a title he was not aware he was promoted to. "I just got off the phone with Sheldon Turner who owns stations in Wichita and Kansas City. Two years ago he came to me with a proposal that I couldn't take on at the time, he was too small for me to handle. Wasn't cost effective, you know. He hired someone else, but they didn't get the job done right. He still wants us to do something for him so I told him I was sending my best man out to take a look. Congratulations Zachary my boy, you've got three weeks to spend out west starting Monday. Use the time as you may." He threw a pile of papers on Zach's desk that had the usual demographic information, Arbitron ratings and such, and was gone like a gust of wind. Zachary didn't even have time to thank him. He sat in his chair and looked at the papers, feeling like he'd witnessed the entire episode from the vantage point of the ceiling. He pulled the pile of papers closer, set his head down on them, and fell asleep.

Two and a half hours later, his creaking office door woke him from a deep sleep. It was Marty bidding him good evening, it was five o'clock and time to go home. "Oh, sorry man," he apologized.

"No, no, thanks for getting me up. I would have slept longer. That's the way to spend the work day," Zach said sleepily. "Time to get up and go home."

"Yea, get some sleep for a change. And don't go sleepin' in no briar patch."

Eight days after setting off for Thomasville, Zach and Emma were on the road again. This time they were heading west to Alabama. At Birmingham they would cut northwest up to Memphis and catch Interstate 40, taking that west to Oklahoma City, then north, cutting back east to Ponca City, head up to the north end of Kaw Lake and once in Arkansas City, head east again out to Burly Olalla's ranch. Leaving Georgia, Zach was singing along with Randy Newman from his album, 'Good Ole Boys'. "Birmingham, Birmingham, the greatest city in Alabam', you can travel 'cross this entire land, there ain't no place like Birmingham." Emma didn't care much for the album, "a Yankee vision of the South," she called it, and had him turn it down a little. She didn't want to dampen his good spirits, they were infectious. She was feeling just as good as he was but the reasons may have been slightly different. All vacations or trips away from work begin in high moods, or should, at least. She was feeling incredibly excited because she was taking the first steps of a grand journey into the heart of something marvelous and mysterious, something unknown, like the Okefenokee swamp. She was bang off the high board, look out gators below. Zachary had been in a great mood the day she had told him on the phone that she loved him, and repeated it to him that night. He told her he loved her too, and they left it there. They were slightly stunned like lovers often are when they first confess love, minds race to say something but what can be said after an admission like that? The awkward, though tender moment, didn't last long; they hadn't explored betrothal or living together. They didn't have time because the phone rang and interrupted them. It was Burly calling again.

He wasn't sure he called the right number the previous call, and given the rather unusual nature of the message, wanted to hand deliver it, so to speak. He remembered Zachary after Zach told him they had met before, at the bull-riding meet. After exchanging normal human pleasantries and observing social proprieties, he brought to the phone a most un-human conversant.

"Dat you, Zachree? I'ze monstus bleedzed w'at t'ere fum you," a not unfamiliar high-pitched voice said. "Dis mos' kuse place. Buhly got mo 'ventions en machines den I kin e'er 'magun. You comin' ter visit?" At first, Zach hadn't responded, it was a bit of a shock; he didn't necessarily believe it to be true. Emma was on a second phone and had to urge him to respond.

"I'm glad to hear from you," was all he could muster until Emma prompted him again. "Umm . . . where did you go? Where's Brer Fox?"

"I dunner, I 'speck he home er up t'Miss Meadows en de gals, since I ain't roun," Brer Rabbit replied. He then went on to tell Zachary how he came to be at Burly's ranch. He started to go into the part of the story where the coyote showed up but Burly cut in on the line. He'd learned a lot about Brer Rabbit in the short span of time he'd been with him and Burly was not about to let him talk long distance as long winded as he was. Burly, Zach and Emma then began a brief conversation of what course of action to take. They could arrive at no other solution than the two had to come out to Kansas, pick up Brer Rabbit, then go back to the church in southwest Georgia, and do the shout again. Or something like that. It was rather vague to them that anything could work, but they felt obligated to return Brer Rabbit to the South, and beyond that plans were a big empty hole. They told Burly they'd be out as soon as possible and got directions.

The next day they were able to call and tell him they would leave Saturday morning. Burly said the timing was right, he'd be in Oklahoma City for a rodeo that weekend, but would be home no later than Sunday afternoon. There wasn't much of a chance they'd arrive before him, if they did; Donovan would be there to let them in.

Emma hadn't forgotten the conversation she and Zach had before the phone call from Burly. She had come to realize she was in love with Zach and when talking to him Tuesday afternoon, had merely added it the list of things she needed to do that day, 'Tell Zach.' It was a fact that had crept into her over time, like a shadow creeping across the yard. She hadn't added up things she liked about Zach and arrived at the sum of I love Zach. The feelings had grown, naturally, over the course of the months they'd know each other, at one point in time she hadn't loved him, move forward and then she did. She now held it like she held other matters of fact and she moved forward. And now she was going to move into this issue of Brer Rabbit with the same quality of acceptance and assurance. Once upon a time there was this story of Brer Rabbit, and now there is a Brer Rabbit, or someone doing a damn good impression. She'd know when she saw him and she would be ready for it. For Zach, she wasn't so sure. But as she looked over at him singing away as they headed toward Birmingham, it didn't matter. She looked at him with the growing confidence that she'd found that someone she was going to move through this adventure called life with. And they sure were off to an interesting start.

The first day of driving they reached the eastern edge of Oklahoma, pulling into a motel around 8:00 that night. It had been a long hard day of driving because they wanted to get out west as quickly as possible. They only stopped for gas and bathroom breaks, and ate fast food they bought from drive up windows.

They hadn't talked about anything serious that long day of driving either. Oh, they'd sung along to an endless supply of music CD's and had remarked on things of interest they'd past, but they crept around the subject of love, and there was only one long conversation on any one topic, and Emma hoped it was *not* illuminating. When they drove through Tupelo, Mississippi, birthplace of Elvis, Emma wanted to stop, Zach didn't. His attitude reminded her of her father. Zachary saw a bloated, self-possessed druggy, not the Sun recording phenom, a black leather in your face establishment rebel. Her father saw in Hemingway a sports writer and animal killer, the Great White Quixote of the Serengeti, not the writer of 'The Old Man and the Sea'. She mentioned 'The Education of Littletree', a book they read together, and Zach saw a drunken white supremacist. The author mattered to him, not to her.

Journeys often begin with a phosphorous fizz and good-natured bantering. Singing, cajoling and carefree wind in your hair whirling laughing high spirits got the road peeling away underneath, stripping away the workday coat of blue and iron spine-blackboot-kick-butt-sunburnt-skin-radioactive-glow-tavern-pale-ashen-smile-deadhead-life-goes-on-give-me-breath-again-momma-I'm gonna make it now. But: the road wears on and the traveler tires and doubt skirts around on the outslinks of thought. Ego ergo ergot.

They made love that night in the motel room, but it lacked the intensity of previous times, it almost seemed perfunctory to Emma. Her mind was on father, Elvis, Ernest, Zachary, Burly and Brer.

They slept in the next morning, having driven so far the previous day they felt they could get up to Burly's in half a day's drive, and they didn't want to get there before he got back from his rodeo. They wanted to meet everyone at the same time in case of . . . what, they didn't know. Fraud, deceit, lies, or worse- truth.

Zach rose to look out the window into the parking lot of their non-descript motel, one of thousands in a chain. The sunlight forced him to squint. "These places never look as good as they do at night when you're tired," he said. He was looking out at the American Interstate System; gas stations, fast food and fast motels. "Ah, America," he sighed, then climbed back into bed and snuggled with Emma.

She rolled over and with her eyes inches from his said, "Zachary, don't turn in to my father. Don't start looking at the world in black and white. Everything's a rainbow." She turned back over and pushed her hips into his. He put an arm over her and held her close around her breasts. He didn't respond; her comment had no context for him. He wondered if she was talking about a dream she had. They lay quietly nestled together until her breathing deepened, and she fell off into sleep again. Zachary lay still, thinking about her statement until he finally drifted off.

They were awakened an hour later by maids knocking on the door. It was nearing ten o'clock, time to hit the road again. They showered and packed what little there was to throw in the car, and drove over to a nearby restaurant for a quick breakfast. After that, Zach filled up his Ford Explorer with gas and got a mug of coffee for himself. Getting back in the truck, he threw a cassette tape on the dashboard that he'd bought inside. It was a best of Elvis collection. He said to Emma, "It's a rainbow." She looked at him and beamed. He was a quick learn, she knew why she loved him.

Less than two hours later the land changed. They were leaving the great forests of the east and entering the great treeless plains. They felt they were finally out west as the rolling hills flattened out and the horizon stretched out for miles. Emma popped the Elvis collection into the stereo system, and they cruised on, singing along with Elvis.

They had misjudged the amount of time it would take to get up to Burly's from the motel they'd stayed in, and it was closing in on six o'clock by the time they got to the Kansas state line. They thought it would be another hour at most to get to his ranch. It had been a warm day driving, and they had the windows down, with silence on the stereo. They hadn't listened to anything for the last two hours. Zach had done all of the driving, and Emma had just woken from a nap an hour ago.

They were quiet, but as they drove into Kansas, anxiety was knotting the air. Following Burly's directions, they passed through the town of Arkansas City heading east until they came to the little crossroad he told them about. They took the right and followed the road as it curled around and swept northeast across the nearly treeless expanse. Just past an old cottonwood stump, still standing some dozen feet off the ground, all one huge round barrel of a trunk, they turned left at the rusty old mailbox, and drove down the one lane road, past a trailer, and stopped behind Burly's old white Ford pickup. They'd made it.

There was a path made of large flat stones leading to the front door, but it had not been used much, judging from the weeds growing at the base of the front stoop, so they went around the side of the house, fearful of dogs and full of anxiety for what they hoped to meet.

chapter eleven

"It's all right, Brer Rabbit. It's all right. He won't hurt you." Burly's words soothed Brer Rabbit's nerves, at least temporarily. He relaxed and set back on his feet. His attention was now focused solely on the penguin. He'd never heard of any such creature as this in all the stories he'd run across. It was about the same height as him, though his own big ears made him seem taller than the black-jacketed figure. His waddling gait was a very curious manner of walking indeed and Brer Rabbit would have laughed had he not thought it rude. The penguin's flippers were an oddity too. Along with the bill and webbed feet, surely this was a bird. But it had no feathers! Its wings were like a fish's fins. "Dis mos' kuse creetur," he said to no one in particular.

"Bart, say hello to Brer Rabbit," Burly asked of the penguin. The penguin, still some six feet from them, spread his wings and nodded his head vigorously up and down while making all kinds of yodels and gronking noises. He made little leaps of half a foot towards them as he did so, bending his head and arching his back, then with a great effort jumping forward with his webbed feet splayed out in front of him. Having the creature come at him in such a cacophonous jangly manner startled Brer Rabbit, who instinctively stepped back a foot. The penguin stopped two paces from him and kept up his chattering even as Brer Rabbit spoke. "I'ze happy to meet yo 'quai'uns," he said, and stuck out a paw for a handshake. The penguin didn't respond, just kept on chattering away.

Burly said, "He's happy to meet you too. He's very excited to meet another intelligent animal."

"Why don' he say so?" asked Brer Rabbit.

"He doesn't talk with his, um, mouth. He has no vocal chords for it. He talks using computers."

"Computers? Is he dumb?"

"No, no. Just different. You'll see. I think you two will get along fine. He lives down there in that storm shelter. It's cooler down there. You see, he's a penguin. They live in a very cold climate down in a place called Antarctica," Burly explained.

"Dat near Lanta?" Brer Rabbit asked.

"No, far from Atlanta. Thousands of miles from Atlanta."

"Hmm," responded a very studious Brer Rabbit. He struck a thoughtful pose, with one paw resting on his chin, the other arm across his chest. "Well," he announced, "Less ha'e some mo un dat beer." With that, and showing complete disinterest in Bart, he turned and headed for the house, the penguin chasing after him trumpeting and gronking.

Back in the kitchen, everyone sat around the table drinking beer, all except Bart, who stood next to Brer Rabbit, watching his every move.

"Buhly," Brer Rabbit asked, "Why don' he ha'e un beer wif de res' un us?"

"He's never had a beer, I don't think it would be good for him," Burly responded.

"Dat ain't right," said Brer Rabbit, who rose and got a beer, opened it up and before Burly could get around the table to stop him and put it in the penguin's bill. Bart leaned back and gulped it down quickly, letting the bottle fall on the table when he finished.

"Damn," Burly cursed. Donovan laughed; he thought it all funny and surreal.

Brer Rabbit smacked the table with his paw, "Dat de way un man does it!" he shouted. "Get he nudder un!" But before anyone could, little Bart teetered on his feet and toppled over on his back, out cold.

Brer Rabbit let out a howl of laughter, along with Donovan, while Burly rushed over to aid the poor penguin.

That was the end of Bart's drinking days, as far as it went with Burly, he vowed not to let Brer Rabbit in the kitchen alone with Bart anymore. In fact, he thought he'd just let the beer run out and not buy anymore. They could all do without it.

Over the course of the next several days, Burly brought Brer Rabbit into the 20th century with all of her technology. The rabbit quickly realized the value of automobiles and tractors and trucks and before long he not only learned how to drive them, to the regret of Burly, he found where Burly had taken to hiding the keys, which led to one unpleasant night when Brer Rabbit drove his truck into a ditch a mile from the house. The night was further compromised by Brer Rabbit's insistence on driving the tractor to pull the truck out of the ditch. He claimed he never saw the car that ended up in the ditch trying to avoid the tractor. Whether the driver drove off the road because of what he saw driving the tractor, or Brer Rabbit forced him off, no one knows for sure to this day. The man was seen heaving beer bottles from the scene of the accident, however, according to Brer Rabbit.

Brer Rabbit thought the phone a marvelous invention too, along with the yellow pages, and soon there were pizza deliveries made twice a day. Burly soon put an end to that and it helped that Brer Rabbit lost interest in the phone when he realized he couldn't call Brer Fox and brag. He was very disappointed that Brer Fox wasn't listed in the phone book, nor was Miss Meadow's place. One time he called a local motel, the Black Bear Lodge, and asked for Brer B'ar. The owner, an immigrant from India, couldn't understand his accent, and Brer Rabbit couldn't understand his. They went round and round until the owner hung up, but not before he had the call traced. The police warned Burly about obnoxious phone calls, but didn't cite him. Another time he managed to call Murdo Bay in Antarctica, trying to call some of Bart's relatives. The scientist on the other end hung up soon after Brer Rabbit asked to talk to any penguin that might be hanging out there, but the call still cost Burly $75. From that point on, the phone was locked in Burly's bedroom.

Other modern day implements and gadgets held his curiosity briefly, like the toaster, the oven, electric shaver and lights and the refrigerator (a favorite), but none held him captive like the television. If he could have dreamed, he couldn't have come up with a more incredible and wonderful machine. He would spend hours in front of it, flipping through channels at breakneck speed, trying to take it in all at once. At first, he thought he was being tricked, that someone was inside it. When an advertisement showed horses running in an open field, he thought he was being conjured, that someone shrank the horses, and he went flying out of the house and ran plum into Burly's mother, who had come up to the house to drop off some baked goods for her son. She shrieked, dropped the platter of cookies and rolls and ran back to her trailer. She had not been informed about her son's house guest. They met later that day when Burly properly introduced them, though whether she truly felt connected to the moment is still a question to Burly. She doesn't ask about the rabbit. Ever.

The other gadget that the rabbit found fascinating was the computer. Specifically, the one in Bart's storm shelter. Burly had a large keyboard made that could be operated by Bart's flippers. The letters and numbers were especially large, the board itself was roughly the size of a card table cut in half. Brer Rabbit soon learned how to use it and it wasn't long before he was able converse with Bart and to log on to the internet, much to Burly's unhappiness. Brer Rabbit and Bart talked for hours down in Bart's little cave, though Brer Rabbit could only stay down there for a couple of hours at most. It was too cold for him. Bart could operate the temperature controls himself, and kept the air conditioning running all the time from spring to fall. Burly had also hauled a used ice machine down there that he'd bought from a gas station and the constant production of ice helped keep the temperature around 45 degrees, still warm by penguin standards.

Brer Rabbit found out that Bart was not a natural penguin, not by birth. To his horror and dismay, he learned that Bart had been genetically altered by scientists in an experiment at the University of Oklahoma. As best he could understand it, they had done 'conjun' on his egg when he was yet hatched. The result was a super intelligent animal, a penguin that they could talk to, could teach, an animal that could reason with them. Bart told Brer Rabbit that as he got older, he became depressed when he found he could not talk to other animals. Either they wouldn't talk to him, or he could not find a way to talk to them. His depression deepened and he soon stopped communicating with the scientists at the university and wouldn't do the tasks and experiments they required of him, so they sold him to a small zoo, which in turn sold him to a small road side attraction in Texas, where Burly found him.

Scientist was a new word for Brer Rabbit and he lumped it into the category that included conjurers and witches and others working magic, good or ill. They were to be avoided at all cost.

As Burly had predicted on that first day they met, he and Bart became pretty good friends, spending a lot of time talking via the computer and cruising the internet, which Bart showed him how to do, and they drank beer that Brer Rabbit obtained from Donovan. Bart soon was able to build up a little tolerance for it, but he couldn't stomach the tobacco Brer Rabbit cherished. He vomited the first time he tried some chew, pretty much the same reaction Brer Rabbit had when he tried to eat a raw mackerel offered by Bart.

The internet was another world for Brer Rabbit. It was an interactive encyclopedia and TV to him. He read up on all things modern and past. He was shocked to discover wars and bombs, shocked to discover how people treated each other, 'wif no 'spect'. The discrepancy between rich and poor was too vast a chasm for him to fathom. It was perhaps an even bigger surprise to him to find that man had flown to the moon and landed on it. He tried, but he just couldn't accept the fact that man had walked on the moon, and his suspicions were heightened by the fact that the 'assronots' hadn't brought back anything to eat. That made the whole thing unbelievable. He also discovered tales about himself and Brer Fox and the whole gang, in a book by a man named Harris. Unless the tale was flattering to him, he called it a damn lie. But some of them were so true that for a several days he was absolutely incapacitated by paranoia, convinced that he was being followed and watched by some evil and malignant forces. It took a lot of effort, a lot of talking and convincing and educating by Burly, Donovan and Bart, to teach Brer Rabbit about literary license and fortuitous story telling that happened to capture the essence of events. In the end, it was Brer Rabbit's short attention span that really helped him recover, though a lingering distrust still shaded his natural wariness.

It was, God willing, another discovery that led him from the path of debilitating paranoia, and perchance with a nod to his species proclivity for regeneration, his favorite web sites were pornographic. He was seduced the first time he stumbled on such a web site, and rarely watched TV in the evenings with Burly and Donovan again, preferring beer at Bart's and the web. He began signing up for free trials to hundreds of such web sites, and in filling out the forms to obtain such a trial, always gave out Burly's phone number. Soon, poor Burly was beset with the overly aspirated voices of women breathing into his phone at all hours of the day and night. It was this little matter he and Burly were discussing when Zachary and Emma drove up to the house.

"But Buhly, dem gals is de fren'liest I nodes. En dey say de mo's aw'dashus tengs," Brer Rabbit was arguing.

"I don't care, I don't want them calling my house. I don't care what you waste your time on, just don't give out my phone number," Burly said in agitation. "And I'm going to take the voice card out of the computer that Bart put in."

"But den dey won' lemme in t'de site. Dey keep axin fo un credit ca'd, en I don' know what dat iz. Duz you got one?"

"Absolutely, positively, no way." Burly shuddered involuntarily at the idea of Brer Rabbit obtaining his credit card.

"Den you got one? Less see it. Buhly, ain't you my fren?" Brer Rabbit would play any angle he could. Not getting any response he pressed on. "Buhly, ain't I bin a good fren fo you. Din't I chase dat coyote feller 'way?"

"I like that coyote 'feller'. He's good medicine."

Feigning hurt, knowing full well Burly's feelings and thoughts about Coyote, Brer Rabbit put on a shocked expression, "You in c'hoots wif dat vilyun, dat's what's going on behime my back. You en he is fix'n t' put ole Brer Rabbit in der pot er bawl'n wadder, ain't dat so?" he accused Burly.

"Oh, stop it, you know that's not true. What's this got to do with Coyote?"

"He done try t' et me."

"All right, all right. But you are not getting my credit card. That is final."

But the cat was out of the bag, and Brer Rabbit was already plotting a way to obtain the cherished item. He was slumped down on the back porch steps like a scolded child when Zachary and Emma walked around the side of the house. Burly, standing in the doorway to the kitchen, vaguely recognized Zachary.

"Zach'ree!" hollered Brer Rabbit. In one giant leap he launched from the steps and landed right in front of them, giving them quite a surprise, since they had been at least ten feet from him. Brer Rabbit gave him a big hug, while Zachary's return embrace was less than enthusiastic, as if he was hugging a beehive. Emma's eyes were wide as the Kansas sky with a smile to match. Noticing her staring at him, Brer Rabbit broke off his embrace of Zachary and spoke to her. "Dis mus' be Emma. You de perdiest 'oman I e'er seed, I mos bleedzd t'meet yer," he said graciously. He moved to shake her hand, which she accepted, but then she opened her arms for a hug, which pleased him greatly. His ears spun in joy. After a long hug that skirted embarrassment, she pulled her arms away. Brer Rabbit's eyes had softened considerably from the initial excitement they had held upon seeing Zachary. A familiar wisp of discomfort of a sexual nature nudged her.

"Zachary and Emma, welcome to my ranch. I'm Burly Olalla," announced Burly as he walked toward them, his hand stretched out in greeting. He was truly glad to see them. For their part, Emma and Zach stood grinning like Halloween pumpkins.

Tired, road weary and suffering from a mild case of shock, the two travelers were led to the kitchen where they were offered refreshments. Burly apologized for not having any beer on hand, but Brer Rabbit said he had some down in Bart's house. Burly was less then pleased to hear this bit of news, but was glad that his guests would at least get what they wanted, an ice cold beer. As Brer Rabbit was leaving to go get it, Burly asked him where he had obtained it. "Fum de innernet," Brer Rabbit lied, knowing he'd get Donovan in trouble with the truth.

As soon as he was gone, Burly said, "Well, the doubt I could hear in your voice when I talked to you on the phone can rest. As you can see, he is very real. Very, very real."

His two guests nodded their heads in agreement, glassy eyes staring at the door that Brer Rabbit had walked out through. "And now the question is what to do about him," Burly said.

Not responding to his statement, Emma asked, "What's he like?"

"Trouble," Burly said quickly, "He is trouble. He's got a knack for finding it. And if he can't find it, he'll create it. That's what he's like. When he first got here, I thanked the creator for his appearance, but lately, I'm not so sure. Maybe he's some kind of test for me. I don't know. What I do know is that he's got to go back. He doesn't belong here, we have to find a way to get him back."

Zachary spoke, "You said on the phone that we had to take him back to Georgia. What good is that going to do? We don't know where to take him. Say we take him to the church, what then?"

"I don't know," Burly said, "But he can't stay here."

"Is there anyone we can go to here that might be able to help us?" Emma asked.

"I haven't been able to think of anyone," Burly responded.

"No one, there's no one? How about a healer, or a medicine man, you know, a wise man or something," she continued.

"I don't know . . . I suppose I can ask my uncle when I see him. He's due to leave the hospital soon. He's just getting over cancer and I don't really want to excite him, but he might know what to do. He's up in Wichita right now."

"I have to go to Wichita for business sometime in the next two weeks. Maybe we can all go together," Zach said and as soon as he finished, Brer Rabbit opened the door with his arms full of beer, holding the door open with his body to let Bart in. Seeing the two strangers, Bart gronked and trumpeted loudly.

"It's okay, Bart, they're friends," said Burly.

Emma laughed and said, "Bart, the penguin. How cute!"

Zach said evenly, "Does it get any weirder?"

The penguin looked directly at Zach and said "Fuh-coo."

Burly couldn't believe that Bart had talked and he didn't want to believe he'd heard him say what he thought he just said. He asked him, "Bart, did you just swear at Mr. Peterson? Who taught you that? Bart!"

The penguin didn't respond, acting as if he hadn't heard him. Burly asked him again, "Bart, I know you can hear me. Who taught you that?"

In the meantime, Brer Rabbit had quietly slid behind Burly to remove himself from the field of candidates for teachers of rude English. Not that it would do any good. Burly quickly saw there could be only one such mentor for the penguin, one pedagogue in particular who was now offering him a cold beer. "Buhly, ha'e un code beer. Hit's nice en code."

"I think I will. I think I will. Brer Rabbit, you wouldn't happen to know where Bart picked up that phrase, would you?" he asked him.

"Pro'lly fum de innernet, er de tel'vishun. Daze mighty disperlite et times," Brer Rabbit said as innocently as he could while handing out bottles of beer. Donovan came in the door, ending the awkward moment. Burly introduced him and soon a lively conversation began. Brer Rabbit entertained the two guests with a highly embellished story of his escape from certain death by the coyote, though 'tis true the coyote's intentions were, after all, gustatorial. Bart joined in now and then with some well-timed grunts and gronks of approval while Burly busied himself warming a lasagna his mother had made a few days earlier.

After dinner, sleeping arrangements were made, with Emma and Zachary getting the spare bedroom, Brer Rabbit slept on the couch anyway since he stayed up late watching TV, while Donovan would sleep in a small tent he had set up in the yard. That settled, Emma and Zach thought it would be good to stretch their legs and take a walk. Burly declined the offer to join them, saying he had had enough exercise down in Oklahoma City working the rodeo. But Donovan went with them to make sure they knew where they were going, and Brer Rabbit went as well. Bart returned to his little shelter.

It was now dark outside. The moon was a sliver in a partly clouded sky, giving just enough light to cast faint shadows. They walked down to the barn and through a fence gate that led into the biggest pasture, where the buffalo were. It would be too dangerous to approach the herd at night without Burly, whom the animals knew and wouldn't harm; and they might recognize Donovan, but the odds weren't stacked enough towards safety, so they would avoid them. When the clouds parted and let the moonlight fall unmolested to the earth, they could see dark objects against the silvery grass a mile away. They walked in the other direction.

They were walking on a finger of a ridge that ran away from the barn for nearly a mile, flanked by shallow washes on either side. The moon was bright enough to give form to the small mounds of buffalo dung to be avoided. As they walked, Brer

Rabbit slipped a paw into Emma's hand, which she at first thought was sweet, but casually let it fall away when she remembered the uncomfortable hug he gave her. He didn't seem to notice; he was asking Zachary what brought him out here to Burly's. Zachary told a partial truth; he was here on business. He had to drive up to Wichita sometime, next week maybe, to do some work for his boss. Brer Rabbit asked him if Wichita was a big city, Zach said he didn't think so, not as big as Atlanta.

"Lemme go wif you, we kin ha'e un reglar jooblee, you me'un Emma," Brer Rabbit said. "I kin drive de cah, too. I got 'speunce now," he added.

"I don't know, I think we'll have to talk to Burly about that," Zach said. To further discourage him he said, "Besides, it will be pretty boring for you, you wouldn't have anything to do. Probably have to just sit in the car all day, for eight, maybe ten hours. Doesn't sound like fun to me."

"Den w'ats Emma goan do?"

"Uh, she's going to help me with my business," Zach lied.

"Well, den I kin des walk 'round en see how de lay er der land is," he stated.

Donovan started laughing, which incited laughter in Zach and Emma too. The idea of Brer Rabbit walking around downtown Wichita by himself, or with anyone, was a ridiculous picture. Brer Rabbit didn't know what they were laughing about, and as anyone else might, he thought they might be laughing at him, but he nervously twittered along with them.

They walked quietly for another twenty minutes until Brer Rabbit stopped dead in his tracks. His nose twitched from side to side while his ears cupped forward. Everyone stopped too, looking at each other with mild alarm.

"Dat coyote's round yer som'ers. I 'spect des down 'n dat li'l holler," Brer Rabbit said, pointing to a dried out creek bed some fifty paces ahead. He spat out some tobacco juice, then said, "He ain't lakly to bodder us none, being a cow'rd 'n all." Then he yelled out "Heyo, Mr. Coyote. I nose yer in dar. Come on oudder

der 'n quit yo swinkin roun' lak some varmint. You ain't projickin wif nobody. Come on 'n sho yo mis'bul se'f."

They waited breathlessly for what seemed like a long time, but nothing moved in the creek bed. Brer Rabbit picked up a stone and said, "I des chunk dis stone en give you a jollop er yo own med'sun," and threw the stone into the hollow, landing it near some short bushes. A reedy voice called out, "You missed me, you little graveyard rabbit. You're lucky you have some help there, or you'd be in my pot tonight."

The humans were stunned; they weren't sure what was going on. Brer Rabbit yelled back, "Don't let dat stop you, come on oudder hidin' en less see yo mangy hide."

"Why don't you come out here, if you're so brave? What's the matter, no buffalo to protect you? You little runt!" the coyote taunted. That infuriated the rabbit, and he started stomping his way toward the creek bed, rolling up his sleeves as he went. When he hadn't gone but ten paces, a dark form came hurtling out of the bushes, closing in on Brer Rabbit with incredible speed. Brer Rabbit paused, thought it better to re-evaluate the situation, and in two leaps was back in the safety of his compatriots. The coyote stopped and began to yell and howl with a mixture of laughter. "I knew you'd run like the rabbit you are. You better stay with your friends, little bunny, or you'll be in my Easter basket." Brer Rabbit yelled back, "I des din't wan' ter show you up in front of un 'oman. Word git out, en make it hard on yo po' soul."

"Ah, gee. Thanks. Come out here and let me thank you properly," the coyote snapped back sarcastically.

"You des better watch yo'se'f round dese yer parts, er you bound t' git in trouble," warned Brer Rabbit.

"Oh my, I'm scared. Why is it that every time I see you you're either with Burly or Donovan. You're never alone. Are you afraid of running into me? You better be, house hare, 'cause if I catch you again, you won't get away. I promise you that."

"You don't skeer me none, you ignunt fool. Hit take a mighty big man ter git der bes' of ole Brer Rabbit, en you ain't ha'f de man t'git de job done. Go on en swink oudder yer lak de snake you is. Go on y'varmint. Git!"

The coyote turned to go, and over his shoulder yelled out one final warning, "I'll go now rabbit, but you better not wander off alone. I'll be watching. I will be watching."

Donovan impulsively yelled, "See ya later, Coyote."

While Brer Rabbit looked over at him with surprise and anger, the coyote yelled back, "Hey Donovan, maybe we'll talk again."

"That'd be great, that'd be great," he said. Turning to Zach and Emma he said, "I can't wait to tell Burly, he's gonna love this. I talked to Coyote! I talked to Coyote!"

As they walked back to the house, Brer Rabbit was unusually quiet, wondering if he could trust Donovan now, maybe he was a spy for that Harris fellow. He knew he had to come up with some plan to remove Coyote from the field of play, or rather, remove himself from the menu.

When they got to the house they told Burly about the incident with the coyote. Burly beamed like a man met his maker. The legends and stories were true, man and coyote could talk as brothers. It reinforced his deeply held convictions that such was truth, and it brushed all of his ideas with a hue of verity, no matter how far fetched or related the notion. With images of ancient legends dancing through his mind he resolved that tomorrow he would go out and seek Coyote and talk to him, he surely knew many things. He would question him on tales and truth and the creator.

He didn't voice his thoughts, and his quietness was a call to bed for everyone. It had been a long day for Emma and Zach, a long two days and they were tired. Yet, tired as she was, Emma was all abuzz with energy, the life pulsing through her measurable in megakilowatts. She felt like a lighthouse for the disenfranchised idea, the odd thought and the lost notion. She was in her milieu now, surrounded by an intelligent penguin, talking coyotes and a live story tale with a bunny tail. Come you sailor on a mystical sea, here lies safe passage to the yonder shore. As she lay in bed next to Zach, she whispered to him, "We're finally in Kansas." Nearly asleep, he mumbled, "Goodnight, Dorothy."

It was not lost on Brer Rabbit that everyone seemed to be in their own little world, playing in their own little puddle, and that he was not the focus of attention now was not acceptable. No matter the event or situation, he, Brer Rabbit, always grabbed the headlines. Even back home, when all the animals held a town meeting, it was either about him, or they came around to needing his help, like the time they needed him to catch old wattle weasel, who was stealing all the butter in the spring house. Slumped down on the couch watching a late night movie, everyone in bed asleep, he didn't like the way things had drifted that night, away from him and towards that damned coyote. He needed to rid himself of the coyote, and his mind eased effortlessly into the intricacies of scheming and plotting. It comforted and soothed him to be on familiar ground, to be hatching a plan. It was spiritual in nature to him, it was prayer and meditation, and he soon fell asleep, cradled in the warm bosom of conspiracy, deceit and destruction.

With the pre-dawn light crowding out the stars, Burly slipped out the back door silently. Avoiding Donovan's tent set up to the back of Bart's shelter, he took a slight detour to the barn, then out into the big pasture. He didn't know where he might find Coyote, but he called out for him in his heart. When he got far enough away from the house, he'd call out aloud. He carried with him his sacred rattle; he would call and sing to Coyote to bring him to council. Burly had been torn between telling Brer Rabbit and not telling him what he was doing. He knew that if he did, Brer Rabbit would not want him to contact Coyote, he'd do his best to keep Burly from going, calling him a traitor or something like that. In his own peculiar way, Brer Rabbit would mess it up somehow. Of course, not telling him would produce the same reaction when he found out, and he surely would eventually. So in the end, he thought it best to not say anything.

He'd deal with the consequences later. And anyway, Brer Rabbit was going back to Georgia, Coyote would be staying around, better to be on good grounds with him, and besides, Coyote was his tribe's myth, Brer Rabbit's was somebody else's.

The morning dew soaked through his deer soled moccasins, which he'd worn for the quiet needed to sneak by the sleeping rabbit on the couch. The cold on his feet was invigorating, as was the morning chill. He was dressed ceremoniously, and wore only a long shirt, more like a robe, that had been decorated with symbols and signs. Around his neck he wore his sacred medicine bundle, and he carried his pipe to share with Coyote if he would have any of it.

He walked toward the area where Donovan and the others had run into Coyote last night. Not finding him, nor any fresh signs he could discern, he wandered further, letting his feet guide him. They would know if he could let go and let spirit guide him. He began to chant and sing and rattle a little as he walked, to release his mind as much as to call Coyote. His soft singing attracted the lone bull hanging out near the gate by the barn. That wouldn't do, Coyote would never come to him if the buffalo was around, especially since this was the bull that chased him off. So he scared the bull away by running toward him rattling and singing loudly. The buffalo turned and trotted back towards the barn, understanding he was not wanted. Burly quickly disappeared down a draw to further discourage the young bull.

He kept on down the draw for a couple of hundred yards. It widened out at the juncture of a rivulet where a spring issued forth from the ground. A small grove of cottonwoods had long ago taken root here, and some were enormous. This seemed as good a place as any, so Burly sat down next to one, laid his pipe on a red cloth, along with tobacco and some other sacred items, such as his eagle feather fan, and sang Coyote songs that his uncle had taught him.

He sang and prayed and chanted and called forth in his heart and in his native tongue for Coyote to come and sit with him, to bless him with his presence, to honor Burly with his council. Along with the rising sun, the singing and rattling warmed him, and he sang for an hour before stopping, listening to the wind for signs, as his uncle had also taught him. The wind sees everything, he remembered his uncle saying, and so it can tell you things if you listen. And it is a chatterbox, the wind is, it can't help telling everyone what it knows. If you want to keep something to yourself, don't let the wind know about it, do it indoors. But here he was outside, trying to hear what the wind knew. "Wind," he called to it, "Do you know where I might find Coyote this fine morning?"

In the silence that followed, he could discern nothing; maybe it was too early for the wind to be up, the sun hadn't sent it scurrying about. So he began to rattle and sing again, this time to the wind. Another quarter of an hour passed, he stopped to listen. Nothing. He began his Coyote songs again, concentrating on the words as he sang, the beautiful sounds of Kiowa rolling around the little hollow he was in, echoing off the great trees surrounding him. Sounds and words that but a hundred twenty years ago were carried on the wind on any given day, now to be heard only rarely, on special occasions, and on little pockets of land, like Burly's.

Burly sang and sang with his eyes closed, riding the rising and falling melodies of the songs. He did not hear the gentle padding of the coyote's feet as it entered the grove of trees and stood on its haunches to listen to him. After finishing one particularly pleasing song, he opened his eyes and was startled to see Coyote staring at him, not four feet away.

"That was beautiful," the coyote said. "I haven't heard those songs in a very long time. My ancestors are very happy to hear them. They thank you for singing them."

"Thank you," Burly said, stumbling a little with his words. "I'm pleased and honored. You, you can hear your ancestors?"

"Yes, their voices are as clear as the notes you just sang."

"Can I hear mine so easily?"

"Of course, you need only listen."

"Thank you for that teaching. I usually hear them when I am in sweat lodge, if I hear them at all," Burly replied.

"That is because you believe you can only hear them in sweat lodge, that the lodge is the only place you can really contact spirit, where they will speak to you. You think you have to create a sacred space in order to talk to your ancestors," the coyote said.

"But the lodge is still sacred?" Burly asked timidly.

"Very sacred. But so is this grove of trees. So is your barn and so is Bart's shelter."

"Then I can talk to them anywhere?"

"Oh yes. Anywhere. There is nothing that is not sacred."

This idea, though not entirely new to Burly (he'd heard his uncle say such things before), had been difficult for him to grasp. If everything was sacred, why bother with lodges and prayers and rituals?

"Then what is the point of building a lodge, of purification and offerings to the creator?"

"It helps you concentrate on the task at hand," came the coyote's response.

"And what would that be if not to pray and ask for healings and guidance from the creator and the spirits?" Burly asked.

"To clear your mind of all the clutter you fill it with."

"I see."

"Are you sure?" the coyote questioned.

"Well, you've just taken centuries of my people's learnings and teachings and minimized them. Said they aren't really necessary," Burly said with a small amount of agitation.

"That's right. Wholly unnecessary, and if I might add, some of them were downright ridiculous."

"Ridiculous!?" Burly said with more agitation. "Name one!" he challenged.

"This whole idea of having to go to another person in order that they might seek divine intervention on your behalf. That someone else has wisdom and you don't. And hanging by your flesh from a pole. Ugh! Well, it's not completely bad, my people have often been fed from some of your more dangerous forms of worship."

"You're not bashing Sundance are you?"

"No, I'm not. I'm talking about really hanging from a pole, not walking around one. No one does that anymore, or some other things that have long since disappeared."

"Like what?" Burly was curious.

"I'm not going to tell you, you might try them," the coyote demurred.

The coyote had irritated Burly to the point where the novelty of talking to him no longer interfered. Burly was not uncomfortable at all, in fact, he was a little agitated. He noticed the coyote didn't always move his thin lips when he spoke, though Burly still marveled at some of the forms his mouth took in order to articulate some of the words.

"Look," continued the coyote. "Times were tough years ago. It took nearly all of your people's efforts to stay alive. They had to work constantly to insure they had enough food and shelter. Can you imagine how hard it was to remove yourself from those kinds of constraints in order to hear the voices of the spirits and the creator?"

"Your point?" asked Burly.

"That is my point. The harshness of life created, even forced, harsh methods to gain wisdom. For some, I might add. Not all needed those disciplines to enter the realm of spirit."

"I thought everything is sacred?"

"It is. But many needed certain rituals and disciplines to break the veil, so to speak," the coyote explained.

"Are you saying some things work, and some things don't? Some are better than others to gain knowledge?"

"No. They all work."

"Okay. They all work but they aren't necessary? Is that what you're saying."

"Yes. Precisely."

"Then why do them?"

"You tell me," the coyote said while yawning.

"So we could all walk around and talk to the creator and the spirits. It's all the same. Seems a little too easy," Burly said with a little suspicion in his voice.

If the coyote picked up on his dubiousness, he didn't show it. "Works for me," is all he said.

They were quiet for a moment, Burly pondering the intent of this great trickster, wondering if he wasn't fooling with him. Changing the subject a little, he asked, "When you speak, you don't always move your lips, like you aren't really speaking. Why is that?"

"I'm not speaking. We could converse without speech, like our people did years ago. But your head is filled with too much noise, too much TV and such. You don't have the clarity needed to communicate without words."

"How would I achieve this clarity?"

"Throwing away your TV would be a start."

Burly muttered under his breath, "Brer Rabbit would go crazy."

The coyote's ears picked up on the mention of the rabbit's name. "That little flea motel is crazy. We'd both be better off with his carcass on a spit instead of on your sofa."

"Wait a minute," Burly said. "Brer Rabbit, or the rabbit, is a great figure in some people's mythology, like you are in our mythology and many other tribe's stories. Are you saying he isn't? To you he's just a rabbit, just food?"

"Well, it would be a sacred meal," grumbled the coyote. "We'll call it his Last Supper."

"You walk a fine line between blaspheming other people's myths and religious figures and not," Burly pointed out to the annoyed coyote.

"That's my job," he replied. "I exist in the marginal gray world between your civilization and the wilds. I trot in and out of your subconscious and conscious. Remember, all is sacred and nothing is sacred. That is truth."

"Oh no, not some zen koan or riddles or word plays. Yea, yea. I get it."

"I don't think you do. I'm the uninvited guest to your backyard barbecue," Coyote said.

"And you want rabbit," Burly said flatly.

"Precisely," the coyote replied, hissing the s. He then stood up and trotted off, leaving Burly sitting alone under the cottonwoods, listening to the wind again.

Walking back to the house, Burly was scolding himself for not asking the coyote the truth of some of the legends and tales surrounding this great figure of mythology. The creation myths, bringing fire to the people, the humorous tales surrounding coyote's sexuality. And what did he know of the creator? Was it possible to see, hear or talk directly to the creator of all? Had he done so? An opportunity blown, and furthermore, he'd upset him talking about Brer Rabbit. What was it about the coyote that reminded him so much of the rabbit? Maybe it was their intense dislike for one another. And after all, they both get in trouble a lot in the stories. And Brer Rabbit is a sort of trickster too. Maybe two tricksters is one too many, they just can't get along with each other, they are too much alike. When he was near the barn, he caught a whiff of bacon, and it reminded him he hadn't eaten nor drank anything yet today, and it must be past 10:00. Everyone will be wondering where he was, except for Donovan. He probably knew where he went.

chapter twelve

"Buhly! Er yo bin?" Brer Rabbit asked as he came through the kitchen door. "We uz et brekkus en all. Miss Emma en Donvun fixed up er mighty fine plate er bittle. Deys sum w'ats left in t'oven, en sum bullace pussuv's in de frigator."

"Thanks, Brer Rabbit. I think I will have some, I'm starving," Burly smiled and gave everyone a warm 'good morning'. They were all seated around the kitchen table, sipping coffee and looking bright and ready to roll into the day. Drinking Donovan's coffee probably had something to do with that, he guessed, Donovan makes it twice as strong as he did, more like espresso. Looking around, he asked, "Where's Bart? Not up yet?"

"He was here, but he went back to his house. He just left," Emma said. Her smile snagged Burly's eyes just as he was reaching into the oven to grab the warm plate of food.

"Ouch!" he yelled when he grabbed one of the hot oven grills. He quickly moved to the sink to run cold water over his hand. Emma had instinctively jumped up to help him and was pressed against him as they looked at the red grill lines on his hand. Last night he hadn't really looked at her closely and hadn't noticed her beauty. Perhaps she had been tired and road worn so she hadn't looked her best. Besides, he didn't really look women over like many men did, especially when the woman was in the company of another man. But God, she was beautiful. With her so close to him, he tried to avoid thinking about her attractiveness, not wanting to send any signals at all, knowing how sensitive women can be to men who show a sexual interest, but he couldn't help but be intrigued and captivated by the aromas and fragrances he was smelling. They were like little wisps of smoke that pulled on him, slender little tendrils stealing into his nose and seizing his brain. Her pale white skin, so soft looking, so sensual. And her touch, so gentle and caring. And the feel of her against him . . . was that a tingle he felt in his groin? Could she feel that? Better shake it off, don't think about it. "It's fine," he said, pulling his hand away. "I'll go put some aloe vera on it. I keep a plant in my bedroom. Thanks for your concern," he said somewhat brusquely. He looked at her for any sign of mutual feelings. If she had felt anything, she wasn't showing it, and all the better for that. The last thing he needed right now was to raise an issue like that with everything else that was going on. He turned quickly and went into his bedroom. When he walked past Brer Rabbit, he sent unseen vapors wafting over the rabbit, who caught the faint scent of something familiar which he couldn't place at first. It took him several minutes before he could categorize it, and the realization of who it was and what it meant sent shivers up his furry back. 'Coyote! That's were Burly went this morning, to see Coyote!' Nothing good could come of that, despite what Burly had told him, that coyote was strong medicine and held a place of honor in his people's history. 'I got history too,' thought the rabbit, 'if only a few day's worth, and that coyote is bad medicine for me.'

Burly soon returned from his bedroom, rubbing a piece of aloe vera on his burns. Everyone was sitting around the table chatting about the things they might do that day. It was decided that Burly would show them his buffalo herd as soon as he had eaten his breakfast.

As hungry as Burly was, it didn't take him long to eat his breakfast, then they all readied themselves for the walk, all save Donovan, who was going to do some chores for Burly while he entertained his guests. And despite the recent admonishments from Coyote, and the smell of the same on Burly, Brer Rabbit went along, to be near Emma more than anything else. He thought he'd be safe in everyone's company. On their way out into the fields, they stopped in on Bart, who showed them his computer, and to the awe of Emma and the seeming disinterest of Zachary, they talked to the penguin. Bart said he was sorry to Zachary for cursing at him, it was a slip of the tongue, he said, a natural reaction to a perceived slight. People laugh at us penguins, he explained. They think us cuddly and cute and we walk funny. My people have a long history. They live hard lives in awful conditions. Give us a break, he said. Get to know us, we're just like humans, just trying to get along in a tough, competitive world. Zach answered that he didn't take any offense, and didn't mean to give any either, he just hadn't run into too many penguins, certainly none that could talk. He'd take better care of what he said in front of animals from now on.

The lone buffalo bull was hanging around the gate by the barn when they came through it. Burly told them not to worry, it wouldn't harm anyone. Catching sight of Brer Rabbit, the buffalo snorted and shook his massive head back and forth. "Hey yo, Mister Buffo! How you come along?" Brer Rabbit greeted him warmly. From deep within the belly of the great shaggy beast, came a rumble that to the astonished people sounded all the world like "Okay." The party of four filed past the buffalo, with the humans smiling sheepishly and saying "Hello", and "Hey, how ya doin'." They didn't notice that Brer Rabbit hung back a moment, but he soon came bounding up to the group.

Moving out into the field, Zach struck up a conversation with Burly. He asked him how large his ranch was and how he got hold of it. Burly explained that the original ranch had been about 1000 acres, which had belonged to his dad, who made his living on the railroad. When his dad died it turned over to his mother and Burly, who had by then saved up enough money working rodeos and bought a couple thousand more acres from a nearby rancher who was getting too old to farm anymore. Since he didn't have any kids to turn the property over to, he sold it to Burly at a good price. Emma remarked that she couldn't imagine rodeo clowns getting payed that much, and Burly said he hadn't always been a clown. In his younger years he was one of the best at riding bulls and broncos. Bull riding didn't pay as much then as it does now, at least the big tournaments, the money was in horses. He also did a lot of ranch work busting horses. He wasn't married, and didn't drink much or gamble, he just saved his money, and the Great Spirit provided, along with a loan from a federal agency.

As they walked, they happened to come by the sweat lodge standing peacefully on top of a little hillock, just a sapling framed dome open to the wind that whistled some ancient tune through the equally ancient house of reverence, prayer and purification. Sacred space in a sacred landscape. The little pouches of tobacco ties attached to the limbs rocked and swayed and twirled in the wind, evidence of playful spirits engaged in an endless game of tetherball. Emma and Zach hadn't seen one before and asked Burly what it was. "It's a sweat lodge, where my people go for prayer and healing. You could call it our portable church," he explained. He went on to describe the process of heating rocks and bringing them into the covered lodge, then pouring water on them to release the heat of the rocks and let their prayers to the spirits rise with the steam, along with the tobacco smoke that would be used later on in the ceremony. "A lot of things can happen in a lodge. This is where Brer Rabbit appeared," Burly said.

"You mean he just showed up?" Zach asked.

"Yea, just materialized. One moment he's not there, the next we start hearing him talking," Burly replied. Emma said she would love to participate in one, while Zach demurred, partly to avoid God knows what showing up and partly because it sounded too hot and uncomfortable. Brer Rabbit didn't seem to care in the least; he'd been in one and didn't care to do it again. Not paying attention, he was preoccupied looking around for Coyote. He wasn't entirely sure this was all but part of an elaborate trick to trap him, but he felt safe with Emma and Zach. And, well, Burly had shown he could be trusted, but that coyote may have done some conjuring on him, turned his mind against Brer Rabbit without Burly being aware of it.

Burly told Emma he'd see about having a lodge, but he doubted it would be today because they'd drunk alcohol the previous night, and spirits usually wanted a full day for the alcohol to leave one's system before entering a lodge. But there'd be a time soon enough, since they were going to be around for a couple of weeks. Pointing ahead he said, "The main herd is over that high ridge. You can see the humps of some of them now."

Sure enough, they could see them, and once in awhile a tail would flick in and out of sight, chasing flies away. They walked up to the next hill to see better, though it was not as high as the ridge the buffalo were on the lee side of. They could see more of the great creatures though, and some of the animals were looking at them, having smelled their presence long before they saw them. The old bull, the protector of the herd, slowly trotted to the top of the ridgeline to get a better view. He knew one of the visitors was Burly; he wanted to see about the others. He'd also smelled the little brown one before, similar to rabbit, only different.

The bull's movement, and size, caused some nervousness in Emma and Zach. "Don't worry, he won't harm us," Burly said to comfort them. "He's never charged me before, nor anyone I've brought out here. He's just checking us out."

Conquering her fear a little, Emma said, "They're magnificent. God, they're awesome!"

Zach added a quiet, "They sure are. Jeez, they're huge. Hey, look! That big one is still coming. Do you give him sugar cubes, like people give to horses?" he asked Burly.

"No, I've never given him anything like that. I wonder what he's doing. He looks a little riled, I wonder what's disturbing him." He turned to look behind them and noticed the young bull standing back some fifty yards. "Why did he follow us? That must be the problem, ole Satanta isn't ready to hand over the reins of the herd to young Tonkonga just quite yet. He's going to chase him off. Let's move off down into this ravine and get out of the way."

The big bull was still some two hundred yards from them when they dropped down into the ravine. Burly said, "This'll probably do, but just in case they get going at each other, let's move in amongst those cottonwoods," indicating a stand of three large trees some fifty yards further up the draw. "When buffaloes start jousting, you don't want to be near 'em." Brer Rabbit didn't need any encouragement, he was nearly there, clearing ten feet with each jump in an easy lope.

The old bull, Satanta, broke into a gallop as he came down the ridge, increasing his speed when the small group started hurrying towards the trees. Turning around, Burly noticed the bull had veered off from the line to the young bull, and was heading straight for them. "What the devil has gotten in to him," he said aloud. "Hurry up, he's coming at us. He must be confused or something. I'll hang back to divert him."

"Like you did those bulls last winter in Georgia?" Zach asked.

"Same idea," Burly said as he turned and held his ground, looking directly at the charging bull and yelling as loud as he could. "Hey, Satanta! SATANTA! It's me, Burly!" He waved his arms and made all kinds of motions, all the while yelling out the bull's name, but to no effect. The beast kept on coming. Looking around, he saw that Emma and Zach were about fifteen yards from the trees, while Brer Rabbit was already peering out from behind one of them. Turning back around, Satanta was nearly on top off him, but looking directly ahead at Emma and Zach it seemed, legs pumping furiously, kicking up big clods of dirt with each stride, head lowered, ready for battle. Like the spirits had taught him, that had worked with the bulls, and that had made him such a success in the rodeo ring, he cleared his thoughts and projected his mind, his consciousness, his perceptions, to the buffalo's mind. He saw himself as bison, felt himself as bison, saw himself as bison bull charging at him as human, little frail human standing in the pasture, no bigger than a fat fence post, the earth moving fast under rumbling power, great surging strength and now two other puny humans running like turtles . . . I am now you buffalo . . . we are one . . . you are now me . . . I you me . . . we will turn. Feeling a successful psychic connection to the bull, Burly took the next step; he tried to turn the bull by seeing the landscape move laterally, change what the bull saw from him as human and Zach and Emma to the rest of the herd, by seeing them, the herd, flash in his mind, he would think of them, would want to return to them. Or at the least it would be enough of a distraction to confuse the bull, giving it pause, perhaps it would slow down, giving Zach and Emma more time. At least that should work. But there was no pause, no change in stride, no wrinkle in the bull's behavior. Satanta kept on coming.

One last time he yelled at the bull and then had to jump aside, the bull not even glancing at him. It didn't look like they'd make it to the trees in time, so he yelled, "Separate! It will confuse him." Which they did, Emma turning right and Zach turning left. If the maneuver confused the bull, Burly couldn't tell, it headed straight for Zachary like it had never a doubt as to its target. "Run, Zach, he's coming after you!" Burly yelled. Zach was moving as fast as he could, but even with a head start, he couldn't out run the charging bull. Burly knew he wouldn't make it to the trees. "On my mark, jump either right or left. Make up your mind now, just jump when I say," hollered Burly. "And don't look back, keep running!" Burly himself was running behind the bull as fast as he could. When it looked like the bull was right on top of Zach, he screamed, "JUMP!" Zach could feel the earth shake as the bull came on top of him, and hearing Burly yell, jumped as hard as he could to his right, losing his balance in the process. The bull went charging right by him in a cloud of dust. Too big to stop right away, the big beast had to turn in a large arc, but knowing that Zachary was trying to get to the trees, he turned toward them to try and head him off, and came roaring back toward Zach, who was getting back on his feet. Burly was still some twenty yards from him and, shouting, "Don't move, stand still. When he gets close, I'm going to yell again to jump. Make your mind up right now which way you're going to go. I'd suggest jumping to your left, away from the trees. He knows you're trying to get there."

Emma was by now in the safety of the trees, three large cottonwoods that grew closely together, close enough that the bull wouldn't be able to get in between them if he tried. She watched in horror as the bull bore down on Zachary, and she yelled as loudly as she could to try and distract the giant animal.

That the bull was after only him didn't register with Zach. Events had unfolded so fast he hadn't time to think about it, he could only react. He could only try and contain his fear, which would have had him jump far too early on the first pass of the bull, that would have given the animal enough time to pivot, and then run him down. Now he stood facing the charging bull, could see the intent in the eyes of the bull, could see its nostrils expand and contract, sucking in huge cubic meters of air, exhaling in blasts that stirred the earth. Saliva foamed up and swept back off the bull's mouth, giving small specks of shine to dusty hooves that slammed into the earth with explosions of grass and dirt. Time seemed to stand still as he watched, he was watching from afar; he wasn't really here, was he? Somewhere in the din of rumbling thundering hooves he heard a small voice. A vaguely familiar voice. It was urging him to jump. Jump now, it said. Jump now. But he didn't respond, there was plenty of time. He was looking into the great beast's eyes. There was no malice, there was no anger, there was no hatred in those black/brown eyes. There was something else, what was it? There was knowing, and there was something akin to one of his college professors, when he was teaching Zach something, and Zach was on the verge of getting it. What to call it? He looked at the bull and realized one more thing was in the eyes of this animal: It was a friend.

With that realization, Zach jumped quickly and easily out of the way, and as it appeared to those watching in horror certain that he was about to be killed, with an air of nonchalance. As soon as the bull was past, Zach ran for safety in the trees. Turning to look, knowing it too late to pursue, the bull ran back toward the herd, ignoring Burly, who stood transfixed by events. Burly could feel that something else had happened here, he felt a surge of power in his solar plexus. This wasn't about an old bull charging someone he felt was threatening. Something else happened, he could almost feel it in the air, like after a lightening storm; that's what power often felt like. What was it with this city boy? For all the world a walking talking L.L Bean clad SUV ad model. He definitely walks that walk and talks that talk, and sometimes talks like a Chicagoan; dese, dem, dose and dat dere, at least when he's making fun of them, his own people. Then Brer Rabbit connects with him, now Satanta, his own buffalo bull named after the great Kiowa chief. And what does a woman as intriguing as Emma see in him? Walking up to the small copse of trees, he could only shake his head. 'Why hadn't I been able to turn Satanta? Why couldn't I enter his mind? That has always worked. Maybe I'm supposed to teach this Zach something. I better get some help with this, it's getting a little tough to figure out,' he concluded.

"You all right?" he asked Zach, who was being held by a teary-eyed Emma. "Yea, yea. I'm fine. Close call, but today's not my day, I guess," Zach answered.

Burly looked hard at him to see if he could detect anything, but couldn't make anything out through the little veil of sarcasm Zach wore. Since his eyes couldn't pick anything up, he looked away and tried to feel with his other senses. He could perceive the lingering effects of power, evidence of interference on this plane of existence by the spirits, that was all. It was vague, amorphous, just slight sensations, flutterings from the wings of a butterfly. They flew away with the wind when a certain creature spoke.

"Zach'ree, dat de mo's suvvigus teng I e'er seed. Stannin' der hol'in yo groun' lak er man, en den jumpin' slonchways des w'en dat bull uz tinkin' he got you dead t'rights," Brer Rabbit said while climbing out of a small cavity he'd found in one of the trees. "You uz bodashus!" he added. "Thanks, Brer Rabbit. Thanks," Zach replied somewhat insipidly, an unusually emotionless response given the events just transpired, thought Burly. It was the first overt sign to him that Zach had felt something happen though it was still hard to separate this response from Zach's usual detached demeanor. But still . . .

Emma was still hugging Zach, shedding a little tear here and there as she stroked his head and told him she thought he was going to get trampled and gored, she thought he was going to die. She saw him getting tossed around by the bull's horns like so much flotsam in a swollen river, like a shirt in the wind clinging to a clothesline in a spring storm.

Cupping his hands round her cheeks, he spoke to her quietly, so that no one else might hear. "I knew I wasn't going to get hurt, I just knew it. Time was standing still, you know what I mean? I could see the buffalo coming at me, but he was in slow motion. I had time to study his face, I could see the veins around his nostrils working, the little muscles, his tongue sliding in and out of his mouth, the saliva dripping from his chin. Blades of grass on his mane. And I could see his eyes. They weren't angry, they weren't mad. They were friendly. He seemed to be telling me something, or giving me something. I don't know." Their eyes were locked, dancing from one to the other. She didn't say anything in response and they fell into silence, holding each other tightly in unspoken gratitude, in grace for having each other.

"Well, I suppose we've seen enough of the herd for today. What say we head back?" Burly asked. He felt neither the inclination nor the need to discuss what had happened. Brer Rabbit zealously took on the role of narrator running over and over the events, all the while regretting that he had gotten stuck in the hole in the tree, otherwise that bull would have really run into trouble, what with him and Zach after it.

Back at the house, Burly announced that tomorrow he was going to Wichita to get his uncle out of the hospital. If that worked out for Zachary and the business he had up there, fine, they could all go together. In the meantime he was going to eat a quick late lunch, then he had chores to do. "Zach, you and Emma can help if you want, there's always work to be done on a ranch. If not, then you can just hang out and do as you please."

The couple looked at each other, and Emma spoke up, "I'd like to do some real work, some farm work. What do you say Zach?"

"The exercise would feel good, I'm game."

"And what are you going to do, Brer Rabbit?" Emma asked him. He already had his head in the refrigerator.

"I des he'p Bart wif some un he own wo'k," he replied.

Burly laughed and said, "That means he's going to log on to the internet and look at dirty pictures."

"Buhly, dat's un damn lie. I'ze goan he'p Bart wif a speshul projeck," he said with a wounded look. Emma giggled under her breath and Zach looked off into the distance through the kitchen window.

"All right, all right. Whatever," Burly said. "Let's make some sandwiches and head out."

Over lunch they discussed what jobs they could do, and Burly decided he'd clear the last of the winter's supply of hay out of the big barn, and take it out into the field for the buffalo. They just might not eat it since the grass was already long enough to graze on, but he needed the room for the fresh hay he would bale in June. With luck there would be two cuttings like last year. Zach and Emma could help him load it on the big flat bed and haul it out with the tractor. Might take two trips, he said, but they should be able to get it done by nightfall.

After lunch and after changing into more suitable clothes, they headed out for the barn. Burly got the trailer hitched to the tractor and backed it into the barn and they proceeded to stack the bales on the flat bed.

"Ah thought bales of hay were big ole round things?" Emma asked.

"They are," Burly agreed, "But I haven't coughed up the money for the machinery yet, so I'm still using my old baler that makes these. You need a lot of help with these bales, from loading them onto the truck in the field to stacking them in the barn. But twice a year I head down to the rez and hire some hands for a few days. You know, unemployment there's so bad, they'll work for near nothing. But I take care of them."

"What do you mean, the rez?" Emma inquired.

"The reservation, or rather, what was the reservation. There isn't one any more for the Kiowa, my people, but they still live on the land where it was, down near Fort Sill and Anadarko. People are pretty poor down there. You either move on, or stay poor. My mother married out and moved away."

"Where are they now?" she asked.

"Well, my father's dead but my mother lives in that trailer you drove past before you got to my house."

"Oh, right, you did tell me that," she said with a grunt as she handed a bale down to a very quiet Zach. She was standing halfway up the stack of hay in the barn, handing bales down to Zach, who was arranging them on the flatbed. Burly was working by himself, grabbing bales and stacking them.

"No," he said to Zach. "Stack them like this, overlapping, so when you put the next layer on, they're interwoven, and aren't as likely to collapse. You can go ten feet high this way, sometimes more." He showed Zach what he meant, and they continued on, though Zach began to work by himself with his thoughts, while Emma handed bales down to Burly.

"So you've lived on this ranch all your life?" Emma asked Burly.

"Pretty much, except I ran off when I was eighteen and joined the rodeo. I spent the next ten years bouncing around the states following the rodeo circuit before coming back home. My father died while I was away, so when I got word, I came home to look after my mom. I haven't left since, 'cept to work rodeo's."

"A faithful son," Emma stated.

"Yea, I guess you could say that," Burly replied. She handed him a bale and he paused to look at her a moment. She had broken out into a sweat, the dark strands of hair surrounding her face were matted to her cheeks, framing them and exaggerating her strong jaw. Wayward bits of straw clung to her face and hair, while her lips were flush and pink. She looked more beautiful than she had in the kitchen. He couldn't help but smile at her.

She admired the ease which he handled the heavy bales, often with one hand, his forearms lean and muscular. He was not a tall man, but was wiry, with great strength, his muscles tight and hard. She had felt them when she had handed him a bale that she nearly dropped, he caught it while she fumbled and held his arm. She found him attractive looking, actually a handsome man, and she had been systematically classifying him in a special niche in her mind the minute she had met him, a category that shaded to the idealized. With his long black braided hair and olive skin, and coal black eyes, he was becoming a noble native. When he smiled at her, she smiled back.

"So now you know about me, tell me about yourself," Burly asked her as she handed him another bale. He looked over at Zach, but he was lost inside, stacking bales mechanically.

"Oh, not much to tell, really. A Southern girl all my life, both muh parents Southerners with a long line of Southern ancestors. Ah haven't done nearly the traveling you've done." Laughing she said, "Ah tried to head north t' go t' college, but that didn't work out, so Ah had to return to my roots and finish at Emory. Ah've been living in Atlanta evuh since. This is my first trip out west."

"Your accent isn't too strong, I've heard stronger," Burly said.

"Oh, it's theyuh all right, but it's been compromised by Atlanta."

"Compromised?"

"Sure," she laughed again. "Atlanta has about as many Yankees as Southerners, so the dialect is getting watered down."

"I see," Burly laughed. "Like everything else in America, it's getting neutralized and standardized. Compromise or die, everyone's middle class. Our television society."

"Don't blame TV, it's just a reflection," Emma said.

"Uh oh. I sense sacred ground. Do you work in television too, like Zach?"

"Yes. Ah work for public TV, but Ah agree with you about television's influence," she smiled.

"Well, it's not just TV, that's just an easy target," Burly said, trying to steer clear of any confrontation. "It's all the media, from TV to magazines and newspapers, popular books and movies. They're all equalizers in the great society," he said with finality. "Well, I think we can stop here," handing her a bale, "Let's take these out and dump 'em in the field somewhere between here and where we saw the herd this morning. They'll find it. What do you say Zach? Zach?"

"What? Yea, yea. Sure," came a foggy reply.

Emma jumped down and hugged Zach. "We can go on a hay ride! Won't that be fun? It'll be safe, don'tcha think Burly?"

"Yea, it should be," he said. "It's not stacked too high. Climb on top, let's go!"

The wagon lurched from side to side as Burly drove out into the field, Emma and Zach sending worried looks to Burly each time he hit a bump and the stack of hay threatened to come down, with them on top. But he would laugh, which gave them some confidence that they weren't going to come tumbling off. Emma asked Zach if he was all right, he being so quiet. He said he was just running some things over in his mind, nothing to worry about, which placated her for the time being.

Burly drove out into the field somewhere close to half the distance they'd walked earlier, then announced he was going to dump the hay right there. They threw off a bunch of bales, then he drove the tractor forward a little, and they threw more down, scattering the hay. If the buffalo didn't eat all of it, it would rot. Then they turned the tractor around and headed back for the next load.

Meanwhile, back at Bart's, Brer Rabbit was cursing the search engine he was using to find something on the web. "Dis su'ch ingun ain't wo'th un damn wiggletail! W'at dis mean, 'No listin's unduh topic?' De damn topic is w'at I'ze axin!"

"Try another search engine." typed Bart. "Try this one." He then opened another search engine for Brer Rabbit. Carefully, slowly and deliberately, Brer Rabbit typed in his request: How to make a bom.'

Bart hooted and shrilled, and typed to Brer Rabbit, "Bomb, with a 'b'."

"Oh, okay. Right," and corrected his mistake.

This time he struck gold, there were 620 matches for his query. "Oooooo, dis uz monstus good," he said.

Bart squirmed and fidgeted in his chair like he was sitting on an anthill. He typed in "I don't like this," on the computer screen over and over, the words popping up in front of Brer Rabbit, but he just clicked on them and they'd fade away. He was too busy perusing the web sites of various hate groups, would be terrorists and anarchists. He was enthralled at the many different kinds of explosive devices that could be built, from the very complex, to the relatively simple. He didn't understand the technology behind many of them, couldn't understand what 'plastic explosive' meant, though Bart tried to explain it. "Dis 'er char uz blastic, but hit ain't 'plodin!" he shot back at Bart. Timing devices were beyond his ken and mixing chemicals that had names he couldn't pronounce didn't seem an option either. He finally settled on a simple pipe bomb filled with gunpowder ignited by a lit fuse. "Dis ull git dat vilyunus coyote," he said to Bart with a wicked smile. "I'll teach him t'mess wif ole Brer Rabbit."

But he needed to obtain gunpowder. A little further exploration on the web provided him with the solution: he could break shotgun shells apart and clean the gunpowder out of them.

He had a vague notion that Burly had some guns that he kept in a closet in his bedroom and there must be ammunition for them. And surely he could find a suitable pipe in Burly's tool shed.

He'd gotten a vague idea about explosive devices while watching his favorite cartoon show, the one in which Wily E. Coyote is always getting his due from the road runner. If there was one TV program he couldn't get enough of, it was that one. And he knew he'd gained the upper hand over Coyote the day before, when he first got the idea about building a bomb. He had stumbled upon the web site of a hate group whose loathing was rather narrowly focused. They didn't like one-eyed bank clerks for some unknown and unexplained reason. He was typing in the web address of a pornographic site when he miss-hit some of the keys. Instead of typing in sexsess, he hit exce$$.

Bart was dead set against it. It was a bad, bad idea, and besides, Coyote hadn't ever done him harm. And in fact, he'd run into Coyote one night walking the short distance from Burly's to his own place, and the coyote didn't show him any malice. No, he'd have nothing to do with it. That didn't deter Brer Rabbit, he was thinking of the first thing he needed: shotgun shells, and he'd better hurry to get them while Burly and everyone were still working down at the barn and Donovan was out fixing fences somewhere. Leaving the protesting penguin, he went to the house.

No one can slink like Brer Rabbit when he has a mind to it, neither weasel nor snake, and a camera wouldn't have been able to record him crossing the yard and entering the kitchen door. In the kitchen, he was startled to hear snoring coming from the living room. Peering around a corner, he spied Donovan asleep on the couch; he'd obviously come in early from his chores. With out making so much as the faint crunching sound of compressing carpet, he snuck past Donovan and crept up to Burly's bedroom door. He tried to turn it, but it was locked. Using some newly discovered and colorful swear words, he cursed his fortune and the door. Though he tried to mutter them under his breath, the noise nonetheless disturbed the sleeping Donovan, but only to the point of missing a couple of beats in his snores. That still alarmed Brer Rabbit, who froze, neither breathing nor batting an eyelash. Donovan soon returned to normal breathing, and Brer Rabbit relaxed and rolled his eyes toward the ceiling, this time blessing his luck for not waking Donovan. A metallic glint on top of the door frame caught his eye and realizing it might be the key to the door, he easily jumped up and grabbed it, landing with only a soft thump that barely registered on Donovan's seismic snore meter.

Feeling like he was entering the great goober patch of plenty, Brer Rabbit trembled as he quietly turned the key. He'd been in Burly's bedroom before it had become off limits and a safe house for the telephone. There on the bed stand was the sequestered treasure, along with Burly's wallet. 'Ah, de credit ca'd,' he thought. He took what he presumed to be the credit card, the rectangular piece of plastic with VISA printed on it, just like the one he'd seen on a TV ad: "Hit's e'erw'er I wants t'be," he said softly. Too bad there's no time to use the phone he thought. Well, maybe he could get two pizzas delivered right quick to Bart's. Being an easily distracted creature, he sat down and dialed the one pizza company that would deliver out to Burly's and ordered two large pizzas with everything on them. "En doan f'git de bacon en anchovies. En betta make dat fo' of um," he told the young person on the other end. "En put 'em on dis 'er credit ca'd."

That taken care of, he looked around the bedroom at all of Burly's personal items. The room was dominated by a large buffalo skull hanging on a wall with sage and sweet grass stuffed into the nasal cavity. Eagle feathers dangled from each horn and hanging between the eye sockets was a beaded medicine pouch. In a corner was an altar with candles, smudge sticks and braided sweet grass, a rolled up deerskin holding Burly's sacred pipe and a number of carved stone fetishes of animals sat mutely in a small circle, including one that looked suspiciously like a coyote, Brer Rabbit thought. That jostled his memory as to why he was there in the first place so he got up from the bed and went over to the closet, slid the door open and poked around behind the clothes until he found a shotgun and a rifle leaning in one corner of the closet, but no shells. Undeterred, he searched until he found what he was looking for on the top shelf, two boxes of 12-gauge shotgun shells, one unopened, and a smaller box of cartridges for the rifle, which he left alone. He paused for a moment, admiring the Golden Retriever that was on the boxes, then threw the credit card in the open box, grabbed the shells, went over to the door, re-locked it, returned the key, and stealthily crept past the still snoozing Donovan and returned to Bart's.

Dancing like a firefly, he showed Bart the shells and sang a new song he'd made up, "Road runner, road runner, road runner goes beep beep, he he he he he he he. En when he catches you, yer BLAM! dat's de en a ole coyote!" He danced around the little room while shaking the shotgun shell boxes like mariachis. Bart was following hard behind him as best he could, trumpeting and hooting to get him to stop shaking the box, but Brer Rabbit was lost in an ecstatic trance, like some ancient shaman prancing round a fire, one foot here and the other in the land of the spirits. This went on until they heard the crunch of tires on the gravel driveway. "Pizza!" whooped Brer Rabbit, throwing the box of shells on the computer desk. Then he dashed up the stairs and out to the car, where a non-plussed acne faced teenager handed the pizzas over to him, saying only, "Nice costume, kid."

Burly grunted as he lifted the last bale of hay on to the flatbed. They'd have to make one more trip with a small load. He couldn't get the rest of it on this trip, so there was no need to stack this one high. The whole time they worked this one, Zach hadn't uttered a word, but he and Emma talked continuously. He was becoming more attracted to her the more they interacted, and unless he was mistaken, she was feeling something too. Then again, maybe it was his imagination; hell, her boyfriend was three feet away from them, though he might as well have been in Zimbabwe. But he'd felt that energy surge again in his groin and he wasn't one given to having sexual urges by and of themselves. No, something was going on, so when they drove this load out into the field, and Zach asked if they'd mind finishing the next one themselves, that he needed to go for a walk by himself, Burly quickly agreed, calming Emma's fears by telling her the buffalo were moving further out, away from them, so it was doubtful he'd run into any of them. She had some quiet words with Zach, nodding her head and stroking his, and the next thing he knew, Zach was marching out over a hill. Burly invited Emma to ride up on the tractor next to him, partly sitting on the tire mud covers and partly leaning heavily onto Burly.

"Is he always so . . ." Burly paused, searching for the right word, hoping Emma would finish his sentence.

"Quiet? No, he's a very social and talkative person. He's just going through a lot of . . . changes. Ah'm sorry if his behavior troubles you," she apologized for Zach.

"Oh, no. No need to say anything. I understand," Burly said.

"These last few weeks he's seen a lot. Startin' with Brer Rabbit at that church 'shout'."

"A what?" Burly asked.

She explained what a 'shout' was.

"The Cherokee's down around Bartlesville do something that sounds very similar, but they call it a 'stomp'. The end results may be the same," he replied. "There are many ways to meet the maker," he finished.

They rode quietly for a while, lurching and swaying as the tractor droned on.

"Meeting Brer Rabbit at a shout, and he ends up out here. I sure don't know how that happened," Burly spoke to end the silence.

Emma laughed and said, "Ah sure don't understand a lot these days. hWhat do you think that buffalo was doin'?" she asked.

"Trying to scare him into or out of something, I would hazard a guess. Sometimes the spirits need to whup you upside the head to get your attention. They sure got my attention a long time ago."

"What?" Emma yelled. The tractor was chugging loudly to get up a hill and it made conversation difficult to hear. She leaned closer as he repeated himself.

"Well," Burly began in a near yell. "There was a time, when I was in my late twenties, I was working this rodeo up in Laramie, and happened to be riding this tough little bronco named Chocolate, I think his name was. Anyway, he was a real ball buster . . . oops. Sorry, I get to talking rodeo and I slip right back into the lingo."

"That's all right," she smiled. "Ah'm not offended."

"Good, but I'll be more careful. Well, this boy threw me hard up against a fence and I hit my head, got knocked out."

He stopped talking, and Emma had to ask him to continue. "What happened then?" They were back at the barn.

"Hang on, I'll tell you when I get this tractor turned around. Here, maybe you should jump down."

He held her around the waist as she searched for footholds to step down on. She did not shrink from his touch. Soon, they were loading hay again, one bale at a time, working together.

"I looked up from the ground," he resumed his story, "and there sitting on the fence rail above me was a man with the body of an eagle. He had wings, but arms too. It was difficult to see him as one thing or the other, he was never all eagle or all man. He said, 'You look good on the ground, but you'd look better up here.'

"'With you?' I asked him.

"'Yes, with me,' he answered.

"I still thought I was in the ring, and looked around for the horse and clowns, but saw no one else. When I climbed to the top of the rail, eagleman took hold of me and we flew off. He took me to these caves on top of some mountain where we set down. From out of these caves came many eagle people, men and women. They stood in a circle around us, not making any noise, until one of them, who I sensed was the chief, spoke to me. He said, 'When you get a sign from us, you will learn our ways and become one of us.' Then they all started to snap at me with their mouths that had turned into beaks, tearing my flesh off. I was terrified, but I couldn't move, frozen, like in a dream. They swarmed all over me, biting and tearing me apart until there was nothing left of me. Nothing, not even bones, I was just a cluster of thoughts suspended in air. That's when I woke up and saw the railings above me with cowboys looking down at me. They had dragged me under the fence to safety. They said I was out a long time."

"That is a marvelous story. Really incredible," Emma said enthusiastically.

"That wasn't the end of it. When I got home several weeks later, after chasing more rodeos, maybe a month, I ran into my uncle. He gave me an eagle bone whistle. That's when I started learning the ways of a medicine man."

"Are you a membuh of an eagle clan?" she asked with such innocence laced with naïveté and delivered so sweetly that he burst into a laugh. She laughed too, acknowledging the simplicity of her comment, which sprang not from a lack of understanding of Kiowa ways as much as revealing a perceived notion, bordering on a stereotype, of Indians.

Their laughter led to playfully tossing straw at one another, Burly assuming a Hollywood pose with one hand covering his eyes, peering into the distance, saying through laughter, "Me see um white woman," which led to more hay being tossed and more stilted, stiff, funny dialogue, until finally they were holding each other and what had been a playful pushing and shoving turned into something quite different, the natural result of such ministrations. They were eye-to-eye, gigglying having given way to smiles, smiles vanishing in preparation for the seriousness of a kiss. But it didn't come.

Emma dropped her arms from around him and stepped back. Without saying a word she grabbed a bale of hay and struggled to get it on the wagon. Burly reached to help her and they finished loading the hay in a forced silence, punctuated by friendly, but inane, conversation.

The last bale loaded, Emma elected to ride on the flat bed. She'd come close to going over a line she wasn't sure she wanted to cross.

Dusk was settling in as they finished unloading the hay, and there was no sign of Zach. Emma was growing a little concerned and Burly said if he wasn't back at the house, he'd go looking for him. Then he spoke directly to her. "Emma, I'm sorry if I was too forward or presumptuous back there. You're a newfound friend and I sure don't want to make you uncomfortable. I can't say I regret anything. I like you. Somehow I think we're kindred spirits."

"No. No. There's nothing to apologize for. Nothing happened. We had fun," she said curtly.

She wasn't exactly in denial, something did happen, though; something was happening. She was as attracted to him as he was to her. She could have easily fallen into his arms, feel his arms around her, stroking his long hair, rub her face on his smooth cheeks, press hard against him. She wanted to. She could feel the draw of sexual excitement; it pulled at her like a tug pulling a ship out of safe harbor. It was confusing to feel such a strong physical attraction to a man she barely knew, and just as she was falling in forever love with Zachary. She felt relieved after having resisted the urge, that incredible wave of sexual energy and pulse. She felt stronger now. She couldn't let it happen. No. It would be a terrible betrayal to Zach and all he was going through. She needed to be there for him. She wanted to be there for him. How could this happen? Just when she was getting comfortable, taking great solace in her heart and in her soul that she had found the partner she wanted to spend the rest of her life with, then this. This unbelievably strong sexual desire for another man enveloped her, washed over her like a spring thunderstorm and wreaking just as much havoc. She would resist it. But oh how delicious the thought of lying naked with this man.

She thanked him for offering to go look for Zach, then they walked back to the house in silence, each in a separate universe of swirling emotions and whirling thoughts, and each longed to hold the other, one ready to admit it, one not.

The only one in the house was Donovan, who sat in Burly's recliner, sipping beer and watching TV in a darkened room. The only light came from the TV, flickering flittering light bouncing off white walls, Donovan's face a mask of moving colors.

"You seen Zach? Burly asked.

"Nope. Not since this morning. I thought he was with you."

"He was till he went for a walk out toward Sand Hill."

Donovan didn't say anything more, just grunted and resumed watching his show.

"Well, I'll get some things together. You want to go?" he asked Emma.

"No, I think I'll wait here."

"All right. Hey, Do. Help me go look for Zach. Hunh? Can the TV spare you?"

"I'll think about it."

"Where's Brer Rabbit and Bart? Down at Bart's?"

"Far as I know."

"Hmm. Must have a good internet connection," Burly muttered to himself.

Moths fluttered around the back porch light like snow in a Christmas globe as Burly and Donovan stepped down the small staircase and out on the lawn. Emma stood in the doorway, then quickly shut the screen door to keep the moths out. The night air was a little too cool for her, so she shut the kitchen door, but as she did, she heard Burly shout, "Hey, Zach! Where you been? We were just coming to look for you. Emma was getting worried."

Emma jumped out of the kitchen and skipped down the stairs. She held herself back a little, she didn't want to appear too eager but she couldn't hide her joy either.

"Been out for a long walk. I'm all right," Zach responded to Burly. "That's nice of you, but I found my way around." Emma was at his side, grabbing his arm. "I'm all right, Em. Sorry I worried you." They embraced and hugged each other with unrestrained affection in front of the two men.

"Ah was gettin' a little worried, it being dark en all, en aftuh this mornin's run in with the buffalo," Emma snuffled.

"Oh, they won't bother me anymore," Zach said, revealing a confidence that did not elude her. "Well, I guess we're off the hook," Burly said. "I'm hungry. Anyone else? Let's see what we can rustle up."

Back in the house, poking around in the refrigerator, Burly asked, "I got these tough ole sirloins I could fry up. How's that sound? We can make blackened ranch steaks," he said with a grin.

"What's that?" Emma asked.

Donovan said, "You burn the shit out of 'em on a cast iron grill."

"Chez Burlee. That's me." Burly laughed.

They sat around the kitchen table laughing at Burly, who was trying to turn a paper towel into a chef's hat. Unable to get the desired results, he said, in mock despair, "I'll just have to stick with my old feed store hat." Then he put on his black baseball cap that bore the insignia of the feed store he got supplies from. In gold letters it read: 'Golden Furrow'.

"Hey! Someone go shake up Brer Rabbit and Bart and see if they're hungry. Bart won't eat this, but I can fix him something else. And I haven't seen anything yet that Brer Rabbit won't eat."

Up until then, Zach had been quiet. He laughed along with everyone else, but he was still a little reserved, so Burly was surprised when he volunteered to go get them. Burly thought he noticed a difference in the way he acted toward Emma, but he couldn't be sure. Something was different about Zach.

It didn't take him long to return. Neither of them were hungry and they were going to stay down there for a while longer.

"Brer Rabbit not hungry?" an incredulous Burly said.

"Well, it looks like they ate pizza. There were empty pizza boxes scattered all over the room," Zach said.

"Pizza! How'd they get pizza delivered out here? Do, you didn't give them any money did you?" Burly asked him.

"Nope. Wasn't me."

"Me neither," Emma said.

Certain his wallet was still safe in his locked bedroom, Burly wondered aloud, "What are they up to? Surfin' the net, I guess."

"That's what it looked like," Zach replied as he moved to help Emma make a salad.

The rest of the evening dribbled away in kitchen cleanup and turns in the shower and early turn ins. They were off to Wichita early in the morning, all save Donovan, who was going to stay behind to keep an eye on Bart and Brer Rabbit, mostly Brer Rabbit, who didn't come up to the house until after 10:00, shivering from the cold of Bart's, and promptly curled up on the couch and fell asleep. Burly had already gone to bed, so he didn't have to lie to him about the money for the pizza.

Lying in bed, Emma asked Zach where he went on his walk. "To talk with the buffalo," he answered.

"You talked to the buffalo? They didn't chase you?"

"No," came the simple response.

"Well, what'd they say?"

"They're worried about Brer Rabbit and Coyote. They said it isn't good that they hate each other so much. It upsets the balance, the circle of life."

"They said that?"

"Yea, the hate is too much like man's. They think man hates himself so much that he treats animals badly because of it. And that's why he does hurtful things."

"What is this hate? Where does it come from?"

"I don't know, they didn't say."

"What else did they say?"

"They said I'm starting to not hate myself. That's why I'm learning to see."

"Learning to see? Like that past life you saw down in Georgia, at Trieste?"

"Yea. That and other things."

"What other things. Are you seeing . . . things? Spirits? Ghosts? That kind of thing?"

"No, just energy. At least right now. Like the white fibers of light that run from your pelvis to Burly's groin."

Emma didn't say anything. Not for a while. Eventually she let the tension drain out of her along with a tear. It helped that Zach said, "It's all right Em. I can see your heart. I love you."

But it didn't help her confusion.

chapter thirteen

"You're not going," Burly said sternly.

"But Buhly, I'ze bleedz'd t'go. Dis my on'y chance." Brer Rabbit laid his ears back and pleaded his case, his hurt eyes puppy dog sad.

"Hit monstus unfair. E'erbody else is goan."

"No they're not. Donovan is staying here with you and Bart." Burly did not look at him as he spoke. "It's just me and Zach and Emma going."

"I hain't ne'er seed un big mod'n city. Bleaze, Buhly. I be awful good."

"That's what worries me. You'll be awful."

"Bleaze, Buuuhhhlllllyyyy. Bleeeeaze?" Brer Rabbit stood next to Burly like a child pleading with his father.

"Oh, what could it hurt if he promises to be good?" Emma offered.

Hope shot through Brer Rabbit like he was struck by lightening.

"I promise, Buhly. I promise I be de bestest you e'er seed. I do anytin' you axe."

"Okay. Let's start with the pizza from last night. Where'd you get the money?" Burly folded his arms and squared off to Brer Rabbit.

"I had coup'ns," Brer Rabbit lied.

"Coupons only get you money off. They don't get you free pizzas. Zachary said he saw a bunch of empty pizza boxes."

"Dems wuz ode uns. We on'y had one pizza."

Burly looked at those big, brown eyes of Brer Rabbit. You could never tell when he was speaking the truth or lying. His eyes always confirmed what his mouth said, as if his words were always truth, no matter what they where or how related they were to events, past or present. Or future, for that matter.

"I don't know," Burly said with a sigh and more than a hint of exasperation, "It just doesn't feel right."

"I'll look after him," Zach said.

Burly cast his eyes down to the table. 'Great,' he thought. 'Zach's going through something, morphing into some kind of butterfly or something , and he's gonna look after Brer Rabbit. I don't think so.' Burly caught himself, 'Christ, when did I start sounding so cynical?'

"All right. You can go," Burly passed the verdict.

"Ai-eee!" yipped Brer Rabbit. He jumped up and spun around. "I go git Ba't. We'll have monstus fun!"

"Hold on," Burly said. "I didn't say Bart's going."

"Buhly," Brer Rabbit opined, "You hain't ne'er taken Ba't anywh'er. Hain't right. He a man des de same as you iz."

Donovan, who up until this time had been quietly eating his breakfast, spoke up, "He's got a point there, Bur. You freed him from a zoo, you can't just make this a bigger cage."

"All right, see if he wants to go," Burly said in a voice heavy with resignation and laced with irritability. He rose from an unfinished breakfast. "Let's get this show on the road. My Uncle's been in the hospital long enough."

"Great!" said Donovan, quickly rising from the table.

"Aren't you going to work on the fence?" Burly asked.

"And miss this? Are you kidding?"

They decided to all go in Zach's Explorer. They'd have to make room for Burly's Uncle, so the return trip would be a little tight, but Bart and Brer Rabbit could sit in the cargo space. They promised to keep a low profile and though they were allowed to sightsee, they had to duck down whenever told to do so and cover themselves with a blanket if need be.

While he drove, Zach called the TV station on his cell phone and set up a meeting with Sheldon Turner, the owner of the station whose ratings Zach's company was going to try to improve. It seemed to work seamlessly: first they'd pick up Burly's Uncle, then have enough time to do a little sightseeing before having lunch. Then he had an early afternoon appointment at the station.

"All set up," he told everyone. "I can slip away to the station while you guys, or as Emma says, 'y'all' drive around town. Maybe we can eat lunch at the downtown park, and I can meet you back there."

"Oh no. We'll drop you off and pick you up," Emma said.

"Yea, all for one and one for all," said Donovan.

"Thank you, D'Artagnon," Burly said sourly and sarcastically.

"What's with you?" Donovan asked him. "Got a burr up your butt?"

Everyone laughed, except of course, Burly.

"Suhly Buhly," said Brer Rabbit, and everyone started to chant 'Surly Burly! Surly Burly!

Burly just groaned.

"Suhly Buhly, poutin' on a pone, din't git a funny bone so he doan go home!" Brer Rabbit sang.

Everyone roared at the little song Brer Rabbit made up and he sang it repeatedly and ad nauseam until Burly pleaded with him to stop. But Bart kept on whistling the tune all the way to the suburbs surrounding Wichita.

"This is it. Turn in here," said Burly, pointing to the hospital caring for his Uncle Remo.

"Looks more like a public housing project than a hospital," observed Zach.

"Yeah, it's a VA hospital. Uncle was in the service, served in WWII. We call it a NWNM place."

"What does that mean?" Emma asked.

"Natives with no money," Donovan said.

Emma made some odd grunting/groaning noise of protest as Zach pulled into a parking space. "We'll wait for you here," he said.

"Do. You coming?" Burly asked Donovan.

"Yea, I'll come in with you."

"We won't be long. I'm sure Uncle is ready to bust out of here," Burly said while he shut the door.

Leaning in an open car window, he pointed to Bart and Brer Rabbit, "And you two stay down. Promise? Promise? Bart? Brer Rabbit?"

"I swear on my po mammy's grave," Brer Rabbit said finally. For emphasis he held up his right paw.

"I'm holding you to it." Speaking to Zach, Burly said, "I just realized that I have to explain to Uncle what we, uh, what we have in the car. So it might take a little longer than I first thought."

"No problem," said Zach as he hunkered down into his seat. "We'll be fine."

"Uncle! The nurses said they are ready to get rid of you!"

Burly teased an old man with long gray braids that hung limply on either side of his head. He was ready to go, sitting on the side of the bed with his small suitcase on his lap. He wore faded blue jeans covering simple brown cowboy boots, and a long sleeved western shirt with plastic pearl buttons set in a field of tan crosshatches over a white base. He was in his late 60's and looked every day of it. Despite that, his blue/gray eyes twinkled with mirth and merriment and life.

He had lived a hard life as a poor farmer raising hogs and a few cattle, growing some corn and some beans, but mostly hogs. He'd always loved hogs.

"They are cold people," he replied. "They have so much to do and have seen so many bad things, they close their hearts like a sunflower at night, only opening them at home, I guess. I hope. It is good to see you, nephew. Hey, Donovan, you came too! How are you?"

"I'm well, Uncle Remo. I'm doing well."

"Good, good. Hey, let's get out of here. We can talk in the truck," Uncle Remo said as he stood to go.

"Uncle, there's something we have to talk about first," Burly said. The serious tone in his voice alarmed his uncle. He knitted his eyebrows together and asked, "Is it your mother? Is she hurt? Has there been an accident?"

"No. No. Nothing like that, but you might want to sit down just the same."

Dejected that he had to spend more time in the hospital, but relieved that his sister was all right, he sat down, his curiosity piqued. "What is it, nephew?" he asked.

"Where to begin," Burly muttered unintentionally aloud. "You know all those coyote stories you used to tell me?" His uncle nodded his head. "And all the stories about how animals and humans used to be brothers and sisters and talk to one another? But man stole fire from coyote and the other animals so they had to grow fur, and how it hasn't been the same since?"

"Yes," his uncle nodded his head vigorously, "there are so many wonderful stories that I told you. Is there one you need to remember?" he asked with great sincerity.

"No, none in particular. I just want to set the stage here."

"Oh."

"You know how you said coyote won't talk anymore because we stole his fire? And he's mad at humans?"

"Yes, the fire he himself stole from Hawakakea," Uncle Remo said matter-of-factly.

"Well . . . I was very blessed to have had a long conversation with Coyote."

"That is wonderful, nephew! That is wonderful! Ha! You are now blessed! You must follow the path we have talked about, with no straying anymore. Ha! Power has spoken, the creator stirs you. Didn't I tell you that you could? Didn't I? Just like you talk to that poor mutant penguin."

"Yes, that's right, Uncle. But Coyote and I talked just like you and me are now."

"Of course! That's natural."

"Right."

"What did you talk about? What things did you learn?" His uncle leaned forward, ready to listen to every word and not miss a thing. He had a rare gift that is becoming rarer.

"I'll tell you later, Uncle. I want to continue with my story."

"Okay. Go ahead." He leaned back, ready for whatever twists and turns Burly might provide.

"Well . . . there is another I've talked to."

"Who? Who? Tell me!" He grew very excited, his eyes dancing between Burly and Donovan.

"Rabbit."

His uncle slapped his knees and laughed loudly. He said, "Oh, he's a wonderful talker, he is. Wonderful stories, he has. But you can't trust him for nothing! No siree! Rabbit as soon lie as take a breath."

Burly and Donovan looked at each other conspiratorially with knowing smiles. If only Uncle knew the truth of his words.

Waiting patiently until his uncle finished laughing, Burly continued with his story. "Well, Uncle, it's not an ordinary rabbit."

"Not an ordinary rabbit? What do you mean? Was it a jackalope?" he asked, breaking out into laughter at his reference to the ubiquitous creature that lurks at every godawful tourist stand in the west; a stuffed jackrabbit with antelope horns attached.

"No, no," chuckled Burly along with his uncle, though he laughed more out of politeness. Well, he might as well get to the point.

"It was Brer Rabbit," he said deadpan.

His uncle looked at him with a mixture of disbelief and earnestness. He wasn't sure if his nephew was joking or not, though he'd never known him to pull pranks.

"Uncle, I'm serious. I'm talking about Brer Rabbit. You know, from the books."

"Yes. I know who he is." Quietly, more to himself, Uncle Remo mumbled, "That's who it was in my dream."

"Well, he's very much alive, and he's very much here. And he's out in Zachary's truck."

"Ah . . . your friends from Atlanta."

"Yes. They're in his truck with Brer Rabbit and Bart."

"Nephew, you seem so serious, I'm not sure what to think."

Donovan joined the conversation, "It's true, Uncle Remo. He's not kidding."

"No foolin' . . . well, let's go! I want to meet Mr. Brer Rabbit!"

"That was easy," Burly said as he and Donovan looked at each other and sighed in unison.

Approaching the truck they could hear Zach reprimanding Brer Rabbit, "You can't whistle at women like that, Brer Rabbit. Women don't like to be treated that way. You have to treat them as equals."

"Equal ter what?" he asked.

"To you and me."

"But I hain't gwine axe you t'dance."

"No, but that isn't the issue. Women today think that being whistled at is not showing them any respect. You won't get any dates that way. Hey! Look, they're back!"

Zach stepped out of the truck to greet Burly's uncle. Uncle Remo was touched by the display of propriety and extended his arm for a handshake. Zach then introduced him to Emma, then said, "And in the back is Bart, whom you know, and Brer Rabbit, whom I 'm sure you'll get to know, for good or ill."

Uncle Remo looked at the pair of ears that stuck up above the rear side windows and saw the upper half of a pair of inquisitive brown eyes looking at him. He nodded his head and smiled and then got in the seat behind Zach and stuck his hand out to Brer Rabbit, "Do you shake hands, Mr. Brer Rabbit?" he asked.

"I sholy do. Put er der," he said, sticking a paw out. "You a mighty perlite man. I kin tell."

"Thank you, sir, thank you." Uncle Remo's eyes were blazing with excitement. He slapped his hands together as if to say, 'this is going to be great, this is going to be exquisitely, deliciously great!'

After everyone was in the vehicle they decided to drive downtown to find the TV station studio and then do a little sightseeing. Downtown Wichita didn't offer much to Zach and Emma, but to Brer Rabbit it was enormously exciting. The huge glass buildings and modest skyscrapers were utterly gigantic to him, they were bigger than his imagination held them after seeing them on TV and the web. And all the people milling about and the traffic, though moderate, were more than he'd ever seen. For perhaps the first time in his life he was speechless. Or nearly so. He still had an annoying habit of making lewd noises at women walking down the sidewalks as they drove by. Uncle Remo thought it was pretty funny while Emma and Zach corrected him.

When they found the studio, instead of driving off, Zach decided he'd run in and see if perchance he could meet with Sheldon Turner early in hopes that would make it a shorter meeting. He pulled into an adjacent parking garage and left everyone to sit in the truck waiting. He figured it might be a quick ten-minute meeting if they were to have one at all. Just break some ground for another more extensive meeting later in the week.

Since leaving Burly's ranch four hours earlier, Brer Rabbit hadn't been out of the truck. While Emma, Uncle Remo, Burly and Donovan engaged in small talk, Brer Rabbit interrupted, "Emma? I gots ta . . . I gots to . . . make wadder. En Ba't do too."

Burly responded instead, "Well, can't you wait until we get to a park or something?"

"I bin hodin' it. I'ze bout t'bust."

"All right. Let's see . . . I guess you'll have to go in front of the truck. We'll watch for you. There doesn't seem to be many cars coming through here now."

"But Mizz Emma kin see."

Emma giggled and said, "I won't look."

"Promise?"

"I promise."

So they carefully and cautiously let Bart and Brer Rabbit out of the truck and watched as they surreptitiously crept up to the front of the truck, which was pulled in close to a wall and was flanked by two other larger SUV's.

"Now doan look," Brer Rabbit reminded Emma.

Burly nervously watched out for people and vehicles, and when he heard tires squealing, as they always do in parking garages, he leaned out the window and said, "Get down. Car coming." But it was really unnecessary, given Brer Rabbit's hearing, his ears had already disappeared below the hood.

The car pulled into a space not far from them, Burly told them to stay down and stay put. It seemed forever for whoever was in the vehicle to get out and walk away. When he was sure they were gone, Burly leaned out the window and said, "Okay. The coast is clear, you can get back in the truck, but hurry up."

Hearing nothing, he spoke in a firmer voice, "All right, you two, come on back in the truck."

Still no answer.

Anxiously he swung open his door and dashed to the front of the truck. Two puddles stained the cement, but the puddleers were gone.

"Shit!" Burly ground the word into his teeth then yelled to Donovan, "Do! Come on! They're gone!"

Inside the station studio, Zach sat patiently in a chair in Mr. Turner's outer office. He didn't have to wait long for the secretary to call then usher him in.

Sheldon Turner was a slightly unkempt man just past his fifty-fifth birthday. He wore a rather cheap suit that did his bolo tie little justice, especially the big chunk of turquoise on it. His nearly white hair reminded Zach of Albert Einstein, though

Sheldon's was a bit better coifed. His voice boomed like a preacher at a Sunday sermon.

Zach moved to the edge of the enormous oak desk Mr. Turner sat behind so they could readily shake hands. Salutations and pleasantries exchanged, Zach sat down in one of two overstuffed leather chairs facing Mr. Turner.

Zach explained that he had not expected to be able to see him until their scheduled time and wasn't prepared for a long meeting as he had people waiting for him in his car that was parked in the adjoining parking garage.

Mr. Turner, a garrulous and forthright, outspoken man, said, "It won't matter. I'm to the point, young Mr. Peterson. I don't waste time on inanities and distractions. Let's see what you've got to put us number one."

"Well, to be frank, Mr. Turner . . ."

"Sheldon is fine."

"Yes sir."

"To be frank, I was hoping to see what you've got now before we make any recommendations. It's easy enough for someone to say change this line-up, plug in this show, play Oprah in this time slot . . . but we don't work that way. We like to see what your anchors are like and spend some time with you. People don't necessarily like changes. We don't want to lose people to gain people if we can avoid it."

"Didn't you get the tapes we sent to you?"

"No sir. We did not. At least I didn't," Zach said truthfully.

"Well, I'm sure we sent them."

"They must have arrived after I left. I left Saturday morning."

"We overnighted them," Sheldon said with a little irritation in his voice.

"I'm sorry, sir. But I did not see them."

"Well," said a disappointed Sheldon, "Let's see what we can do anyway. Let's go into the conference room so I can show you some tapes. It's a better machine in there."

"That would be great, Sheldon. But I should let my party know it might be a while."

"Good idea, I'll get the tapes set up."

Zach went out to the truck, only to find it empty. 'Strange,' he thought, 'They must have gone for a walk, but with Brer Rabbit and Bart, I can't really see them doing that.' There wasn't much he could do so he returned to his meeting with Mr. Turner.

They began to watch tapes of various news shows the station ran; from morning editions to noon and evening programs to the 10:00 o'clock news. Zach took notes while he also scanned their entire programming schedule along with what their competitors ran.

They were at it for at least an hour before Mr. Turner's secretary, a middle-aged woman with a rather plump and plain face, stuck her head in the door. "Mr. Turner, I'm sorry to disturb you, could I have a word with you?"

"That's all right, Margie, what is it?"

"Well, sir, there's a big ruckus in studio 3. You better come look right away."

He looked at her quizzically, "Come again? Margie."

"There's something going on in studio 3 that you're not going to believe. You'd best see for yourself."

Zach had a sinking feeling in his stomach as he stood, along with Mr. Turner, and made for the door.

"I'll take care of this, son," said Sheldon.

"If it's all the same to you, sir, I'd like to go along," Zach replied.

"Suit yourself. See us with our pants down and all. Well, let's go."

Studio 3 was a large room the station utilized for live shows, like the morning talk show hosted by one of their more popular news anchors. The room was set up like a theater and was large enough to accommodate a live audience of a hundred people or more.

Sheldon, Margie and Zach entered at the front of the hall, the audience entrance. The stage had just recently been vacated by the morning show, and the cameras were still set up, along with the setting, which included one small sofa and two chairs, along with a coffee table that still held fresh flowers in a vase. However, the set was mobbed by cameramen, soundmen, anchors, sports reporters, regular reporters, secretaries, janitors and a few delivery men. Everyone was visibly excited, gesturing wildly or putting hands to faces or shaking heads, but what they were struggling to see was not visible to the trio, except for Zach, who saw two large ears sticking out of the middle of the crowd. He groaned audibly. As they walked toward the crowd he saw Burly come through a side door and mouth the unmistakable words, "Oh shit!" He was followed by Donovan, Emma and Uncle Remo. Zach veered off to meet with them. It was obviously too late to stop things now.

"What the hell are we going to do?" Burly said loudly over the buzz of chatter and exultant cries. His eyes danced with desperation.

Donovan looked on with a bemused grin. Emma looked concerned, but had a smile fronting it. She could do that, he thought, it's her posture and eyebrows that are worried. Burly's uncle looked positively ecstatic and his face beamed 'This is great! This is really something!' His smile was so wide it swallowed his wrinkles. He was straining to get a good look, his neck stretched out like a tortoise trying to eat the sun.

"Nothing," Zach replied to Burly, "We can do nothing."

Seated on the couch next to each other were Bart and Brer Rabbit. Two reporters were sitting directly in front of them on the edge of their chairs, microphones thrust out. Two more reporters flanked the two objects of fascination and awe, also with microphones. At least five cameras were recording them, and another two were covering everyone covering the whole thing.

Bart looked terrified but Brer Rabbit was holding court. A born entertainer, he loved to be the center of attention. If he knew what politics were, he would storm the White House.

The reporters were firing questions simultaneously, volley upon volley of rapid fire shots. "Who are you really?" "Where did you come from?" "Who's behind this?" "Are you movie stunt men?" "Is this a joke?" "Are you mutants?" "Are you terrorists?" And on and on.

Bart wasn't making a sound, but Brer Rabbit was holding up as best he could with the unruly behavior of the people, some nearly screaming their questions.

"I des tol' you. I'ze Brer Rabbit en dis 'ere 'z my bes fren Ba't. On'y he caint' tak lak no'ml folk."

"I des sed I'ze Brer Rabbit."

"I cum fum Buhly's."

"I live at home."

"Hit's 'bout un good lik fum Brer Fox, he home."

"Ba't live at Buhly's."

"Buhly nudder good fren."

And so the riot continued until Sheldon, who was standing on the outside of the melee and until this moment had been trying to get a grasp on the situation, finally yelled, "Who are these children? Let me in here!"

He pushed his way into the center of the storm and sat down on the edge of the coffee table, knocking over the flower vase in the process.

"Now look here," he said in a fatherly tone to Brer Rabbit, then to the reporters, his own reporters, he shouted, "Get back! Give them some room for Christ's sake!"

"Now look here," he began again, "I don't know who you kids are, but the jokes gone on long enough. I appreciate all the efforts you put into your costumes, and they are the best I've seen, but I've got a business to run, and you two are going to have to leave now. If you just get up and go, I won't call the police and have them contact your parents and get you into a lot of trouble. Okay?"

Brer Rabbit looked at him suspiciously. It was one thing when someone didn't believe him when he was lying, but it was another when he told the truth. He gave Bart a conspiratorial look and Bart bleated out a hearty "Fuhh Cooo!"

The whole place exploded in laughter, except for Burly, who looked alarmed and frightened, and Sheldon, who fell back in shock, stunned that a child would talk to him like that. He leaned forward and grabbed Bart by the shoulder and shook him, angrily saying, "Listen here you little brat . . ." but he didn't finish his statement. He stared at his hand on Bart's shoulder as if it belonged to someone else. He realized he was feeling real skin, and real bones underneath that. Real penguin bones. A look of amazement came over him. "What the . . ." but again he didn't finish his statement as the house went quiet. He leaned over and touched Brer Rabbit's leg, pinching the flesh beneath the coveralls.

"Yow!" Brer Rabbit yelped, then slapped at Sheldon's hand. "You bes leggo dere, Mista," he warned as he laid his ears back and narrowed his eyes.

Sheldon did not heed the warning. He was too stunned. An alarmingly large fissure was growing in his brain. On one side was his view of reality, nurtured by his hard, nose to the grind stone pull 'em up by the bootstrap Robert's Rules of Order. On the other side was the receding cliff of this reality. There goes the shore! Lifeline!

He grabbed Brer Rabbit again.

"AH! GODDAMN IT!" he howled, pulling his bloodied hand back. The flesh of his index and middle fingers had been peeled back like a carrot from the knuckle to the fingertip.

Brer Rabbit spat Sheldon's blood on to the stage floor and said, "Suhve's yer right t' mess wif un man. Make he downright suvvigus." Then, as if nothing unusual at all had occurred, he turned to one of the prettier female reporters and with an endearing smile and lustful eye said, "You kin axe me mo qweshuns."

The reporters pounced again, unmindful of Sheldon, who was their de facto boss. A good story is a good story, but a great one: ah Pulitzer! For his part, Sheldon stood up, wrapping his hand in a soiled handkerchief, and ordered the cameras to keep rolling.

"It's time," Zach said. "Let's try and get them out of here. Donovan, could you pull the truck around front and wait for us? Here're the keys. We have to do this fast so that no one will be able to follow us. Uncle Remo, maybe you better go too. If we have to run . . . well, it might be hard on you."

"No way am I missing any of this," he responded firmly.

Zach smiled and said okay but Burly quickly interjected, "Uncle! This is serious! You should go with Donovan so we can move fast. You just got out of the hospital! Think of yourself!"

"Burly, what has gotten into you," his uncle replied. "Why are you so concerned that people see these two? Do you think the creator doesn't know of this? Do you think the creator does not see?" He swept his arm around, taking in the entire room. "Maybe the creator willed this. I will not go." For emphasis he folded his arms across his chest and stood tall and erect.

Burly bit his lips and turned away silently, brooding, while Donovan sprinted back the way they'd come, through a side door heading to the parking garage.

"What's your plan?" Emma asked Zach.

"I don't know, but somehow we've got to distract all these people so we can grab those two."

"That's going to be hard with all those cameras and all this excitement," she said.

"Well, I suppose I could just fight my way through the crowd and grab them, then run like hell."

"Too dramatic. You've been watching too many old TV shows. Then you ride off into the sunset?"

"Nothing else comes to mind," he said.

"How about we bring Brer Rabbit over here? To us?" Emma offered.

"No way is he going to leave all that attention, especially that one woman he's latched on to."

"Oh," Emma said somewhat idly, "I think I can get his attention. Uncle, would you hold my purse? Burly and Zach, get ready to grab Bart."

"What are you going to do?" asked Zach, full of curiosity.

"Just go on and work your way close to Bart. Uncle, get ready to run back out the way we came. Zach, once you go through this door, there's a hallway to your left. Head down that way and you'll see doors leading outside. There's a sidewalk that goes right to the front of the building. Now, go over and get ready to grab Bart."

Burly and Zach moved to the edge of the mass of people. The crowd was growing bigger as more and more people came rushing in as word spread that something fantastic was going on in studio 3.

Brer Rabbit and Bart were busy fending off questions and a few groping hands. Many wanted to touch them, especially Brer Rabbit, as if they were touching divinity. To see was one thing, eyes are an unfaithful couple, but touch has no disloyal mate.

Others clasped hands together, prayer-like, perhaps asking to be delivered from such perplexity and befuddlement.

As the two men worked their way through the crowd, Burly noticed that Bart was starting to look very scared, nearing panic. Having been in a zoo, he was used to having people stare at him, but he had the space the bars provided. Stressing him too, was the fact it was way too hot for him, big lights were focused right on him and Brer Rabbit. Even Brer Rabbit seemed to be getting annoyed, especially at the people who were quick to steal a feel. He was nervously looking to his left and right and squirming in his chair.

Getting as close as they could, yet still be able to clearly see Emma, the two men waited for her cue. Zach could not imagine what she was up to.

As they waited for her signal, or whatever it was she was going to do, Bart caught sight of Burly and started to trumpet and whistle excitedly. Brer Rabbit didn't notice, but many in the crowd did, and they turned to see what had the penguin so galvanized. With so many heads already turned, this was the opportunity for Emma. She grabbed the bottom of her long sleeved blouse and pulled it up and over her head. Then she unfastened her bra and set her breasts free. For emphasis, she jiggled them.

Every single face in the house was soon looking at her, many of the cameramen had the wherewithal to view the image from the perspective of the lens, still rolling the tape. Not being able to see above the heads of the people, Brer Rabbit stood up to see Emma, her body lit up by many Klieg and camera lights, topless, and calling out to him.

At times likes these, Brer Rabbit's natural instincts take over, nay, tyrannically mutiny and overwhelm him, and without further thought about cameras and reporters or Bart, with a magnificent leap that had only one brief visit to a man's head, he was soon holding Emma. And she held him too, tight. Very tight, to his pleasure.

"That's our cue," a hysterically laughing Zach said, "Let's go!"

He cleared a path through the crowd for Burly, who reached down and grabbed Bart. They tore out after the fleeing Uncle Remo and Emma, now disappearing through the door with Brer Rabbit safe in tow. Most of the reporters started to give chase, so Zach, Burly and Bart were effectively running with the tide.

Outside they reached the waiting truck and piled in. It all happened so fast that the reporters could do nothing but stand in the street and watch as they sped away.

Inside the car there was jubilant and riotous laughter.

"I can't believe you did that," Zach said through peels of laughter. Uncle Remo was nearly choking, he was laughing so hard. Even Burly wore a smile. Emma was laughing along with everyone, too, as she slipped her shirt back on. It was a small struggle because Brer Rabbit didn't want to let go, but her firm entreaties forced him to, and with a dejected look, he crawled in the back to rue what might have been.

"What on earth made you think of doing that?" asked a still laughing Zach.

"Wayull, my daddy told me when Ah was a little girl, that the way they caught monkeys in the jungle was to put somethin' sweet in a coconut that had a hole drilled in it. The monkeys would reach in and grab the sweet, and when they clenched their paws into a fist, they couldn't get theyuh paws back out the hole. Not wantin' to give up the treat, they'd get caught that way."

"I hain't no mohnkee," said a pouting Brer Rabbit.

"No, but I knew you wouldn't let go either," said Emma, with a laugh.

"Hmph!" was his grunted response.

"Oh, Brer Rabbit. Don't be sore. I just wanted to get your attention and couldn't think of any othuh way," she said reassuringly. She reached back and rubbed his ears, which brought a smile back to his dour demeanor. So close to paradise, yet so far.

chapter fourteen

On their way out of town they stopped at the drive-through window of a burger joint and bought lunch. Zach took the wheel again as they headed back down south to Burly's ranch. It was full in to the warm afternoon and with their bellies filled with the all-American meal of burgers and fries, the electric charge of the preceding events fizzled into irregular somnolent snores. Even Uncle Remo, excited as he was, had his face smooshed against the side window, fogging it with his breath. More than one person driving by thought it odd for an old man to be making faces at them. On his shoulder lay Emma's head, who slept with a peaceful smile adorning her face, the first smile since Zach had let her know he was aware of the exchange between her and Burly. In the back dozed Donovan and behind him Brer Rabbit schemed in his dreams while Bart snored like a busted flute.

Only Zach was alert as he drove. Sitting next to him, Burly found a little peace and quiet in sleep, though Zach noticed he twitched a lot, still unable to escape his apprehension, even in sleep.

Zach wondered why Burly had become so edgy. Maybe he'd always been that way, Zach just didn't know him well enough. But when he'd first met him way back in what seemed so long ago, just this past winter, he'd seemed so . . . together. So sure of himself, so at ease and comfortable with who he was. The kind of guy you'd go to for guidance. But he'd become nervous and edgy, second guessing things. Well . . . maybe Brer Rabbit was becoming too much, was driving him crazy. He was a handful. But then Burly had called him good medicine. Maybe he'd better leave it at just medicine and bitter at that. He liked his Uncle

Remo. There was a good man who wore his warm and generous heart on his sleeves like chevrons, insignias for the blessed and well earned stripes for lessons learned after a life of strife. He had gained wisdom from his wounds, a rare man indeed. And wise to the point of being infused with joy and full of humor. The man exuded happiness and cheerfulness, and, maybe even more importantly, contentment.

And Donovan? A free floating spirit with few cares. A butterfly sipping nectar at blossom after blossom, each a taste of different experiences.

Thinking of blossoms and flowers made him think then of Emma, and he looked at her in his rear view mirror. So beautiful in sleep, so serene. He had thought her nearly perfect before, someone like Burly, or pre-Brer Rabbit Burly, in complete acceptance of who they were and what they did. Her views always seemed to come from some deep well of understanding about humankind. Like some old soul who knew the intricacies of the human mind and human behavior, had seen it all through lifetime after lifetime. He'd thought her understanding of things beyond his ken and never failed to agree with an opinion she held, not out of some weak submissiveness, or worse, to get some desired end like her bed. But because she always seemed to hold the good and right assessment of things. Her notions and ideas about life on planet people always seemed wise, certainly deeper than he'd dared to admit for himself. He'd always crack jokes to avoid looking directly in to his soul and expose the chamber pot that held the clippings and post-it notes that were his thoughts. His fear had been that she'd find out how shallow he truly was and discard him like a broken eggshell. Somehow, she'd never uncovered him, and now, as deep an ocean he thought she was, she was sounding still.

His musings brought him back to the wild and tumultuous events at the studio. He'd left without talking to Mr. Turner. Don't worry, Sheldon, roll those tapes and you'll be number one in no time! Another great job by the J.J. Johnson Company!

And this one by J.J.'s own wonderkin, his boy Zach. 'Attaboy, Zach!' He could hear him now, and the new Zach saw the old Zach swell with pride. Good dog! Give the lad a bone!

But the new Zach wasn't distanced enough from the old Zach to look at his changes any closer, at least yet. He knew he was a little different, he knew he was changing, he knew he was seeing people a little differently and just now himself. When does an oak tree know it is no longer an acorn or the stream into the river into the sea know it is no longer the brook? Are there boundaries to awareness, or is that an oxymoron? I am the thought, I am the star, earth, cell and bug, slug and snail, monkey mandrill man, lion whale and back to snail and earth to star again. Circles. Cycles. Busted.

A siren startled Zach from his reverie.

"Please pull the vehicle safely off to the side of the road," a tinny voice barked through a loudspeaker.

Zach looked down at the speedometer and groaned, he had sped up to 85 mph without being aware of it. The passengers woke as one.

"It's okay," he assured everyone. "I'm getting pulled over for speeding. Brer Rabbit and Bart, you pull those blankets over you and don't move. Don't make a sound! This isn't like earlier. I don't know what the policeman would do if he saw you. Just don't do anything!" For insurance, he added, "Brer Rabbit, he might throw you in jail. I mean it!"

"Jail? Wha' fer? I hain't done nuffin'."

"He may not know that."

"I be still as stone."

"Good."

They waited on the side of the expressway while the cop ran the usual checks on the license plates. Finding no blemishes or warrants on them, he stepped out of the squad car and approached the truck.

Alert and wary eyes searched the vehicle as the cop came up to Zach's window, who was ready, window down, with a smile and a friendly, "Afternoon, officer!"

Being a somewhat amiable soul, though of necessity a bit jaded from a dozen years on the force, the officer returned the greeting with his own salutation. "Afternoon. Registration and license, please."

As Zach got the items together, the cop looked over the sleepy faces looking back at him. After checking the documents, and while waiting for a return call from the dispatcher concerning Zach's drivers license, he asked him. "Do you know how fast you were going back there?"

"Yeah," Zach said sheepishly, "I kinda drifted up to 85, I think."

"You admit to driving that fast?"

"Yea," Zach said, drawing 'yea' out like a fishing line. "I just kinda . . . did it."

"Just kinda did it," the cop said a little mockingly. "Do you know what the speed limit is through here?"

"Umm, 65?"

"No, that would mean you were driving more than twenty miles an hour over the speed limit, and I would automatically have to take you in. It's 70 through here. But I still have to write you up a ticket."

"Thank you," Zach said absently.

"Oh, you are most welcome. Anytime," the cop said.

While the cop wrote the ticket he asked Zach where he was going in such a hurry. With a thumb pointing to Burly, he said, "His place."

"And where would that be?" the policeman asked as he stood, head bent over the clipboard he was writing on.

"Does it matter?" an irritated Burly interjected.

"It might," the cop said as he leaned into the window, his once indifferent and slightly sarcastic attitude now turning to one of growing interest. Zach quickly piped in, "We just picked up his Uncle Remo here at the Veteran's Hospital in Wichita, and we're driving him home to his," pointing to Burly, "Burly Olalla's, ranch outside of Arkansas City."

"Thank you," the cop said without a drop of gratitude. "Your friend here seems a bit touchy."

"He's just shook up about his uncle, the hospital and all, you know."

"I see."

The cop went on to explain Zach's payment and/or protest options for the ticket. Thanks to modern technology, he was able to use his Visa card and pay the $75 right on the spot, and they were soon on their way again.

"Shoo, that was a close one," allowed Zach. "Brer Rabbit and Bart, thank you for being so good. Burly, what were you trying to do? Get us back in the news with 'Police arrest alien smuggling gang . . . news at 10'?"

"It's none of his goddamn business where we're going," Burly said sorely.

"True. But he could make it his," Zach replied as he looked through the rear-view mirror. He could see Uncle Remo shaking his head. Everyone else was quiet.

Unfortunately for them, the entire city of Wichita was busy making their business theirs. There is a strata in American society that likes to while away the hours listening to police radio frequencies. Now, should they be looking, they had a police report to help them find one Zachary Peterson, owner of a Ford Explorer with Georgia tags LCD 48637. And interested parties merely had to find the records of a certain Remo from the Veteran's Hospital, and then to track down his nephew, Burly Olalla, who lived on a ranch outside Arkansas City. Heck, they could skip Uncle Remo altogether, if they wanted. Bigger bread crumbs could not leave an easier trail to follow, and many indeed were looking for their spoor.

They did not know it, nor did the policeman, but they were now the most sought after people in the Wichita area, soon to be Kansas, and soon enough, America and the world. They also did not know their pictures were being shown constantly on television, though, if they had thought about it, they certainly should have known. All of Kansas, and, since CNN had picked up the pictures, America was just waking to be treated to shot after shot of Brer Rabbit, Bart, Zach and Burly, and lots of very good pictures of Emma, from all different angles, often with certain features slightly besmirched and blurred for the (in)decently challenged. Little did they know they were getting their fifteen minutes of fame. And maybe a few minutes more. Fortunately for them, the rest of the drive back to Burly's ranch was uneventful. But that would soon change.

They found the ranch as they left it, so peaceful and relaxing now in the fading, late afternoon sun. Long shadows darkened gullies as golden light danced farewell to daylight on hilltops. The sky was turning salmon pastel and clementine orange as the sun set about making its bed, sending small, multicolored puffs of cotton ball clouds huffing from east to west to awaken the moon. Birds chattered to one another about the day's gossip while lone whippoorwills sang their lonesome dirges. Out in the pastures, contented buffalo were quietly stalking tender spring grass, living tanks mowing down armies of green recruits.

As the weary travelers spilled out of the truck like melting wax, Zach asked Emma to take a walk with him while Burly announced he'd start fixing supper. Uncle Remo said he was going to visit his sister while Bart went to his shelter to literally chill out from the hot ride in the truck. Brer Rabbit honed in on the couch and the TV. Donovan said he'd head for the barn to do some chores.

"It's absolutely beautiful right now, isn't it?" he said to Emma.

"That, and a little cool," she said, wrapping her arms around him. Spring days on the plains were often warm, but they gave way to cool nights.

They walked out behind the house to sit on a fallen cottonwood tree, half of it cut for firewood, but leaving plenty left to sit on. They watched the glorious good night-kiss to the day from the sun.

"What do you think is goin' to happen?" she asked Zach.

"With us or Brer Rabbit?" he replied.

"Well, Ah meant Brer Rabbit, but Ah suppose us is as good a question."

"Well, I don't think anything has changed between us, has it? I still love you, in fact I love you more each day. And I think you still love me. Ain't that raght, hon?" he said in his best imitation of a Southern drawl.

She smiled at his attempt at humor, more so because he said he loved her, and loved her more.

"This thing with Burly," she began.

"Thing?" he said with mock alarm.

"Well, Ah don't know what else to call it. Ah have this . . . Zach, it's more lahke just a sexual . . . draw. Just a sexual draw. But Ah don't feel connected to him at all. Ah don't feel . . . love. Certainly not in the sense Ah do for you." She spoke almost apologetically, and haltingly.

"Emma, then I think that all you're feeling is sexual energy unrelated to love. Maybe it's just his desire for you, you feel his longing for you and feeling that, it confuses you because they are not your own feelings. I think that we can have sexual desires for someone that is entirely a physical draw that is not matched, or caused, by love or emotional . . . what shall I call it . . . soul connection. Or how about this: What if your feelings are based on some past life connection? Hmm? Boy, that clouds the picture."

"When did you get so wise," she playfully teased, but she meant it.

"Oh, when I was with the buffalo, they kicked me in the head. Said it would help me." They enjoyed a laugh, and trying to maintain that he asked her, "Hey, they sure got some good pictures of you and the girls," he teased, nodding to her breasts.

"Yes, Ah suppose they did," she laughed.

"That was out of character for a Southern girl!"

"Not so! We ain't shy! We ain't all lace and petticoats. We can get down in the dirt and mud same as any pimple headed boy!"

They enjoyed their own laughter and lightheartedness while watching the sky turn green and purple and red as the sun sank behind the Flint Hills, taking with it some of the day's more taxing moments. And they enjoyed being alone together, sharing tender kisses and caresses.

It was dark when they left the old cottonwood log and started to make their way back to the house.

"You know, they're probably looking for us," Emma said.

"Who, Burly?" Zach asked.

"No, that Mr. Turner and them. They won't quit, it's too big a story."

"I know," Zach responded with a sigh of resignation.

"Hmm, smells good," Emma said as they entered the kitchen. "hWhat's for dinnuh?"

"Spaghetti," Burly said as he raced around. "Mom made it and sent it over with Uncle Remo."

"Oh, is she going to join us?" she asked.

"No, she won't do that. She's pretty shy."

"Too bad," Emma said. "What's that you're drinking?"

"Cheap red wine. Want some?"

"Love to."

"Zach?"

"No, I'll pass. But thanks." Zach looked into the living room where Donovan and Brer Rabbit sat on the couch watching TV, feet propped up on the coffee table, each nursing a beer. A little plastic cup sat next to Brer Rabbit's feet. 'Probably using it to spit tobacco juice in,' thought Zach. Ugh. According to Donovan, he'd learned quickly that if he was going to chew tobacco in the house, he had to use a cup. They almost had rabbit stew the first time he spat on Burly's carpet. Donovan had to take the baseball bat from Burly. That was on day three after Brer Rabbit's arrival. Burly had swung quickly from thinking Brer Rabbit a gift from spirit, to a test and a pest. Zach reckoned the pendulum was registering curse or beyond by now.

"Brer Rabbit," Burly called from the kitchen, "Go give this to Bart. He won't eat spaghetti. And hurry back, dinners almost ready." He held out a plate of thawed carp, the meat pulpy and rubbery.

Slowly, and with great drama and many groans, Brer Rabbit lifted himself from the couch and took the plate of food.

"Ugh! What dish 'er iz dis? Hit smell monstus bad," he said, face contorted in a grimace.

"Well it's goddamn hard to get good fish out here in Kansas. We're a million miles from the sea, in case you hadn't noticed," Burly snapped.

Brer Rabbit didn't bat a long eyelash, he just trudged to the door.

Sitting at the kitchen table, Emma, Zach and Uncle Remo looked at each other in quiet alarm. Emma offered to help make a salad.

"No greens left, spaghetti's it. I haven't had time to shop," Burly said, anger still lingering in his voice.

"We'll go shopping tomorrow," Zach said as softly and evenly as he could. "We'll pick up a lot of supplies."

"Oh? You're planning to stay a while?" Burly said a little sharply.

"I guess not. But I don't think we're ready to leave tomorrow. Unless you want us to go." Zach looked at Emma as he spoke, trying to read into her silent eyes if they should leave in the morning, but before they could come to an understanding, Uncle Remo spoke up.

"Nephew! Where are your manners? We always welcome guests!" he said, sharply rebuking Burly. "There's always enough to go around. The creator always provides."

Burly's defiant posture weakened as they watched the anger visibly leaving him. At last he spoke, ending the uncomfortable silence. "You're right, Uncle. Look, I'm sorry. I'm just a little frazzled." He took a long deep pull from his wineglass.

"And careful with that stuff. We might have to do a ceremony tomorrow," Uncle Remo warned.

"Too late. I've already had two glasses," Burly replied.

"Then stop now," Uncle Remo said.

Burly just shrugged his shoulders and turned his attention to the boiling noodles.

"What ceremony, Uncle Remo?" Emma asked.

"I dunno. I'll ask the spirits to speak to me in my dreams tonight."

"Dinner's ready," Burly announced.

"Nephew, if it's all the same to you, I'll take my plate and go eat with my sister," Uncle Remo said.

"Suit yourself. She probably ate already, but I'll give you enough for her, too."

Zach grabbed Emma's hand and spoke to Burly, "If it's okay, we'd like to go there too. We'd like to spend some time with her, get to know her a little. She must be a little lonely there."

"Okay by me," Burly replied. "No problem, I'll just split the spaghetti and the noodles. Do, you wanna go too?"

"Nah, the beer's better here," Donovan yelled over the TV noise.

"Good idea," Emma whispered into Zach's ear as they closed the kitchen door. "He needs some time to himself." She was glad to be away from Burly. It was uncomfortable being around him and Zach at the same time, especially since Zach was aware of the pull between her and Burly. But he was being so good about it, so wonderful and wise, and understanding. Knowing there was sexual tension, or something, between them didn't seem to be bothering Zach at all. How can that be? He was changing so much, yet it wasn't scary or threatening like it is with so many people when one changes while the other doesn't. No, Zach was like some flower blossoming. She couldn't quite put her finger on it, but it was certainly for the good. And Burly, what's going on with him? Is it related to her? Maybe it was his feelings for her. Maybe she was somehow the cause of his erratic behavior, his misbehavior. Ah, guilt. Maybe it would be better if they left in the morning. Just pack up Brer Rabbit and hit the road for home. Drop him off at the church and say "Here you go, Esther! He's all yours! Ta ta!" No, no, they still had a lot to do. Maybe Uncle Remo could help.

Burly's mother's life revolved around two things: her garden and her TV set. And with spring in full bore, the TV was mostly neglected, except at night. She had just turned it on when the three knocked at her door. She smiled warmly at her brother but gave a wary smile to Emma and Zach.

"We're here to share dinner with you, sister," Remo announced.

"I've already eaten, thank you, but you're welcome to come in." She stepped back from the door.

"You didn't wait for me!" Uncle Remo said with exaggerated surprise.

"Well, I wasn't sure when you'd come back from the house." She took the food from them and prepared to warm it up. Quickly, she cleared off the table and turned the TV off, then invited everyone to sit at the small table. Emma and Zach listened as brother and sister continued their discussion about his stay in the hospital, a topic they had not heard much about since Uncle Remo's story took a back seat to the adventures they'd had with Brer Rabbit. Their attention was diverted by all the dried plants that hung from just about every available space in the small trailer. They hung from the ceiling and walls, behind the TV, above the refrigerator, over the sink, in front of windows. The cabinets must be stuffed with them too, Emma thought, and she couldn't imagine what her bedroom looked like.

But Burly's mother seemed very nice. A little quiet, but two strangers sat in her house, and Emma was well aware of how quiet country people can be in front of strangers. She had very long hair, which had once been coal black, Emma was sure, but was now speckled with plenty of gray. She wore it braided into one long plait that trailed down her spine. She had on a simple, flower print dress, the kind often worn by older women in the mid-west, or in small towns and out in the country. Even now, in early spring, her face was tanned a dark brown. Great rivers and tributaries of wrinkles carried her age downstream to a turkey neck busily working on a delta of more wrinkles. Her hands were dark too, with fingernails forever stained from the earth. Her voice was deep and slightly hoarse and reedy from years of smoking cigarettes, which she chain smoked still. Even though it was well after the supper hour, she was drinking coffee, black as espresso and nearly as strong, Emma was certain.

"You have a wonderful home," Emma offered with a smile.

"The trailer's a piece of shit," was her surprisingly raw response.

A slightly flushed Emma quickly recovered, "With all these plants, I wonder if you're not a herbalist, or a healer of some sort," she gently said, still smiling. No need to stir the old gal up.

"Many are good for that," she replied. "I give some to those in need. Woulda' helped him," she pointed to Remo, "if he wasn't so damn set on gettin' to them doctors."

"Wasn't much I could do about that," Uncle Remo said in defense. "The doc's threw me in there without a 'How d'you do'."

Burly's mother took a couple of deep draws off her cigarette and let the exhaled smoke surround her like a cloud. A noxious cloud, thought Zach, who was doing all he could not to cough.

"You goin' t'go home, or you gonna stay around here a while?" she asked her brother.

"Oh, my, no! Things are too interesting around here to go home. Have you met the rabbit?" he asked, eyes twinkling. Emma thought Uncle Remo's eyes had so much humor and life in them that it was at times hard to look straight into them. It was like he was seeing you naked, looking deep into the cellars of your life and soul. She'd seen flashes of it lately from Zach, and she'd seen it sometimes in Burly's eyes when they first got there, but she was sure now he wanted to see her naked! It had nothing to do with spirit.

Burly's mother nodded her head to indicate that she had met Brer Rabbit, but she offered no further elaboration.

Uncle Remo went on to relate the day's events to Burly's mother with obvious pleasure. He was a great storyteller, emphatically shaking his head or gesturing with his hands and swinging his arms about. Emma couldn't help but be smitten by the dear old man, even Zach was charmed by this kind soul. He glossed over how Emma attracted Brer Rabbit to her, just telling Burly's mother that she got Brer Rabbit to come to her, grabbed him, and they all ran to the waiting truck and sped off, leaving dozens of people standing stunned and bewildered in the street.

Burly's mother didn't say much, nothing in fact; just puffed away on her cigarette and sipped her coffee.

An awkward silence ensued, at least to Emma and Zach. Having followed proper protocol for visitation, it was time to eat. The food was plenty warm.

And good, too, in the filling way even bland spaghetti can be. But this was far from that. There were spices in it that neither Emma nor Zach could name. There was a hint of flowery something or other on top of pungent, fresh oregano, basil and thyme. The only unpleasant aspect of dinner was the pall of cigarette smoke that choked the air. But Burly's mother kept puffing away, oblivious to the obvious discomfort and displeasure of her guests.

Dinner entertainment was provided by Uncle Remo relating stories of his stay in the hospital, or confinement, from the food to the nurses to the waking up healed and back to the nurses, especially the pretty ones.

Of his healing, he told how he had dreamt one night that he was in a strange land, with plants and trees he didn't recognize. Big pines growing straight and as tall as skyscrapers he'd seen in Wichita, of huge trees spread out over an acre of land with small rubbery leaves the size of big almonds. Great garlands of odd green/white plants hung from the great tree limbs like towels on a bathroom peg.

Emma and Zach recognized the southern oak with Spanish moss, and the pines were probably turpentine pines.

Uncle Remo said he was walking down a path made of crushed white shells, it seemed, when he ran into a man and a woman, both with skin as dark as night. One of them, the woman, spoke to him in a language he didn't understand, but the man spoke to him in English, though with an unusual accent, like some Texans, only different.

Anyway, they asked him to follow them to their house, which turned out to be just a log cabin in the woods. It was very clean and tidy inside though pretty bare, just one table with four straight-backed chairs and one rocker by the stone fireplace. A single, small bed sat in one corner along with a crudely built set of clothes drawers. The walls were cluttered with all kinds of implements and tools and cooking stuff and what not. From the rafters bracing the roof hung many dried plants, "Just like here in Sis'." Some were recognizable as food plants, others were probably herbs.

Uncle Remo continued with his story, "The woman said something to me, and though I couldn't understand the words, I knew what she meant. She said there was a sadness in me, a big dark sadness that was robbing me of life. I didn't know at first what that could have been, but then I realized it had to be about my wife. She died a long time ago, at least 20 years ago. It was a bad accident at work. The woman said she would take the sadness from me, if I wanted. I agreed, and so she got a rabbit's foot from somewheres and worked it over me, just like some old time doctorin'."

"A rabbit's foot?" Zach interrupted.

"Yea, a rabbit's foot. You know, lots of folks think they bring good luck. Maybe they do more than that," Uncle Remo said.

"Not for the rabbit," Zach said.

"I don't know," said Uncle Remo, then continued with his dream.

"When she finished working the rabbit's foot over me, there was a knock at the door. The man opened it up, and there standing just like you and me was this rabbit. Standing just like a man and dressed just like a farmer. Without saying a word, he walked up to the woman and took the rabbit's foot from her, and walked right back out the door. That was it. That was the end of the dream. Next day, I wake up, and the cancer's gone. Just like that."

Emma and Zach expressed amazement at Uncle Remo's story, but his sister didn't say a word, just rubbed her cigarette out, stood up, and grabbed the dinner plates to start cleaning up. Emma stood to help but she motioned her not to bother. Then she said, "You know, them TV people that took your pictures, I bet they're playing 'em all over Wichita."

Uncle Remo said, "Nah. Who's gonna believe them. Everybody will think they're made up, fakes, like special effects or something they did for better ratings."

"I hope you're right," Zach said. "I hope you're right."

Emma was still smiling at Uncle Remo and his story. She asked him, "You must have loved your wife very much, Uncle Remo. Do you feel any sadness left in you?"

Burly's mother cut in, "She was a gift from God. They don't come any better than Angie."

Uncle Remo said slowly, "You're right there, sister. Creator wanted her back." No one said anything and after a moment of silence, he went on, "Yes, Emma, I did love her very much. You can't help but feel pain when you love someone that much and they're taken from you. But I don't feel it eatin' at me like it did before. I'm gonna see her again, I know that."

After another quiet moment that seemed to be in honor of his dead wife, Zach asked Uncle Remo what he thought they ought to do with Brer Rabbit.

"Nothing. Spirit will tell us if and when we need to do something."

It was getting late, so they thanked Burly's mother profusely for putting up with them, and left to go back to Burly's.

The night was beautiful, the air crisp and cool, the stars as sharp as crystals. Uncle Remo looked up at them and said, "It's cracklin' out here!"

"What do you mean, Uncle Remo?" Emma asked him.

"The night is full of power. Full of power. Lots and lots of power, like electricity."

Emma and Zach looked at each other, wondering if the other could feel what he was talking about.

"Be a good night for working with spirit, that's for sure," Uncle Remo continued. "Too bad this old man's just going to bed."

They shared a good laugh and went in the house. It was quiet, Burly must have turned in and Donovan was asleep on the couch. Brer Rabbit wasn't in, but that wasn't unusual. Emma and Zach looked forward to falling asleep in luxurious exhaustion after making love.

Down in Bart's little dwelling, making love was not on the agenda. Making war was. They, or rather, Brer Rabbit, had managed to obtain all the necessary items for battle now; gunpowder, pipes and fuses. Into the wee hours of the night he worked, Brer Rabbit shivering from the cold as he poured the black gunpowder into the lead pipes, spilling some here and there with each twitch and spasm of shiver. But he didn't care how cold he was, the end of coyote was near.

"Der gwine be coyote bits all o'er dis ere lan'," he said. "Ere un toof, dere un toof, e'erw'er un toofy toof," he sang gleefully to the rythym of a song he'd heard on a children's television show. Then, to the rhythm of the show's title song, he sang, "Hit's un boo'ful day in der naybuhood, un boo'ful day in der naybuhood, cu'd you be dade? Wu'd you be dade?" as he laughed and laughed and sang and snickered evilly. Bart was forever waddling and pacing back and forth in the room, making little clucking sounds.

He was worried sick about everything Brer Rabbit was up to. He was afraid that Burly would return him to the zoo or sell him back to some university research program for allowing this to happen here on his own ranch. He feared Burly would think it some kind of betrayal for all he'd done for Bart, rescuing him, taking him in, caring for him and giving him his own shelter. And just to have it all end up with his medicine animal blown to bits by Brer Rabbit, aided and abetted by Bart. This wasn't right. He didn't have a violent bone in his body, save what he thought of fish, and this was unspeakably violent, horribly mean and violent. But, he tried to reason, wasn't Coyote mean to Brer Rabbit? Didn't he want to eat him? What if the fish he ate turned on him? They do! He shuddered at what sharks do to his people. That's it! This is like penguins eating sharks! The tables are turned, the victim is becoming the hunter, the eatee the eater. But Brer Rabbit isn't going to eat Coyote, he's not going to use his flesh so that he may live, for his own life needs. He's going to give him to the plants, the grasses and the weeds. He's going to recycle Coyote, just a little differently. But Coyote! He'd never hurt Bart. Oh, damnable conscience, why do humans cherish the cursed thing?

These thoughts tormented the little penguin, like crows on an owl, sending him from one end of the room to the other, seeking solace from his pursuers, as if walking, or more properly, waddling, would whisk them away. One more turn, one more step, and surely they'd miss their mark and he'd be free from them. Meanwhile, Brer Rabbit merrily kept to his mission.

At length, Brer Rabbit had a dozen pipe bombs, each nearly a foot long. He was ready for battle, but he needed to sleep: tomorrow was going to be one hell of a great day. 'Dey gwine tak bout dis fum ere t'Miss Meadows en back!' thought Brer Rabbit as he pushed himself away from the table and hopped down off the chair.

"Ba't, I'ze doan go ter bed, I'ze done in fo'. Doan let no one git dis 'ere stuff. Morrow gwine be mo' fun dan der biggitiest joob'lee you ere seed. But we bes' git some res' fuhst." With that, he skipped up the stairs and went to the house.

Unlike the soon slumbering Brer Rabbit, poor Bart had trouble falling asleep, and when he did he had awful nightmares. People in white coats and black bellies kept grabbing and poking him, forcing him to perform stupid, simple, repetitive tasks and tricks, which he did to perfection, but it was never enough for his tormentors. Over and over he would put square pegs in to square holes and round pegs in to round holes, or match the color green with the image of grass, or blue with the sky and white with clouds. He was suffering in a hell of monotonous simple mindedness, stuck in a room of suffocating tedium with pedantic bores. An endless ennui. But at precisely 5:37 a.m., he was released from perdition.

The sun was just rising, sending out trembling, tentative fingers of light to touch the sky and earth, shadows still held sway as the ritual battle of light and dark unfolded. One never loses, one never wins, when both have their sway twice a day.

All were cozy and snug in warm beds when the world stopped her spin, unleashing the most horrific, stupendous and stultifying storm that threatened to break her in so many pieces, like a shattered crystal goblet. And the storm was right over Burly's house.

Uncle Remo, a World War II vet, rolled out of bed yelling, "Take cover! Hit the dirt! Incoming!" Donovan fell off the couch, hitting his head on the coffee table, sending him back into sleep after a brief second of awareness. Burly leapt out of bed and crashed in to his closet, breaking the doors in the process, while Emma and Zach clutched each other, wide eyed in fear.

Only Brer Rabbit had heard the storm coming. With his sensitive ears, he'd woken long before it broke over the house, and he'd gone to the window to watch it. As it approached with thunderous, air compacting concussions, and lightening flashes that nearly blinded him, he looked up to see the colored logo of the TV station they'd been at the day before. A search light danced across the lawn until it landed on Zach's truck, where it stayed.

As everyone raced into the living room, it dawned on some that the earth-rending sound was made by a helicopter, and Brer Rabbit helped to confirm that all was well, or at least they weren't going to be scattered across Kansas from a tornado, because he shook a fist at the machine and scratched his rump with the other hand. Ah, paradise. Lost.

chapter fifteen

Sheldon Turner was in the helicopter, commandeering what amounted to a small invasion force comprised of reporters, cameramen and technicians. And one helicopter pilot. The main force, the ground troops as it were, were barreling down the little gravel country road that led to Burly's, in toto: eight vehicles. Sheldon regretted the heavy handedness, not for scaring the hell out of Burly, Zach, Emma and whoever else might be in the house, but for possibly alerting rival media as to Burly's, and thus, Brer Rabbit's, whereabouts. But he knew he did not have the luxury of time. Every TV and radio station, every newspaper and magazine, were hot on this story, and so far, the only tape they had was his. He was going to keep it that way as long as he could. 'It's my goddamn story,' he thought. 'They walked into my goddamn station.'

He had the pilot bring the helicopter dangerously low to the ground so they could positively identify Zach's truck. They couldn't make out all the letters on the license with the searchlight, but they could tell they were Georgia tags. "That's got to be it. Looks like the same goddamn truck to me," yelled Sheldon over the roar of the helicopter. "Land this goddamn thing in that field over there," he commanded the pilot, pointing to the big field on the other side of the barn. He winced in pain as his heavily bandaged hand struck the window of the helicopter.

Safely on the ground, he ran out from underneath the still spinning blades and made for the house. Two of his attorneys accompanied him. "Remember," he yelled at them, "I want this all legit and above board. But if they don't bite to exclusives, we'll threaten 'em."

"I still don't understand how. With what?" one of them asked. The other said, "Sheldon, you can't sue Mr. Peterson, or this Burky fellow for the rabbit biting you unless we can prove either one owns him, that he's their pet. And I dare say, after seeing the videotapes, that is going to be a difficult thing to get a judge to agree on."

"Come on! Support me here, damn it! Then give me some options! Options! You two have had all night. You're lawyers! You should be able to scheme up some pretense or legalistic mumbo jumbo, and you better hurry because we're almost there. I can see lights on in the house, and people moving about. There! Look! It's him! The goddamn rabbit! Look at that sonofabitch!"

Brer Rabbit was peering at them through the kitchen window, already contriving how he could get a ride in the machine that just landed behind the barn. Or better yet, fly it.

Sheldon strode right up to the back door and knocked hard like his request was the most pressing issue on earth. Brer Rabbit was staring at him through the window not two feet away, but Sheldon would not look at him. The lawyers, not having met Brer Rabbit before, certainly were looking. Brer Rabbit rolled a fresh wad of tobacco in his mouth while the lawyers stared slack-jawed at him.

Zach opened the door and somewhat sheepishly said, "Mr. Turner, sir. Glad to see you! Good thing you woke us up, my alarm clock broke. Oh, sorry about your hand."

Dismissing his hand with a wave of it, Sheldon said, "Zachary, son, you're a goddamn genius. I had confidence in you, my boy, but I didn't think you'd be able to do so much in one day! You should see last night's ratings! They're off the charts!"

Zachary was chagrined and a little confused, but it didn't take him long to see that Mr. Turner thought yesterday was all part of a plot to better his ratings. He quickly played along.

"Well, okay. I'm busted! I'm glad it worked! I wasn't sure how it would all come together, but it seems it worked just fine. Whew!" Zach said, drawing puzzled looks from Emma and Burly, who stood behind him. Donovan had regained consciousness, and sat on the couch rubbing his aching head while Uncle Remo was still getting dressed. Brer Rabbit scratched his chin. He didn't know exactly what was going on, but he could smell deceit in the air and attributed it to this fellow, who he now remembered as the one he bit yesterday. That would fit, he thought, better keep an eye on him.

"You bet it did! The whole country is buying my tape!" Sheldon said enthusiastically. "The whole goddamn world wants it now! Goddamn Chinese paying through the nose for it. And the Japanese are throwing dollars at me like confetti. How'd you do it? Where'd you get the idea? Where'd you get the rabbit?"

Still standing in the open doorway, Zach looked over his shoulder at Emma and Burly. Burly looked to get ill while Emma had a smile that said, succinctly, and rather precisely, 'This is cool.' Turning back to Sheldon, he had to ask him, "What'd you say?"

"I asked where you got him?" Sheldon said again, pointing to a non-plussed Brer Rabbit, who, bored by the conversation, sat down at the kitchen table and idly picked his teeth with a fork.

"He, uh..he, uh . . . came from Georgia," Zach finally managed to get out.

"What . . . like he was living there, in some kind of circus?"

"No. No. He just . . . yeah, he was living there. You know, with Brer Fox and everyone." Zach was getting a little unnerved. What to say, really? The truth?

Sheldon laughed. "Yea, sure son. Of course, Brer Fox. I forgot." He turned to his lawyers. "Get that boys? Brer Fox and all." The lawyers laughed uneasily. Tense little flitters and twitters.

"Say, Zachary," Sheldon asked, "Do you mind if we come in? These are my attorneys, Guildenstern and Rosencrantz."

Behind Zach came an audible groan from Burly at the mention of 'attorneys'.

"No. No, of course not. Come on in. This is actually Burly's house. Burly, meet Sheldon Turner. Sheldon, Burly Olalla. And I think you might remember Emma?"

"Oh, yes. We certainly do," said one of the attorneys.

God, she's great, thought Zach. Didn't bat a lash nor blush.

"I guess we can sit around the table here," said Zach. "Brer Rabbit, make some room. Do you remember Mr. Turner? This is Mr. Guildenstern and Mr. Rosencrantz."

Brer Rabbit looked very disinterested, though he managed to mutter a weak "Howdy," followed by a wan smile; he showed more interest in his teeth. The two lawyers were in thrall and didn't take an eye off him for long, only to look at each other, or steal a look at Emma, but never her eyes. She was busy helping Burly make some coffee. Burly was trying to stay calm and out of the way. Donovan walked into the kitchen rubbing his head, nodded to the visitors, and went to the icebox to get some ice cubes to put on the rising bump on his head.

In his loud voice, Sheldon said, "I s'pose I owe y'all an apology for waking you up this morning, but I had to be sure it was you. Goddamn chopper makes more noise than a freight train and a twister."

"How'd you find us?" Zach asked him.

"Police report. We monitored the police radio after you sped off yesterday just hoping something would turn up. And there you were getting a speeding ticket."

"But how did you find my place?" Burly asked from over by the sink.

"You pretty well told us everything. Your name was mentioned, and the fact that you lived outside of Ark City. Now the whole world is tracking you down, I'm just the first to get here."

Burly and Zach did not like the sounds of that. Burly turned to face the sink as if he might get sick.

"Which brings me to the reason I'm here," Sheldon continued, glancing at his attorneys.

"Let me guess," Zach said, "You want more pictures of Brer Rabbit."

"That's right, son. I want more pictures of the rabbit."

Even though he was being talked about in the third person, while sitting at the same table, it did not bother Brer Rabbit. Not in the least.

"And I want to make you an offer," Sheldon said

"An offer?" Zach asked simultaneously with Emma, who was standing behind him.

"Yes. An exclusivity offer."

"What does that mean? Sole rights to filming and interviews?" Zach asked.

"Exactly. But we can put a time limit on it of, say, ten days, or if you want, one week."

"To talk with Brer Rabbit? Sheldon, you have to ask him."

"Ask him? Ask him? But who's in charge of . . . who owns, uh, someone must own him. Don't they?"

Even Burly joined the laughter that erupted at the thought of someone owning Brer Rabbit. The lawyers joined too, at least until a scowl from the slightly embarrassed Sheldon silenced them. He pressed on.

"All right. All right. Now listen. Things are going to get messy in a hurry, believe you me. This place is going to be besieged by the press. And I mean assaulted, hounded and harassed. Everyone who wears a press badge from around the whole goddamned globe is gonna be on your doorsteps, camped out until they get something from you, circling overhead in choppers and planes and balloons. It's gonna make the Superbowl look like a family gathering. Don't kid yourselves. This is the biggest story since World War II. Hell, it's bigger. What I'm offering is some protection, some distance and a sense of privacy. I can do this if you let me. Your world is going to bust wide open."

They all looked at each other, the men with grim looks. Even Donovan managed to pipe in with a frown. As Uncle Remo walked in to the kitchen, Emma told Sheldon, "Well, you're still going to have to ask Brer Rabbit for permission. It's him they want, right? Go ahead, ask him, he won't bite. Again." She couldn't help but giggle at that, which raised her to improbably higher levels of esteem in Brer Rabbit's eyes.

Sheldon turned to Brer Rabbit, "Well, Mr. Brer Rabbit. You've heard all we've had to say. What do you say about giving me some exclusivity?"

Smiling at Emma for her thoughtful concern for him as well as the dig at Sheldon, he said, "Hit mo samer t'me. You kin ha'e all de pixchurs you wan' en all de takkin, I des wan t'get up in dat big whirlybuhd."

"Great!" said Sheldon. "We can easily arrange that." He shoved his good hand forward for a handshake, his normal gesture to conclude a deal, but thinking better of it, withdrew it. He turned to his attorneys and nodded ever so slightly, which prompted them to open their briefcases and pull out a stack of papers.

"Now wait a minute," Zach said. "Brer Rabbit, you have to be careful here. They are going to want you to sign some papers which will legally bind you to your agreement. You can get in a lot of trouble if you don't follow through. Sheldon, is this really necessary?"

"Zachary, my boy. It's just an agreement. The usual stuff."

"Let me see." Emma said, sticking her hand out. One of the attorneys handed her the documents, smiling warmly at her. Or was it an embarrassed leer? she wondered.

While she looked over the documents, Burly served everyone coffee, which gave her time. It was quiet for a moment while everyone sipped the hot morning medicine. But silence was an abhorrent vacuum to Sheldon, especially when he was working on a deal.

"Now you can see they're just simple agreements, you can trust me on that. But we don't have a lot of time. I'm trying to help you folks here."

As if for emphasis, his hard driving contingent of reporters, et al, roared on to the driveway, kicking up a cyclone of dust along with the crunch of gravel sounding like some giant chewing chalk.

More looks of concern were shared by the beleaguered as car doors slammed and an excited crowd gathered outside, which began to move towards the back porch en masse.

"As I said, we don't have a lot of time," Sheldon reminded them as he casually slid a pen across the table to Brer Rabbit.

"Hold on, Brer Rabbit," Emma said, showing Zach a particularly odious passage. "Sheldon," she said, "This is not agreeable," and read off the clause that allowed Sheldon to extend the time period as he saw fit.

"We'll change anything you don't like," he said as feet trampled on the back steps.

"And this, about financial terms. You've got to be kidding! This gives Brer Rabbit only 5% of possible profits. No way!" she said. "Sixty percent or nothing at all!"

"Sixty percent! Ma'am, that's unreasonable. The most I'll go is twenty percent, the norm is ten if there is one at all."

"Forty percent then," she countered.

"Now I'm not here to play games. This is a reasonable offer. I'll go twenty-five and that's it. That is my final offer," Sheldon said with as much finality as he could muster. He needed to get them to sign as quickly as possible. He was hoping to use the sense of urgency that the reporters milling about on the porch would bring, before they realized they were his reporters. Camera lights were shining through the windows and there came a rapping on the back door frame.

"Thirty-five," Emma counter offered.

"Done!" Sheldon said and slapped the table. "You drive a hard bargain, Emma." He took the papers and changed the numbers. "Here, go ahead now. It's all set," said a smiling Sheldon to Brer Rabbit as he thrust pen and paper under his nose.

Not giving a whit about law or contracts or even obligations posed by giving his word, Brer Rabbit took the pen and set about making some kind of mark signifying his name.

Uncle Remo, who had been studying the vans and cars, said, "Hey! It looks like all them cars and trucks have your logo on 'em."

Sheldon did not flinch; besides, no one seemed to hear or understand what Uncle Remo said. "Go ahead, Brer Rabbit, go ahead and sign," Sheldon said, much too eagerly now.

The reporters were knocking and Burly was pacing and Sheldon was grinning and the lawyers were leering.

Brer Rabbit said, "But I doan write. I cain't sign dis 'ere doc'munt."

Sheldon said, "Just make your mark, we'll be witnesses."

Emma finally tuned into what Uncle Remo had noticed, and said, "Your own reporters? So there's no rush? Your own reporters? You were trying to pressure us, and him!"

Sheldon's head fell toward the table in resignation. He slowly brought it back up and turned to Emma, "Yes, they're all mine right now, but trust me, soon they won't be. You can't blame me, I'm a businessman. I can still help you though. I think you are all naive, you don't know what you have unleashed. There is still time, and I can help you all."

Small little mustard seeds of doubt and distrust had quickly sprouted into redwoods among Emma, Zach, Burly, Uncle Remo and Donovan. But Brer Rabbit, sensing he could deal with Mr. Turner now that he knew for sure the kind of man he was dealing with, and could make a more favorable deal now, spoke up, "You a pert' trustful man, des lak me," he lied. "Less strike up un gennermans 'greemint. I gives you all de pixchurs en innervoo's fer now, en you let me drive dat der whirlybuhd. En if days any money, half un it goes on Buhly's crd't ca'd. What say yer?"

Defeated, Sheldon had no alternative but to agree to Brer Rabbit's offer. He turned to his lawyers and snapped, "Go tell them goddamn reporters to shut up. A waste of payroll, most of 'em. Like you." Both of them scooted out of their chairs and went outside to the clicks of cameras and a rush of reporters menacing microphones, until they realized who the two were.

"All right, Mr. Brer Rabbit, you've got a deal."

Brer Rabbit seized the man's bandaged hand and squeezed it hard before Sheldon could retract it.

Above the gasps of pain from Sheldon, Brer Rabbit said, "You got my shorance prop-en-tickler."

The pain nearly separated Sheldon from consciousness, but he managed to hang on and say, through clenched teeth, "Great. Goddamn great," and then sank into his chair when Brer Rabbit let go.

Shot from dreams like a bird in flight, Burly's mother woke with a start and a stutter of terror to the sounds of thundering helicopter blades. She realized fairly quickly what they were and why they were there. She had thought them all foolish last night for not preparing for the inevitable. Slowly raising herself from bed, she dressed in the dawn darkness, not wanting to turn any lights on and draw attention to her trailer. Then she went out to the kitchen and carefully closed the curtains as tightly as she could and then turned on the television. Fearing, or rather sensing, the worst, she turned on CNN. There, for all the world to see, was Brer Rabbit, surrounded by reporters. They had so called film experts, she noted with distaste, talking to the anchors about the reliability of the video, whether they were real, or fraudulent. There were, of course, those who were certain they were a product of Hollywood, and those who were just as certain and convinced they were real, couldn't possibly be faked. What they all agreed were real, to her amusement, were Emma's breasts. Beautiful, full, rounded young breasts, like hers once. She wondered if older men ever felt the same about young men's penis'. Probably not, they all start out wrinkled, was her conclusion.

Quietly, she made herself a pot of strong coffee, stronger than usual, and sat down to a breakfast of that and cigarettes and TV. Occasionally, she caught glimpses of her son as they replayed the tapes over and over again. But mostly it was different angles of Brer Rabbit and Emma's breasts seen again and again. It was difficult to tell which was of more interest to the station showing the pictures. Little boys, she thought, giggly over boobies and bunnies. Poor Emma, she seems so nice.

She followed as the TV switched from this location to that location, this reporter to that reporter, this country to that country. From this politician to that politician, and no comment from the White House, scholarly monologues from professor this and professor that. Debunker here and believer there. All a big alphabet soup of alibi's and Allah's wise and Christ's alive and films a lie and kiss it all goodbye.

'Boy, this world's nuts,' she thought.

She watched as demonstrators in Chicago and Detroit and New York marched, both black and white, protesting the obvious hoax perpetuated by racist Nazi's or bigoted Southern white robed morons, using a hated symbol of slavery: Brer Rabbit. 'No Uncle Tom!' and 'Down With Remus', 'Brer Rabbit=Brer Bondage', signs read. Elsewhere, smart looking college types, both black and white, many wearing horn-rimmed glasses, spoke of the value of Uncle Remus as a recorder of history.

Boy, did they open a can of worms. She looked skyward, up through her ceiling, and wondered what God was up to. Hearing the crunch of gravel on the road that clatter crashed into their driveway, she muted the TV and peered out to see all the cars and trucks charging like hungry lions. "And so it begins," she muttered aloud, 'better lock my doors."

It wasn't long before someone knocked very insistently on her door. The camera crews were fanning out over the ranch, and two were now at her door, replete with two reporters complaining about the morning chill, but they could wait until next winter before she would answer the door. She didn't move and barely breathed. She could hear some smarty saying they could smell cigarettes, so someone had to be in there. But she'd be damned before she'd open the door.

Another crew was carefully making their way down into Bart's cellar. They had knocked, carefully following reporter's protocol, and not getting any response, followed the next step in reporter's rules of order, and let themselves in. They really had no idea what they were entering other than a shed with a door, therefore something to be explored.

They slowly went down the stairs, camera lights flashed about like some robot submarine illuminating the dark ocean depths, objects appeared sinister and threatening, suddenly they were spooked by a blanket that seemed to be alive. It pulsed and undulated like a jellyfish. The two reporters jumped behind the cameramen, who, well trained as they were, kept on filming. Reality was in the lens.

The trembling, quaking blanket, gray in the spotlight of the camera lights, was mute as one of the cameramen braved a query, "Hello? Is anyone there? It's all right, we won't hurt you."

He asked again, to no avail, then one of the reporters gathered enough courage to move close to the violently shaking figure huddled beneath the blanket. That scared the creature so much that it threw the blanket off and dove under the bed. Unfortunately, the bed was only three inches off the floor, and the poor creature could not fit underneath. Little orange webbed feet frantically tried to gain purchase in the cement floor.

"The penguin! It's the penguin!" shouted the one female reporter as the male jumped behind the cameraman, terror on his face.

Poor little Bart. All the forces of good and righteousness had descended on his hamlet to mete out his deserved justice and punishment for aiding and abetting Brer Rabbit in his evil deeds. "I'm done! I'm done! I'm done!" he hysterically cried to himself as he tried in vain to wedge under the bed. But the futility of his efforts soon dawned on him, and gradually he went limp, panting and gasping for breath. Slowly, he pulled out the only part of his body that he was able to get under the bed, his head, and turned to face his certain death, or banishment and imprisonment. He thought he heard someone yell, but as he turned, all was quiet, not a breath could be heard over his pounding heart, echoing like a drum in the cold dark, the only light the blinding beam in his eyes. He had run across such things on the web. He was going to be interrogated and tortured. He would be brave and face his pain like a hero, maybe they would sing a song of praise in his honor during the long deadly winters in Antarctica, when his brothers watched over and kept their babies warm in their eggs. The Ballad of Bodacious Bart, they would call it.

One of the interrogators came forward and spoke. A woman! She said he would not be harmed, everything was okay. Right! They always say that before they blindfold you. She asked if there were any lights they could turn on. What for, he wondered, so they could better see him suffer? Sadistic humans! He pointed a flipper to the wall switch.

When she turned on the lights, Bart realized the evidence, the bombs, would be seen. Well, it didn't matter, he was already up to his beak in trouble. To his immense relief, he saw that he'd kicked the box of pipe bombs under the desk when he tried to get under the bed. They wouldn't discover it for a while, hopefully. By then maybe he'd be able to escape.

The woman spoke to him again. She sounded nice for a torturer. "It's okay, little penguin. We're not going to hurt you. We're just reporters, you know? We just want your picture. I know you understand me. Do you remember me? We met yesterday." She came in closer to him and bent down eye level to him. "We talked yesterday. It's okay," she said in a very soothing manner.

He began to remember her and when she saw his tightened shoulders relax, and some of the fear leave his eyes, she spoke again, "There, there," in a very soft, comforting voice. "It's okay. See? I'm not going to hurt you. Can I touch you?" she asked. He didn't know about that. Maybe she was going to strangle him and throttle a confession out of him. Maybe, but she sure is nice. Barely, almost against his will, he nodded his head.

She extended a hand and carefully touched the top of his head. Gently, so very gently, she patted him, and then slowly stroked his head, caressing and coddling it with her hand. He soon forgot about possible pain. If this was it, he'd allow himself to be tortured to death. His cooing signaled the end of hostilities.

Ripped from a dream of freshly killed rabbit by thundering hooves, Coyote woke with a snarl: the buffalo were running. He was safe in the old fox den he usually slept in on cold nights. He hadn't needed to do much work on the hole, just widen it a bit, that was why he took it from the original owner. Valiant fellow, that fox was. Fought hard, but in the end, ran off.

Now the buffalo were loosening the ceiling as they stormed above him. Big clods of dirt came crashing down as the earth shook. Big oafs, what's spooked them now? he wondered. He strained to listen above the din of hooves and bellowing and bawling, and could make out a rare, but not unheard of, sound. It was one of man's flying machines heading directly to Burly's house. This could prove interesting, something well worth investigating.

As soon as the buffalo were past, he carefully stuck his nose out of the entrance and waited until all was clear. Then he trotted out and in no particular hurry, loped off toward the barn. There was a vantage point inside it from which he could watch the comings and goings at the house. And if he was lucky, he might be able to catch one of the chickens that roamed freely around the barnyard. It was early enough that they might still be snug in nests burrowed in to the leftover hay. It would be as easy as pulling food from the refrigerator, like he'd seen Burly do.

As he neared the barn, he saw three men leave the ugly, gawky machine and head up towards the house. They seemed to be in bad moods, must be trouble. He watched as they stood on the porch for a while, talking to Zach and the woman. Behind her stood Burly. Postures were stiff, they must be strangers. When one of the men motioned to the window, he could make out Brer Rabbit's silhouette. Instinctively, he growled.

They didn't linger there long, and when everyone went inside the house he lay down: time to get comfortable and wait and watch. If he was quiet long enough, maybe a chicken would poke a head out of the hay.

It didn't seem very long and unfortunately before any chickens surfaced, that the silence was broken by a pile of vehicles rattle bang jangling into the driveway. He braced to run as people spilled out of the cars and trucks. There were a lot of them and some carried odd-looking machines. Most ran to the house, while others fanned out over the ranch. He watched as some broke into Bart's house, and nervously watched one person point his way. Two people began walking toward him, and before they got too close, he stole out the back way and made off for safer grounds.

The indefatigable Sheldon Turner rose to orchestrate his minions, the battle was lost, but the war raged on. Having obtained permission for further filming from the reluctant occupants of the house, he had the front room looking like a TV studio in fifteen minutes. Of course, cameras were rolling the whole time, recording the entire process like a documentary, and at least two cameras followed Brer Rabbit's every move, filming every habit, good or bad, and preserving them for posterity, including his itchy posterior.

The studio now ready, in one section sat Brer Rabbit being interviewed by several reporters, while across from him, at various times, sat Emma, Zach, Burly, Uncle Remo or Donovan.

The questions posed to Brer Rabbit had a monotonous sameness to them, from the inane: "What's your favorite color?" "Toebacker." To the sane: "What do you think of modern life?" "Dat in'net iz sum'in." Back to the inane: "Do you believe in God?" "I reckon he un pert smart fell'r."

The particulars of how Brer Rabbit came to be in Kansas still couldn't be deciphered from the actually straightforward and truthful answers he gave. The reporters wanted the mechanics of it, something that he didn't know himself. So they went round and round as illustrated by the following ellipse from one reporter's attempt to get to the heart of the matter:

"So you were at home, in what would appear to be Georgia, with Zachary Peterson?"

"Dat co'rek. I uz tied t' he big toe."

"Yes. And this was in Brer Fox's house. On his bed?"

"Dat ut I sedz."

"And then you woke up in Kansas. How did you get there?"

"I woke up dere."

"But how did you get there?"

"I des tole you."

"No. You said you woke up there."

"Dat right."

"Then how did you get there?"

"I des tole you. Iz you dumb? Dis iz r'dickluss. I gotsa take un ho'se fo un walk."

"You what?"

"I gotter pee."

"Oh."

And so it went.

The reporters interviewing the others weren't having much luck either. They told their stories truthfully, which led to some confusion concerning time and space. On the one hand, they had Zach meeting Brer Rabbit in some kind of dream on a church house floor in Georgia, and on the other they had Burly meeting Brer Rabbit in some kind of odd Native American ritual. The exact transporting mechanism was as much a mystery to the reporters as to Emma, Zach, et al. No new ground broken today, just the facts.

And many did want to discuss those facts with Emma, and to linger like naughty little schoolboys and twittering little schoolgirls. Giggiggily ha ha hoowe atta girl oh boy oo la oui, zit snap postules tapioca hormones, never did grow much give the dogs a bone.

On his way to the bathroom, Brer Rabbit ran in to Uncle Remo, and said, "Dem folks cream ain't riz all der way."

Uncle Remo didn't quite hear him, and asked him to repeat what he said.

"Dey candles hain't none too bright."

"Oh," he laughed. "I don't know about that, but this is all pretty new stuff to them. It isn't everyday they get to talk to a myth. It's a shock that you exist at all. It's a shock that they can talk to an animal. Wait till they start talking to Bart." As he spoke, a camera crew came up and poked a camera into their faces. The intrusion ended the brief conversation.

Brer Rabbit stayed in the bathroom for half an hour before Zach, at the pestering insistence of Sheldon, coaxed him back out to be hounded by reporters and cameras once again. It was about this time that the phone began to ring.

At first, Burly answered it, acknowledging that it was him indeed, Burly Olalla. But once he heard they were either a reporter or journalist of whatever sort, famous or not, academician, filmmaker, local or national politician, cranks, racists, novelists, civil rights organizations, reverend this or reverend that, or sweet old Aunt sorry I never heard of you, then he would swear they'd called the wrong Burly Olalla, never heard of Brer Rabbit, wrong number, wrong state and wrong country, wrong planet and wrong universe. And all of these in an hour. Eventually, he let the answering machine take the calls. God bless the answering machine, he vowed to build an altar to it and make daily offerings when things settled back down.

Two hours after Sheldon had arrived, two hours into the madness, Burly thought he'd better go and check in on his mother. Slipping away through the unused front door, he walked to her trailer. No one was hanging around it, but he noticed her phone lying in some weeds outside her bathroom window. He sighed, knowing it meant they'd found her out. He was just about to knock on her door, when he noticed a county squad car sitting out on the road. It was a county deputy whom he recognized from somewhere, so he ambled over to strike up a conversation. It would be nice to talk to a normal human being.

"Mornin'," he said in a friendly manner.

"Morning," the youngish deputy responded.

Maybe 30 years old, he looked young for his age, wore de rigour mirror sunglasses and sported very short hair.

"What's up?" Burly asked pleasantly enough.

"Not much, just saw all these vehicles pulling off the interstate like some kind of convoy and followed 'em here. Sheriff asked me to sit and keep an eye on things for a while."

"Yea, crazy TV people," Burly said. "Hey, don't I know you from somewhere?"

"You might have known my brother. He was about the same age as you, Bert Lawrence."

"Of course. I knew him in high school. Ain't seen him in years. How is he?" Burly didn't catch the use of the past tense: he was remembering Bert as a mean sonofabitch, always picking fights. He steered well clear of him.

"He's dead. Died in Desert Storm." The cop looked off into the distance as if to remove himself from the death and the memory.

"Sorry to hear that. He was a good man," Burly lied. The cop didn't say anything, just grunted.

"Say," he asked, "Are the rumors true?"

"Depends on what they are," Burly smiled.

"They say you've got a talking rabbit in there, that's what all the fuss is about."

"Well, that rumor is true. Any others?"

The cop looked a little embarrassed and uncertain, but Burly knew something was burning on the man's brain.

"It's none of my business, but they say he sleeps with women."

"Decidedly untrue. Very untrue. Jeez, what will people say," he shook his head in mock disgust, knowing that in Brer Rabbit's heart of hearts, he wished it were so.

"So you really have a talking rabbit? No shit? Where'd you get him?"

Burly could see the child-like innocence in the man trying so hard to be stoic, the imperturbable and dispassionate public guardian. "Why don't you go and see for yourself, ask him these same questions?" he suggested.

"I could? You don't mind?"

"Not at all. Go right ahead." Burly nodded toward the house.

"Thank you," the cop said, then drove his squad car into the driveway and got out. Burly could hear him muttering to himself as he walked to the house, "I don't believe I'm doing this."

He paused at the door, so Burly yelled, "Don't bother knocking, just go right in." Nice kid, he thought, not like his lunatic brother.

Released from the tension induced by living under a microscope for the past few hours, his thoughts floated and meandered like dandelion seeds in the wind. The zephyr causing the diaspora seemed to be the universe straining for some kind of balance. Walking to his mother's trailer, the apparent contrast between cop and brother had him wondering if there would ever come a time when the universe no longer needed the mechanism of duality to exist. Sure, males and females would be needed, but would we need hate to know love? Poor to know rich? Illness to know well-being? Looking at the press cars, he wondered if humans need meddlesome to know not-meddlesome.

He knocked on his mother's door, but she didn't answer, so he tried the knob. It was locked, so as quietly as he could and yet still be heard, he hiss-pered to her, "Mother! It's me, Burly! Mom! I know you're in there. You okay? Let me in."

No voice answered, but he waited and sure enough, the soft and gentle sounds of carefully placed footsteps padded to the door.

"Shhh! They'll hear you. Go away! I don't want them to know I'm in here. Go away!"

So much for his show of filial concern. Burly turned away and looked at all the vehicles parked in his driveway, his pickup surrounded by news reporter's vans and cars, some perverse inversion of wagons pulled in a circle to fend off Indian attacks. Maybe they'd all been here before, say 150 years ago, his ancestors and theirs. They were all repeating the act of attack as quickly as you can, take what you can, and leave just as fast. No hard feelings, nothing personal, just doing my job. My job as raiding Indian, your job as raiding newsman. A gentleman's genteel guerrilla war. Change the years, the same story. Cycles and cycles, he thought. This is pay back for that arrow you nailed me with right on this spot, I limped for the rest of that life. The camera flashes, gotcha! Now your life will never be the same. Tit for tat. He smiled at the fluidity of it. One big web of relationships and events rolling through time like some karmic tumbleweed flitting and darting and careening around and through space. The same actors doing the same tumbledown dance. There's that wind again, that breeze that tugs at poles and old barbed wire fences and souls. For the briefest of moments, for the thinnest of seconds, he caught a fleeting peek at a plan so vastly immense and complex he reeled from it. He'd been given a glimpse through a keyhole, and it stunned him. It was too big, and too simple. Too hard to grasp and believe, and take in. But thank the gods of the parking lot for trying. It was also too personal.

Two reporters or technicians approached him, he couldn't remember who was who. The fear that he had been able to elude for this brief recess returned, boiling up in his blood. He recognized it as the flight or fight mechanism, but they seemed friendly enough. Endure, he had to endure and suffer through this. Maybe he'd scalped one of them once. News at 10:00, this coup's for you.

He smiled back at the two men and stuck his hands in his pockets to signal he was available and accessible, though his legs wanted badly to tear turf between here and the next ranch.

When they were about ten paces from him, someone poked his shoulder from behind, which caused him to jump off his mother's doorsteps from surprise. He turned to look, expecting to see his mother, but instead saw a black woman standing on the stoop. She was dressed very neatly in a clean, crisp, dark, pinstriped business suit. But her hair did not quite fit the serious demeanor the clothes demanded; it was a large, somewhat wild, afro.

"I'm sorry," she apologized in a soft voice. "I didn't mean to startle you like that."

Burly stuck his shaking hands back in his pocket, it was the only way to get them to stop trembling. He was a little too stunned to speak, though his glaring eyes were doing a good job of relaying a message. The two men came up to him and one of them asked, "Are you okay? Did you get stung or something?"

Burly looked at him as if the man were related to a mollusk, and said slowly and sarcastically, singing the words like a nine year old boy might, "Nooo, I didn't get stung by anything. I was just scared out of my wits by her," and pointed a menacing finger at the woman. "She snuck up behind me and jabbed me with her finger! You people . . ." he let his words trail off and shook his head. She was obviously one of them.

"Who did?" the other man asked pleasantly. Must be careful, he was thinking, you never know about these country people.

"What do you mean, 'who?' Her!" Burly angrily shouted at the woman. The two men looked at each other a trifle conspiratorially, to Burly.

"I guess we missed her," one of them said.

"What do you mean you missed her? She's standing right the fuck in front of me, for God's sake!" Jesus, he thought, what kind of stupid game is this? He watched as the two men bowed slightly, then politely but insincerely said, "Sorry we couldn't help," and walked off.

He turned to glare at the woman, who just smiled back at him, very innocently, actually. And disturbingly sincerely.

"All right," Burly asked her as even toned as he could choke out over his annoyance, "What gives? You know those two guys?"

"Never met them before in my life," she replied, still smiling.

"Well, they must know you the way they pretended not to see you."

"An interesting twist of logic. Anyway, they couldn't."

"Couldn't what?"

"See me."

"They couldn't see you?"

"That's right."

Burly laughed and mockingly said, "So you're invisible? That right?"

"Yes. Exactly."

"And only I can, I suppose?"

"Right now, yes."

"I guess that would make you a spirit then, yes?"

"Correct again. You are doing wonderfully!"

She almost gushed that out. Burly looked at her with a disbelieving grin. He mulled over the possibility that she could be a spirit, after all, they do appear to people, that much he knew, but . . . her?

She stepped off his mother's stoop and walked right up to him and looked directly in to his eyes, unflinching and unblinking despite the intimacy of her action.

"Okay. I'll play along," Burly said, breaking eye contact and stepping back. "Though I think you're just another reporter trying another angle. If you are as you say you are, why can't I feel you? Why can't I feel your power like I sometimes can when Spirit is about? I don't feel anything from you."

"What would you like? Thunder and lightening?"

"No, I didn't say I need dramatics," he replied.

"But you want proof all the same," she said.

"No, I'm not really saying that," he argued.

"Sure you are! It would better fit into your perception of things. The old 'This is how things are' bit. I'm familiar with it."

"You are twisting my words. I only said I feel power when it is about and I don't feel anything with you. Nothing. Like meeting a fertilizer salesman."

"Okay. Okay," she said thoughtfully. "Well, this is how it is," then brought her right foot up quickly and powerfully, kicking him viciously square in the groin.

Burly howled and doubled over, his hands trying to cover his exploding testicles, then his feet gave out and he fell to the ground in a fetal position. He lay there curled up, groaning in agony and racking anguish for several minutes, it seemed, until he gradually caught hold of his breath and stopped moaning. His eyes popped open, looked about, then he scrambled to his feet as if nothing had happened. Dusting himself off, he said, "Nice trick. I thought for sure you kicked me in the balls. I saw your foot buried in my crotch."

"I did kick you."

"No way," he said stubbornly, "I didn't feel a thing."

"Because I'm spirit."

"Now why would spirit kick me in the balls?"

"To get your attention."

"That you have," he replied as he began to study her more closely. She was a good looking woman, he thought, actually quite attractive in her own way, considering how incongruous her hair was with her clothes. Still . . .

The sound of his mother opening up a window distracted him. She hissed at him, "What's the matter with you? Who are you talking to? Are you losing it? Get the hell away from here, you're making too much noise." Then she closed it shut again and disappeared behind a swirl of curtains.

The woman said, "Your mother is something else! Mmmhmm!" Then she looked directly back to him and smiled widely, "Hi Burly. I'm Lucidity Jones."

"How do you know my name and that she's my mother?" he asked suspiciously.

"I'm your tutorial."

"My what?"

"Your tutorial, your preceptor, the teacher of our clan."

"My clan?"

"Yes. Our moiety. You caught a glimpse of it just a moment ago. You opened the door just enough for me to come to help you. That's what I'm here for, to help you. We're family, Burly."

"Unh hunh," he responded slowly. "Well, I don't remember calling you, and while things are a mess right now, it's nothing I can't handle." Understanding was creeping slowly into his awareness, like a vine up a barn. She could be who she says she is.

"Is that the way you want to struggle with fear? By becoming sarcastic and distant? And paranoid too?" she asked.

"These are difficult times . . . that rabbit . . ."

"Is not the cause of your fear. It is already there, he just lets you see it," Lucidity finished his sentence.

"I'm not so sure about that. He can cause quite a bit of . . ." Burly's eyes became unfocused as his thought trailed off.

"Remember when you first met him, you thought he was a gift from spirit. He was and is."

"No! He's a self-centered lazy nuisance, a trouble maker," he said harshly. As his anger rose, his eyes became focused again. Ah, anger. Another mechanism for which to return from flights of fancy to hard boiled reality. Purloining poached incursions into a prodigious purview.

Silence followed as his ire waxed and waned, and as it receded he was able to study Brer Rabbit a little nearer to his original perspective, that of blessed wonderment. Yes, there was his miraculous appearance in the sweat lodge, and Uncle Remo had coincidentally recovered from cancer, but still . . . No! He couldn't let go of the black, acidic fog that surrounded the name Brer Rabbit in his mind and lay embedded in his body like so much shrapnel.

"What is this moiety you speak of?" he asked Lucidity, who stood in front of him, very patiently and very smilingly. "You say you're my tutorial or whatever."

"Teacher is a good descriptive word too," she replied. "It is the circle of family, of souls that you and I belong to that is in turn part of a larger circle of souls. Circles and circles and cycles and cycles, just like you thought, we're all riding the same tumbleweed."

'Jeez, she read my thoughts', he realized. "I thought a moiety was a half or something like that," he asked.

"It is. Our circle and the bigger circle, the intersection, the shadow of the two, the penumbra of the Great Spirit."

"Don't confuse me any more than I already am. What of the other circles? How can they be half again?" Burly asked.

"They are not. There is their circle then the other half, which we are in."

"That doesn't work out too well mathematically but I won't quibble the point with you, I get the sense of it. Now answer me this: How come you aren't a Kiowa god or legend, some spirit I've been praying to? How come you're not Earth Mother or Eagle, or Hawk?"

"They are all here, they are all around you. I see them as we speak, like Coyote, he's right here with you now. You could see him if you tried."

"Why aren't you like them? Part of my belief system?" he asked her.

"Why would you need another Coyote?" she asked rhetorically. "You talked to him, you know him. And what about your belief system? If I came to you in the form of, say, Santanta, you would believe me, but then would you grow if he verified what you already know in your heart to be true? Would you push and expand your envelope of belief system? I do not say your Kiowa system is limiting, only your understanding of it. People codify and concretize systems until they no longer function as methods of renewal and understanding and growth. Also, remember, you called me. We grow as a team."

He didn't respond, just looked at the ground and shuffled his feet, like a schoolboy guilty of some refraction of the rules and now paying the penalty of a lecture. He gestured to all the vehicles and asked her, "What is all this about? Can you tell me the meaning of this?" While waiting for a response, he realized they had been talking a long time but they had not been bothered by anyone at all, save his mother's quick rebuke. Sensing his thoughts, or avoiding his question, Lucidity laughed and said, "Time is of so little consequence. Such a trifling, a toy to play with."

No sooner had she finished her statement, Emma walked up to Burly.

Lucidity spoke again, "I love coming back here. I love the wonder, the beauty and power, and the magic of physicality. What a gift this place is!" With that, she walked up to, and melded right into, Emma. Burly thrust a hand out and yelled, "No!" but it was too late. Lucidity was in Emma.

Emma smiled coyly at Burly and asked, "What did you say? I've been looking all over for you." She grabbed him and pulled him tight to her, pressing her groin in to his and kissing him full on the lips.

Mumbling through her lips, he tried to protest, "No! No!" he said.

"Oh God, Burly! I want you so bad!" she said passionately.

"No! No!" he repeated. "This isn't fair. You can't manipulate people like that. It isn't right!" he protested further while he tried to pry Emma's arms off him.

"What are you talking about, Burly? Just take me. Here. Now." she pulled back and tore her shirt off, then unbuttoned her jeans, letting them fall to the ground. "Now, Burly. Now. I want you now." She grabbed for him but he pushed her away.

"Stop it!" he yelled, and she was gone. Only Lucidity and Burly remained.

"What are you doing?" he said angrily. "She's not a puppet for you to control!"

"Oh, it happens all the time. Who do you think really pulls the trigger? Besides, isn't that what you want? Don't you want her?" Lucidity asked.

"Yes, but not that way. It should be with her consent, her own free will," he stated.

"Then it'll never happen," she said with finality.

"It won't?" Burly looked concerned and disappointed.

Lucidity laughed gleefully, fully, with the freedom of a child. "Oh, I just love it back here. You know, you just can't get the same feeling of touch back home like you can down here. You should be spending all your time making love and savoring it."

"That wouldn't have been love," Burly said sourly, "That would have been sex."

"Not true!" she exclaimed. "Don't you have feelings for her? She has them for you."

"She does? Didn't you just say that I, I mean, we, would never . . ."

"Hearts don't always get the head to hear, the body's message isn't always received at headquarters, though you men seem to have less trouble with that. But everyone down here has little rules about things like that. Choices, choices, choices," she tsked tsked. "Well, it's time to go back to here."

"Go back to here?" a puzzled Burly repeated.

"Right. Correct. Time to be here now."

"Wait!" Burly interjected quickly before whatever she meant happened. "What about Emma. Was she really here?"

"Oh yes."

"Will she remember?"

"Oh yes."

"That's not good."

"Oh, she'll not be sure it really happened. Everyone here keeps doubt about to squash memories non grata and other things. Times up!"

Burly looked around to see if anything had happened, wondering if they'd be transported somewhere else or God knows what. His feet had not moved, he was still standing on the same plot of ground as before, in front of his mother's trailer. Only there were more cars in his driveway. Lots more cars. Way, way lots more cars, and many, many people milling about. Hundreds of millers milling. Some walked in circles carrying signs, many looked like homeless people, others seemed starry-eyed and homeless in another way, and there were more reporters and more cameras and helicopters flying overhead and people speaking in foreign tongues in front of more cameras. Vendors were selling hotdogs and drinks as if it were a ball game, there was a police line demarcated with yellow tape. And more police and more people and more protesters and more . . . Burly felt sick and looked over at Lucidity Jones, who still stood next to him. She was very excited, and said, "Oh! I want a hotdog! I want a hotdog! Get me a hotdog, would you?"

Burly looked at her incredulously. Some angel, or tutorial, or whatever. He wasn't very sure about her.

They made their way through the throng of people and up to the police line. Burly went up to one of the policeman and said, "I'm Burly Olalla. This is my house. Could I come in?" He was very polite.

The cop glanced to another one standing near him, then back to Burly. "What do you mean, 'us?' There's only you."

"Oh yeah. I meant me."

With a grunt the cop lifted the tape and Burly went under it and walked toward his house. He had not taken ten paces before a different policeman appeared at his side, and asked, "Are you Burly Olalla, of Arkansas City, owner of this property?"

"Yes. Yes I am, sorry to say."

"Could you come with me?" the cop asked.

"Sure," Burly replied. They must have some kind of strategy they need to talk to me about, he thought. Some kind of crowd control or something, need my permission. Or to complain about all the fuss. He followed the cop into his own house, and upon entering the kitchen, was greeted with the very dour faces of Emma, Zachary, Uncle Remo and Donovan. All were sitting around the table, with as many cops standing around them, and several others arguing with Sheldon Turner, who was trying to keep his cameras rolling, but the police seemed to be trying to stop him. He turned to look at Lucidity, who was all abeam with happiness and joy, but she didn't return his look. In marked contrast, all at the table had grim countenances.

Donovan was the first to speak up, "Bur, where you been? They've been looking all over for you."

"I was right out front of Mom's. Who's been looking for me?"

Uncle Remo looked at the table, Emma at Zach, and Zach at Burly.

"The police," Zach replied.

A man dressed in civilian clothes who had been arguing with Sheldon stepped forth. He asked, "Are you Burly Olalla, owner of this ranch?"

"I am," Burly said with authority. "What's going on here?"

"I'm detective Stevens of the Chautaqua County Sheriff's Department. You are under arrest for the possession of incendiary devices."

"What?" Burly asked incredulously. "What incendiary devices? You mean bombs? What are you talking about?"

"You claim to have no knowledge of these? Officer!" he barked out and the younger brother of Bert Lawrence came forward holding a box of pipe bombs.

"What the hell is that?" Burly asked. "Where'd those come from?"

"You don't know? Is that what you're telling me?" the detective probed.

"I've never seem them before."

"They were found in your storm cellar, with a penguin. Is that some kind of zoo animal? Do you have a license to keep it caged down there?"

"License for Bart? Why would I need a license for Bart? Bombs down there?" What anger Burly had for being accused of having bombs was turning into confusion by the topic of licenses.

"You claim innocence?" the detective persisted.

"Honestly," a bewildered Burly said, "I don't know anything about this." He looked at the others sitting around the table and got sympathetic looks, though Uncle Remo still stared at the table.

The detective said, "It is a very serious felony offense to make or have in your possession such devices that can cause explosions and bodily harm. Pipe bombs, Mr. Olalla, are very, very illegal. You have the right to remain silent . . ."

While he read Burly his Miranda rights, two cops handcuffed the purported offender. Burly turned to look for Lucidity Jones, but she was gone. Just like a spirit, he thought, the minute you need them, they're outtahere. He turned to Bert Lawrence's brother and asked, "Was it you? You did this, didn't you?"

"No, Mr. Olalla. I just did my job."

Burly shook his head, his eyes accusatory for the perceived act of betrayal. Turning to go with the cops, he realized Brer Rabbit was missing. It dawned on him that he had to be in on this. The strain of the past few weeks finally wore him down and he snapped. "Of course!" he nearly shouted. He looked at all seated at the table and said, "Where's that fuckin' rabbit? He did this! I'm gonna kill that . . ."

"Let's go!" a cop said, pushing him roughly out the door.

Donovan followed behind, shouting encouragement to Burly. "We'll get you out, Bur! We'll get you out of this! Don't worry! We'll straighten it out!"

"First kill that fucking rabbit!" Burly shouted back.

They led him away through the cheers and jeers of the crowd, and the cameras rolled on.

Inside her trailer, Burly' mother watched it all on TV, watched on the little box while they took here son away to jail not twenty-five feet from her front door. There were at least six different camera angles, she noted.

A few moments earlier, bored and tired of the same dumb questions asked over and over and over again, Brer Rabbit needed a break. Maybe he could steal away to Bart's and get on the internet or call some of the 900 numbers he knew. 'Dem gals prolly bin callin n' callin missin me. Dey ne'enter worry er be sollumcolly, I be dere soon,' he thought. Nobody would be at Bart's, he was sure, since he was obviously the center of attention. No, Bart's, would be quiet, a refuge from the pestering people.

Slipping away was no problem: into the bathroom, out the window, creep along the grasses and weeds that lined the fence, duck behind the propane tank, then behind the pear tree, slink around the small knob of dirt marking the storm shelter, and home safe through the wooden entryway.

And so he excused himself for the umpteenth time and went into the bathroom and propped the window open and slid out, making sure no one was outside to see him. He dropped to the ground, easily jumped the fence, waited a few minutes to be sure the coast was clear, then crept along the wire fence from grass tuft to grass tuft. Getting within sight of Bart's, his heart stopped when he saw a policeman come out of the storm shelter carrying his box of bombs, with poor little Bart close on his heels flapping his arms and trumpeting in protest. The darned cop then kicked Bart with his foot, sending him tumbling down the stairs, back into the shelter. Being gifted with a preternatural self-preservation instinct, Brer Rabbit fought the impulse to rush after the cop, not for mistreating Bart, but for stealing his bombs. Instead, he lay low in the grass, only his ears visible as he peered between blades of grass. He watched with anger as more policemen came, then watched with curiosity as they led Burly into the house. 'Kuse,' he thought, 'dems mus be Buhly's frens de way dey stick to um.'

The coast was clear, though, for him to make a break for Bart's and salvage what he might. He tensed his muscles to vault the fence but something blasted in to him, knocking his breath away and nearly breaking his bones as he was sent tumbling. Something bit painfully hard into his shoulder. The force of the charge left him dazed and flat on his back. When his senses returned, and his eyes cleared, he opened them to see a most unwelcome face looking down upon him. Teeth were bared and ready to bite again, yellow eyes were full of hate.

"Mr. Coyote, I des cum out fer t'find you! Buhly wants t'see yuz. How you bin, ole fren?" Brer Rabbit quickly lied as fast as the blood flowed from his shoulder.

"Fuck you, rabbit."

"Dat'd be mos unnatal lak, see'un we bofe men."

The coyote snapped at his head, Brer Rabbit turning just in time to avoid getting part of it ripped off. But the razor sharp teeth still raked across one of his ears, drawing blood.

"Hole on der, Mr. Coyote, afore you mak mice meat out'n me. You bes year de message fum Buhly."

"There is no message from Burly, you lying soon to be hair ball. He hates you as much as I do. Get ready for bunny heaven."

Coyote's eyes narrowed protectively as he brought his jaws down on what he thought was Brer Rabbit's neck, only to get a wad of grass in his mouth. The rabbit had managed to squirm out of the way again.

"You're a slippery one, maggot. But you'll slide down easy enough," he spat at Brer Rabbit.

A commotion at the back door followed by a roar from the crowd out front distracted Coyote from his task of tearing Brer Rabbit apart, but he still held him in a vice grip between his legs. Burly was being hauled away by the policemen, handcuffed. Coyote looked on in alarm as Burly disappeared in a crowd of blue uniforms. He could hear Donovan calling out to him, saying he would get him out of this mess, and he heard Burly very clearly yell, "Kill the fucking rabbit!"

"You little bastard! Look what you've done now! You got Burly arrested! It's time for the end of your tale, Little Brer Asshole!"

He coiled his head to give him more power to drive his muzzle down and his fangs deep into the rabbit's throat, but Brer Rabbit took advantage of Coyote's exposed neck and quickly sunk his long front teeth into it. He couldn't afford a wrestling match, so as Coyote scrunched back in surprise and pain, he slid out from underneath and lit out over the field as fast as he could, with Coyote in hot pursuit.

Brer Rabbit was not in good form, though. He was a couple of six-packs and a few pizzas too slow, and Coyote quickly caught up to him, sending him sprawling with a well timed swat at his hind legs.

Coyote was back on top of him, breathing hard and madder than Brer Rabbit had ever seen him.

Dire had become direr yet, and Brer Rabbit was about to become the die-ee on Coyote's diet. Noting the blood spilling out from the wound he'd opened on Coyote's neck, Brer Rabbit said, "I'ze monstus sorry t' bite yer, but I bleezed to he'p it git betta."

Between pants, Coyote said, "You will make it better by dying." He readied to tear into Brer Rabbit again, but tremors in the earth stalled him. To his profound dismay, the lone buffalo bull was charging hard at him and would be on top of him in seconds.

"You lucky little shit," he snapped at Brer Rabbit, "but I've still got a few seconds." And he clamped his jaws tight on Brer Rabbit's neck, missing vital vessels by fractions as Brer Rabbit twisted as best he could.

Luck and Brer Rabbit have been partners forever, and his confrere provided the good Brer with another boon as a stinging nettle plant happened to be at his paw tips, which he seized and ground into Coyote's open wound.

Around and around they spun, Coyote's jaws clamped down firmly on Brer Rabbit's neck, while Brer Rabbit twisted and mashed the stinging nettle and the earth shook as Lone Buffalo Bull rumbled forward. Finally, Coyote had to let go or be trampled by the bull, so as the bison came in, head lowered and horns inches off the ground, Coyote let go and spun out of the way as the buffalo stopped right on top of Brer Rabbit, standing protectively over him.

But Coyote was not going to leave; he'd run circles around the buffalo until the bull tired, then he'd finish off Brer Rabbit. He was not going to give up; Brer Rabbit was going to die today.

So, while Brer Rabbit lay on his back, propped up on his elbows and nursing his wounds, Coyote and Lone Buffalo Bull circled around each other endlessly. Each time Coyote moved in, the bull would chase him off, always staying between Brer Rabbit and him, like circled wagons of another day, like cars around a certain truck, like reporters around a story. Circles and circles and cycles and cycles.

They kept at it for hours: feinting, rushing, probing, charging, darting, until they could barely move. Lone Buffalo's sides were lathered white with sweat, his tongue sagging to the ground. Coyote was severely weakened from loss of blood, the pain of the stinging nettles still tearing and burning at his throat. His tongue lolled back and forth like a noodle. Eventually, they were reduced to crawling: the bison on its knees, Coyote on his belly.

Refreshed and pretty well recovered, Brer Rabbit, who could have finished off Coyote right there had he a mind to, stood up, stretched, and said, "Iz you fell'rs done? You pert near done in as t'is. Man git mighty hongry watchin you two go atter it." He smacked his lips as the two antagonists lay crumpled on the earth, breathing heavily but still watching the other warily through glazed eyes. The standoff was on the same hilltop where Burly had his sweat lodge, and Brer Rabbit ambled over to it, picked up an old bucket, and walked down to the creek to fill it up with water. Struggling to bring it back up the little hilltop, he spilled half the water, then set the bucket down between the two gladiators.

Coyote crawled up to it, managed to prop himself up on his front legs, and drank deeply. When finished, he dragged himself off and collapsed four feet away. Brer Rabbit walked over and picked the bucket up and set it down under Lone Buffalo's mouth.

"Der you go, big fell'r. Ha'e a heppin er dat."

As the sun sent its multi-colored light heralds across the sky announcing the end of another day, Brer Rabbit tended to the weary warriors, bringing them water, and for the bison, clumps of grass. With Coyote he shared a left over pizza he'd found in Bart's. He had snuck in to the shelter without drawing anyone's attention. Now he was nursemaid to his protector and antagonist. As the stars woke from their daily sleep and opened their shiny eyes, Brer Rabbit announced to the two recovering combatants, "Gennerman, we uz got t'git Buhly outter trouble." He held up two pipe bombs the police had missed.

chapter sixteen

Around the kitchen table sat Zach, Emma, Donovan, Uncle Remo and Sheldon Turner. Four were discussing ways to get Burly out of jail, of getting legal counsel, posting bail and other pertinent details relating to the freeing of a jail bound soul. The other, Mr. Turner, to be precise, was more focused on the filming of events for his docudrama. But he was also busy with his other tasks, as he had become their de facto media consultant and chief ranch house press secretary. It was he who was liaison between the other four and the army of reporters, writers, photographers, policemen, the newly arrived National Guard colonel, professors, students, spectators, curiosity seekers, state senators, U.S. senators and other undesirables. The world was setting up camp on their doorstep and clamoring for interviews, but it had to go through Sheldon.

He was also their advisor, and, when prodded by Emma, allowed the four the use of his lawyers, the same two who had accompanied him in the helicopter. Sheldon said they were kept corporate ninnies, but should know what a jailhouse looked like. And at any rate, he had waived their fees, which made Emma suspicious.

She argued to the others that Sheldon must expect to make a lot of money off them to not charge for his attorneys. Lawyers do not come cheap and she cautioned them to take another look at their agreement with him, but her words fell on deaf ears; the others did not care.

Their newly anointed barristers thought it would be a foolish waste of time to go immediately down to the county courthouse cum jail and try to release Burly. It would take some time to properly book him, then to get a judge to set bail. They might as well wait a few hours, they argued, then they could call the jail and find out if bail had been set. No need to rush, they advised, they might as well have dinner first. Besides, they argued, Mr. Olalla was better off spending the night in jail than in this madhouse.

That was their counsel, so Emma summarily fired them. She was taking control, and her decisiveness was appreciated by Donovan and Uncle Remo, who didn't want Burly to spend any more time in jail than was absolutely necessary. Uncle Remo was especially pleased because he'd spent a night or two in the drunk tank, and though that was years ago, he couldn't imagine conditions would have improved all that much.

Zach liked it too. For some reason, though everyone had been targets, reporters had focused in on him. He'd given what seemed to be a hundred interviews in just this one day, and the questions were mind numbingly similar. How did you meet Brer Rabbit? Is it really Brer Rabbit? Does he really talk? Is he intelligent? Did he meet Brer Fox? Is this some elaborate hoax? Are there more like Brer Rabbit? Is he genetically engineered? And on and on. After Burly's arrest, the questions had taken on a darker tone, and even though the police had thoroughly interrogated them, and found no reason to detain anyone other than Burly, the presses grilling was far worse. Are you certain this isn't part of some terrorist plot? Did he know about the bombs? Is he in on it? Is Brer Rabbit in on it? He, and everyone else, stopped giving interviews soon after the police left. He was tired and worn out, and very glad Emma was taking control of the lawyer issue and Burly's release.

Donovan set a phone book down in front of her and she looked over her options for lawyers. In a small farming and ranching community there wasn't a great need for lawyers, nonetheless, the U.S. is still fertile breeding ground for attorneys and so her choices were numerous enough. She skipped over those advertising specialties in divorce or injury, or even those offering help with bail bonds. Relying on her gut instincts, she chose one without an ad, just a name and phone number, a Mr. R. C. McDowell, Attn. She dialed the number, but when a recorded message clicked on she cursed and hung up the phone. She needed help now, not later, she muttered, but within seconds, the phone rang. It was R. C. McDowell. "Caller ID, Ma'am. I been harassed enough in my time, at least now I know who's doing the harassin'. What can I do you for?" a friendly enough voice said. Definitely a cowboy, thought Emma.

She explained the situation, which he already knew about from the TV. He said he'd be glad to head on over and get Burly out. He knew the judge who would likely be setting bail, and thought "Burly'd more'n likely be back at the ranch by 9:00 that evening. Couldn't imagine bail being more'n fifty thou' seein's how Burly's been livin' round these parts fer so long. And hell, everyone knows him and allowin' that he ain't never been in trouble or nothin'. And call me Bubba, everyone does."

'Great,' thought Emma, 'Bubba, my lawyer,' but she had a good feeling about her lawyer Bubba.

Lawyer procured, they set about getting something together for dinner. Though there were many people milling about the house, they were strict about who got fed; the media had to provide for themselves, even Sheldon. They had also started limiting the number of people in the house at any one time, allowing only Sheldon's top crew, never more than half a dozen, and that included the newly arrived national film crew from Sheldon's parent network, along with their well known popular nightly anchor.

They'd gotten somewhat used to the constant infringement in their private lives. Inside, it was manageable, but outside, there madness lay. The police were doing a good job of keeping the growing crowd from getting to the house and were lately directed by Sheldon to have people removed from the property entirely, which put more people out on the already overcrowded and jammed gravel country road. But it would mean fewer intrusions on those inside the house, and at least they wouldn't hear the crowd so much-all the taunts, cheers and pleas. Besides, it also narrowed the field of competition for Sheldon.

The insistent popular news anchor made them all realize that Brer Rabbit had been missing for hours now. They also wondered how Bart was getting along, and so, since dinner was ready, Donovan went to Bart's home, finding the penguin merrily chatting away with a female reporter, via computer, of course. They were alone; the other reporter and the film crew had drifted off somewhere, and neither had seen Brer Rabbit all afternoon or evening. Bart would happily come to dinner as long as his newfound friend came along too. Donovan had no problem with that, as pretty as she was.

The dinner table was crowded, even so, the network news anchor insisted on being seated. He was very disappointed that Brer Rabbit was not around and he was almost accusatory about it all being a hoax, he nearly demanded that he be granted an interview with the supposed rabbit. He'd flown all the way from New York in the dead of night to meet the hare and now he was nowhere to be found. Of course it was a little suspicious, he argued. Wouldn't anyone think so? The 6:00 o'clock news was a bust, but they could still get something on for the 11:00 o'clock news. Maybe a special for 9:00 o'clock. And no, he wasn't hungry, he was on a special diet that appeared to consist of green tea, coffee and cigarettes.

Dinner was quiet. Everyone ate leftovers within the realm of their own thoughts-minds and bodies fatigued from the demands of the day. Emma was thinking she'd never watch that asshole again on the nightly news, nor his newsmagazine. What a jerk!

The phone rang, intruding into the silence, but no one acted startled. It was Bubba the lawyer bringing bad news. The judge wasn't going to set bail, at least not yet, she wanted to see if more facts turned up. She was afraid it might be bigger than just Burly, though the police seemed fairly confident that no one at the house was involved.

The news angered Emma and annoyed the others, but there wasn't much they could do about it. She thanked Bubba for being prompt and asked to be kept informed. Anything further would have to wait until the morning.

After dinner, Uncle Remo and Donovan cleaned up with some assistance from Emma while Zach readied himself for two final interviews for the evening. The first was with the Right Reverend Thadonious Calcedon Thumpton of the First Baptist Evangelical Church of Our Lord Jesus Christ from Beulah, Mississippi. The Right Reverend had gotten past Sheldon with earnest, yet forceful insistence that the matter of Brer Rabbit was of utmost concern to the fine Christian church-going black population of America and that he, Reverend Thumpton, would be able to soothe their troubled souls if he could but meet with the creature. Sheldon relented over the phone and the meeting was set, and the Rev's name put on the police list for access beyond the yellow tape.

The man that now sat across the table from Zach thanked him profusely for the opportunity to be heard on behalf of his congregation back in Beulah, a little ol' river town on an oxbow of the Arkansas River in northwest Mississippi, and on behalf of black people all across America, nay, the world.

"No problem, Reverend," Zach told him, "I just wish Brer Rabbit was here so you could talk to him directly."

Reverend Thumpton smiled widely, his excessively white teeth looking slightly phosphorescent in the dull kitchen light. And a little too wolf-like, Zach thought. Where's the camera lights when you need them, he wondered.

The Right Reverend launched into a prepared speech of biliousness, bombast and vituperation lambasting the Uncle Remus character as a pathetic, stereotyped slave, "a shuffling yassir master I sho will, characterization and perpetuation and the demonization by an evil slave nation of the African kingdom to further the subjugation and terrorization of the black nation that will lead to the eternal damnation of white America and poison the budding relation of black and white just coming to fruitation and equalization." He slammed the table with his fist to signal the end of his speech, only his timing was a little late for full effect.

Zach nodded his head thoughtfully and said, "I guess I never thought about it that way, but I can see your point. But I think it would still be best for you to talk to Brer Rabbit. By the way, that's an interesting accent you have, Reverend. You're not a native Southerner, are you?"

"No sir. I'm not. I grew up in Brooklyn."

"Moved south, hunh?" Zach said.

"Yes sir, God called me to my flock, to a beautiful community in the Deep South."

"I see," said Zach. "Must of been hard for a Yankee to fit right in, specially a white one."

"My brothers and sisters took me in with open arms."

"You're a lucky man, Reverend," Zach said.

"Indeed I am. Indeed I am," said the Right Reverend. "What can I take back to my brothers and sisters, Mr. Peterson?"

"I don't know," replied Zach. "God bless, I suppose."

Mr. Thumpton rose from his chair and with a warm smile, thanked Zach for his time and left. Zach called out to him, "You're welcome to come back, Reverend, when Brer Rabbit's around."

Turning and bowing, looking ever so dapper in his three-piece suit with fedora in hand, the plump Right Reverend Thadonious Calcedon Thumpton thanked Zach once again and took his leave.

When the Reverend reached the police line, he was swarmed by reporters and cameras. Puffing himself up and looking as angry as he could, his fat jowls shaking like jelly, he launched into the same diatribe he'd hurled at the non-plussed Zach. But the cameras were rolling and this was his big moment. His performance was much better after having warmed up inside the house and even better executed than the practice runs done in front of his mirror at home.

"... and to think we have set just one foot into the promised land before once again we have seen the door close ... for the irrational hatred of a man for his color ... the evil empire did not collapse with Russia, and the Berlin wall fell, but not for my brothers and sisters ... segregation remains alive and well in America, it is an institutional infestation of a moral degenerational turpitudation that will not let the black man rise up as equals to his white brothers. Nay, I say to you, for when he does look o'er his ivory brows and sees the ebony framed eyes of a black man looking square in to his, the white demon does lash out and cause his black brother to falter. We saw this yesterday, and we see this today with the arrival, once again, of old steppin' fetchit Uncle Remus, the eternal reminder where the black man should stand. This perfidious and odious man is a traitorous and deceitful purveyor of the devil's truth and we shall stand up united, and again we will overcome him with the shining sword of God's laser light and smote this treachery down and cast him back into hell. Where he belongs! Where he belongs! Where he belongs!"

A slender black man in his early thirties, wearing wire rimmed glasses and sporting a goatee, made his way to the police line. He'd been listening to the fat white man give his speech. Quite stirring at times, he thought. But a little too pompous and staged for his tastes. Good points, though. Couldn't argue with most of them concerning prejudice and discrimination, still alive and well in America on both sides of the fence at that, black and white. But the fat boy's style was a little dated. It was as stereotyped, perhaps even more so, than Uncle Remus. Totally unnecessary and actually a bit of an embarrassment to him. The truly great speeches of Martin Luther King distilled to style and a smattering of substance. His mind flashed on the images of a few more notorious, well-known black 'orators', façades of falsity. Fakirs and publicity hounds, always mucking up the truth, shadows of the real light. 'Get that!' he thought, 'One stereotype accusing the other of being false.' At least Uncle Remus served a purpose beyond literary expression, giving real value to something other than himself, unlike these dime-a-dozen pulpit pounders. In the end, Remus served as a vehicle for the more important stories about the animals, Brer Rabbit and Brer Fox and the crew, and of the relation of his ancestors to the animals, and of his ancestor's relation to the white man. No, you've got it all wrong, fat man. You've done Martin wrong and you've got Remus wrong.

The defender of Remus was Dr. Timothy Bottoms, associate professor of ethnography at the University of Chicago. He was running a little late for his interview with Zach and Brer Rabbit.

The policeman at the gate checked his ID's after seeing his name on the visitation list and let him pass. Walking the short distance from the gate to the house, he trembled with excitement. He wasn't sure whether to believe in all this or laugh at himself for being so gullible, the duped academician. But those pictures on TV were so real, so incredibly real. And the man he talked to on the phone, Zachary, seemed so nice, so down to earth or something, certainly believable. He sure didn't sound like any con artist he'd ever run into. Not that he'd run into many con artists before, having grown up in Bloomfield Hills, Michigan, the son of a wealthy medical doctor. But the whole thing seemed so fantastic, as preposterous and outlandish as the stories of Brer Rabbit himself. He felt like a child again, the same excitement that ran through him like a current when his mother or father would read him the tales of Brer Rabbit at night before he slept, and he'd fall into sweet dreams with Brer Bear and Brer Fox and Brer Terrapin and of course, Brer Rabbit. How many times had he met him in his dreams! How many capers did he and Brer Rabbit pull off! How much fun they had! Oh, the blissful magical innocence of childhood. Is it gone? Can he reclaim it? He wasn't sure as he knocked on the door.

An attractive woman opened the door, "Hi!" she said, extending a hand, "Ah'm Emma. Come on in."

He took her hand and stepped in to the kitchen. There were people sitting around a table with what looked like a penguin that was gesturing very animatedly to another good-looking woman. She seemed rapt in attention with it. Rather odd, he thought. The two men at the table were looking idly on. One was an older looking man with long braids, probably an Indian, he thought, the other a younger white man, who stood up and said, "You must be Dr. Bottoms. Hi, I'm Zach, the guy you talked to earlier. Come on, sit down," he said pleasantly enough.

After exchanging cordiality's, Zach said, "The first thing I'm going to tell you is that Brer Rabbit is not here right now, and frankly, I don't know where he is."

"Of course," Dr. Bottoms said stiffly, while thinking 'I smell scam.'

"I know what you're thinking, and I guarantee you, he's real," Zach said.

"Damned real," a different man said, who walked into the kitchen from another room, crushing an empty beer can and getting another fresh one from the 'fridge. Looks like another Indian, Dr. Tim observed.

He heard another man, who had been working on some kind of recording device just outside the kitchen, mutter, "Little bastard," just loud enough to hear. He could see a bandaged hand, but not the man's face.

Zach spoke again, "Well, you'll see."

"Of course," was the only thing he could think to say in response.

"Hmmm," Zach said. "Anyway, I promised you an interview with Brer Rabbit and you'll get it as soon as he shows up. In the meantime, ask me anything you like."

"Well, I presume," began Dr. Bottoms, "that you've been asked all the pertinent journalistic who, what, where and when's a few thousand times. But if I could just press on you to relive a few of those questions for my own bearings on this, I would greatly appreciate it."

"No problem, Doc. Fire away," Zach said, sliding back from the table getting comfortable. Then, as one would recite the alphabet, he told Dr. Bottoms how he met Brer Rabbit, and how Brer Rabbit turned up in Kansas.

"Interesting," Dr. Bottoms said when Zach was finished. "You met him at a 'shout', it seems."

"Yes, that's what they called it. Didn't I say that?"

"No, you didn't. But I recognized it as such. I didn't think those were being done anymore, but I'm glad to hear otherwise."

"Yup, it was definitely off the beaten path down there in Georgia," Zach said.

"Oh, it ain't that far out in the sticks," Emma said from the sink, where she'd been doing some last minute cleaning.

"She lives near there, she's been to lots of them things out in the boonies," Zach teased.

"Really," an obviously pleased Dr. Bottoms said. "That really is wonderful news. I'd be grateful to hear more some time. Only, right now, if you'll forgive me, I'm more interested in hearing about Brer Rabbit. That he is . . . real, is, well, extraordinary news. I'm sure you realize the enormity of this, the implications . . . that a myth, a fable, lives and breathes. It implies . . ."

"That the tobacco growers and breweries will have jobs into eternity," intruded Uncle Remo, who had been silent.

A bemused smile curled around one corner of Dr. Tim's mouth as others laughed. "What do you mean?" he asked.

"He means," Zach said, "that Brer Rabbit has some unusual habits for your run of the mill, garden variety rabbit. Which he is none of."

"Oh. I see. So he likes tobacco and . . . beer?" Dr. Bottoms offered rhetorically. To himself, he thought, 'Just like the books.'

"Yeah, chewing tobacco and beer," Donovan said as he came into the kitchen for yet another beer. Dr. Bottoms grimaced at the mention of chewing tobacco and settled back into his chair. In the meantime, Bart, who had settled down to study the good doctor, suddenly hopped off his chair and started to trumpet and coo, then grabbed part of the table cloth and shook it violently. And just as abruptly, he dropped it from his beak, pointed at it with a flipper, and began to coo again. Whatever he was trying to tell the onlookers, the message was not getting across. No one seemed to understand what he wanted, and they kept asking him: What is it? What is it? What is it? Which provoked more furious gnashing of the table cloth and spasms in his little body. Finally. Uncle Remo understood what Bart was trying to communicate. "He wants a blanket for his friend," he stated simply. Bart jumped up and down as his message was finally comprehended. "He wants his friend to be warm down in his cellar," Uncle Remo finished.

Everyone looked at each other as Donovan went to grab a blanket. He had to step across a room full of sleeping technicians and reporters and cameramen to make his way to the linen closet to look for a spare blanket. Gratefully, the invaders had left everything. They were so tired they were falling asleep on the floor, or if they were lucky, on a chair or the sofa, except for the anchorman from New York, who sat in a chair staring out the front window, chain smoking cigarettes from a faux ivory cigarette holder. He was looking out over the road, at the cars lining it with people milling about. It was carnival like, but he didn't seem to notice, he didn't seem to notice anything, he was wrapped up alone with his thoughts.

The female reporter blushed at the looks she was garnering from those sitting around the table. They were eyes of curiosity and eyes of disbelief. Realizing what they were thinking, she blurted, "For gods sake, people! He's a penguin! I'm not going to sleep with him! Jesus! How could you! We're just friends!"

No one said a word as she and a doleful looking Bart ambled out the door. She had them, until she said the thing about only being friends.

The sound careened and ricocheted down the concrete and stainless steel corridor like BB's in a blender. Echo smashed into echo, sound wave piled up into sound wave but Burly could still discern the tinny and muddled sounding notes that reached his cell. The guard, a big oaf of a farmboy, was watching his favorite movie, 'Apocalypse Now'. Burly knew from the music what scene he was watching: helicopters were rising above the Viet Nam jungle to the sounds of Wagner's, 'Ride of the Valkyries'.

Something rose up in him as well, he paced around his little cell, shaking his fists and singing, "Kill the Wabbit! Kill the Wabbit!"

As he droned on, a mist swirled out of nowhere and congealed into a prostrate form languishing on the jail cot. Lucidity Jones casually asked, "What are you saying?"

"AAAA!" a startled Burly cried and jumped backwards into the cell wall, slamming his head and elbows painfully into it. "What the . . . oh, it's you."

"What was that? What were you singing?" she asked again.

"Nothing. It was Elmer Fudd."

"Friend of yours?"

"Not yet, but who knows tomorrow."

"Yes!" Lucidity said with relish. "Who knows tomorrow!" She looked around the cell with glee in her eyes. "So this is a modern jail? How nice! In my time it would be straw on a stone floor, if you're lucky. My, how times have changed!"

Gathering himself, and annoyed at the break in his meditation on murder and mayhem, Burly angrily responded, "And when would that be? Never mind! Where have you been? You're an angel, get me out of here! Do some magic!"

"Orders, orders, orders" she tsked tsked, ignoring his demands. "The last time was in a castle dungeon in southern France. I was marching against Roland, in the eight century, I believe, to counter the Christian king, Charlemagne. We lost, and I was imprisoned and tortured in the name of Christ. We were a lovely forest people. What a shame . . ." her voice trailed off with a wisp of sadness and regret. Then she abruptly sat up and dangled her feet off the cot. "But that was a long time ago and things change, don't they Burly boy?"

Burly looked at her, eyes blazing with anger and dancing like a possessed ferret. His fists were clenched, bleaching his knuckles, and his jaws were clamped shut, the skin spasming like an army of moles was marching under it. His shoulders were rigid as a metal rake and his head was lowered like a bull ready to charge.

"You're looking a little loony these days, Burly. Hanging on to anger is not doing you any good. Look at yourself." She stood to turn him to the sheet of polished stainless steel that served as the mirror, but he shrank from her.

"Oh, Burly. Where have you gone," she sighed.

"I've gone to goddamn jail because of that little tobacco sucking runt!" he snapped.

"You don't need to be redundant," Lucidity said.

"What?" a puzzled Burly snarled.

"Little and runt mean much the same thing, so one or the other and your meaning will sing," she said.

"And roasted and basted is good a hare tastes," Burly sneered.

"Oh! Clever!" Lucidity squealed with delight. "There's something left up there after all!" She pointed to his head. "It hasn't all given way to anger and hatred. We can salvage you yet! We'll babble and jabble until you can chatter from all of our blabber and wordy good prattle, like Cicero speaking to the senate of Rome, we'll keep at it anon, you'll be back at home!"

>"Oh, I don't give a whit for my conditional fit,
> If I'm loony or moony I couldn't care-oony!
> Until that rodent is dead, defunct and extinct,
> My life has no meaning, it's dull and insipid.
> I'll get my revenge and the hare will be limpid,
> A soul left to wander on dark t'other shore,
> Whilst I dance in joy and sing, 'nevermore'," Burly
>   chimed.

>"Tis never the season for any such reason,
> You'll poison your heart with the black little fart.
> So open the door and let the fresh air in,
> Or stew undercover and foul your clean linen.

Forgive and forget, they're the good lessons,
Open your heart and receive the good blessin's,"
   Lucidity responded.

"Why should I care for that little hare,
Who's done me more harm, the cursed dark charm.
I'd rather he sit upon roasting spit
Than ever in fair, I call him my brer,
I'd rather be dead, than having such said."

"You wish you may, you wish you might,
Be very careful what you ask in spite,
The creator has a great gift chest
And doles it out with grand largess
And gives you what you ask in spades
Even tis your shallow grave," Lucidity admonished.

"Higgery diggery hula hoop,
You can't scare a man now a nincompoop.
So leave off and exit, go leave me alone
If you won't do my bidding and get me back
   home.
Where is your magic, your voodoo, Miss Jones?
Is something amiss, my dark alchemist?
Or don't you do house calls, the doctor's not in?
No hocus pocus for souls out of focus?"

"There's more to this tale than sad Burly's wail
Against his misfortune, importune I will tell.
Come hither and sit, of the chosen I talk,
Though at the moment, you do seem to balk.
It was you who did ask for the blessing of task,
Of caring for rabbit, the rascally shit
Who put you in jail, against whom you rail.

I tell you the truth, 'tis you have the blame,
You and your spirit, they're one and the same,"
   she told him.

"So esoteric, this ethereal spiel,
This powwow profundo is more mumbo jumbo.
If such is the gift from heavenly hosts,
They must hold me a lemon to give me such
   venom,
Lest heaven has humor as black as a tumor.
No, I never did ask for said little ass,
Don't tell me I'm chosen when the gift is a poi-
   son."

"A lesson learned is a lesson earned
And the merit inherit is worth it enough,
Though human it is to whine and complain,
Grumble and gripe about everything.
Yet high and above their spirits do roar
Into the ears of their deaf earthly whore,
Who sell themselves out for trinkets of ore
And never do hear the heavenly voice
Of their own blessed souls, thus is the choice.
But hark now the feet of your jailer creeps,
And so I will go, our talk now complete."

"More drivel and drool and nonsense you spout,
You're more of a pain than that little furred lout.
The bean addled wind that breaks from your
   tongue,
Falls on my ears, chit chat from a gnat.
So take my advice all rolled in a ball,
And shove it far up, where never it fall."

"What? What did you say, Olalla? You talking to me?" the approaching guard said, anger rising in his voice.

"Shut up, you big clod," Burly snapped.

"Oh, feeling a little sorry for oneself? Poor little boy. Well, let's see if I can help. I've got something to shove all right." The guard opened Burly's cell door and thrust his fist out, which hit Burly's snout, knocking him out, and heavy he fell, we hope to dream well and freshen his soul and to think of parole.

"Essentially, there are two main camps of thought about Brer Rabbit," continued Dr. Bottoms, who had been discussing, actually lecturing, the gang about Brer Rabbit and the other characters in the Joel Chandler Harris stories. "In general, sociologists consider him to be a proxy for the slave, from whom the stories emanate. They are he, the small, essentially defenseless and vulnerable rabbit, target of the carnivorous animals of the forest and farm, the prey of the predators, who are the white slave owners, of course. But the wily rabbit is able to outwit his would-be tormentors, he always ends up on top, always outshines his would-be oppressor. He always wins in the end. So there is an element of him as hope and aspiration. And there is no story where he loses, at least in the tales we know of, and there are other sources beyond Harris.

"Anthropologists, on the other hand, prefer to think of him as a metamorphic entity, a distilled version of the archetypal trickster figure, who, through his foibles and misdeeds, ends up giving boons to the world, or creating the world, or saving it. His misguided efforts, always for his own gain, end up going awry for him, benefiting mankind or the animal kingdom at large. For instance, he'll steal fire from the gods for his own purpose, but then loses it to humans. There are stories and tales concerning rabbit in Africa, considered the original home of Brer Rabbit, where he has some of these attributes. However, his role in mythology shifted; it changed when he came over to America with the slaves. He became Americanized and may well have been a proxy for the slaves who brought him. Certainly, he did evolve into something a bit different from his original African genesis."

Emma asked him what camp he belonged to.

"I think both have elements of the truth, though I suspect the anthropologists are probably closer to the mark. I was hoping Brer Rabbit could shed some light on the matter," Dr. Tim winked as he said the latter.

"The only light he'll shed is from the refrigerator door," Donovan said.

They all chuckled at that, then Zach said, "I'm afraid he only knows himself. He can't identify himself as something other than who he is, not what he may have been. Did that make sense? He does have self-awareness, but I can't see him being of much help to you."

"Oh, yes," Emma said. "He is very self-aware. Self-involved may be the bettuh term."

"That he can't separate himself from the world around him, from a perspective removed from his own, is not a problem. Most people can't, let alone an intelligent, er, animal, or legend, myth, or whatever," Dr. Tim said.

"Yes, it is hard to classify him. But once you get to know him, he becomes just Brer Rabbit. Not animal, not human, though he has characteristics of both. He is just, well, Brer Rabbit," Zach said.

"Here! Here!" Donovan said as he popped the top off a beer can. "Hey Doc! You want one?"

"Well, sure, if you don't mind."

"Not at all. We try and keep some handy, and mostly hidden from Brer Rabbit so we can have some for ourselves and guests," Donovan said.

Uncle Remo had been listening to Dr. Bottoms with great interest. "You know," he said, "folks are making such a fuss about this here rabbit talking, but animals are talking all the time. You just have to know how to listen. Take Coyote. Now there's a talker, but he don't talk like you n'me. Well," he paused, scratching his head, "that ain't quite right. Burly said he talked plain as day to him. I guess it just depends on how he's feeling." He stopped, his mind suspended, caught on a thought.

"Buffalo talk too," Zach offered in the silence that followed Uncle Remo's comments.

"I had a dog once that could bark 'please'," Emma said earnestly.

Everyone laughed. Dr. Bottoms was intrigued by Zach and Uncle Remo's comments and he asked Zach, "How do you mean that, buffalo talk? Did you have a conversation with one? Did they use words?" He sipped on his beer while waiting for the slow and deliberate response that eventually came from Zach.

"Well, not really. It was more in my mind. I could . . ." he paused, carefully choosing his words, "it was more like the words formed in my mind. But they were clearly not my own. I would answer them and the response would come back different than what I would have said. Or thought. No. They were not my words. We were communicating."

Dr. Bottoms would not look at Zach, instead, he rested his eyes on his can of beer. "Hmmm," was his only reply.

"I know you don't believe me," Zach said. "That's all right. Hey Do! I'll take a beer."

The house was quieting down. Zach, Emma and everyone talked in hushed tones, occasionally having to raise their voices over the snores coming from the front room where many of the film crews were hunkered down for the night. Sheldon was still sitting in a chair near the kitchen, but his head was bobbing up and down as he fought sleep. Eventually he announced he was going to bed, to sleep in the special cot that was kept in one of the vans. No doubt someone would be sleeping in it, but surely they'd relinquish it for their job.

Outside, all was quieting down too as night deepened. Only a minimum number of police manned the lines, drinking coffee and telling stories and jokes as stale and ancient as ever were told when humans first stood watch over cave entrances or people, cows, horses, sheep or rabbits. Out on the road, headlights had dimmed as most people tried to sleep in their vehicles. The police had made sure the road was still open, though tightly jammed, so anyone could have driven back toward town and tried to get a room in a motel, though they were booked for miles around. Most just stayed put. Perhaps tomorrow they'd get to see the miracle they'd come to witness.

Back in the house, enervated by the beer and the friendly conversation, Emma, Zach and Donovan, weary as they were, stayed up longer than perhaps they should have. But they enjoyed Dr. Timothy Bottoms and invited him to sleep in the extra bed freed up when Uncle Remo went off to sleep in his sister's trailer.

Most people were asleep by now, with the exception of a few people sitting around small fires burning in the ditch along the road. They were some of the last to go to bed; save three figures creeping forth from behind the barn.

They had waited until the lights in the ranch house had been out for nearly an hour before leaving the protection of their gully hideout. Then they carefully made their way to the barn from up the same ditch Buffalo had chased Coyote down on the day he'd escorted Brer Rabbit up near the house. Now they were all working together with one common goal: to free Burly from jail. But they were far from congenial to one another.

"If I get hurt because you can't drive, I swear I'll rip your throat out," menaced Coyote to Brer Rabbit.

"You'll do nothing of the sort," rumbled Buffalo, who walked between the two natural antagonists.

"I was just being rhetorical," lied Coyote.

"What?" Buffalo said in a very serious tone, swinging his massive head to the comparatively puny one of Coyote.

"I was kidding, just a joke, and a poor one at that," Coyote said, lying again but managing a smile for effect, which always looked like half a sneer, a tempered, insolent fleer.

The insouciant Brer Rabbit, having yet again escaped serious harm and death mere hours before by the thin margin of a buffalo's horn, and perhaps thinner still, by a fold of his own skin or by a singular hair on his chinny chin chin, matched Coyote's lies with one of his own.

"Buhly lemme drive all de time. I des a natchul bo'n autumbo'lee drivuh," he said.

"Natural born liar," Coyote corrected him.

Poor Buffalo was surrounded by two liars; a stalwart mount of truth and integrity sandwiched by two prefabricating prevaricators. An odd sort of oreo.

Ignoring Coyote, Brer Rabbit went on, "Lessee ef'n we kin git un big ole truck fer Mr. Buffo. De mo biggity de mo betta. Hit de on'y way we'z gwine git t'town en git Buhly outter de calaboose."

As quietly as they could, they made their way to the front of the house where a fleet of choices sat parked for the taking. While Buffalo lay back in the shadows, Brer Rabbit and Coyote crept out into the parking lot of hope. Unfortunately, the lack of keys narrowed the field of options.

However, Brer Rabbit and luck have been partners longer than man and fire, and someone had left the keys in a large van, probably assuming no one would be foolish enough to steal a large vehicle under the watchful eyes of the police, and one with the side emblazoned with the logo of Sheldon's TV station to boot. It was late, the police tired or engrossed in old tales, and so none thought it unusual when the engine turned over and the truck began to move. Media trucks and vans and cars had been coming and going all day and night, and so the few police awake paid it no mind.

That changed as the truck lurched and swerved and moved about in a herky jerky manner. One young duty-bound officer decided he'd better take a look and began to walk after the truck.

The problem was caused by Brer Rabbit's size. He had moved the seat up as far as it went, and sat on a coffee can the crew used for cable connections and whatnot. He could see out the window but he had to stretch to reach the pedals, and thus he kept sliding off the can, alternately hitting the gas pedal and the brakes and jerking the steering wheel around.

He had managed to jolt and rattle the vehicle to within twenty paces of the waiting Buffalo when once again he slipped off the can and instinctively grabbed hard on the steering wheel, turning the van into the side of another van. The sounds of crumpling metal and the jolt of the hit woke the sleeping occupant of the sitting van, knocking him off the little cot he slept on.

Inside the now resting truck, Coyote was hissing and spitting venom at Brer Rabbit. "You stupid little moron, you can't drive any more than I can, you lying hare brain. You're going to get us all killed."

"Dis goll danged gimber jawed cans gwine git chunked out'n de winder," and he threw the can out the window where it struck a just awaking Sheldon Turner in the forehead as he stepped out of the van that had just been damaged. The can glanced off him, leaving a small cut in the process. It did not knock him out, but it knocked him to his knees, nonetheless.

The policeman, meanwhile, who could not see the vehicles, nevertheless heard the collision and quickened his pace.

Back at the site of the accident, Buffalo came from the shadows. He stood over Sheldon and rumbled a warning that even a dazed and addled mind could comprehend.

Sheldon, peering through eyes impaired by trickling blood, looked up into the face and felt the warm breath of the bison bull. He thought he was either dreaming or about to die, or both. So he closed his eyes. When he opened them again, he was looking directly into the angry eyes of a snarling, growling coyote, teeth bared and inches from his throat. This must be hell, he thought, or a very, very bad dream. So he closed his eyes again, the only thing real was his throbbing head, he reminded himself, that he could be certain of. But he prayed anyway, to a god that he had always taken for granted.

When he opened his eyes again, it was because of the urgent pleas from someone calling out his name and shaking his shoulders urgently.

"Mr. Turner! Mr. Turner! Are you all right?" the young policeman asked. "Hey, are you all right? Sir? Sir?"

"Yes. Yes, I am. Thank you," came the slow reply from a man who just now came to the unmistakable conclusion that God was not dead after all.

"Where'd they go?" Sheldon asked.

"Who? Where'd who go? Where you assaulted, sir?"

"Yes. I mean, no. Wasn't a buffalo just here?"

"Not that I saw, sir. I saw only you when I got here. I saw the van . . ."

"The van! Yes! The van!" Sheldon stood on wobbly legs and looked at the two vehicles.

The bigger one had its left front bumper embedded into the side of the one he'd been sleeping in, and the engine was still running.

"They wrecked my goddamn trucks!" he muttered in disgust.

"Who, who wrecked them, sir?" the policeman asked.

"The, the . . . I don't know. I thought, I thought . . ." but he couldn't finish the sentence because he didn't know the 'who' of it.

The cop said, "Listen, it's on private property, so I can't write a ticket on this anyway unless there's a complaint. So it's all right if you did it. I won't write you up, unless you purposely lie to me."

Sheldon's mind was clearing, and he realized that the cop had not seen anyone and thought Sheldon had been driving, so to make matters easy, he confessed.

"Okay. It was me. I was, you're not going to believe me, but, you know how some people sleepwalk?"

"Yes sir," came the brisk reply.

"Well, I sometimes sleepdrive."

"Sleepdrive, sir?" came the incredulous response.

"Yes. Sleepdrive. My wife and I try and keep it to ourselves. At night, at home, my wife locks the keys to the cars in a drawer. But here, well, you can see how the problem could come about."

"I guess," the cop said laconically and slowly. "Well, it's none of my business and since they are both your vehicles, so . . ." he was trying to get away.

"So I'll take care of this in the morning," Sheldon said hastily. "Thank you officer. And if you could, I'd appreciate it if you kept this between us."

"No problem," the cop said and turned to walk away. When he was safely away, the large truck clumsily jerked free from the other one, forcing Sheldon to jump backwards in fright, and then, gears grinding badly, it lurched forward and drove off.

The back of the van nearly scraped the ground as it disappeared in to the night. But before it drove off, Sheldon got a good look at one of the occupants, so he knew the other must be driving. "Guildenstern and Rosencrantz, you two jackals. What in the hell are you up to?" He cursed them as the vehicle sped off.

chapter seventeen

Inside the van, space was at a premium. Fortunately, the larger equipment usually stored there was in the house. Still, there were a lot of cables and other stuff lying loosely in the back, leaving just enough room for Buffalo, though on his knees, and all the jostling and jerking and rocking did not suit him. Not very well at all. When he jumped into the van, he'd nearly crushed the two lawyers who were crouching in the shadows in silent terror.

They had not woken when Brer Rabbit and Coyote first started the truck up, though Rosencrantz had stirred, but thought the noises came from an adjacent van. But they certainly came to when Brer Rabbit hit the other vehicle and they'd jumped up demanding to know just what on earth was going on. Their imperious queries were quickly quelled by Coyote, who, in very good English, told them to shut the fuck up. They acquiesced most agreeably since the proffered option was to have their throats torn out. Thus, when the huge bison leapt into the back, nearly flattening them up against the forward console, they only whimpered in alarm, and when Sheldon Turner saw Guildenstern, he was mutely pleading for his life.

And so the quintet made their way into town, the mission a go to save Burly from a life of hard labor, as they saw it. But their journey was not without mishap. The van was large, the road narrow, and the driver poor.

Like a fallen pinball wizard, Brer Rabbit drove the van down the gauntlet of cars that lined the little country road that led to the highway, slightly, or greatly, denting, scratching, nicking, demolishing, damaging, scraping, grazing or lacerating twenty-three vehicles in the process. A ping with too many pongs. When they finally reached the highway, Coyote took one look at all the cars whizzing by and said, "There is no way that I am going to let you kill me on that road. Let's get one of the humans to drive."

"Wha' fer?" Brer Rabbit asked. "Hit monstus big road. Mo biggity'n dat lil bitty teng we des come fum."

"I'm not giving you a choice, rabbit. Get out and let one of them drive. You!" he pointed a paw at Rosencrantz. "Drive!"

"Yes sir!" a very responsive Rosencrantz replied. "I'm a great driver, don't you worry." He climbed into the driver's seat that Brer Rabbit gave up with a woeful look and sour countenance, and sat next to a wide-eyed Guildenstern. He folded his arms and pouted as he leaned back against Buffalo, whose only wish was to get into town so he could get off his aching knees and stand up.

"Which way?" asked Rosencrantz.

"That way," said Coyote, pointing with his muzzle. And so they were off.

Though the comparison is a poor one, Rosencrantz was indeed a much better driver than Brer Rabbit, much to the comfort of Coyote and Buffalo, though for both, human contraptions always made them uneasy and uncomfortable anyway.

Despite the lateness of the hour, there was still a fair amount of traffic on the road, gratefully, it was heading the other way, towards Burly's, so they drove without anyone taking notice of the dinged up vehicle, the darkness of the night helping to hide Brer Rabbit's artistic flourishes.

Coyote had a general idea where the jail was, but since it was a little outside of his wanderings, he didn't know the exact location. He'd certainly heard about the place humans send each other when one is bad, though the concept of bad was difficult to grasp. Stupid, he could understand, but not bad. There was necessity, and from that, there was a good for him, a good for coyotes, a good for other creatures, but an act that was not good did not translate into bad. Stupid could be an opposite, but the whole idea of duality was not a readily acknowledged force at large. The large grazing animals, like Buffalo, had a similar understanding of good and bad. Bad was something like fences, and smaller fences, pens, must be what jails were like. But bad behavior was troublesome to fathom. After all, what had they done to be jailed in fences and pens?

Being a good civic-minded municipality, the city had posted many signs alerting drivers to the whereabouts of the county courthouse and jail, so the issue of directions resolved itself as they neared town.

Getting to the jail was not a problem. Getting in the jail was another matter. And they needed to because although they planned to blow up a section of it, they had to make sure Burly was not in that section, nor anyone else. They intended no harm to anyone; they were on a rescue mission.

They pulled into the nearly empty parking lot, empty because most squad cars were out at Burly's, and parked the van behind a garbage dumpster, trying to hide it. The effort was futile, like trying to hide an elephant behind a telephone pole, but it gave them some measure of security while they discussed ways to get inside.

They thought about storming the front desk, crashing through the doors behind the charging Buffalo, who, not being very keen on the idea, convinced them it was perhaps an unwise choice since the police would likely shoot them. To that, Brer Rabbit suggested they tie the two humans on his back, because surely they wouldn't shoot their own kind. The lawyers broke their silence on that proposal, vehemently arguing the opposite, that humans would shoot first and ask questions later. Their agitation over the matter strengthened Coyote's wavering support of the idea, and he thought perhaps they should tie the lawyers to the front of the van. Buffalo countered that the two captives were probably right, the humans inside were apt to shoot at anything and anyone, one person's as good as another.

Brer Rabbit then suggested that he walk in the front door, saunter up to the counter, and ask to see his friend, Burly. "Man 'low wha' t' see he fren, hain't he?"

"Yea, sure," said Coyote in acid sarcasm and mimicking a human, "You can go talk to Burly, Mr. Rabbit. Here's the key. And, oh! Take him some hot chocolate from me, would you? Ha!" he laughed. "Or, 'Of course! Mr. Buffalo. Go on in, just don't poop in the hallway. Okay?' That ain't going to work, hare brain," he spat.

The notion that he wouldn't be able to deceive anyone wounded Brer Rabbit's pride. "Dey hain't er man 'live dat what I cain't bamboozle en projickin wif. You des set der en wa'ch en see how er man git der job done." He rolled up his sleeves and started to open the door, but Buffalo's rumbling voice stopped him.

"Brer Rabbit, please sit down. We all know your gifts are plentiful and your abilities great, but let's not be hasty."

The two lawyers were impressed by the wisdom of this giant creature that they heretofore thought of as a humongous buffaloburger, but his next words torpedoed their rising admiration.

"Why don't we send one of these men to parley with the police while we hold the other hostage so we won't be deceived."

"Great idea, Buffalo! Great idea!" yipped Coyote. "And we'll eat him if the other doesn't come back!"

"Not what I had in mind," said the large vegetarian, but to make sure his point was perceived as the threat intended, he tipped a horn to Guildenstern's chest and said, "But I could make him easier for you to eat."

The two men cowered, Brer Rabbit pouted, and Buffalo continued. "What do you two do in your work with humans?" he asked them.

They did not want to be discovered as lawyers, lest they be further involved in whatever shenanigans these animals were up to. They didn't know the full plans of the creatures, just that they wanted to see Burly. They glanced at each other to communicate the need for quick thinking.

"We're clergymen," replied Rosencrantz.

"Clergymen?" asked Buffalo.

"Yes, um, like priests, you know? Ministers of God," said Guildenstern.

"Men of faith," said an earnest Rosencrantz.

"Is that so," Buffalo said slowly and thoughtfully.

"Liars!" yelled Brer Rabbit and Coyote simultaneously.

"No! No! It's the truth!" Guildenstern quickly said.

"Yes, we are followers of God, preachers of divine truth and the holy word," added a slightly panicked Rosencrantz.

"Liars!" yelled Brer Rabbit and Coyote again. The two accomplished storytellers certainly knew a tale when they heard one, and Guildenstern and Rosencrantz had to retreat and retrench upon threats from Buffalo.

A dejected Guildenstern, whose proximity to Buffalo's nudging horns put his neck more perilously on the line, confessed, "We're lawyers. That's the truth."

"Lawyers! I knew I smelled . . ." snarled Coyote. He was cut off by Rosencrantz.

"Emma hired us to help Burly," he blurted out.

"So you work for Emma?" Buffalo asked.

"Well, no . . . not now. But we did! Briefly."

"What happened?"

"She hired us to get Mr. Olalla out of jail, but apparently she didn't care for our counsel."

"Why not?" asked Coyote.

"I don't know. I guess she didn't think we were acting quickly enough on behalf of Mr. Olalla. We thought he might have to spend the night in jail, but she didn't want him to," Rosencrantz continued.

"Hmm," was the slow response from Buffalo, who said eventually, "You can help us."

"Well, do you mean to hire us?" Rosencrantz chuckled just a bit as he spoke.

"No. I mean to tell you," menaced Buffalo.

"Of course! Of course we'll help you," interjected an agreeable Guildenstern.

"Good. A wise choice," Buffalo said. "You," he spoke to Rosencrantz, "will stay here with us while he goes in to talk to the police."

Rosencrantz's face paled as the verdict was rendered. It was a death sentence as far as he was concerned. Had he been the one picked to go inside, he would have told the police everything as soon as he was inside the safety of the jail house doors and abandon Guildenstern to the fates. Damn! Oh cursed luck, he muttered silently to himself. He knew Guildenstern would do the same.

"What am I going to say?" asked a guileless Guildenstern.

"Yea, wha' he goan say," echoed Brer Rabbit.

"I think he should only ask where Burly is being held, then come back out. Then, we drive to where that is and blow the walls down and get him out. Then we drive back to the ranch," Coyote said. "Make it real quick so they don't have time to react."

"Yea! Blam! Boom!" Brer Rabbit agreed loudly.

"Blow up? Blow up? What are you talking about? Are you all nuts?" the incredulous voice of Rosencrantz dared to say.

"Shut up!" Coyote hissed, baring his fangs. "If you hadn't listened to Emma, Burly might be at home right now."

"As if I had anything to do with this!" he cried.

"All right, everyone. Let's be quiet. We're losing the cover of darkness," Buffalo said. "We have to keep moving on." He swung his massive head to look at Guildenstern. "You will go in and tell the police you represent Mr. Olalla and wish to see him. You will bring him to the front of the building, right by the front desk where we can see you. We will cause a diversion and you will bring Burly out the front door in the confusion that is sure to follow."

Brer Rabbit and Coyote thought it a fine idea and said they were lucky to have such a fine thinker with them. The two lawyers looked at each other, Rosencrantz searching for some hint of conspiracy in Guildenstern's eyes that, disappointingly, he could not find. He'd gone over to their side, he could see it in the softness of his eyes. 'That's why he'd never be a great lawyer like me, never fall in love with your client, you'll go down with them.'

Before Rosencrantz could stop him, Guildenstern said, "That won't work, they'll never let him out of the confinement area."

Rosencrantz groaned and rolled his eyes around, which of course betrayed the truth in Guildenstern's words to the trio of liberators. Guildenstern continued, "The best we can hope to do is get him near a window somewhere in the jail. I don't know where that will be, but I know how I can let you know. We," he indicated Rosencrantz and himself, "both have cell phones with us. I'll take mine with me and then call you when I have Mr. Olalla, and I'll tell you as best I can where we'll be. That's the best I think we can do if you are going to try and bust him out of jail. You realize, don't you, that this is a very, very illegal thing to do?" he finished, looking at the three conspirators very sincerely.

"What will they do if they catch me? Return me to the pasture?" Buffalo opined.

Coyote snickered, "There's no way they would ever be able to catch me."

Brer Rabbit said smugly and with a loud harumph, "Cotch Brer Rabbit? Dats un hoot. Ole Scratch be frozed fo' un man e'er cotch me up."

"Well, I just want you all to be aware of what you are doing, and that the consequences are once, I mean, should you, be caught, very severe. For the record, I advise against it," Guildenstern concluded.

"Wha's dis 'er fo de recuhd?" Brer Rabbit asked.

"It means he does not support our course of action and should we get caught, he can tell the authorities that he warned us against it. He won't get in trouble that way, or as much, I should say, knowing humans," Buffalo related.

"Run out on us, is that it?" Coyote snipped.

"Not in the least, lads," Guildenstern said. "I'm going in, aren't I?" he smiled. "Remember, it's my plan and the best one you have."

Coyote grumbled and chewed on some unintelligible oath while Buffalo said, "Well, let's get going, it's getting late and I have to get up and stretch my legs. Brer Rabbit, would you go around and open this backdoor so that I can get out?"

Guildenstern checked to see if he still had his cell phone, which he did, and he had to reach over and check the uncooperative Rosencrantz for his cell phone. Bending over to pat Rosencrantz's jacket pocket, he winked at him. By the twinkle in Rosencrantz's eyes, he knew he got the message. Hope bloomed like a mushroom cloud in Rosencrantz's chest.

When Guildenstern got out of the vehicle, Buffalo ambled up to him on stiff, sore legs. "Remember," he rumbled, "any betrayal and he will suffer horribly. Horribly." He shook his head menacingly.

With a serious but innocent look, Guildenstern responded, "He's my best and only friend. Please take care of him. I can trust you, I really feel that." Then he boldly patted Buffalo on the head, right between his horns. "I'll be waiting inside with Burly, you can count on me." Then he turned and walked to the entrance of the jailhouse.

Something had come over Rosencrantz. Brer Rabbit didn't know what it was exactly, couldn't quite give it a name, but Rosencrantz wasn't acting any different now that Guildenstern had entered the building. Watching him disappear out of sight, escorted by a policeman, Rosencrantz seemed very peaceful, almost happy. Too calm for someone involved in a caper with him, Brer Rabbit. He didn't say anything, just held it to himself and stayed on guard. 'Der's sumpin jubous 'ere,' he thought to himself as they all watched another man walk into the police station not five minutes after Guildenstern.

"Wake up, Olalla. Your lawyer's here." The harsh voice and cold clank of metal of the unlocking door brought Burly from his dreams. He groaned from the dull pain that throbbed in his head and his eye. 'Ow! Damn, that hurts!' he grunted as he rolled to sit up on his cot. Slowly the memory of how he obtained the pain came to his consciousness. 'Smartin' off to a guard. Brilliant, ya' dummy,' he berated himself. As the guard swung the door open, he remembered Lucidity and looked around for her. "Gone, of course," he muttered.

"What's that?" the guard asked brusquely.

"Nothin', just talkin' to myself," Burly replied.

"Hold your hands out, you gotta be cuffed leaving the cell, and hurry up. You ain't got all day. Nice shiner, Olalla. Fall out of bed?" the guard teased and then laughed.

He wasn't the one who punched him, but he probably knew who did. "Yup, fell out of bed," Burly agreed. He thought the better route would be to agree to whatever these mean sonzabitches said. Compliantly, obediently, he held his hands up.

Properly hand cuffed, he was led into a windowless room where a thick sheet of bulletproof glass separated him from a man he recognized as one of Sheldon Turner's lawyers. Still groggy from sleep, he sat down awkwardly and grabbed the telephone receiver, the only means of communication.

"So you're my lawyer," he said.

"Yes, one of them, Mr. Olalla. But I no longer wish to be. I do not want to represent you. How is your cell?" Guildenstern asked.

"You aren't my . . . my cell? What about my cell? Listen, Rosenstern, I'm a little sleepy still. Let's start over, beginning with you're my lawyer and you're not my lawyer. Then we'll get to my cell. Okay?"

"Sure, sure," Guildenstern said, his mind racing. He had decided not to tell the police the truth until he was well inside the jail, get deep in to the building so that if the crazed animals drove the van into the building, or blew something up, there would be less of a chance he'd get hurt. And not getting hurt was highest on his priority list. The next was getting out of this mess without getting implicated, or as little as possible. A small guilt, you can always deadlock a jury with wee guilt. And the hell with Rosencrantz. God knows what the loonies would do if they didn't get his phone call, but they'll get it all right, from deep within the security of a jail cell. Then he'll spill the beans to the cops, and should they rush the van and the animals are somehow able to slam the van into the building, he'll be safe. Yes, that's the best plan.

"Mr. Olalla, we need to, I mean, I need to visit your cell. You seem to be hurt, and I, um, I need to gather evidence, there could be police brutality on top of everything else. Judges are always more lenient in sentencing . . ."

"What the hell is this cell thing? What evidence? Are you, or are you not, my lawyer?"

The guard monitoring the two couldn't hear what was being said, but he could see Burly getting agitated and the guard was quite good at reading body language. Obviously, the two could not agree on something. Curious, he turned on a small listening device (that was hugely illegal) they had installed to listen in on the supposedly private conversation between lawyer and client.

"Are you nuts?" he heard Burly say to the lawyer. "Why do you care so much about my goddamn cell? Are you queer or something? Look, if you're not my lawyer, then who the hell are you?"

The lawyer kept repeating his need to visit Burly's cell. Finally, the guard watched as Burly, visibly agitated, stood up and announced the time was up. As he did, another man, escorted by two cops, entered the visitation room. The two cops immediately surrounded Guildenstern as another cop, the Captain of the Guard, came in quickly and spoke to Guildenstern. He had in tow another man, a civilian, who grabbed the receiver from Guildenstern and spoke to Olalla, relating something quite confusing to him.

"Mr. Olalla, I'm your lawyer."

In a short course of time, the police were able to uncover these pertinent facts: Mr. Guildenstern was not Burly's lawyer, Bubba here was, and he had signed papers for Burly's release from the judge, who had decided, based on Burly's past civic record and on Bubba's reputation (she knew him quite well), that Mr. Olalla was not, in truth, a threat to the community, though his release had some rather strict stipulations attached. Mr. Olalla allowed that his conversation with Mr. Guildenstern did not make a whole lot of sense, and in fact, it disturbed and distressed him. For some unknown reason, Mr. Guildenstern wanted to accompany him to his cell.

For his part, Mr. Guildenstern allowed there was a bomb threat, which they took very seriously and quickly took measures to counter that threat. Why Mr. Guildenstern had not alerted them earlier could not be readily explained, and so they had to detain him for false representation and for a far more serious charge, potentially: implication in a bomb threat. And should a bomb be found . . . well, Mr. Guildenstern would visit a cell after all.

Outside, the three would-be emancipators were growing restless and uneasy because it was taking too much time, and their position was getting vulnerable as the dark cloak of night was giving way to gray, predawn light.

Rosencrantz was uneasy too. He was beginning to doubt the sincerity of the conspiratorial wink from Guildenstern. He still sat in the driver's seat, nervously tapping his foot on the gas pedal.

The first to notice the police stealthily fanning out over the grounds was Buffalo. They hadn't noticed the van yet, but they would soon enough. He sent a warning rumble to Coyote and Brer Rabbit, who understood immediately, though to Rosencrantz, it was an innocent enough sound. Buffalo was still standing outside the van, and he quietly slipped behind the dumpsters and disappeared into a copse of trees and bushes that ringed the perimeter of the parking lot. Just as silently, Brer Rabbit snuck out of the van with a nod to Coyote, then melded into the waning shadows to meet up with Buffalo.

Coyote was going to wait until the last minute, until there would be no escape for Rosencrantz, who, he knew, would get into trouble for something. Humans always found something wrong when they were looking for it.

While Rosencrantz tapped away at the gas pedal and glanced at his watch, Coyote could see more and more police moving just out of sight, guns ready. This could be tricky, he thought.

"Better start the engine, they're bound to be calling any time now. I'll get everything else ready," he told Rosencrantz. Then he slipped into the back of the van, and as he did, he caught sight of Burly leaving the building through another entrance, with the man who went in soon after Guildenstern. He could tell they were walking in a forced, calm manner. 'Better get out of here,' he thought to himself, 'this is going to blow one way or another.'

Rosencrantz was as tight as a wire so when the phone rang in his pocket, he jumped up in his seat and jammed the truck into gear. At the same time, Coyote jumped out the back of the van, which Rosencrantz happened to see in the mirror. Knowing he was alone, he slammed the gas pedal down while the police officer on the line told him he was surrounded, and to give himself up. Rosencrantz whooped in joy, he was safe now, but the cop misinterpreted his elation as a sign he was going to carry out whatever nefarious deed he had planned, so he yelled to his fellow officers to employ plan B.

Every cop who had a gun or rifle opened up and started blasting away at the speeding van as squad cars came tearing around the corner, lights flashing and sirens wailing, trying to intercept Rosencrantz. They all succeeded.

At the first hail storm of bullets smacking into the truck, Rosencrantz slammed on the brakes and jumped out of the van, unhurt, but slightly puzzled as to why the police had opened fire. Surely Guildenstern had told them something of the truth. He was rudely thrown to the ground by the first cops who ran to him, and treated rather roughly, but within legal bounds, he noted with disappointment. His befuddlement would give way to anger, then something beyond anger that would meld into depression as he was handcuffed and booked, along with two pipe bombs.

The police had noticed what appeared to be a dog jumping out of the back of the van just before it jumped from zero to fifty, but as Coyote expected, they paid him no mind. He soon joined his mates in the shadows of the trees.

"Burly's out of jail," he hissed at them. "I saw him leave with that man who went in after the asshole we sent in. He may still be in trouble, we have to get to him. Buffalo, you stay here, Brer Rabbit and I will run after him. Come on!" And off the two sped after Burly and Bubba.

The two men had just pulled out of the parking stall in Bubba's Ford F150 pickup when gunfire erupted, so fearing the worse, Bubba urged the truck on with a little more gas to the pedal. Coming around the corner of the somewhat long police station drive, Brer Rabbit and Coyote appeared in the headlights, running right at them. Burly grabbed hold of the steering wheel and slammed his foot down on Bubba's (who screamed in pain), and yelled, "Hit him! Hit him! Damn you little bastard! Hit him!"

"No you don't!" a voice cracked like a thunderclap. Lucidity Jones wrestled the steering wheel from Burly and pulled hard right, tipping the truck on two wheels. It jumped the curb and crashed into a tree, the front grille parallel to the trunk. The vehicle lurched and groaned as it toppled back over on to its wheels, knocking the occupant's heads into the ceiling on the rebound. When the truck stopped bouncing and shaking, Bubba looked out the cracked windshield and said, "This ain't Kansas no mo."

A very angry Emma shouted at a very meek and apologetic Brer Rabbit, whose sagging chin nearly touched the table. It made him absolutely miserable to have Emma yell at him. It didn't matter that he hadn't done anything to deserve it, just her being mad at him was misery enough. Time and again he told her the same thing, "I doan know 'ere he went. He us drivin' right fo' us en den he uz gone. Des gone. De truck too. I des ez sorry ez you iz, en maybe mo."

It had taken him, Coyote and Buffalo nearly six hours to get back to the ranch. They had to cross fences, streets, cut through backyards, cross highways, walk through drainage ditches. It would have been easy enough for him and Coyote, but with Buffalo along it was quite a job to walk back to the ranch unnoticed. Especially the ranch, as surrounded as it was. It had been quite a feat, but they managed to pull it off, naturally.

All the way back they had talked about the car and its occupants. They couldn't figure out what happened. As soon as the truck jumped the curb, it had disappeared. All they remembered seeing was a man behind the wheel with a terrified look on his face, Burly sitting next to him yelling and looking wild, and a dark form sitting behind, but between them. The dark form was troubling. The manner in which the pickup vanished made them suspect the creator wanted the two men back, and the dark form was the messenger bringing the creator's message. Coyote regretted he wasn't able to send Burly off under better conditions, but it wasn't his call.

Coyote and Buffalo had promised Brer Rabbit they'd remain in the barn in case the people in the house wanted to verify Brer Rabbit's story that he alone would deliver to them. Soon enough, Emma, Zach, Donovan, Uncle Remo and a very excited Dr. Timothy Bottoms came to the barn. Brer Rabbit was too out of sorts to protest the lack of trust they showed in his words.

"Des axe dem fell'rs. Dey ull 'greenamint wif me," Brer Rabbit said, sitting on a bale of hay and folding his arms across his chest. Dr. Bottoms sat next to him.

When Brer Rabbit had entered the house with his story of Burly's disappearance it was the first time Dr. Tim had seen him. He couldn't take his eyes off the creature, which of course didn't bother the attention-loving Brer Rabbit. He followed every word Brer Rabbit spoke, savored every inflection, every syllable, every pronouncement for the rarity that his speech and language was, long since vanished into the mists of history. He was feasting on a sumptuous meal; well seasoned words. He was enthralled, even enchanted, a creature he knew only as fable had risen from the printed page living and breathing, and cursing, for that matter. Dr. Tim was a new man, he'd seen the light, he'd seen the work of God. He'd seen the sacred.

And now sitting on a bale of hay next to his childhood hero, he was a boy reborn.

The two animals stood and faced their inquisitors. They were a little intimidated standing in front of the humans, who in turn were intimidated standing in front of them, especially Buffalo, whose head was square even to Emma's. No one knew how to start things, so an awkward silence followed their meeting. Zachary had his eyes closed, trying to pick up any thoughts the animals might be sending him, but if his facial contortions were any indication, he was having a hard time tuning in. Finally, Uncle Remo stepped forward and spoke to Coyote in the old tongue, Kiowa. He asked him how he was. In perfectly good Kiowa, Coyote responded, "I am well, Uncle. And you?"

"My heart is heavy. I seek my nephew, who has gone somewhere and we cannot find him. Do you know where he might be?"

"I think the creator might have taken him."

"Are you not the creator?"

"No, I am not."

"There are many tales of you creating this turtle island . . ."

"Ah . . . many, many moons have gone by, many, many stories have been told by many different peoples. But always, there was the creator."

"We'll have to adjust some of our tribal stories then, I think," Uncle Remo said with a sigh.

"No. They are all correct."

"How can that be?"

"I'll explain it this way," Coyote stopped speaking Kiowa, and in perfect Brer Rabbitese, said, "De im'p'cashun by dis 'er statemint hain't dat one un de folks tales en miffs ez mo troof den yenny d'yudders, deys all troof."

His dead on Brer Rabbit imitation surprised everyone, including Brer Rabbit, who shot him a scowl, but only Uncle Remo responded. "Hmm. I'll have to think about that one. So the story this trickster rabbit tells is true? Burly disappeared into thin air?" he asked in Kiowa.

"I'm afraid so. Vanished into thin air."

"Does that big buffalo talk?" Uncle Remo asked, their conversation still in Kiowa.

"Ask him," Coyote replied.

"Gadalpa," Buffalo bull, he addressed him in Kiowa, "I humbly ask to speak with you."

Turning to Uncle Remo, Buffalo, also speaking in Kiowa said, "I am honored and pleased for your courteous manners. It has been so very long that we buffalo have been treated with respect, even by those who would eat our flesh. I know they call you Uncle, but I would prefer to call you Grandfather." Uncle Remo was pleased and bowed his head slightly in acknowledgment of the honorific title, then asked, "What do you know of my nephew?"

Buffalo said his nephew was a good man but apparently still had some things to learn, and unfortunately the things he heard about his disappearance were true.

Everyone else could tell by Uncle Remo's reaction from both animal's words that Brer Rabbit had been telling the truth. Knowing they hadn't understood Kiowa, Buffalo repeated everything said between him, Coyote and Uncle Remo, including the part about respect.

Emma, non-plussed about either animal talking, said, "The drivuh must have been that lawyer, but what about this dark form y'all been talkin' bout?"

Buffalo looked at Brer Rabbit and Coyote, but neither seemed inclined to say anything, so he spoke, ""We think it might have been Death, come to take them back home."

"That don't make no sense," she said. "Why on earth would it take the truck?"

"Maybe it was its time, too," Donovan offered.

"Don't be silly," she said in scorn.

"Hey, machines have spirits too," he argued.

"Donovan, we're talkin' 'bout Burly's death, or abduction or somethin'. Try en be helpful," she admonished, drawing 'try' out like traaa.

"I am," he protested.

Since his efforts to communicate non-verbally had failed, Zach had been quiet, listening to all that was said, now he turned to Uncle Remo and asked, "Is there anyway for us to find out if they've, um, crossed over? Is there someone or some spirit, what do you call it, an oracle, that we can talk to, that maybe has an ear in the spirit world, or something?"

Uncle Remo concentrated hard, but apparently to no avail, he could rouse no notion from the murk of memory that would work. "A sweat might work," he slowly let the words go as if he held them underwater, "but you never know with them. A vision quest most likely would, but that'd take four days. I dunno . . ."

Coyote, in an act that betrayed boredom, had been sitting on his haunches, but lay down on his belly and said, "Uncle Remo, you forget about the Dream Dance."

"Of course! Why didn't I think of that! It's perfect! The Ghost Dance!"

"De Ghos' Dance?" Brer Rabbit stuttered in unmistakable fear. His ears drooped down his back. "Mebbe hit time I'ze git t'der house. I'ze pow'ful tired."

He was about to get up and leave, but Uncle Remus' words calmed him, "Oh, we can't do it right now. There'll be some preparation, but we should be able to do it tonight," he said.

"Ah, the Ghost Dance, that's perfect," he said more to himself as hope and joy blossomed in his heart.

"The Ghost Dance?" Zachary said. "I thought you Indians did that to make yourselves invisible or invincible, so bullets wouldn't hurt you?"

"That was the Sioux," Uncle Remo said. "They used it for war, and they were pretty good at it, but it wasn't meant for that. Not originally. It was meant to contact ancestors and to bring back the buffalo, and the past, too."

"So if Burly's dead, some dead ancestor's goin' to tell us?" Emma asked.

"Something like that. Who knows, maybe it'll bring Burly back," Uncle Remo said.

Coyote, who had brought up the subject, didn't say anything, just nodded his head and smiled, or sneered. No one could tell which.

Dr. Tim was especially happy for now, on top of meeting a literary, mythical/historical personnae, er, creaturrae, he was going to re-enact an authentic, documented historical ritual, one that had fanned hope for a people that needed it as their culture and way of life, their world, was coming to an end. For the plains Indians, the Ghost Dance had promised a return to life as it was before the white man came, the be'dalpago, or 'hairy mouths', as the Kiowa called them, before the buffalo disappeared and land became something bought and sold, a commodity, not a being. It was a dance that promised a return, too, of all the ancestors who had lived before, and now it held promise of yielding information and the possible return of another Indian, and a white lawyer named Bubba. And maybe his pickup.

chapter eighteen

"Where in the hell are we?" Bubba asked aloud.
"What in the hell have you done?" Burly asked Lucidity.
"Who the hell are you?" Bubba asked Lucidity.
"Uh oh," Lucidity said to both.
"You can see her?" Burly asked Bubba.
"Kind of hard to miss her when she's practically sitting right on top of me," he replied.
"That helps," Lucidity said.
"What helps? That you're sitting on him? Lucidity, what did you do? Where are we?" Burly angrily demanded.
"Well, I'm not sure," she said, looking around.
"Great. Just great." Burly said in disgust and pushed back against the front seat then looked out the side window.
The landscape was not entirely unfamiliar. There were trees and plants and rocks and grass, and birds could be heard chirping and peeping. The sky was still the sky; big puffy cotton ball clouds hung suspended in a bright blue vault. But it sure wasn't Kansas. The trees looked familiar, but they were not of any species he knew and none of the plants were familiar either, nor were any of the flowers that many had. And neither did he recognize any of the birds he caught glimpses of. No, there was something different about everything. The whole place had a surrealistic quality to it, even the light, the sunlight, seemed tangibly different somehow. Somehow . . . he couldn't put a finger on it. He turned his attention back to Lucidity. Though a collar of constraint strained his voice, he began as calmly as he could, "Lucidity, obviously this is not where we were. You have done something, you have transported us somewhere. I admit to being wrong

about you, you have greater powers than I gave you credit for. My apologies. Now, since you got us here, one would surmise you could get us back. Yes?" He looked at her but there was no friendliness in his eyes, no regret in his voice.

"If that's as clear of an apology, dear,
That ever I hear you'll ever near,
Then never not ever will I endeavor
To set things aright and rot you will here," she sang.

"Not now, Lucidity. Not now," Burly grimaced through his teeth.

"Hey, who are you?" Burly asked Lucidity.

"I'm Lucidity Jones," she answered forthrightly.

"What the hell happened to my truck? You wrecked it! You drove us right into that tree . . . that was here in front of us," his voice dropped as he realized there was no longer any tree in front of them.

And so they sat for a moment, all three shoulder to shoulder in Bubba's pickup, quietly assessing the situation in their own minds until reverie was broken by Bubba, who got out and inspected the front end of his truck.

"There ain't no damage! Nothin'!" he exclaimed. "Don't that beat all. I saw the hood crumble round that tree and now there ain't a scratch on it. Hell, ain't no tree neither." Puzzled and befuddled, he walked back and stuck his head in through the open side window. "I don't pretend to know what's goin' on, but something peculiar, mighty peculiar is goin' on. Suppose someone lets me in on it. Have I been drugged or something?"

"Go ahead, Lucidity. You heard the man. Tell him what's going on. Tell him what you did," Burly urged.

"What you did!" she challenged. "If you hadn't tried running over Brer Rabbit we wouldn't be here!"

"Well that's just classic. It's my fault. How come I didn't know. Duh. In case this isn't clear, I didn't bring us here, you did!" he shouted at her.

"When are you going to accept some responsibility for your actions?" she shot back.

"Oh, sorry mom. I'll clean my room up. Who the hell are you to lecture me . . ."

"Stop it!" Bubba cut in to the argument. "Y'all sound like an ole married couple."

"Mr. R.C. McDowell, do you mind?" Lucidity looked at him coldly.

"How do you know my name?" he asked her.

"I know more than you can imagine, Bubba. Which, by the way, is something you could use a little work on."

"What? You're telling me what? That I'm not . . . imaginative?"

"Oh, she's good at pointing out other people's short comings," Burly piped in.

"I did not say you lack the capacity for imagination, I implied you need to flex some atrophied muscles," Lucidity said, carefully measuring the words.

"Well excuuuuse me! Who the hell are you to talk to me that way!" he cried.

"Go get her, guy! Go get her!" Burly prodded.

Lucidity rolled her eyeballs and chimed,

"Always a wall whenever at all

There's a threat to the ego, no matter how small.

Get off my turf, don't stand on my toes,

You're crowding me now, I'm a giant, you know."

Burly leaned forward to see Bubba around Lucidity and said, "Bubba, this here's my angel. This is what God sent me." He chuckled and leaned back again.

"An angel?" Bubba sounded as if the words tasted bad.

"To be factual, a tutorial," Lucidity said flatly.

"An angel," Bubba repeated himself. "Well, if you're an angel, or tutory, or whatever, can't you just get us back home, or at the least, tell us where we are? Like maybe, some directions?"

"It's not as easy as that," she replied.

"Don't play games, Miss Jones," Burly spat. "You know you can just twiddle your thumbs or twitch your nose or snap your fingers and Bam! we're back home. Hell, I bet you could click your heels together and we'd be home. Let's try it! I'll say, 'There's no place like home' and you click your heels. Come on! Let's try it! 'There's no place like home, there's no place like home' go ahead, click 'em!" Burly laughed hysterically and a bit too maniacally, even for Bubba, who asked Lucidity if he was all right.

"A little close to the edge, but he hasn't slipped over yet. Just don't encourage him."

Bubba leaned back in his seat and blew air out of his mouth. Burly was still laughing with himself. Bubba, in a concerned voice that no longer held anger, asked Lucidity "You really don't know where we are?"

"I have my suspicions, but I need more information, more clues. Let's get out and take a look around."

They all got out of the car, Burly following them, and as soon as he stepped out, said, "Look! There's feet under the tires! Ding dong the witch is dead," he sang. "Which old witch? The wicked witch! Oh! She's not!" he looked at Lucidity, mock horror on his face. Then he began to laugh hysterically again.

"I don't think he's going to be of much help," she said to Bubba. "Let's look around."

"What about my truck?" he said.

"What about it?" she responded. "I don't think it's going anywhere. It's not like someone could drive off with it."

True enough, for it sat in the middle of a little forest glade, completely surrounded by trees.

"Well, I guess you're right. But let's lock it just the same."

"Americans," Lucidity muttered under her breath.

They walked to the edge of the trees, whereupon Lucidity paused and asked them, "Ready?"

"For what?" they asked in unison.

She smiled sweetly and stepped into the line of trees.

They had not walked long before Lucidity observed a large, bright blue colored plant with long tubular flowers suspended at the end of short spiky stems. "What incredibly beautiful flowers!" she exclaimed.

"Wow!" Bubba said, "I never seen such a shade of red like that before! Man, that's something!"

Lucidity turned to Burly and said, "Ding," to which he responded, "Dong," and pealed off more maniacal laughter.

Continuing on, the drier woodland environment started to give way to a more humid and hot one, moss could be seen hanging from tree limbs and little mushrooms grew at their feet, which, the further they walked, they got bigger until eventually they were enormous, some three feet high and at least four around. The air was now very humid, they were dripping sweat; it was very jungle-like. Huge ferns with giant fronds grew at the base of humongous trees with trunks as thick as a man is long. Vines grew everywhere, spiraling around anything that would stand still long enough to be seized. Multicolored birds flitted from branch to branch and insects, some as big as birds, noisily buzzed around, flashing gossamer wings and painted bodies. Unknown and unseen noises peeped, chirped, sang, called, growled yowled and squawked all around. It was a world primitive, beautiful and awesome to behold. Stepping around a giant toadstool, Lucidity spoke to the two awestruck men as they walked, "Any thoughts, gentlemen?"

Burly gasped when a mushroom he accidentally kicked jumped out of his way. "It moved! My God, it moved! What is this place?" Stepping back to avoid the mushroom, he stumbled on a tree root, but a vine caught him before he fell. Purposely, he noted.

"Um . . . Lucidity! Wait up!" he called out. He quickly caught up to them as they entered a dense stand of mushrooms, or herd, as it parted for the trio. The two men were silent, eyes wide open in wonderment.

The skin of the mushrooms was iridescent as though a thin film of oil covered them. Underneath the crown, the color shaded to purplish brown. The caps were not big floppy hats, but peaked, like a bell. The stems were thin in proportion, a long slender leg. They were obviously not rooted; they moved, shuffling out of the way like celeritous snails.

"What are these?" Bubba wondered.

"Mushrooms," Lucidity replied.

"Duh," Burly said sarcastically.

"I've never seen mushrooms that move around, and they're so damn big!" Bubba exclaimed. "What are they called?"

"Ask them," Lucidity told him.

"Ask them," he said, "How?"

"It won't do to talk to them like you and I are conversing. Sit down next to one and gently touch it. Don't grab, reach out like you're making first contact. Gentle is the key word. Okay?"

"Gotcha," Bubba replied and sat down next to one cross-legged, his belly spilling over his belt buckle like jelly leaving a mold. Gingerly, he reached a hand out to the mushroom.

It trembled slightly, as if troubled by a whispered wind, but did not retreat from the finger that nudged it, then the palm that lay on its crown. In fact, it seemed soothed by the contact. Bubba felt foolish as his grin belied, but it was not long before his discomfited smirk gave way to a broad and beaming smile.

"I know what those are," Burly stated with an air of smugness and a bordering hubris, "and I don't need that."

"You know what they are? Clever you! Maybe you do need them," Lucidity said with her own tang of sarcasm. "Or better yet, why don't you go talk to the vines?"

"Why?" he said suspiciously. "What are they?"

"Oh, I don't know. They just seem everywhere, maybe they're like the you know whats that you don't need."

"Do you want me to?"

"It could be good for you."

"Then I won't," he said. "I don't see that you've been much help to me. Not at all."

"Oh, you know, you think you're right,
And always ready for the fight,
But I tire of your fire,
Petty, irksome, little ire.
Then do not talk with vine of dead,
Better off with whining head," she shrugged and sighed.

Burly looked as if he'd bit on something very sour, and folded his arms across his chest defiantly. They both stood in silence, waiting for Bubba, who was in cruising communication with the toadstool. Eventually he stirred, lifted his hand from the mushroom and looking at them with glassy eyes and moonbeam smile.

"Well how do you do, Bubba Buddha?" Burly said nastily. "Have a nice flight?"

"Yes, I did," he said as he grunted to his feet, standing none too steadily. "Man, that was something. I mean, that was something! I can't . . . I don't know . . . it's hard to describe . . ."

"I know," Lucidity smiled at him. "I know," patting his shoulder affectionately, "You don't have to say anything. Just be with it. Well, shall we get going?"

"Off to see the wizard," grumbled Burly.

They carefully picked their way through the toadstool tribe until they'd left them behind, and the vines for that matter as the land eventually shaded from dark jungle ecosystem to a bucolic and pastoral open land. Worked and cultivated fields began to appear, which raised the spirits of the two men, obviously, they felt they were finally getting somewhere. When they came to a rather ordinary house, they cried for joy and complained of hunger and thirst, conditions they had not mentioned prior to seeing the house. They ran to the front door.

"Let's do it!" Bubba said, his eyes dancing with anticipation of food and drink. A big golden knocker hung from the center of the door begging to be banged, which Bubba did with enthusiasm.

No response. So he wailed on it.

That got someone's attention. They heard the sounds of footsteps coming quickly toward the door, and watched anxiously while the door lock was unlatched and the door swung open.

Standing in the doorway was a very large and very fat black cat with a big white belly that bespoke of idle time in a well-stocked kitchen. The cat easily stood five feet tall on its back legs and wore a red bow tie. On top of its head sat a very large stovepipe hat, bent in the middle so the top sagged forward. The hat was striped horizontally with broad bands of red and white. It sported white silk gloves on its front paws, giving it an air of daintiness and ludicrous genteelness.

"Jesus Christ!" Bubba spat as he stepped back.

"Oh no!" cried Burly.

"Oh yes!" said the creature.

> "I'm so glad to see you,
> You've no idea how,
> I missed you so much,
> And here you are now!"

"Lucidity, stop this. Stop this right now!" Burly demanded as he staggered backward.

> "I don't think I'm mistaken,
> You seem somewhat shaken,"
> Said the fat cat in the hat.
> "The last time I saw you,
> You played with a toy,
> Now you're grown up,
> A man from a boy!
> But now you seem surly,
> Could it be the same Burly?

> And Bubba as baby,
> Was little Bob then,
> And Ooh! all the fun,
> We had in the sun!
> You would look,
> At me in the book,
> And I would look back,
> With a nod and a wink,
> And I know that you saw me,
> You saw me, I think."

"Man oh man," Bubba shook his head from side to side. "What the hell is goin' on," he said softly. "What the hell is goin' on. How do you know my name? You look like . . . but it ain't quite right . . ."

> "You knew me by another name,
> But I had a life before I found fame.
> I lived in the mind of a mad mouse named Moose
> With all of my friends we ran around loose,
> The mind of mouse Moose was our house home
>   and roost
> Until a bad day that we all fell away,
> Caught in a wind that did the mouse in,
> We tumbled and turned and we bounced and we
>   jounced
> Until we were snagged by the sharp eye of one,
> A doctor he was and a language masseuse.
> He saw us as different but just by a shade,
> And gave us new names, thus we were made.
> Such is the past, enough of all that!
> So glad to see you, I'm Fat with the Hat!"

"Jones! This isn't funny. I'm warning you!" Burly said angrily.
"What would I do? There's nothing I *can* do!" she shot back.

"You could give him a loan,
Or a phone or a tome.
That's what you could do," said Fat with the Hat.
"If you really want to.
Or give him a bone, on that he could chew.
And so it's Miss Jones! How do you do?"

"I'm doing so well, sometimes I can't tell,
If I'm going to burst like a balloon from a pin,
All I can do is drool and grin," she chimed.

"Oh how delightful,
To meet someone insightful.
You must come inside,
In here we can play,
In here you can stay
As we play,
      play
        and
          play!"

"Oh no," Burly said ominously, "We're not going in there."

"But some friends have come over,
Come here they have,
From places nearby and some quite far away.
They would be very sad,
If you went away mad,
They just came to play
On this very same day!
So please come inside, put your troubles aside,"
   said the cat.

"Oh, Burly's so grumpy, Mr. Fat with the Hat,

> You'd think he was Humpty, who fell over and splat!
> No more a Dumpty, he was flat as a mat," Lucidity said.
>
> "Oh me! Oh my!" said Fat with the Hat.
> "Then you really must come
> Into my house, have you had any lunch?
> Meet some of my friends, you'll like them a bunch.
> There's one on the run,
> He likes to stay hid,
> He tried to steal Christmas!
> That's what he did!
> He'll do as a friend, but just in a pinch.
> Burly and Bob, meet Mr. Lynch!

"Oh, Jesus!" moaned Burly, who turned away in a mixture of disgust and anger. "I'm getting out of here, I can't stand this! You coming Bubba?" Burly started to walk away, but Bubba couldn't help but stare at the little, green furred, hunched over creature that came to the door and blinked hard at the sunlight that seemed to burn his eyes.

> "I don't think they can play,
> Mister Fat with the Hat.
> Once you grow up, you can't,
> So they say.
> But I know that they're hungry,
> On top of the grumbly,
> Burly the surly may even stay," said Lucidity.
>
> "If the need is to eat,
> I've a friend you must meet.
> He always has food,
> You could say it's his mood,

If empty the belly, the brain 'come a jelly
He understands, do something he can!
Please greet the fellow we call,
'Simply Man'."

A little elfin creature came to the door carrying a plate of food held high aloft his head. "I am Man," he said. "Would anyone care for dreamed pleas and ham?"

Lucidity clapped her hands in delight while Bubba was still struck dumb in shock and disbelief at the parade of creatures he was witnessing and the conversation he was hearing. Burly was not so mute, "What the hell, you little fool" he snarled, "It's green eggs and . . ."

"I see a noise and you hear a color,
Such is the prism of the prison of Ism!" said Fat with the Hat.

"Onomatopoeia, I see prosopopoeias!" squealed Lucidity.

Burly groaned loudly and turned away in disgust. Simply Man followed, which annoyed Burly, so he broke into a trot, which turned into a run that served as an irresistible invitation for Man to hard sell his menu, and he sped off in hot pursuit, calling to Burly as they ran;

"Would you eat them in a sweat?
Would you, could you, on a bet?
Would you like them on a jet?
Or upside down in a net?"

They could hear Burly's responses for a little while, before both voices faded, "Get away from me you evil little imp! Get away from me!"

"Until they're back, Burly and Man,
I'll have to stay right where I am.
And so my lawyerman and friend,
We might as well just go right in," Lucidity
rhymed to Bubba.

And so, arm in arm, they entered Fat with the Hat's house, much, much to his joy.

Bubba and Lucidity sat at the kitchen table, while the owner, Fat, manicured his nails and talked incessantly in rhyme. Good rhyme, thought Bubba, just like the good ole country songs he listened to back home, while in the shadows lurked the green Mr. Lynch.

> "There's so much to do," droned Fat with the Hat,
> "Just fresh from the zoo,
> Let's play with garzubus' and hexmegalulus'
> Who love to eat ice cream yaktoohloos'
> And fried portlezyzs' on sizzling thyss'."

And there again in the shadows, Mr. Lynch, moping about, never revealing himself, never taking part in any conversation, just forever pacing and slinking. Now and then Bubba could see his blood stained eyes sneaking a look at him. They made him uneasy. Lucidity didn't seem to notice, she was enjoying herself so much. Of course, all the other odd creatures that came and went weren't exactly calming influences. Big and small, fat and thin, black and white and all colors in between from purple to orange and red to blue, from one leg to many and some none at all. He weighed in that he was holding together pretty well. Remarkably well, in fact, given he'd walked into a living breathing children's library. But it was wearing on his nerves, eroding his will, breaking down his barriers that said this wasn't real. This was madness and would end soon, he'd be back to his world eventually. Just hang in there, guy! Chin up!

In other words, he was dodging it.

Timorously, over the singsong voice of the cat, he asked Lucidity if she knew where they were now.

"Why, yes. I believe we are with Fat with the Hat," she answered with no hint of jest or sarcasm.

"Weeeellll, thanks for that bit of information, Ma'am. I was a'wonderin'. I mean bigger where!? You said you needed to know more, you needed more bits and pieces. Do you have them now?"

"Uh hunh," she grunted affirmatively.

"Good. Great. Then you can tell me? Hey?"

"Sure."

"Well?"

"We are in the world of imagination."

"The world of imagination?" he repeated her statement as question.

"That's right, Bubba. The world of human imagination, to be more precise."

"Isn't that interesting", he said distractedly. "Good. Good. You know where we are. Then you can get us back home, right?"

"No," she said flatly.

"Why not?" he nearly yelled out.

"It isn't my place, it's yours. And I work in God's place anyway."

"Excuse me? Wouldn't that be everywhere?"

"No, not really, but then again; yes. The other place is God's imagination, this is yours, all of yours. It's really quite simple."

"Oh. Of course. 'Really quite simple', she says. Then how simple is it to get back home?" his voice angry and disappointed, and a little fearful.

"Ooohh. Simple enough."

"How simple enough?"

"When Burly likes dreamed pleas and ham!"

chapter nineteen

"Emma, buhleeeeeze. Ah doan wanner be no pa't er no conjurin!"
"You chicken shit. Just do as you're told," Coyote snipped at Brer Rabbit, who was trying to gain sympathy from Emma by using all the best whining tactics he could employ, including half closing his eyelids and puckering his lips like a hurt child. But she would have none of it. Everyone there, including him, Bart, Coyote and Buffalo, were going to participate in the Ghost Dance, or Dream Dance, as Uncle Remo called it. Brer Rabbit, as soon as he heard it called a Ghost Dance, had tried to get out of it so they'd asked Coyote to keep an eye on him, a task he gladly accepted.

They were all gathered in the barn in the late evening, or, more accurately, the early morning. The people had begun to come from the house around midnight, one at a time, to draw the least attention. Burly's mother and Uncle Remo had come early in the afternoon to get the barn ready, then returned along with everyone else as night set in.

They had cleared a big area in the center of the barn, carefully cleaning the dirt floor as best they could and laying down fresh hay all around. They created a circle, a sacred circle some fifteen feet in diameter, marking it off with sage and cedar sprigs that Burly's mother had tied into bundles. Ceremoniously, they had blessed the space by burning one of the smudge sticks while Uncle Remo invoked helping spirits, sending the purifying smoke off in all directions with a fan made with the tail feathers from a red hawk. Then he rattled and sang using an undecorated rattle made from deerskin tied to a branch, the bark still on it.

Uncle Remo had everyone standing around him as he stood in the center of the circle; Emma, Zach, Donovan, Burly's mother, Dr. Timothy Bottoms, Brer Rabbit, Bart, Buffalo and Coyote. No film crews either, everyone had been careful all day not to let Sheldon nor anyone else, not even Bart's new friend, know what they were up to. Emma gave Brer Rabbit one last look that warned of serious retaliation and further revocation of privileges if he did not shut up. He did, and everyone waited for Uncle Remo's instructions.

The barn was secure, the doors locked or otherwise secured, the few windows covered and the only light came from a kerosene lantern hanging from a nail in a support pole. Shadows danced uneasily in its flickering light, adding an eerie ambiance to an already expectant and electric atmosphere. Everything was quiet, save for the few odd noises coming from the road, or the stereo they'd left on in the house to muffle the sound of the drum Uncle Remo would use.

It was a single frame, hand-held drum sixteen inches across and about three inches deep. An elk hide had been stretched taut over a circular wooden frame and a crude image of the sun rising over a symbolic prairie had been painted on it. Uncle Remo held it by the sinews that crisscrossed the open-faced side. In his other hand he held a beater, the business end being wrapped in strips of old flannel shirts.

He would use the drum only at the beginning of the ceremony, when he sang the first song. After that, during the dance, there would only be the voices of the dancers offered to the ancestors.

In the very center of the hoop of man and animal, Uncle Remo had placed a cedar tree he'd cut earlier that day. It would serve as the fulcrum, the axle of the dance. It was the world tree that held the sky up and the path from which the gods come down to earth, the bridge between our world and theirs, the road to earth for spirit.

Uncle Remo wore a ragged white deerskin shirt that hung to his knees. He told everyone it was his grandfather's and had been originally decorated by him. Uncle Remo repaired it as best he could now and then, occasionally adding designs according to his own visions.

It was a long sleeved shirt with a line of feathers attached quill end to the underside of the arms, various shiny metal objects dangled here and there, spotty, like hairs on an old man's head. Many seemed to be old silver coins tarnished almost black. Around the neck it was stained blue, a dark blue sky color down to the top of the chest and back, and half-way down the shoulders like a dark cloud settling on a white sky. It was magnificent and powerful like a rumor, old and venerable like a collective dream.

He wore no pants, no ornaments, nothing but braids in his hair and an old pair of moccasins on his feet. Faded patterns of some mysterious design could be seen if one looked closely enough. Long gone were the colorful beads that had helped decorate the deerskin.

Uncle Remo walked around the sacred tree, brightly colored ribbons hung from the limbs, along with various bird feathers. At the base of the trunk unknown leather-wrapped bundles lay in repose, offerings to guests celebrated, but unnamed. "We are going to do this as my grandfather taught me," he spoke to his rapt audience. "We have not had the time to prepare properly, but I think because we have some powerful medicine here in Coyote and Buffalo, it won't matter too much." A protest from Brer Rabbit forced him to amend his statement, "And of course, another type of medicine in Brer Rabbit."

"What is important to remember," he continued, "is we dance and sing with our hearts. That the creator understands, always knows the heart. Now, because we do have these four leggeds blessing us, it will be a little difficult to do the dance proper. But we'll try anyway. Sister," he looked for Burly's mother who was dressed in a simple white dress made from heavy, coarse cloth that she had painted with nature symbols. The sun, moon, birds and animals, trees, even stones were represented. She broke from the circle and walked to her brother. In her hand was a stick wrapped in red string with two crow feathers tied to one end, flaring from each other so they formed a Y.

Uncle Remo took it from her and said, "This is a guatoton. If we were doin' this right we'd have seven of 'em, but this is all we got tonight. We'll make do. These are tail feathers from our brother, the crow. Someone has'ta wear this. You, Zach. You wear it."

Zach wasn't about to turn it down. Uncle Remo handed the guatoton back to his sister, who walked over to Zach and tied it to the back of his head with a strip of red cloth so the feathers pointed to the sky, and the instrument itself pointed to the earth, another pathway inviting the spirits to come down.

"You may have heard many things about this here thing, the Dream Dance. Many years ago, my people sent a messenger, Apiatan, to talk directly with Wovoka, the Paiute holy man who was given the dance by the dakinago, the spirits. Apiatan brought it back to us and we were given our own songs to sing, along with some Arapaho ones. For my people, it is a way to talk with our ancestors, to gain their wisdom. They have crossed over the great divide that separates us from the spirit world. They know many things. Tonight we ask them if they know where Burly is, and this other fella, what's his name? Yeah, right. And Bubba."

Uncle Remo paused, looking at his feet, gathering his thoughts. "So . . . like I said, this ain't gonna be easy, following the dance just right. But we'll do the best we can. It's important that you touch the person in front of you when you're goin' round the circle, like this." He pulled Emma from the line and turned her to face away from him, placing his hands on her shoulders. "Like this. And she does the same to the person in front of her. The animals, well, I guess you'll have to touch somehow. It's important that everyone be touching, the power is created by touching and walking around the circle, and singing. We go round clockwise, so I guess Coyote, you'll be behind Buffalo, so you can hold his tail in your mouth, but don't bite. He might knock you out of the barn!" he laughed, setting everyone to ease as they laughed along with him.

"Brer Rabbit, you'll be behind Coyote, you can hang on his tail, and Bart, you get behind him . . . No, let's change all this. Let's put a person in between the animals," he decided.

He counted out four animals and five humans, so it would work it perfectly that the circle was balanced in the manner of one human then one animal. "The stuff will flow better that way," he said.

Between Emma and Zach he put Bart. Behind Zach was Coyote, followed by Donovan and Buffalo, then Dr. Tim, Brer Rabbit, then Burly's mother, who would have Emma's hands on her shoulders.

"This should be something," Uncle Remo breathed to himself. "This should be something."

"Okay," he said after lining everyone up to his satisfaction. "Here's what we're gonna do. First, I'm gonna sing a song invitin' the spirits in. Then . . ."

"Now dem iz frenly spir'ts, ain't dey?" Brer Rabbit interrupted.

"Most friendly, Brer Rabbit, most friendly. Likely be your kin," Uncle Remo said.

"Ah doan lak sum'ers um," he replied, causing some laughter.

"Just ask your granny, rabbit. You're not afraid of her, are you?" Even though they were in a sacred circle, Coyote couldn't help but snap at Brer Rabbit. He was about to say something else, but a hard look from Buffalo emptied his tongue.

"Okay, now," Uncle Remo began, "After that first song everyone'll start moving clockwise, startin' out kinda slow, then gettin' faster. Try and sing the songs as best you can, they're in the old tongue and we'll sing some of 'em over a lot. I don't know how many times right now, whatever seems right. Now, when you start getting tired, keep goin'! It's gonna get pretty fast after a while, and when you really can't keep goin', drop out and try and lay in the middle of the circle, as near the sacred tree as you can. The circle will close in a little tighter, cause you still want to try and touch the person, er, animal, in front of you. Okay, everyone understand?"

"Uncle Remo," Dr. Tim asked, "What do you do when you lie down?"

"Maybe you fall asleep, maybe you dream. Whatever comes in your head, just let it come. Don't fight nothin'. Anymore questions?"

No one said anything, even Brer Rabbit didn't have anything to say to stall what seemed the inevitable, so Uncle Remo continued, "Good. Let's get goin'."

He had everyone face west, then sheepishly said, "I guess it doesn't start with me 'n the drum, first I gotta sing this." Then he began to sing very quietly:

> "Heye, heye, heye, heye. Aho ho!
> Heye, heye, heye, heye. Aho ho!
> Nadag akana,
> Nadag akana,
> Degyagomga datsato
> Degyagomga datsato
> Aonyo! Aonyo!"
>
> Heye, heye, heye, heye. Aho ho!
> Heye, heye, heye, heye. Aho ho!
> Because I am poor,
> Because I am poor.
> I pray for every living creature,
> I pray for every living creature,
> Aonyo! Aonyo!

When he finished, he grabbed the drum and beater and had everyone continue to face west. Then he began to beat the drum, very softly at first, then louder as he sang, a steady unwavering single beat that rose from the ground up and about him, waltzing around the silent circle, weaving in and out between them, then turning upward, to the sky, to the ears of the creator.

"Data i sodate,
Data i sodate,
Dom ezantedate,
Dom ezantedate,
Deimhadate,
Deimhadate,
Beamanhayi,
Beamanhayi."

The Father will descend,
The Father will descend,
The earth will tremble,
The earth will tremble,
Everybody will arise,
Everybody will arise,
Stretch out your hands,
Stretch out your hands.

He had them all sing that twice, so that each line was sung four times, then he lay the drum down and said, "Now join together and we'll start dancing, slowly at first, and sing this:

"Dakinago im zanteahedal,
Dakinago im zanteahedal,
Dedom ezanteahedal,
Dedom ezanteahedal,
Deimgo adatodeyo,
Deimgo adatodeyo,
Debekodatsa,
Debekodatsa."

> The spirit army is approaching,
> The spirit army is approaching,
> The whole world is moving onward,
> The whole world is moving onward,
> See! Everybody is standing watching,
> See! Everybody is standing watching,
> Let us all pray,
> Let us all pray.

Many times they sang that song, and many times they shuffled around the circle, over and over, until they knew the words by heart, even in Kiowa. Round and round the odd assortment of creatures went, singing, stepping, plodding, and singing and dancing more.

For Coyote, it was an easy lope, a near perfect pace. For Brer Rabbit, the steady pace was not his normal mode of movement, steady for him meant something more along the lines of a steady stream of beers and tobacco. For Buffalo, it was not physically challenging at all, he had more trouble making sure he didn't knock Donovan down, who walked in front of him. But for Bart it was agony, he had difficulty after only a couple of turns around the circle. It got too hot and the pace was far too fast, his small legs just couldn't maintain the gate everyone else could. Zach was forced to help him along most of the time and he was the first to go down. Breathing like a trombone, he tucked his head down and rolled into the circle until he came to the center tree, leaned up against it and fell backwards, tumbling head over heels in a blinding light, frantically flapping his wings in a futile effort to stabilize himself, but his wings no longer served to move air. Down he went, little Alice the Bart, but no Mad Hatter did he find. Breaking through some thin wispy clouds he saw beneath him a vast expanse of white surrounded by brilliant blue waters. On the expanse of white, and darting about in the water, he could see little black dots. Little black penguin dots. Bart was going home.

The humans were moving along fine, the pace, up until then, was easily followed. But soon after Bart left the circle it quickened and they broke into a slow trot while singing the same song, only faster.

A trench was being worn into the dirt floor from the feet, hooves and paws. The dirt was being ground into a fine talc dust that rose about them like a mist, clinging to hair, fur and clothes, and clogging breathing passageways.

But still they sang, still they danced, rhythmically swaying back and forth, sending shadows prancing across the barn walls echoing scenes painted on cave walls by hunters and shamans thousands of years ago. They would have felt right at home had they been participating that night. Perhaps they were.

Uncle Remo cried out, "New song!" which did not break the dancer's steps, only the voice of the serpent that writhed around the cedar tree.

"Dakina bateya,
Dakina bateya,
Guato ton nyaamo,
Guato ton nyaamo,
Ahinaih nyaamo,
Ahinaih nyaamo."

The spirit is approaching,
The spirit is approaching,
He is going to give me a bird tail,
He is going to give me a bird tail,
He will give it to me in the tops of the cottonwoods,
He will give it to me in the tops of the cottonwoods.

They sang this song for what seemed an eternity to them, perhaps nearly an hour. They had worn the ground into a trough several inches deep, the dust limning their mouths and noses. Throats were dry and cracked, voices faltering now but still straining to sing, bodies sore, tired, dehydrated and cramping, but still the legs managed to put one foot, one paw, in front of the other. Sweat poured down foreheads making patterns like cracked terra cotta on the dust-caked skin. Tongues hung low for Coyote and Buffalo and Brer Rabbit too, his stained from chewing tobacco. But he did not notice, he was mesmerized, lost following the footsteps of Dr. Tim, as hypnotized as Tantalus.

He dug his paws under Tim's belt in order to keep up, often allowing himself to be dragged along, but Dr. Tim did not mind. His eyes were closed, his focus on the moment, trying, striving, making certain he would get all he could out of this dance, this truly *ancien regime*.

And still they kept going at a pace just under a run, a quick trot.

Burly's mother showed no signs of breaking rank, though her breathing was labored and her voice harsh from years of smoking cigarettes. Emma and Zach, now touching because of the loss of Bart, were moving in perfect synchronism, though fatigue often misplaced a foot, they would stumble, but catch each other before they fell. They were good dance partners, good for a marathon.

And on they danced, stumbling, gasping, wheezing, bellowing, moaning groaning foaming their way to numbing ecstasy, oblivious to the shadows on the barn walls that no longer reflected their movement, their shadows. They moved of their own volition.

But Uncle Remo saw them. "New song!" he cried.

"Ninaa niahuna,
Ninaa niahuna,
Bitaawu hanaisai,
Bitaawu hanaisai,
Hinaathi naniwuhuna,
Hinaathi naniwuhuna."

I circle around,
I circle around,
The bounderies of the earth,
The bounderies of the earth,
Wearing the long wing feathers as I fly,
Wearing the long wing feathers as I fly.

When everyone seemed to have learned the song, Uncle Remo picked up the pace, singing faster to urge them on. When he had them at a rate that was too hard, too fast, too much after all they'd been doing, he took a white handkerchief that had been tied under one of his sleeves, and began swinging it around in a big circular arc, like a windmill. Everyone's eyes naturally fixed on it as he walked around the inside of the circle, moving in front of individuals to the point of distraction. He wanted them to focus on it. They were exhausted and spent from physical exertion, even Buffalo seem tired. For him, it was a dizzying little circle they walked around, singing songs his bones knew, the maddening dust choking his throat and clogging his lungs. He badly needed water, as did everyone else. The white handkerchief offered an oasis of diversion, ransoming pain and agony for the moment.

And Uncle Remo saw to it that Brer Rabbit's mind was held captive too. He and Dr. Tim were as one, Brer Rabbit being the tail that hung limpid and shamed from Dr. Bottoms.

Emma and Zach shuffle-stumbled one-foot, two-foot, round and round and round and round in sweat-stained agony, panting, sticky dry glue in mouths and eyes burning from salty sweat and dust, little motes scratching eyes like rakes. But still they moved.

As did Burly's mother, singing the songs of her ancestors, fixated on her moccasins, 'Look one foot get in front of the other, white handkerchief a blaze of light, look feet . . . Listen! Self! This is nothing! My ancestors did this for hours, starting in the morning and all day under the hot prairie sun, dancing late in to the night! Do not shame them! This is nothing! Don't be pitiful! Do not shame them!' she told herself over and over.

Dr. Tim shared the same mantra, do not shame your ancestors, but he included a bit larger kin group in his thinking. His ancestors included all the people who had come before him that had put themselves through self-inflicted pain in order to gain spiritual revelations. No, he was not going to let his aching legs, sore feet, heaving lungs or parched throat keep him from achieving some sense of understanding how it felt to suffer, how it felt to torture oneself in the name of enlightenment. How many times had he read about it? Many more times than he'd danced around this circle. How many times had he wondered what could one possibly gain from doing such things to oneself? And why did they continue to do these things? Why did some of these practices continue well into this modern age, when so many alternatives were available? Alternatives? Like a TV sermon? A weekend workshop of owning your pain or letting go of some group psychosis? No, the old seemed better. Maybe there was something to them, maybe there was something to be learned from the ancient ways that you couldn't get any other way. Maybe it wasn't some delusional notions wrung from the agony of pain. The old forms, transmuted into modern methods, or nearly modern, like the relatively painless 'Shout'. Extremes on a sliding scale. What can you tolerate? What does it take to separate you from your senses? Cleave the mind from body with an axe of blazing sun or hot stones in a small space and water, parboiled to perfection, you and your soul. Dance till you drop or starve for days and sit on a mountain top waiting for a vision, or prance around a tree that you're tied to with sinew that's pierced through your skin and wrapped around your flesh, your own blood dripping down your belly, pull until you break free and your spirit soars while your body collapses. He'd read and wondered, wondered and read. What was it he heard somewhere, the shortest route to belief is experience? He wasn't going to let this opportunity to participate in something ancient and noble, this ceremony that had roots reaching down into mankind's past, veins coursing from deep within the earth of his existence. He could hear the voices of the ancestors in his blood. All of them. He was going to put everything he could in this experience, he wanted to remember everything, each agonizing step, each labored breath, relish the cracked throat, hoarse from singing and parched for water. He was going to dance until he dropped and had a dream.

The only one not suffering was Coyote, who still spent much of each day loping about the prairie unencumbered by the fences that confined Buffalo. He could trot for hours, and did each day in search of food or driven by his insatiable curiosity. This Dream Dance was not an ordeal for him, it did not tax his legs or burn his lungs. The dust was bad, but he'd seen worse during drought years. And he didn't need to exhaust himself to dream, his ancestors were always in his ear.

He watched the swirling white handkerchief while his ancestors told him what Uncle Remo was doing, what he was trying to accomplish.

The people trudged and stumbled on, their bodies too spent to continue without a very deliberate and conscious effort. And that effort, that stealing of attention from the mind by the body put all the mind's focus on all the insistent nagging voices of distress in the body, from an itch to a blister, from a sore toe to a cracked lip. By gathering focus to the blurring white of the handkerchief, Uncle Remo was purloining their consciousness long enough that their bodies would quit on them. Just give up and collapse, a knee-buckling crumpling breakdown when the stilts of awareness were kicked out when they weren't looking. Uncle Remo was trying to distract them at the right moment, when they were ripe to flounder and run aground on that distant shore, the same beach Zachary had grounded on not so long ago back in Georgia. And he hit the beach again.

Most others did too. One by one they fell, staggering into the center of the circle or collapsing where they were, some to be hauled into the center, if they were small enough for Uncle Remo to drag.

Like a drunk, Zach spun wildly as he fell, careening with arms flailing to land in a jangled tangle of arms and legs near the sacred tree. Emma managed a few more steps before she went down, and when she did, it was a very graceful landing, a supple swoon nearly hitting Donovan, who had slipped out just before her, landing just inside the circle mumbling, "I'm seein' white." Burly's mother went soon after, first falling to her knees before the rest of her embraced the earth. Brown skinned arms folded around her.

Dr. Tim sagged under the weight of the unconscious Brer Rabbit, who had tangled his arms so well into Tim's belt that he would not fall to the ground, at least not by his own accord. It was a deliberate act to avoid touching the ground. He had the idea that if he didn't touch down, then he would probably avoid meeting any ghosts, kin or not. So like an Indian dragging a buffalo skull tethered to his back muscles in the sacred Sun Dance, Dr. Tim kept going, dragging Brer Rabbit along like a rag doll, stumbling along in a stupor until his body would take no more and a cease and desist order was issued to the brain so that his soul soon joined the shadows dancing on the wall that he noticed just as he collapsed.

Buffalo went next, his massive body slowing to an imperceptible shuffling of hooves, then he stopped altogether and fell to his knees, then down on his belly, his big head leaning forward like a locomotive nodding curtsy to a deer crossing the tracks.

As soon as Buffalo went down, Coyote stopped and sat back on his haunches. He knew the dancing part was over, now it was time to dream, if they were lucky. Uncle Remo sat down too, his work almost complete. He would wait until most had stirred from their dreams then he would softly sing one more song. Until then, he would wait, distracted by his own thirst.

The barn was silent now, even the spirits dancing on the walls were resting, or had gone back to their homes, Uncle Remo wasn't sure which, though Coyote knew. The voices in his ear told him they were busy at work, teaching the lucky few the mysteries. He shook his head slightly in disdain as he looked around at the crumpled mounds of flesh and bones. So much work spent trying to reach out and touch the past. Working oneself beyond any reasonable sense of exertion into exhaustion and nearly into expiration. Humans. A good thing this Dream Dance, very effective, but so dramatic! So hard! There were easier ways to talk to the spirits and to the ancestors, but he could not tell them how. He could not say unless they asked, and no one talks to coyotes anymore, they only talk to their dogs, and they don't know dog poop.

There was one last shadow on the wall and Coyote watched quietly as it peeled itself off and slither-flickered over to the kerosene lantern and extinguished it. "Thanks," he whispered.

chapter twenty

"Frightfully complex cathedrals are cathartic to the Christian mind as Byzantine mosques are to the Muslim. But for the life of me, I can't get elevated one stitch of an eyebrow in them. Give me a forest or a field full of flowers. Now that's inspirational!" said the little old man who sat cross legged in front of the rather prostrate Dr. Tim, who was flat on his belly. Rising to an elbow he appraised the little gnome of a man. His ebony skin was as polished as shoe leather on a drill sergeant, sunlight glinted and sparkled off the top of his hairless head, but turned away from his short gray beard. Through the man's wire-rimmed glasses Dr. Tim could see the remnants of coal black eyes behind the yellow gray discoloration of cataracts. 'What does this wizened wee elf want from me?' he wondered.

"Just to greet you and talk with you, you know," the old man said, surprising Tim.

"So you can read my thoughts," Tim noted.

"And more importantly, your heart," the gnome replied factually, them smiled extravagantly, exposing a mouth full of mistakes and bad habits. What teeth he had were yellow and broken. Dr. Tim wasn't sure if any of them were any good.

"No. I don't think they are. But it doesn't matter here, thank goodness," the elfin man said, again reading Dr. Tim's mind.

That comment nudged his memory of the Dream Dance and he quickly turned and reached behind him for Brer Rabbit.

"He's gone. Dreaming somewhere else," the old man said.

"Do you know where?" Dr. Tim asked.

"Oh, not far away. Not far away a'tall," came his reply.

"Hmm," Dr. Tim puzzled, "Dreaming. Dreaming," he repeated. "Am I dreaming you?"

"No. No. You're remembering me."

"That's curious. I don't believe we've ever met. I don't remember that we have," Dr. Tim observed.

"Oh, and you have a great memory, don't you?" said the gnome smiling.

'Sarcasm,' thought Dr. Tim.

"No no," interjected the old man waiving a bent nub of a finger. "You pride yourself on your memory, I was just letting you know that."

"Letting me know something I already know?" a puzzled Timothy asked.

"Precisely," said the gnome, baring his sorry array of ivory.

"And that isn't sarcasm?"

"Not at all. It is a complement to your vanity," the elder said with finality.

"Vanity is excessive pride in one's accomplishments or appearance. It is most definitely a pejorative aspect of a person's personality. To posit me with such an attribute is either an insult or sarcasm, which are quite related," Dr. Tim said coolly.

"Really? My, my," said the elf, shaking his head in apparent internal dismay. "All I meant to do was praise the efficase of your aura, or is it the edifice of your oreo? I can't remember. Well," he slapped his thighs, "It doesn't matter. Here we are at last, your heart's desire."

"My heart's desire, hunh," Dr. Tim repeated as he sat up. "Then I must have made it. I must be in the Dream Time," his voice rising with joy.

"Yes! Yes!" encouraged the old man, rocking back and forth on his buttocks. "You've finally made it!"

Dr. Tim took in his surroundings for a moment, which looked rather ordinary, actually. The two men sat in a field of wildflowers surrounded by deciduous trees. Beautiful, but ordinary. That fact did not dampen his rising good mood. "If you're what I've been dreaming for, maybe I have to go back to the beginning and rethink all this," he said laughing. The gnome seemed to enjoy the humor and readily laughed along.

Dr. Tim leaned back to savor the elation that rose like air bubbles escaping from some deep ocean vent. All the work he'd done, all the books he'd read, lectures he sat in on, papers he'd read and written, people he'd talked to, stories he'd heard, everything he'd ever run across about humans searching for, and reaching, through fasting, feasting, feting, or flogging or whatever, the other side, looking through the veil, entering the land of myth, the land of the spirits, the realm of the Gods, whatever, whether real or imagined, he was there now. He'd made it.

"So then," he looked at the little man as if for the first time, "Who are you?" his voice carrying confidence with no arrogance.

"I'm your many times great grandfather."

"Well, Many Times, have you a name?"

"Hmm, yes. Somewhere back there. But I know you're hungry for something. That's why you came. Here," he offered him a hitherto unseen wooden bowl that appeared to be empty.

Dr. Tim took the bowl with both hands, holding it carefully as if it were filled with a broth that might spill. But no broth did it hold, when he brought it close to his mouth a startled gasp escaped from his lips. The faces of Zach, Emma, Donovan, Uncle Remo and Brer Rabbit were looking back at him.

Emma said, "I don't know what I want out of life. I just don't know. Maybe it's better that I don't know, then there's no anxiety about not knowing, wondering what it would be like if I didn't know. My anxiety is from knowing that I should know that I should know what I want out of life, not what I don't know. I don't know, maybe I'm not sure. What do you think, Doc?"

As he tried to stammer out a response, Zach said, "I want to be a dog. Just a dog. Four legs and smell your crotch please and I'm happy. Oh, to be a dog. You know Timmy, it wouldn't be all that bad. You think?"

Brer Rabbit was noisily puckering and smacking his lips in exaggerated kisses. "I des luvz de dickin's outter dat man. He de bes." Kiss kiss smooch smooch.

Uncle Remo spoke up, "You've got a point there, Brer Rabbit. Black holes aren't very good in soup, they leave it a little too thin for my tastes too. But a stellar crop, now that I can sink my gums in."

All the while, Donovan was blowing bubbles with a wad of chewing gum. He'd blow a big bubble until it burst, 'SMACK!', 'SNAP!', 'POP!' Dr. Tim watched as he blew one so big if filled the bowl. Fearing it would pop all over him, he leaned away, but still it grew. Bigger and bigger it got, until it filled the whole bowl, overtaking and covering up the other faces. 'Jesus Christ!, he wondered, 'How big can it get?' Then 'POW' it blew with an amazing force that sent pink ribbon strings of bubble gum in all directions, but none hit Tim.

"Hey! Timmy. Let's go!" said old Mr. Many Times, and the little gnome of a man picked him up and threw him in the air where he blew around like a balloon losing its air, flbtlbtfltbssssssssss.

He went streaming and racing and tearing over the countryside until he came to a small wooden cabin in a clearing. Unable to control his flight path, he closed his eyes expecting to fly smack into a wall and be splattered like a bug on a car windshield, but instead he zoomed in through an open window and landed on a bed. He was dizzy and disoriented from his flight and it took him a moment to gather his senses; his bearings would return much later. When he was able to regroup, he realized a large red fox dressed in bib overalls was standing over him. In an awe-shucks kind of manner, the fox said, "Brer Tim! 'Er you bin?"

"I'd guess you'd be Brer Fox?" Tim hazarded.

"Co's I iz. Doan be infoolin' wif me, now git outter dat bed en git a move on. Brer Tarrypin gwine be 'er sho'tly, en dem fish ain't gwine wait all day fer de laks un you'n."

A knock at the door underscored his urge for haste. Brer Fox yelled out, "Dat you, Brer Tarrypin?"

A small nasally voice responded, "It be."

"C'moan in. We uz fix'n t'git a'gwine."

Dr. Tim, sitting on the edge of the bed still, watched as the door unlatched and a tortoise not more than two and a half feet tall on the hind legs on which it stood, sauntered in to the cabin, a cane fishing pole in one hand.

"Lo, Brer Tim," it said. "Hit one fine mawnin fo cat'n, but you hain't gwine kotch nuffin in dat dar bed."

"I was just getting up," Dr. Tim replied. He bounced off the bed and helped Brer Fox untangle the lines of two fishing poles leaning in one corner of the cabin. The initial confusion he felt when he plopped down on the bed, which had then given way to a little trepidation and fear, now moved into an altogether new emotional state; a burgeoning enthusiasm, the likes of which he hadn't experienced since childhood, though meeting Brer Rabbit had dusted it off, now it came full shine. He was a born again child, and he was goin' fishin'. He was, as they say, in the moment.

Gathering what little in the way of equipment they needed, Brer Fox said, "I nose right 'er t'git some snake doctors. Dem cats doan stan' er chance. Less' skaddle."

While they moved to leave the cabin, from the woods came the sounds of something large crashing through undergrowth and branches. Spooked, the three quickly pulled back inside and locked the door.

"Hit pro'lly des Brer Bar gittin' gnawed on by de brumblybee's fo messin wif der honey 'gin," Brer Tarrypin speculated.

"He makin' nuff racket t'raise ole scratch, dat fo sho," Brer Fox allowed. "Den agin, it might'n be dat fool Brer Rabbit. Lawd node wha' trouble he up ter."

Footsteps quickly came to the little cabin door, along with heavy labored breathing from lungs gasping for air, they must have been running a very long time. Whoever it was banged hard on the door as if their life depended on it.

Bang! Bang! "Hello!" they hollered. "Hello! Is anyone home? Hello! Hey!"

The three looked at each other to formulate a strategy. Brer Fox shrugged his shoulders and said, "Who dat?"

"Oh, thank god! Someone's in there," the voice cried. "Let me in, please! I won't hurt you, just let me in!"

"Wha fo?" asked Brer Fox.

"Someone's after me. Please, let me in."

"Wha' dey call you? Wha' tcher name?"

"It doesn't matter, I'm not from around here, you won't know me from Adam. C'mon! Let me in," the voice pleaded.

"How I doan node you ain't Brer Wolf gwine gobble me up? How I doan node dat?" Brer Fox asked. "En why you joon roun hether en yan causin' sech un rippit?"

"I'm not a wolf, for Christ's sakes. I'm just a man. Open up, I'm not going to hurt you," the man said.

Brer Tarrypin said, "He seem all right. 'Sides, Brer Tim un big fell'r. He proteck us."

"Alrighty, hol' yer hosses endurin I'ze open de do," Brer Fox yelled, then he unlatched the door and the person outside quickly jumped through the doorway and just as quickly slammed it back shut. His speed alarmed Brer Fox, Brer Tarrypin and Dr. Tim. They all moved back away from the newcomer.

"Thank you!" the man gasped as he bent over and put his hands on his knees to help him catch his breath. "Thank you so very much," he rasped. He had not really seen his saviors when he came through the door, and his eyes were mere slits as he refreshed his lungs. Between gulps of air, he said, "My name . . . is . . . Burly . . . Olalla," when he opened his eyes fully, he said, "Oh, shit!"

"Oh won't you stay, don't go away,
If it's boredom you've found,
I have a new playground.

> We'll have fun, you will see,
> We can play with cats alpha through bee's"
> Said the cat, as he took off his hat.
> Then all the little cats showed up in hats,
> Smaller and smaller until only a speck,
> "Take my word," said the cat,
> "The little one's there that carries the broom,
> That sweeps away gloom."
>
> "No, no. Thank you so much,
> But we really must go,
> We have to find Burly,
> While it's still early,
> He's been gone far too long,
> We'll look all around,
> Until he is found,"

Lucidity said as she stood up and bowed,
    And grabbed Bubba's hand
    Then they left, and everyone cheered.

    Thanks, Lucidity," Bubba said. "I was going crazy in there, I couldn't take it anymore. All those weird creatures and odd things, all of 'em so different. Man, I can't take different like that. And the way they talked and everything was getting to me too. I can only take so much."

    They were walking along a path that took them directly into the woods. "And that cat," Bubba continued, "whose gonna believe that! Fat with the Hat! If that don't beat all!"

    Lucidity wasn't responding, no um's or ah's or hm's to show she was listening, and so Bubba, having the somewhat normal human proclivity to talk rhetorically, or at least to his own ears, asked her if she was all right, had she heard what he said?

    "Yes," she replied. "Such wonderful and delightful beings. All they want to do is help and have fun!"

"Well, I'm not so sure about that Mr. Lynch fellow. He looked kinda nasty to me," Bubba grumbled.

"To help or to teach, it is one and the same," she said.

"I don't know what you'd learn from that green booger," he said.

She fell silent again and seemed kind of despondent to Bubba, who was yearning for conversation so he asked her if they were really going to look for Burly, to which she affirmed they were indeed, and in point of fact, would happen upon him shortly. They walked in silence after that, an irritable noisy silence to Bubba. The crunchy kind of quiet.

They walked through a patchwork of cleared fields and timbered stands, a very pleasing and bucolic countryside. Eventually they came to two men sawing a tree down with a long double handled saw. One was a short, tending to plump, pale white man, the other, an older, gray haired and bespectacled dark-skinned man.

"Mawnin'," the black man said in a friendly manner. His rolled up sleeves revealed strong muscles despite his apparent age. The other man did not so much as look up, only wiped sweat from his brow with a handkerchief he pulled from a pocket.

"Good morning," Lucidity returned the friendly salutation. Bubba nodded and smiled a greeting.

"A bit warm to be working so hard, don't you think?" she asked the man.

"Hit alluz hot fer doin' de right wuhk," the black man replied.

"What do you mean, 'doing the right work'?" she asked.

"Well," he stopped and rubbed the grizzled hairs on his chin. The quiet man took this as a cue to rest and sat down with his back to Lucidity and Bubba. "We'ze cuttin' fence rails t'lay down de paf so'ze folks kin fin' der way."

"Oh, so they won't get lost!" Lucidity said brightly. "To your house?"

"Yes'm," he smiled. "So'ze dey kin fin de troof."

"Well, then you have a big job ahead of you, but the good one. Your friend seems kind of shy. Doesn't he talk?"

"No'm. I taks fo de bofe ud uz."

"I'm Lucidity Jones, and this is my friend Bubba. What're your names?"

"Folks callz me Uncle, en dis er's Joel."

"Do you need any help?"

"No'm, I reckon we kin han'l it we'ze bin h'at it fo' so long, but thanks des de same."

"Suit yourself," Lucidity said and they parted ways after a few more pleasantries.

They walked on for a couple of miles through the same quilt work of fields and trees until one pasture yielded a path that rolled up a small hill and then disappeared out of sight down the other side. "I'm thirsty," Bubba said, "Let's see if that leads to water."

They followed the trail to the top of the hill and looked down on a little wooden cabin standing in a clearing. "Look, a well!" Bubba cried jubilantly, then started to walk toward it, but Lucidity grabbed his arm and whispered, "Wait!"

A small imp of a creature wearing a red hat emerged from the trees opposite where they stood and approached the door of the cabin. He carried the platter of dreamed pleas and ham. "I guess we found Burly," Bubba whispered.

The moans and sighs and loud exhalations accompanying the rustle of clothing indicated people were stirring, coming back from their dreams and wanderings. Emma and Zach seemed to rouse at the same time, reached out, found each other, cuddled up, and waited for instructions. They did not need to speak to each other, they did not need to confirm where they had been. Looking into one another's eyes was enough: they'd been with each other.

Donovan stirred and rolled over with an audible groan, which woke Uncle Remo and Bart, who had his head on Uncle Remo's lap. Burly's mother then sat up abruptly, a leaf shook loose from a dreamtree.

Only Buffalo and Brer Rabbit slept on, but only for another five minutes or so before a loud yawn from Buffalo sent Brer Rabbit's ears a'twitching. Getting impatient, Coyote thought to go over and kick him in the head, but Brer Rabbit propped himself up on his elbows, saving him the trouble. How unfortunate, he thought.

Someone is missing, he realized. Shouldn't there be a human between Brer Rabbit and Buffalo? Yes, of course! The doctor! He got up and trotted to the space left between the two. Empty as a grouse nest. He sniffed around, but could not find any scent trace of him, not fresh at any rate. The spirits took him!

"Someone turn the lights on," Coyote said. "I think Dr. Tim is missing."

Audible gasps filled the air as Uncle Remo stumbled over to the lantern and lit it. Sure enough, no Dr. Bottoms.

"Uh oh, that's not good," Uncle Remo wisely observed.

While everyone rubbed their eyes and yawned themselves alert, Uncle Remo spoke with urgency, "We have to keep going. We have to go back and find him. Oh, Grandfather," he implored the heavens, "What the hey is going on? Here, everyone sit in a circle, we must sing and pray to the spirits. Come! Come! Bring the circle in closer. Someone turn the light back out!"

They were all moving slowly, too slowly for Uncle Remo. Their bodies were stiff, tongues dry and cracked, some had headaches, some felt nauseated, all felt done in, done out and done down, the last thing they wanted to do was sing more. At least they didn't have to dance, or so it seemed. Grudgingly, they tightened the circle and waited for Uncle Remo's commands. All except Brer Rabbit, who refused.

"I des bone tahrd. I des cain't. I cain't! I won't!" he said. If they all wanted to work further with the haunts, they could, but he'd had enough. All he had done was sleep, which was the best of all outcomes to him. Despite Uncle Remo's entreaties and the pleading from the circle, he refused to participate and said he just had to go to bed. Uncle Remo finally said to let him go though some still pleaded for him to stay.

"Let the useless piece of dung go," Coyote sneered. "He's no good to us anyway."

The ever sensible Buffalo said, "Everyone has their place, Coyote. You know that."

"We don't have time to argue, let him go," Uncle Remo said again. While Brer Rabbit slowly walked out of the barn, Uncle Remo kept talking. "If we are going to bring Dr. Tim back, we have to act now, he might be hovering between worlds right now, one of his spirits still wanting to be here, not sure to go, while the other may have already crossed over." He grabbed his rattle and began to sing, but he started out too fast for the others, so much to his annoyance, he had to start over:

> "Gomgyadaga, Gomgyadaga,
> Donyazango, Donyazango,
> Godagya inhapo, Godagya inhapo,
> Dagya inatagyi, Dagya inatagyi,
> Animhago, Animhago."
>
> That wind, that wind,
> Shakes my teepee, shakes my teepee
> And sings a song for me, and sings a song for me,
> My song is a good one, my song is a good one,
> He gets up again, he gets up again.

Brer Rabbit could hear them sing as he left the barnyard, could hear them even as he passed the sleepy policeman standing near the yellow tape that served as a fence. He ducked under it while the cop looked at him as if he were dreaming, wide-eyed and jaw sagging. Brer Rabbit didn't say a word, just left the cop staring at his rear end as he scratched it on his way in to the house.

He went straight to the faucet and drank directly from it, making loud gulping noises as he greedily drank his fill. Then he went into the living room. His favorite sleeping spot, the couch, was taken, serving as a bed for three crewmen. No matter, he was too tired to even watch TV, so he hopped over sleeping bodies and went into Zach and Emma's room. Ah, the smell of Emma enveloped him as he sank his head into her pillow. One final yawn and he was ready for blissful sleep, just like the sleep he had in the barn. No ghosts, no spirits, no haunts, no apparitions had tormented nor terrorized him, just a lush dreamless sleep. He smacked his lips one last time and briefly opened his eyes for the small security of surety knowing he was alone. A moonbeam fell on something in Zach's dufflebag, something that tugged at his curiosity, it seemed vaguely familiar, what small part of it he could see. He slipped out of bed and reached into the bag and could not believe what it was. He leapt and hollered for joy! He'd found his lucky rabbit's foot, given to him long ago by Aunt Mammy-Bammy Big-Money!

"Now who dat?" wonderd Brer Fox. "Dis gittin mo kuser en kuser by de minit," he said as yet another insistent knock knock knocking came to his door.

"Don't let him in," pleaded Burly. "You'll be sorry. You'll see!"

"Whysomever I be sorry? Wha' fo?" asked the fox.

"He'll pester you until you go crazy," Burly warned.

"Ef'n hit ain't Brer Rabbit, I speck I git 'long tol'bul well," he replied. "No un drive de ca't er crazy lak dat fool."

"You open that door and you'll be forced to do things you don't want to," Burly kept warning him but it wasn't having any effect on the stubborn fox.

"Fo un man, you mighty a'scear't," Brer Tarrypin observed.

"Yes, why all the fear?" Dr. Tim asked.

"You just don't get it, do you," he said to them all. "All right, go ahead. Open the goddamned door!"

Brer Fox opened the door to look down at the little creature holding a large platter. He chuckled and said, "Dis itty bitty fell'r wha' gotcher dander up? Hah hah! Hey dar, lil fell'r. Wha' cho name?"

"My name is Man. I am Simply Man. Would you like dreamed pleas and ham?"

"Ah doan reckembembunce 'er eatin' 'em b'fo," Brer Fox stated, hooking his paws in his overall straps. "But I specelate I kin try 'em. C'moan in, Brer Man."

Lucidity and Bubba left their hiding place as soon as Simply Man was let in the door and carefully and quietly snuck up to peek through a window.

"Oooo, I like him," Lucidity squealed as she lay eyes on Dr. Tim. "Physicality has its promises."

"Hush!" hissed Bubba. "They might hear you! And what the hell you talkin' about? You're supposed to be an angel or something and here you are drooling over someone. Maybe Burly's right about you."

Inside, Burly was talking to Brer Fox. "You're going to eat that? It looks rotten! You'll get sick!"

"Mo' samer t'me," Brer Fox said. "I done et wurst. I'll axe him den. Say lil fell'r, dis 'er bittle good?"

The funny little creature said, "Of course they're good. They are good here. They are good there. Dare I say, dare I might, they are good everywhere!"

"Dat's good nuff fo me," Brer Fox determined and reached to grab the plate that was held so tantalizingly close to his nose.

"Wait a minute," Burly said and rushed to intercept the plate of dreamed pleas and hams, but he knocked Brer Tarrypin over in his haste, sending the tortoise spinning on his shell, his little arms and legs flailing about to stop himself.

"God, I'm sorry, turtle," Burly apologized. "Here, let me help you."

Brer Tarrypin's unfortunate spill didn't stop Brer Fox, who was intent on eating dreamed pleas and ham. He had a piece of ham cut and was placing a bit of pleas on it while Burly lifted Brer Tarrypin back up.

Burly stood next to Brer Fox and said, "Now just hold it. I'll try the goddamn things."

"Wait yo tu'n, deys plenty mo," Brer Fox said as he brought the deftly arranged morsel to his mouth, but he stopped when a loud thump and crash came from outside the kitchen window.

Lucidity had lost her balance and fallen awkwardly, knocking into the cabin wall as she fell. Bubba caught her but she still scraped a good portion of skin off her elbow and forearm. He was holding her in his arms when everyone from inside came out to investigate the noise.

"What happened, Lucidity, what happened? You just crumpled up like paper. You alright?" Bubba asked her.

"I don't know, something has happened, Bubba, something has happened. I don't know what it is, but something has come to pass. It's good, that much I know. And strong, too. It just sent me spinning, is all." She struggled to her feet and as graciously as she could, said to the people and animals gawking at her and Bubba, "Hey, y'all! What's up?"

Sitting at Brer Fox's table, Lucidity had everyone's attention. "It doesn't hurt, and as soon as we're out of here, the scratches will go away," she told Bubba, who looked concerned, as did everyone else save Burly.

"I thought you couldn't get hurt, being an angel, or a tutorial," he said, though with a little less venom, Lucidity noted.

"I am, but remember, this isn't my place, it's yours."

"What is that supposed to mean?" Burly asked as everyone puzzled over Lucidity's words.

"Oh, right. You weren't there when Bubba and I were talking about it. You were being chased by Simply Man."

"Whatever," Burly said irritably, "Go on."

"What I mean is, this is mankind's place, not mine. I belong in God's imagination, unfiltered, you might say. I'm natural, God's organic. This," she said, sweeping her arm about, "is God's refined thought through your mind."

Burly looked at her as blankly as the rest of them. Brer Fox took the silence as an opportunity to move to more important matters. "I got some lim'mint awl t'gawm on it, ef yer wanner," he offered. Then he looked longingly at the platter of food.

"No thank you, Brer Fox," Lucidity said. "That is very kind of you. But I think I turned a muscle in my neck. Would anyone like to massage it, like you?" she smiled coyly at Dr. Tim, who had been smitten by her the second he saw her outside. "You look like you have a healing touch, would you mind?" Lucidity cooed. Bereft of words as a teenage boy when the prom queen calls, he hastily humbly mumbly agreed and clumsily began to knead his fingers on her neck.

While everyone watched Lucidity's eyes close in pleasure, Brer Fox slid the platter of food in front of himself, and picked up the fork again, saying, "Less 'ave a-baiter dis ham" but before he could sink one fang in it, Burly rudely snatched the fork from him and said, "No you don't! I get the first bite. Give me that knife," he demanded.

Unaccustomed to quarreling with anyone but Brer Rabbit, and least of all a human, Brer Fox meekly handed over the knife. Burly wasn't going to eat Brer Fox's piece, instead, he set it down and went about cutting his own slice of ham, or rather, mangled a piece off the ham bone then grabbed a whole dreamed plea with his hand, slabbed it on the ham slice and looked around as if to dare anyone to challenge him. No one did, he looked especially at Lucidity, but she couldn't care less, she paid him no mind at all. She had a rapturous look on her face that bore a striking resemblance to the one Dr. Tim wore. In the small cabin crowded with everyone, they were alone.

Dramatically, and with great show, Burly slowly brought the mouthful of food toward his open jaws.

Agonizingly slow, thought Simply Man and Bubba, the more so Bubba because he thought as soon as Burly ate that mean looking shit he'd be back home in Kansas. Silently, he tapped his heels together.

Brer Tarrypin just wished to heck the fool would eat the darned stuff so he could get on with the more serious business of fishing and get well away from this monkey business.

Brer Fox's only thought was the wish there would be plenty left.

Burly spoke to Lucidity to get her attention, "Well, here goes. Don't you want to look? Isn't this what you want? Hey!" But she didn't open an eyelid, just rolled her head back and forth as Dr. Tim worked on her neck and shoulder muscles, with an occasional foray down her back.

"Ah, for Christ sakes!" Burly shouted. "I thought you were my angel!"

Lucidity only smiled and softly said, "I was, or will have been."

"Jesus! More mumbo jumbo," and he crammed the lump of ham and runny pleas in his mouth and chewed, slowly at first, then faster.

Around the room, Lucidity paid no attention, Bubba clicked his heels together furiously and Brer Tarrypin said aloud, "Swallow, dagnabbit!"

Brer Fox leaned in close for a vicarious taste, his muzzle mere inches from Burly's mouth, just a bit closer than Simply Man, who was leaning forward, full of expectations.

Burly chewed and chewed and chewed, then abruptly stopped, screwed up his face, puckered his lips and spat the food out in one godawful green slime stream, spraying Brer Fox and Man to boot.

"Blech! This shit sucks!" he blurted. "Water! Water!" he demanded.

Everyone was too stunned to move, except Brer Tarrypin. He grabbed his fishing pole and slipped out the door. He'd had enough of humans, especially that one.

Brer Fox licked his splattered muzzle, concluded Burly was in error, grabbed the plate of dreamed pleas and ham, and sat down to eat as Burly ran out the door to the well to rinse his mouth out.

Poor Man. He was crushed. Totally, utterly destroyed. He slumped in a chair mournfully sobbing:

> "I do not, do not, understand,
> How this human, how this man,
> Could not, could not, ever like,
> Good, delicious, dreamed pleas and ham,
> What is this thing that he calls Spam®?"

His little body shook with grief, rocked by spasms of woe until the noisy sounds of lips smacking opened one of his eyes. The sight of Brer Fox greedily and happily eating the rest lit a candle of joy in him, he brightened immediately.

But the room held another still clouded in gloom; Bubba. He sat down on the edge of Brer Fox's bed, head in hands, fearing all was lost, he would forever be stuck in this place of odd creatures and cartoon characters, never to see his wife and children again. He found some consolation thinking of the place of the large mushrooms. Maybe he would build a little house there, it'd be all right for a while.

Lucidity was still getting a massage, technically. She was on Dr. Tim's lap and they were massaging lip muscles now, but no one in the little cabin noticed, each was in their own little sphere, occupied with their own undertakings, interests or hurts.

Burly heaved the bucket down the well and it didn't take long for it to splash down. He let it sink for a moment to fill with water, then hauled it back up, sloshing full of cool, clear, mineral laden water. It was immediately refreshing, not to mention palate cleansing, quickly taking away the taste of that awful green mess. The taste-the taste. How long had it been since he could actually taste water, water that tasted good? He was on a city tap at home though he was out in the country, some damned county ordinance about safety and such and modernizing. Sure, city water had a taste, but it wasn't really water he tasted, it was chlorine and god knows what. Can you taste fluoride? he wondered. And the salt to soften it! And bottled waters were usually insipid tasteless nothings. But this, this was full of flavor, full of the taste of minerals and rocks and stones and earth. Yes, that was it! It tasted like earth! He rinsed his mouth again, now remembering an old well his grandfather had on his little farm further north. It was his father's father's place up toward Emporia. He could taste the water now. It wasn't much of a well, just a cistern, really, that would collect water that seeped out of the prairie grass, down through the deep rich top soil that was created over thousands and thousands of years by prairie grass growing and dying and growing and dying. What was that grass? It was the true native prairie grass. Bluestem, that was it. The water came from the clouds, fell to the grasses, down through the loam then down into the limestone, the earth's outer crust there in the Flint Hills created by a vast ocean he'd been told by some professor type had been there first. An ocean sea turned prairie sea. There on top of the limestone shelf the surface water mingled with spring water that came from deep within the earth, maybe it was all that was left of the inland ocean. Maybe there was a lake down there the size of Lake Superior. And just as cold. Thus united, flavors mingled and taste made, the water then flowed out into the bottom of the little wash where Grandpa collected it in an old claw-footed bathtub.

It nearly ran dry in drought years, but there was always a trickle that would run like a busted faucet, the prairie sod dripping like an old soaked rug. The cottonwoods made off with that, water thieves that they were.

Oh, the taste of that water! All mixed up with clouds and grass and dirt and the old seabed and the fishes and creatures that swam and lived and died in it, and granite far below and even old buffalo bones. Grandpa said his people, my people, at least his side of the family, the Kansa, used the steep drop off of the little valley there for a buffalo jump. How many thousands died at the bottom of this little wash, rolling and tumbling, grunting and bellowing to their death so that his people could live, so that he could stand there now, drinking water from Brer Fox's well. A cycle. A very big cycle. One within a cycle which was within a cycle which was probably within another cycle. Cycles and cycles and circles and circles.

He turned to go back to the cabin.

Everyone was preoccupied, doing their own thing, rotating in their own cycle of doing. Brer Fox was patting his fatted swollen belly while Simply Man kept asking the obvious, 'Yes, Man, he would like some more'. Bubba sat on the edge of the bed lost in thought, a stony smile on his face and Lucidity and Dr. Tim were all entwined, their lips mutely, but effectively, communicating all they needed to say.

Well, he thought, I guess I'll pull up a chair and do mine.

He sat down on a chair opposite Lucidity. She opened one eye, parted her lips from Tim's just enough to say, "I see you like dreamed pleas and ham."

Burly shrugged his shoulders, "Whatever."

Dry, cracked voices sent harsh broken words careening off the barn wall. The wood did not want the words, did not want the notes, they were too grating, too piercing and scratchy, discordant save for the steady cadence of Uncle Remo. His one voice netted the off-tones and pulled them back into something resembling harmony, a near-unison, enough to lift the singular choir's efforts up through the agony of sore, tired and deprived bodies into a whole that could be discerned a song, that could reverberate and be heard as one voice, albeit a curious one, that asked the spirits for the return of Tim. And Burly and Bubba too, if they wouldn't mind.

On and on they sang in the dark. Coyote sang too, but he sang for Burly alone. As he called for the Great Spirit, his sharp ears heard the familiar thump thumping of someone's paws on the earth, so when the barn door was opened with a crash and a bang, he was not alarmed. But everyone else was. The interruption of their meditative chanting was as riotous as pins getting smashed by a bowling ball. Strike! Voices slammed into walls, veered off into the gutter with a clatter and clang and spun about before falling flat and silent.

'You little demon,' thought Coyote as Brer Rabbit crashed the prayer party.

"My lucky rabbit's foot! My lucky foot! I got my lucky rabbit's foot back agin! Emma! Zach! Do'van! Look! Look!" he yipped and danced and jigged about.

Unfortunately, no one shared his joy. For one, they could not see in the dark.

"Brer Rabbit! Please, we're praying to the Creator and the Spirits to get everyone back. This is not the time," Uncle Remo admonished him.

"But I got my lucky rabbit's foot back! I got it back!" he cried as he kissed the musty old thing. "I got it back!"

Murmurings of discord were breaking out through the ranks, concentration was lost.

"A light. Turn on the light," Uncle Remo asked. "Zach, are you there?"

"Yeah, sure, Uncle Remo. I'll get it," a tired voice responded.

Zach got up and stumbled around looking for the matches. When he finally found them and struck one, the flaring light illumined two bodies lying next to the cedar tree. Everyone gasped, including Coyote.

The light didn't last long. His attention turned, Zach let the match burn down to his fingers. Howling, he put it out then lit another as voices cried out, "It's Burly! Wasn't it?" "Hurry up!" "Light the lantern!"

This time Zach got the lantern burning bright before he, too, tried to see who the two bodies belonged to.

A groggy Burly sat up to cries of "Hurrah!" and "Oh my god!" The other person sat up too, but no one knew who he was until he said, "I'm his lawyer."

"Bubba!" Emma hollered.

They rushed up to touch them, to make sure they weren't a mirage of some sort, to insure they were real and perhaps to weigh them down so they didn't float away. Sometime after a mother's tears and Emma's too, someone thought of Dr. Tim.

Burly, arms wrapped around his mother, said, "Um . . . he's going to stay awhile. He said not to worry, he can get back any time. He's going to experience another real myth for a spell: true love, he said."

epilogue

The night air was heavy and hot. It lay around the sleepers like a wet wool blanket warmed by the breath of a dragon, steaming them like boiled potatoes. As the first gray herald of dawn crossed through the turgid, humid sky, a piercing cry from one of the sleepers lanced the last of the night.

"Aieeee!" screamed the dreamer, jack-knifing bolt upright in bed.

His sleeping mate woke with a start and grabbed her husband, comforting and yet shushing him, telling him it's all right, but don't wake the children, it's trouble enough when one's awake, but when all fourteen . . . well, you can imagine.

"I des had de mos monstus ho'bul dream," Brer Rabbit panted.

"What was it, dear?" his concerned wife asked.

"Dey wuz dis 'er fell'r, name Buhly, I reckembembunce, en he weren't fit t'ter, no, he wuz needin' sump'n. En er wuz dis gal, Emma, en nudder fell'r Zachree, en lots un udder folks, sumunemz unner de enfloons of deze er machines. It were bodacious en suvvigus!" he trembled recounting his dream. "Er's my . . . der hit'iz." He took his lucky rabbit's foot from the spot on his bedpost where he always hung it.

"Dats it. Dat mo lak hit."